UNDEAD RECKONING

MIKE SLABON

All rights reserved. No part of this book may be reproduced or transmitted in any form or by any means, electronic or mechanical, including photocopying, recording, or by any information storage and retrieval system, without permission in writing from the copyright owner.

This is a work of fiction. Names, characters, places, and incidents either are the product of the author's imagination or are used fictitiously, and any resemblance to any actual persons, living or dead, events, or locales is entirely coincidental.

Copyright © 2011 Mike Slabon
ISBN: 978-0-9869203-1-8

For those who have tried to make sense of all the absurdity and inexplicability in the world.

AHSAAN,

ENJOY THE APOCALYPSE... MAY YOU NEVER BE ZOMBIE BAIT!

ACKNOWLEDGEMENTS

Although I plan to write other novels, since this is my first, I better make my dedication count. I wish to thank the following people on this particular adventure:

My amazing wife Kate Goring, for the cover design. Thank you for your love and your encouragement. Since I met you, every day is an amazing and awesome adventure, the likes of which no epic tale can even begin to rival. If you thought my book was beyond your comprehension, then the light and love you bring into this world is beyond words.

Maximus, Sophia and Syrus, for sharing stories, laughing, singing and dancing, and for giving me cool character names and ideas. I look forward to the day when you are old enough to read this book.

K.A. Corlett, for editing my manuscript, for supporting me in my writing endeavors, for working with me to slay demons, and for sharing my story in this and in other worlds.

Mom, for introducing me to science fiction and fantasy media at such a young age - it screwed me up in a good way. Thank you for also supporting me and encouraging me to explore my creative interests.

Dad, for enlightening me with your views of the world. Don't worry… someday everyone will get it right.

My brother Chris, for sharing and making up crazy stories with me, both real and fictitious. Also, thanks for letting me sneak into your room when you weren't around to "borrow" your Dungeons and Dragons 1st edition boxed set. (Heh! Heh!)

My Grandparents, for keeping me well supplied with Lego and other toys; for worrying about me yet encouraging me to be myself; for sharing fascinating bedtime stories, and for providing me with lots of anecdotes.

Tom and Marie Goring, for your support, your encouragement, and your generosity. Thanks for believing in me! Thank you for your open minded approach to all the zaniness I have introduced into your lives.

My family and friends who took the time to read my story, and provided feedback, suggestions, reviews, translation, and commentary. Thank you for the support and encouragement. Thank you for laughing, cringing, screaming, furrowing your brow, getting all confused to hell, and trying to keep up (whether you were being sincere or just polite). There will always be "one time" when I have a story to tell. Thank you for taking an interest.

Summer Burton, for last-minute heroics, suggestions, revisions, edits, and support.

CONTENTS

1	The Downward Spiral	1
2	A Painful, Burning Discharge	10
3	Things that go Chomp in the Night	19
4	Recipe for Disaster	27
5	The Afro Saxon	36
6	Jim's Story: An Eye for an Eye	50
7	Grave Yardage	53
8	A Million to Juan	70
9	Hero's Welcome?	93
10	The Autocthon	107
11	Home Advantage	126
12	Shed for Brains	143
13	Keek to the Head	157
14	Frontlinebacker	177
15	Tempus Fugitives	195
16	From Hero to Eternity	214
17	Jim's Story: I Am Legion	228
18	Scoot to Kill	254
19	Jim's Story: Dismembers Only	293
20	Pair O'Dice Lost	315
21	Paradise Found	345
22	The Quantum Mechanic	368
23	The Excrementalist	404
24	Noetic Justice	430

1 THE DOWNWARD SPIRAL

Men can never cheat death.
How sad it is when one man can live a thousand deaths,
And never really die.
          -The Book of Amaltheon

"I'd take a bullet over a splinter any day," I mumbled as I pulled my thumb out of my mouth and stared at the dark spot just below the surface of my skin.

"That's one wish you may regret," Jim muttered.

I rolled onto my back. Dark clouds limped across the sky. Rain was coming. Finally, some relief from the heat. Rain wasn't too common anymore. The world sure could change a lot in nine months.

I stared at my thumb again, but that didn't stop the piercing throb. "At least with a bullet," I began, "there's peace of mind knowing you're going to die unless they operate. And even then you still may die, but you knew you had it coming. With splinters, you just live with the pain. And if you can't dig the thing out, it'll either fester, or come back to bite you in the ass later in life." Jim raised one eyebrow and glared at me like he always did when it was time to shut up. I jabbed the sore digit back in my mouth and thought of Pete Hinze. Poor bastard woke up limping the morning of the season opener. At first, there was no sign of what was causing him the pain. By mid-afternoon, he couldn't put any weight on his foot. His toe swelled up bigger than a kishka. He was feverish too!

The team doctors soaked his foot in Epsom salts. By game time, he was bleeding from around the nail bed. The doctor picked around in there and pulled out a piece of metal. *"Probably been there for years,"* the doctor said. Hinze felt better almost immediately. With less than a minute remaining in the game, his toe kicked the winning field goal. To think we could've lost to a splinter. I shuddered.

"See anything?" I nudged Jim with my elbow.

"No. But there's a sign in the window advertising the *Super Bowl Special*. They must've known you were coming."

"Hmpf..." I snorted. Seemed like ages ago since I'd won the Super Bowl... almost like it was a dream. After all, I hadn't even started playing football until junior high, but I had this natural athletic prowess, or so the coach said. Guess he was right, because eventually the scouts came after me. That's when I became the youngest player ever to be drafted first overall. In my first season, I'd been named Rookie of the Year, and MVP, and led my team to the Super Bowl. Heck, I even made the cover of *Time* magazine. And the fucking zombies took all that away from me.

I looked at the sky again. No birds. I couldn't remember the last time I'd seen one. I raised my head and looked around. No zombies, either. You learned quickly to never drop your guard... not even for a minute. Those scrawny little fuckers would sneak up on you. And not like they intended to. They shambled along so quietly – no breath, no moans, no groans. And no stink either, so you couldn't even smell 'em. *Suspended Decomposition* was what the scientists called it. These weren't your standard crawl-out-of-the-ground-partially-decomposed type of zombies. They'd been people once, just like you and me. No brain activity, yet a head-shot would put'em down for good. All zombies wanted to do was eat – rip a man to shreds, they would. It made no sense. Yep... zombies were a modern-day cancer waiting for a cure.

Jim set down the binoculars and rubbed his eyes.

"Well?"

He shook his head.

"Aw, c'mon," I huffed. "We've been lying here for half an hour. Surely we would have seen something by now!"

"Think back to your training - UDs generally congregate in habitable areas."

UDs - that's what the army called the undead. There were so many other names to choose from: meat sticks, flesh bags, zombies, skinnies, necrons, deadites, shamblers, boners, chompers, flesheaters, ghouls, no-brainers, zeds... to name a few. Leave it to the US army to keep it simple.

I rolled over onto my belly and grabbed the binoculars. We were up on a ridge overlooking the highway. I peered out at the service station: three vehicle bays, a diner, and eight cars in the lot. A small shed sat approximately seventy or eighty yards to the north, next to a windmill. A tattered American flag hung sadly from the top. A few hundred yards up the road was a motel – The Skull Rock Inn. And there was no movement.

"They're in there," Jim said softly, biting his lip.

"Can't we go around? I mean, is going into that garage part of this 'secret mission' we're on that you're so reluctant to tell me anything about?"

"No and no. And you agreed to be on a need-to-know basis. Besides, we may scavenge something useful from that garage."

"We gonna check out the motel, too?"

He smirked. "Why? You tired of sleeping outdoors?"

"Are you kidding? I love the jab of the odd rock in my back." We returned our attention to the building. "You sure there're UDs in there?"

"Yeah, I'm sure... I can feel it."

Lieutenant Jim Shrike had the most uncanny intuition. He was a former special ops agent, and veteran of numerous conflicts, or so the stories told. I trusted Jim's danger sense more than he did at times. He was also green, as in skin color. I don't know what happened to make him change color, but back in the bunker, there'd been more conspiracy theories about Jim's green skin than about Area 51. He patted me on the shoulder as he stood up.

"Let's move, Ed!"

I got up and released the safety on my assault rifle. We skidded down the steep slope towards the highway. I kept looking back to make sure there was nothing behind us. On the horizon, the sky flickered and thunder rumbled in the distance. A cool breeze licked the sweat on the back of my neck.

Jim ran ahead and took up a position on the edge of the parking lot. He crouched down behind a pickup truck: a Dodge Tailgater, just like the one my Grandpa used to drive. He waved for me to close in. As I did, he sped across the lot to the diner. He leaned up against the door and drew his pistol. I was surprised at that. Normally, Jim preferred using his knife because he was an 'edged weapon' specialist. I once heard Jim killed a man with that little blade from inside a pencil sharpener.

"Circle around to the rear!" he ordered. "I'll clear out the inside and meet you in the back." I nodded. With pistol in hand, he disappeared inside.

I traversed the front of the building, passing the service bays. Somebody had spray painted *Rev 9.6* on the bay door. I stopped when I saw that. *"And in those days shall men seek death, and shall not find it; and shall desire to die, and death shall flee from them."*

The sky darkened. Dust and debris swirled around my legs as the wind picked up. The windmill screeched and the flag flapped to life. I closed my eyes and took in a deep breath. The air was clean and refreshing – not like that recycled shit we breathed while in the bunker. I am so happy I got out of that place.

***

I was in Texas when UD-Day[1] arrived, paying a post-Super Bowl visit to the troops stationed at Fort Hood. I would have rather been at the Billy Rubin[2] Film Festival in Manhattan, but my agent had felt the troop visit would boost my public image. I couldn't have gone to the Film Festival anyway. The plan had been for me to go with my Grandpa... but he had died a few days before the trip. Going without him to see a Billy Rubin film just didn't seem right,

---

[1] UD-Day *(slang)*: Undead Day – The day the dead rose.
[2] Billy Rubin: A fictitious New York City detective; main character in the critically acclaimed series of award winning films.

even though they were all re-shot with uMe[3] technology for the festival.

The deafening wail of the warning sirens filled the air and I was suddenly pulled aside by a military aide. He said there was some sort of 'incident' and asked that I come with him. I didn't even get a chance to say yes, before he had his hand on my arm and was leading me across the compound towards the Soldier Service Center. Things seemed tense: troops ran about wearing gas masks or Hazmat suits.

The man next to me released my arm and fell to the ground, convulsing. I wanted to help him, but he began to puke up blood. I backed away. Then I realized it was happening all around me - people thrashed about in pools of bloody vomit - moaning, screaming, gagging, gurgling, silence... death. It happened so fast. Even the ones with masks and suits lay dead. And just like that, it was over. The ground was littered with bodies: sallow, gaunt bodies. Those of us who were still alive just stared at one another.

"What the fuck just happened?" a soldier yelled. "What the fuck?" Nobody responded. But then, the real horror began. All those dead people, the very same people that died moments ago, began to rise! Seriously! The dead were rising! Every hair on my body stood on end and the skin on the back of my neck was crawling. This dead guy lying on the ground in front of me slowly got to his feet. His eyes were the first thing I noticed – there was this dull yellow glow in them. It was very wrong. My heart was racing and my legs shook. I could feel my pulse in my neck. His mouth opened and closed, blood dripping from the chin. He stumbled towards me, reaching. Then I heard the yelling and screaming... and then gunfire.

---

[3] uMe: Ultimate Movie Experience - A 3D holographic projection which enabled viewers to observe the film as if on set. The holographic characters were also programmed to interact with the audience, delaying scene transitions. The dialogue programming always tried to steer the conversation into resuming the film.

My feet came unglued. I turned and ran. I ran and I ran. All around me the dead were rising, coming towards me. I dodged from side to side, pushing my way past the corpses. I never stopped... not even to help the ones who were swarmed and torn to shreds. A truck pulled up alongside me.

"Get in!" the driver yelled.

The soldiers in the back grabbed me by the arms and pulled me in.

"Holy shit! It's Eddie Griffin," one of them realized.

But the others said nothing. Like me, they sat and stared at the horror we left behind.

Gradually, we hooked up with other vehicles. I don't know how long we travelled. We made periodic stops to pick up survivors and to shoot the dead. Nobody really knew what was going on. Stories ranged from aliens to biochemical terrorist attacks.

We arrived at a fortified gateway. Once we got past the guards, we entered a tunnel and continued our journey, descending deep into the ground. We emerged into the largest underground parking lot I had ever seen. The convoy broke formation and military personnel directed the vehicles into designated parking spots. Other soldiers ordered us to proceed to an assembly area, just outside a set of steel doors. Civilians were separated from the crowd and escorted off to the side. There we waited. We waited until the last vehicle pulled in and drove up right alongside the crowd. An officer emerged and ordered everyone to attention. The troops immediately fell into formation.

"At ease," he began. "As many of you may have realized by now, there's been an incident. Information is limited at this time, but we understand this to be an event of global proportions. We have been ordered to seek shelter immediately inside the Emergency Services Bunker. Once we get settled, we'll establish contact with the other bunkers, coordinate our plan of attack and get this situation under control. America has and always will be the land of the free and the home of the brave. We intend to keep it that way. And we will do our part. Until then, this is your new home. Welcome to Bunker 57!"

And that's how it all started. One minute, everyone was going about their business. The next, nearly everyone was dead and risen. The military estimated ninety eight percent, plus or minus a percentage point margin of error of the world's population were walking dead. I didn't know what was worse: not knowing why it happened, or not knowing why some of us survived.

***

CRACK! CRACK!

The shots startled me. I guess Jim was right about the zombies inside. It started raining. I gripped my weapon a little tighter – my thumb was throbbing. A bolt of lightning sliced through the sky, followed by deafening thunder. I picked up my pace and headed down the side of the building.

I was about to round the corner. *SMACK!* The shed door swung open. Another flash of lightening… I thought I saw someone in the shed. The thunder cracked. The rain started coming down. There was a blur out the corner of my eye. Nails raked my shoulder. I twisted to my right, and leaned back as the zombie moved in on me. I stepped back and lost my balance, taking the corpse down with me.

We hit the ground and the rifle fell from my grasp. My right arm shot out and I caught the zombie by the throat. He was just inches away from my face. I stared into his gaping black mouth. It was full of yellow, snapping teeth. His eyes glowed fiercely from within their sunken pits. That glow…yet another thing the scientists couldn't explain. Mind you, it did make it easier to kill zombies at night. You'd just aim for the spot between the two specks.

With my left hand, I drew the combat knife from the sheath on my chest. "Not today, asshole!" I buried the knife to the hilt under the jawbone. The body went limp. I threw him off me, got up and pulled my knife free. The shed door smacked again. And there he stood! I could see the yellow specks just inside the doorframe.

I picked up my rifle, aimed and fired. Nothing happened! "What the...?" I fired again. Still nothing! I stared at my weapon... like that would somehow solve the problem. "Godammit!" I repeatedly squeezed the trigger. The zombie lurched forward out of the shed. A short, squat, scraggly bearded little... "Fuck!" I dropped the rifle and stared at him, while I thought of all the different ways I could brain him. In the end, I decided I would just have to charge at him, knock him down, and kick his head in.

But then I noticed an elliptical shaped rock on the ground. I picked up the cold stone and it... it felt like a football. I ran my fingers over the smooth surface. It was a little hard to hold with my sore thumb. I tilted my head back and felt the rain on my face. This was just like the Super Bowl game: down two points, twenty-five seconds on the clock, seventy five yards and goal, fourth down, pissing rain and roaring thunder. The sky lit up and I felt the adrenaline surge through my body.

I took a deep breath and as I exhaled, I hurled that rock with all my strength. The sky continued to flash and grumble. But to me, it was camera flashes and a riotous crowd. The rock spiraled perfectly, slicing an arc through the air. I swear, the zombie stopped and looked up. It was as if he noticed the rock too. *THWACK!* His head exploded. Brain matter scattered everywhere. The body stood there momentarily before crumpling to the ground. I jumped into the air and ran around in circles, sending fist-pumps and cheers into the stormy sky.

"Nice throw," Jim said.

I turned to see him walking towards me. "That's what won me the Super Bowl." He gave me a high-five. "Ouch!" I stuck my thumb in my mouth.

"Still prefer a bullet?"

"Oh... fuck off!"

Jim grinned. His teeth shone brightly against his pallid green skin.

UNDEAD RECKONING

The rain stopped. The clouds still murmured as they hurried away.

"Hey, Ed... I think you might want to see this," Jim said, crouching over the zombie I had just brained.

I ran to over to him. Jim had removed the dead guy's army jacket. My jaw dropped when I saw the torso. The body was wearing a tattered crimson and gold San Antonio Rattlers football jersey. I pulled it off and held it up in front of me. My heart was racing. The logo was in good shape – I could clearly see the image of a coiled snake, baring its fangs and ready to strike.

"Wait until you see what's on the back." Jim pointed.

I turned the shirt around. "Holy shit." I stared at the gold block letters on the back of the jersey, reading the word in stunned silence – *Griffin*.

"Poor bugger," Jim said, picking at the dead body's gaping head wound with his knife. "He probably would've just settled for an autograph."

2 A PAINFUL, BURNING DISCHARGE

Cowardly men run from death, and leave others in its wake.
Courageous men face the unmaker and live to share the experience.
                                        -The Book of Amaltheon

I always expected, or hoped rather, to meet survivors once I went topside[4]. According to the military, the odds were slim. So you can imagine my surprise when we ran into somebody Jim actually knew. Lieutenant Hoss Arnold didn't strike me as the army type. With his shaggy blonde hair and a face full of freckles, the portly man looked way too comfortable in overalls. Had he not shown me a picture of himself in uniform (standing next to Jim, I might add), I would've never believed it. Hoss and his two close friends, Tom *Handbeef* Thomas and Jack Nelson, had left the bunker near Fort Carson a few days earlier.

KA-POW!

The shot echoed through the valley. The round blew out the zombie's neck and he slumped to the ground. I set down the binoculars. "Nice shot."

"Thanks," Hoss replied. "Your turn." He handed me the rifle. "How's that thumb?"

I stuck out the bandaged digit. "Feels much better, thanks." I pointed the rifle and aimed at the pair of remaining zombies in the distance. "Which one do you want me to hit?"

"The one in the red shirt," Jim pointed.

BOOM!

"Ooohhh... right through the top of the head," Hoss winced. "Jesus, Ed... your shot is as good as your throw."

"I bet I could hit him with a pass from here."

"I don't doubt it! Your turn, Jim."

---

[4] **Topside** *(military slang)*: To go above ground; leave the bunker.

"I'll take that last one in the blue shirt," Jim said. He put a round right through the center of the zombie's forehead. Daylight shone through from the other side.

"Still a good shot," Hoss said, clapping Jim on the back. "Why you insist on close combat when you got a shot like that is beyond me!" He downed his beer, crumpled the can and threw it into the sand. "That's the last one," he lamented.

"No more zombies, either," I added, pointing at the pile of dead bodies lying in the desolate field.

"Why the hell would a buncha zeds wander around out there in the middle of nowhere?" Hoss asked. "I thought they liked the big city life."

I shrugged. "You know, all that UDEATT[5] they drilled into us ain't worth shit in this world. We've been topside long enough now to know what it's like in the real world."

"Real world, my ass," Hoss said. "Shit!" He sat down on the deck of the MARL 750[6] and wiped the sweat off his brow with his forearm. "I still can't believe I ran into you boys," Hoss started. "I mean, I seen a few survivors here and there since we left our bunker near Fort Carson. Mostly I just saw them fuckin' meat sticks. But what are the odds of running into an old army buddy and an NFL future Hall of Famer? I damn near shit myself! I guess it was fate that this here piece of shit broke down." Hoss pounded his heel against the deck. "Well, as soon as Professor Yao fixes this fuckin' thang, we'll head out. It'll be nice to have you boys along."

---

[5] UDEATT: Undead Engagement and Tactics Training: a military program designed to resocialize individuals to survive in a post-UD world; training also includes UD identification, engagement and combat skills.

[6] MARL 750: Mobile Army Research Lab – A heavily armored, tracked research and reconnaissance vehicle specially designed for hazardous environments. The vehicle has two distinct sections, similar to rail cars: a forward command and operation section, and a research section. Maximum crew capacity: 8

"Negative," Jim said. "We're not coming with you."

"Why the hell not? Why you wanna get yourself deeper in the shit, huh?"

"We have our orders. Our mission…"

"Oh, Jesus Christ, Jim," Hoss began, "Fuck orders! Fuck the mission! Nobody's in charge anymore! Who's gonna care if you carry out your orders? Central Command is gone - overrun with UDs, just like all them bunkers. Heck, even Area 51. There is no more continuity of government. You heard them emergency broadcasts…and now the radios ain't pickin' up shit. There's nobody left. When did you lose contact with your bunker… huh?"

"We never had a radio."

"No radio?" Hoss took a deep breath. "Shit. Bunker 57 was lost a few days ago. It was the last one standing, too." There was a moment of silence as the weight of that remark sank in. "I'm sorry Jim. I wish I had your sense of duty. I admire that – I really do! But you know as well as anyone the situation is fido[7]." He stopped talking. Jim's stern look said it all - he would never abandon the mission.

Hoss turned away and wiped his brow. He threw his arms up in the air and said, "Ah heck… I reckon if any one man can save this country, it would be you, Jim. I damn near figured if I ever had grankids, they'd be sittin' on my knee, out there on the screened in porch, listenin' to stories about the mighty green Jim Shrike." They both laughed. "Now tell me how you went about changing color…"

Just then the roof hatch at the back opened and the infamous Professor Yao popped his head out. "Hoss," he said as he climbed up on the deck. He dabbed his sweaty forehead with his hanky before speaking. "The power relay in…" *blah blah blah*… whatever he said. I can't remember exactly. It was all technoshitspeak, just like the engineer on that TV show my Grandpa used to watch called *Space Chase*.

---

[7] Fido (*acronym: Fuck it, drive on!*): To leave a hopeless situation or problem behind.

"Okay, already!" Hoss blurted, silencing the little man. "Enough with the bullshit and just fix it!"

Yao stood there and clenched his fists. "I'm burning," he spat in disgust. "I can't wait to be discharged!" He stomped across the metal plating and disappeared back down the hatch.

"Where did you find that guy?" Jim asked, scowling.

Hoss chuckled to himself, "He's a civilian – a scientist of some sort. He was already in Bunker 21. From what they tell me, he was working on some sort of 'top secret' project. Anyways, the day comes when the zeds show up and me, Handbeef and Nelson meet up in the motor pool. So here we are, loadin' all the fuel and shit into the MARL, you know. And all of a sudden, I hear this angry voice comin' from inside the cab. The three of us went in there and there's Yao, lyin' on his back, with his head under the pilot's console - wires all over. So Nelson sticks his head in real close and all and says, 'Can I help you?' And all we get is this loud, 'I'm burning!' Damn near woke the undead, I'm sure of it."

We all burst out laughing. "You mean he was trying to hot wire it?"

"Somethin' like that...," Hoss replied. "Heck, what he lacks in social graces he more than makes up for in smarts. He can damn near frankenstein[8] anything. Anyways, I made a deal with him that if he enlisted, with me as his commander, we would protect him. In exchange, he had to keep the engines running and his mouth shut. I promised I would discharge him once we got him to safety. And he's been damn near the biggest pain in my ass ever since."

Jim raised a hand and shushed him. "Hear that?"

"Hear what?" Hoss asked.

"Quiet!"

It sounded like a like a swarm of mechanical hornets in the distance. "Is that a dirt bike?"

"Sounds like it... more than one, I'd say."

---

[8] Frankenstein: The ability to fix or build something using spare parts.

The buzz drew closer.

"Aw shit!" Hoss spat. "Turdburglars![9]"

The first bike jumped the dune and sped towards us. Five or six more bikes followed. Hoss got down on one knee and yelled into the hatch. "Get your asses up here – we got company." A shot rang off the armor plating. "And they're comin' in hot!" The big man ran to the front of the vehicle and threw off the tarp concealing the gunner's cupola. He squirmed his way in.

"What the hell's goin' on?" Handbeef shouted as he emerged on deck.

"Incoming at three o'clock!" Jim yelled. Several more dirt bikes were racing towards us, followed by two pickup trucks.

I made my way to the back of the vehicle and crouched down behind the radar dish.

"Take that you fuckin' wahoos!" Hoss barked. The .50 caliber roared to life, tearing up the ground, whipping up dust and smoke. Everyone opened fire. Hoss cut down two of the bikes. I took aim and fired, taking out another.

"More bikes at six o'clock," Nelson yelled. "They're swarming us!" Before I could fire another shot, a volley of bullets danced around my position. The men in the trucks sprayed wildly at us, giving the bikes a chance to close in.

One of the bikers leapt from his mount and grabbed the exterior ladder. Before he could pull himself on board, I stood up and fired three rounds into his chest. Nelson screamed. I looked over just in time to see his gut explode. He doubled over and dropped. Two more bikers were already climbing up the side. I ran over and planted my boot in the face of one of them. He let go of the rungs and fell back. I shot him in the face and again in top of the head for good measure. I turned just in time to duck the other man's machete.

"We've been boarded!" Jim shouted.

"Tell me something I don't know!" I shouted back.

---

[9] Turdburglars: People who steal your shit or take it by force.

UNDEAD RECKONING

The biker swung the machete again. Instinctively I raised my rifle, and the blow tore it from my hands. Another biker snuck up behind me. Jim grappled with someone and Handbeef provided cover fire for Hoss. I exchanged glances with my two attackers. A third was climbing up the ladder. The situation did not look good.

Something rumbled deep inside the vehicle. I could feel trembling under my feet. The bikers seemed to be as surprised as I was. Thick black smoke belched from the exhaust vent, which I happened to be standing over, engulfing me and one of my assailants. I blindly threw a punch. My fist connected and flattened a biker's nose. I grabbed him by the arm and shoulder and hurled him towards the other man. Both fell off the deck. I took a blow to my kidney and fell to one knee. I twisted and put my arm up to block the follow-up kick, but the impact sent me sprawling onto my back.

I felt the rumble again. The MARL 750 suddenly jerked forward. The biker lost his balance and fell on top of me. The engines roared to life and the vehicle lurched forward. I threw the biker off me. But he grabbed hold of my jersey and both of us went over the side. I managed to get one hand on the ladder. He held on tightly – his feet kicking at the treads.

"Aaargh!"

Holding up your own weight plus that of another man with one hand wasn't easy. The pick-up truck accelerated, drawing in alongside us. The man in the bed grabbed on to the guy who was holding onto me. The pick-up veered away. With my free hand, I punched the biker in the head. He let go. Lucky for me and not for him, the man holding onto the biker was leaning out too far. Both of them fell under the treads, where they were turned to pulp. A hand grabbed onto my wrist.

"C'mon!" Jim pulled me back up on the deck.

"Thanks!"

"Don't thank me just yet. We got bigger problems."

I looked up and saw the other pickup: it was barreling head-on towards us. Two men were leaning on the cab, firing automatic rifles. The passenger was also firing out the window. Handbeef took a few rounds and dropped. Hoss fired back, filling the windshield and the vehicle's occupants full of holes. But the pick-up kept charging toward us.

"Brace yourself for impact!" Jim and I got down, grabbing any hand holds within reach.

Suddenly the rear roof hatch opened. Yao rushed out of the hole. "Hey Hoss," Yao said excitedly, "I fixed the... what the..."

"Get down Yao!"

I clenched my teeth. The MARL slammed into the pick-up throwing the crumpled heap back a few meters. Both gunners in the bed flew forward and got pasted against the armor plating.

"I'm burning!" Yao screamed as he was thrown forward. He hit the deck face first and then rolled off the side, landing in the bed of the pickup truck that was driving alongside us.

"Yao!" I shouted.

The pick-up and the remaining bikes sped off. The MARL rolled right along, crushing what remained of the wreck. Eventually, the engine sputtered and died.

"Well that was quite the ride!"

Jim didn't hear me. He was crouching over Hoss in the gunner's cupola. It wasn't what I wanted to see. Hoss was a bloody mess.

"Easy, Hoss," Jim said, gripping Hoss' shoulder.

Hoss coughed. Goo dripped from his chin. He was breathing heavily. "I'm all fucked up, eh, Jim?" Hoss wheezed. Jim didn't respond. "Where's Nelson? And... Handbeef?"

"We lost them," Jim responded, "And Yao."

Hoss forced a smile. "Ah, shit... remember... how I said I'd tell them stories about you?"

"Yeah."

"I guess..." he coughed. "I guess I'll be sharing them with the good Lord himself." Hoss started to laugh but his breath gave out on him.

"Just take it easy."

"Jim, do me a favor? I don't wanna become one of them fuckin' meatsticks. You know what to do."

"I understand."

"I damn near thought I was gonna make it," Hoss sighed. And then he lowered his head.

Jim stood up. "Ed... why don't you go find a weapon and make sure the dead stay dead." He drew his sidearm and aimed it at the back of Hoss' head.

"Yessir!" I turned my back to him and shuddered. You know, you never think twice about killing a zombie. But killing someone who was about to become a zombie, that wasn't easy.

POW!

By dusk, we had salvaged just about everything we could carry. We had all the necessities: food, water, weapons, and ammo. I also found a crate with an AT-4 antitank missile. We laid out our gear on the deck. After I conducted a final sweep of the interior, I headed back up. Jim lay on his stomach, and he was looking through the binoculars. I got down and crawled right up beside him.

"Wassup?"

"They're back!"

He handed me the binoculars. A truck and a few bikers stood guard up on a hill a few hundred meters away.

"Jim, did you see that before?"

"If you're referring to that catapult... no."

The truck had been modified. Mounted onto it were wood and steel beams, lashed together, and an intricate network of ropes and pulleys. A shallow basket hung from the long, extended arm. It looked like the giant spoon you used to see on the billboards advertising *Mossey's Mostly Meat Stew... Mmm, Stew!*

The man standing on the hood pressed a megaphone to his face. "OCCUPANTS OF THE ARMORED VEHICLE! JUST LEAVE EVERYTHING AND WALK AWAY OR THE HOSTAGE DIES!"

Hostage? I looked at the catapult again.

"Hey Jim… there's someone strapped to the end of that thing. Jim?" Jim already set up the AT-4 and was taking aim. "Jim, wait! That's…"

WHOOSH! The missile took off and spiraled towards its target. Men scattered. The vehicle erupted into a ball of fire. The blast caused the catapult arm to fling forward, hurling a bright fiery mass across the sky towards us.

"I'M BUUUUUURRRRNNNNIIIIINNNNGGG!" Professor Yao's angry monotone voice screamed. His flaming body sailed over our heads and landed in dirt.

I turned to Jim. "We could've saved him!"

"We did! He got his wish, didn't he?"

3 THINGS THAT GO CHOMP IN THE NIGHT

Even the darkest of designs holds light.
-The Book of Amaltheon

    We travelled most of the night and well into the day. A few zombies roamed the countryside here and there, but it was nothing a clear shot couldn't fix. Zombies weren't a common sight in the country – they seemed to like the big city life (or lack thereof). Around midday we happened upon some high ground that was easily defendable and provided a clear view of the surrounding terrain. We took that as our cue to rest.

    I slept away the rest of the day. Jim only slept once every three or four days. And when he did sleep, it was anywhere from eight to twelve hours. He said it was conditioning he received from when he was in the Special Forces. By dusk, it was my turn to take watch.

    The night sky was an incredible sight to behold. I really wished I knew more about constellations. The only one that I recognized was the Big Dipper: three stars in the handle and four in the bucket. I gave myself a little jiggle, shook off the pee-shivers, and zipped up my fly. When I turned, it was just there: a shadow crouching over Jim. The adrenaline surged through my body and I grabbed my rifle: safety off, aimed and ready to fire.

    The shadow rose and stood still. It was taller than most linebackers I had encountered. "Nice night," it said. The voice felt like ice water down my back – my skin broke out in goose bumps. And it had this strange accent, like a creepier version of our grade school janitor, Mr. Kecskemeti. "Men have spent so much time looking at the stars. Ever wonder if they... look back? Think of what they have seen... what they know."

    "Step back!" I ordered.

    "Where?" it asked. "In space? Or in time?"

"What? Just get back!" I repeated, "As in, away from my friend there." It looked down at Jim, who lay asleep on his bedroll. Then, it looked back at me.

"And if I don't?"

"What? Hello? I'm holding a gun. What do you think I am going to do? I'll shoot!"

"I don't think you will," it said confidently, inflecting every word in such a strange way that... it made me feel... drowsy. The shadow took one giant step over Jim and stopped short of the fire. There was just enough light to illuminate it. It was a man... and he was hideous! If he hadn't talked, I would've sworn he was undead. His eyes were completely black (no whites in them at all), and deeply set in a pale, gaunt face. Dark, greasy hair hung down from his scalp. And then he smiled, revealing a mouth filled with row upon row of sharp teeth. The hair stood up on the back of my neck.

He moved forward very quickly – his long coat swept over the fire - until he stood right in front of me. He cupped a hand over the barrel of my rifle, leaned in and said, "But if you REALLY want to shoot... then go ahead." My head was heavy. I knew what I wanted my body to do and it didn't do it. The world seemed to move much more slowly than it should - like I was dreaming.

I suddenly came to my senses and pulled the trigger. He pulled his hand away, held it up in front of me, and looked at me through the hole in his palm. "Feel better?"

I lowered my rifle.

"Good! I would hate for you to feel... uncomfortable."

"Wh-What are you?" My legs were trembling.

"I am Upior[10]."

"Did you just say, *up yours*?"

It smiled coyly, revealing those god-awful teeth. I almost had to look away. "Careful... I can easily pull that smart ass of yours out through your mouth." My blood instantly ran cold. "Please, don't give me a reason to ... kill you... Mr. Griffin."

---

[10] **Upior** (*Slavic, pronounced oop-yoor*)**:** Undead; vampire.

"No... I won't. How, uh...," I cleared my throat. "How did you know my name?"

He raised a long, bony finger and drew a jagged nail along my jersey. It snagged and pulled at the fabric. "It is written... on your shirt. I saw this when you were... peeing." I felt stupid. "Do you know what a Griffin is?"

"A mythical beast... half lion and half eagle sort of thing." I only knew that because my best friend in high school, Carlin Frenke, got me into playing AA[11].

"Ah... impressive!" he smiled. *Those teeth!* "Griffins are tough to kill. They put up a good fight. Guardians of great... treasure, or so it is said."

He returned to Jim's side and crouched down. He ran a finger along the letters on Jim's army jacket "And your friend... J. Shrike," he read. He cocked his head to one side and rubbed his chin, as if deep in thought. "Do you know what a Shrike is?"

"No... I mean, other than Jim, I don't know what a Shrike is."

"It is a type of... bird," he said. "The Shrike impales its prey on a thorn bush, making it easier to... tear apart." He waited for the concept to sink in. "Does your friend like to tear things apart?"

In an instant, Jim had the Upior by the wrist. With his other hand, he held a knife to his throat.

"Actually, I do," Jim seethed.

Now, Jim had the fastest reflexes I had ever seen. But quick as a flash, the Upior rose, with Jim dangling from his arm. And just as

---

[11] Anomalies Amok (AA): The award-winning fantasy role-playing game, created by Larry Goldlake. The game used the d20 wave system, whereby a series of 20-sided dice would be thrown. Success on the first throw would add cumulative modifiers to the second, and so on. A similar mechanic was used in determining combat damage. The number of d20s required to determine success was left to the discretion of the Game Master. However, the common practice was to use three.

quickly, he hurled him... I'd say maybe ten feet. Jim hit the ground face first.

Instinctively, I charged at the Upior, and ran right into his hand. He had me by the throat and I was gasping for air. His grip was ice-cold. My knees weakened. "You want me to change my mind about killing you, hmm?" I clawed at his fingers. My eyes bulged from my head. Everything went dark. He threw me to the ground and I landed so hard on my ass, it measured on the Richter scale. But I ignored the pain – I was too busy welcoming the cool night air into my lungs.

The Upior shifted his attention back to Jim. He kicked him over with his boot. Then he dropped to one knee and clutched him by the face. Jim struggled, but it was of no use. It seemed as though the Upior was pushing him into the earth.

"Whatever happened to a hand shake, hmm? Perhaps I should kill you after all." He leaned in and opened his mouth wide. There was a pop and his jaw extended even further, revealing more of those horrific teeth. But then he quickly drew back. "What's this?"

He twisted Jim's head from side to side. He stood up, still holding Jim by the head, and dragged him closer to the fire. He stared closely at his forehead. I know what he saw – the bloody abrasion on Jim's forehead was healing before his eyes. The Upior grinned.

"You can regenerate! Truly, you are the Green Man! The prophecy must be true!"

With that, he let go of Jim, dropping him to the ground. The Upior crouched down and stared at him with those two black pits. I hobbled over and joined them.

"You, okay?"

"Yeah," Jim winced. I could tell his ego had been bruised more than his body.

The Upior grinned. His teeth gave me a little jolt, but I was getting used to it. *"The Green Man will walk among the dead. And Death will kneel before him. And he will rule as Lord of the Dead."*

Jim looked at me, and then back at the Upior and said, "I'm not familiar with this prophecy you speak of."

"Nor should you be. It is taken from the Book of Amaltheon. It is... ancient."

"Like you?"

"Ha, yes! Like me!" The Upior looked directly at Jim. "Where did you come from?" Even though the question was not directed at me, my head felt heavy.

"Bunker 57," Jim answered.

The Upior stood. He closed his eyes, tilted his head back and continued, *"For when Darkness feeds upon the living, the Green Man shall be found. And never again shall Darkness be sated. And with the aid of his champions, he will spill the blood of salvation. And into the belly of the dragon he shall go."*

The Upior opened his eyes, and looked down at us. "For weeks now, I have wandered these wastes... travelling from bunker to bunker. Yours was the last to fall. And that is when I found you."

"What is this reference to the blood of salvation?" Jim asked.

The Upior nodded. "It is the blood of Christ that was shed at... Golgotha."

"Golgotha?" I repeated.

"Yes," The Upior said matter-of-factly.

"Uh, no offence," I started. "But you can read anything you want into holy writings, if you're desperate enough. My Uncle, the Reverend, he could always explain away shit with a biblical passage."

The Upior flared his nostrils. Slowly his teeth crept out of his mouth. I think I pissed him off. But Jim grabbed me by the arm and raised his hand, as if to stop the Upior.

"If I am the Green Man as the prophecy says, then where do I find Golgotha?"

The Upior turned his attention to him. "Travel north! Then deep...into the earth."

"And there we find the blood of salvation?"

"Yes."

"Then what?"

"Keep going! "The dragon's belly runs long... and deep. *And he shall walk through the fiery halls of Nabisusha."* The Upior grinned.

"Nabi-what?" I asked.

"Worry not of this! First, find what you are looking for, and then, be found... by what looks for you. Together, you must break the jaw of the blind mouth. Only then, may you... continue."

Jim stood up, approached the Upior and said, "I believe I am the Green Man you are looking for."

The Upior raised his eyebrows and smiled. "Excellent!"

"What?" I gasped.

"I'll explain later," Jim said out the side of his mouth.

The Upior clapped Jim on the shoulders. "You should leave immediately."

"Why?"

"The undead like to congregate in deep, dark places. It is... comforting to them."

"We'll move at dawn."

"Ah, yes," the Upior responded. "I have no desire to travel in... daylight."

"You can't, right?" I asked. "Vampires can't stand the sun."

"The sun cannot stand me. It does not like to see what... I do." He grinned. "You watch too many movies, Mr. Griffin. It is possible to stand in full sun. It takes... discipline. The night is more... accommodating."

He turned to Jim. "I shall leave you now."

"That's it?" I gasped. "You're leaving? What the hell?"

"I have done what I set out to do... I found you."

"Right... so I trust we'll meet again someday?"

"Indeed!" He looked at me and showed me those awful teeth one last time. "It was a pleasure, Mr. Griffin. You seem much taller than you did on the cover of... *Time* magazine." And with a sweep of his cloak, he was gone.

I took a deep breath. Jim was staring at the ground.

"Well, that was fuckin' weird! He knew who I was. I didn't know vampires liked football."

"Obviously, this one did."

"Yeah, that's kind of freakish." I put my hands on my hips. "I thought we were just dealing with zombies here. What the hell happened to this world?" Jim didn't respond, so I pressed on to the next issue on my mind. "Hey... what's all this shit about you and the prophecy?"

"He knows something."

I scowled. "Knows what?"

"What's another word for Golgotha?"

"Golgotha? What does that have to do with this?"

"C'mon... all those stories you told me about your Uncle... surely you learned something from him."

"Okay... um... Golgotha is an Aramaic word. It means *The Skull*. It was where Christ was crucified. The Latin word for it is *Calvary*."

"Calvary Research Lab."

I shrugged my shoulders. "Is that what the Upior was talking about? I've never heard of it."

"I don't think the Upior was directly referring to it. It's a top secret military facility. But it is underground. And it's where we're headed."

"Which is where, exactly?"

"Dulce, New Mexico."

"Hmm...in that case, the Upior's words kind of make sense then, don't they?"

"Yeah, that's what I found so odd."

"But what about the blood of salvation? And the blind mouth? And the something that will find us?"

"I'm not sure about that. I guess we'll find out when we get there. We'll leave at dawn. You okay to continue watch?" Jim made his way to his bedroll.

"Yeah, I'm okay." I sat down on a rock and fiddled with my rifle. "Hey, Jim?"

"What is it?" He was lying on his back staring at the starry sky.

"I dunno." I kicked at the ground. "It just seems like there are always more questions. And the answers we got just lead to more questions."

Jim titled his head back and looked at me. "Does that bother you?"

"Yeah, I guess. Doesn't it bother you?"

Jim grinned. "Not really."

"Not really?"

"I'm not bothered by the questions. I'm bothered by the answers," he said, as he rolled onto his side, putting his back to me.

"Hmph!" I chuckled. "So I guess you're not going to tell me why you're green?" Jim didn't respond. I sighed and looked up at the stars. "Well, I'm not bothered by answers," I whispered.

4 RECIPE FOR DISASTER

Even the hands of men cannot be stayed by death.
In time, that very hand will reach for death's grasp.
                                            -The Book of Amaltheon

Dulce, New Mexico was dead quiet. Actually, it was more like *undead* quiet. But for a town that once housed approximately 2500 people, zombies weren't much of a concern. In fact, Jim and I took out the ones that stood in our way rather easily; there weren't many on the barren outskirts of the town. This wasn't a scavenger mission. We weren't as interested in what was in town as we were in what was hidden somewhere under nearby Dulce Rock. In all, it was very uneventful, and a bit disappointing, considering the area was known for UFO sightings and cattle mutilations.

Jim led the way, taking us deep into the rocky terrain, until he found what he was looking for.

"Here it is," he said, pointing to a small cave. It was just big enough for someone to crawl into.

"What is this?"

"A back door." Jim said, as he squirmed his way in. I followed. Gradually, the cave expanded enough so we could hunch over.

Nestled deep within the hollow rock was a round hatch with a wheel in the center. Jim crouched in the small opening. It took a few tries, but he finally managed to force the wheel and open the hatch. We squeezed through about fifty yards of metal pipe and emerged inside a much larger cave. Set in the rock wall was a large steel door, similar to an airlock. Next to it, a wall-mounted panel with a screen and keypad.

"Restricted Area," I read aloud. Most of the lettering had rusted out, but typical of military signage, the wording was all the same. "Use of deadly force authorized."

"This is it."

"That's it? A top secret government facility with a back door? You're kidding, right?"

"Sometimes the best kept secret is where you least expect to find it." Jim tapped at the keys and the panel came to life. Just above it, something that looked like a pair of goggles lit up. He pressed his face up to them. Data danced and flashed across the screen.

"ACCESS GRANTED," a pre-recorded voice droned.

Jim stepped back from the panel. A green light lit up above the door. It hissed open. When the dust settled, we were staring into an elevator.

"You're serious?"

Jim gave me a nod, and stepped inside. "Going down."

I shook my head in disbelief. "This better be worth it. What floor we going to?"

"Level 7: Calvary Research Lab."

"What kind of research do they do in this lab?"

"Genetic engineering."

"Have you been here before?"

"No... all I know is how to get in and what level to go to."

The door slid shut. The elevator made no mechanical sound nor did it seem like we were moving. Seconds later, the doors slid open opposite to the side we had entered. Moist stale air filled my nostrils. It didn't smell right, like old Moses Calhoun, after he spent a summer's day in the alley next to *Walstein's Thrift Shop*, drinking and pissing all over himself. Poor old fool used to drink antiseptic mouthwash – never smelled minty though.

I stuck my head out in the corridor. It stretched endlessly in both directions, lined with various pipes and conduit, and dotted along the way with sections of bare rock. Peeling *Caution* and *High Pressure* stickers hung from the pipes. The only sound was the hum of the dull yellow emergency lights. I have to admit, I was a little nervous. Even with emergency lights, it still seemed so dark. Jim stepped out, and I followed hesitantly.

"Okay, Jim... uh... which way now?"

"You go that way," he replied, pointing. "And I'll go this way."

"What are we looking for?"

"You mean the blood of salvation? I honestly don't know."

"Oh, fuck off... you're shittin' me, right?"

"No, I'm not."

"What the... that's it? We just wander around until we think we've found something?"

"That's all I know."

I stared at Jim in disbelief. But he was serious! I threw my arms up and huffed. "Whatever!"

I flipped on the light on the barrel of my rifle and slowly paced down the corridor. Jim headed off in the other direction. Drips echoed through the halls. As I walked forward, I tried to keep my breathing and my rifle steady. The dripping grew louder. An eerie green glow emanated out from around the corner.

I turned right. The entire wall to the left of me appeared to be a single pane of glass. The glow was coming from the other side. A laboratory, the likes of which I had only ever seen in sci-fi movies, was on the other side. I entered through the main doors.

The whole room smelled like Moses Calhoun. My breathing was heavier and my heart thumped rapidly. Cables, piping and servo arms hovered over stainless autopsy tables. Rusting saws, surgical blades and needles rested in their storage trays. Computer terminals idled – the odd blinking diode indicating the only sign of life. Rows upon rows of huge clear vats lined the back wall of the room. The vats contained the glowing liquid and - the hair stood on the back of my neck – zombies... about a dozen in each one. They were hairless, naked and all shriveled, like grotesque raisins. *Yuck! I hate raisins.* Barcodes had been laser-scribed across their foreheads.

"Holy shit!" I whispered. "What the fuck were they doing down here?"

Interwoven cables and leaky hoses connected the vats to a variety of electronic equipment. Puddles of green liquid covered the floor. The zombies in the vats appeared to be, pardon the pun, dead. They had been *neutralized*[12], as Jim put it. Some were even showing signs of decomposition. All the vats contained dead zombies... except for one. And the zombies inside it noticed me. They pushed their squishy skin up against the vat, tapping their nails on the glass.

TINK! TINK! TINK!

I took a deep breath and headed towards some sterile-looking steel storage units. Through glass paneled doors, I saw hundreds of vials sitting in racks, arranged in rows, and labeled with bar codes. Each label also had a batch number and the word *Failure* in red ink. I set down my rifle and opened a door. I scanned over the homogenous little containers. Then, I saw it: a rack of five vials with *Bunker 57* written on them in pen. I grabbed one, and that's when I heard the splash. My heart jumped.

"Jim?"

I heard the splash again and turned just in time. The zombie descended on me and we locked arms. I dropped the vial in my hand. He wasn't saturated like the others. His skin felt like rotting bark and his parched teeth snapped at my face. I fell back into the cabinet, smashing the glass shelves. Vials fell out all over the floor.

"Shit!"

I wrestled with the zombie until I got back on my feet and threw him. He stumbled back against the vat filled with live zombies. Before he took another step forward, I drew my sidearm and put a bullet right through the center of his forehead. The bullet exited the back of his head, splattering his brain against the glass. The zombie slid to the floor. Green liquid spouted from the small hole where the bullet had entered the vat. Tiny cracks spider-veined out from the hole, popping and creaking their way across the glass.

"Oh... Ffffuck!"

---

[12] Neutralized *(military terminology)*: To kill a zombie by destroying the brain.

I quickly sorted through the vials, trying the find the ones labeled *Bunker 57*. I looked back at the vat. Liquid seeped through the cracks. The glass bulged.

"Fuck! Fuck! Fuck!"

Glass snapped and shattered. A wave of green liquid spilled forth, washing the vials across the floor and out into the hall. The zombies took notice of their new-found freedom and shuffled through the exit.

"Fuck!"

I ran to the entry doors and stared down anxiously at the sea of green.

"C'mon, Bunker 57! Where are you?"

The zombies were getting closer. And then I remembered that my rifle was leaning against the cabinet.

"Fuck!" I liked that rifle. It was a Bushmaster ACR, not like the standard issue stuff the other guys in the bunker had carried. It even had a red dot sight and a grinning skull decal on the stock.

I frantically searched the floor. There it was! I reached for the vial and closed my hand on it. Right then, a pair of soggy decaying feet appeared. I looked up at the zombie standing over me. I avoided looking at his crotch – being dead and shriveled was especially unkind to genitals. The rest of the crowd was gathering behind him. I pushed off the floor and ploughed my shoulder into his chest. His skin slid across his rib cage and sloughed away. At least I put enough force into him to send him sprawling into the crowd. The zombie entourage tumbled like bowling pins.

I took off down the corridor while stowing the vial in my belt. When I felt I had gained enough ground, I slowed down. The corridor was dark. "Jim? Hello?" Pairs of dull yellow lights emerged from the darkness. Zombies were shambling towards me from the other direction as well. They were all naked. Some were kindling dry, and others sopping wet. I felt like the odd man out at the Zombie Nudist Resort. I drew my sidearm. *BANG! BANG! BANG! CLICK!*

"Crap!" My hands were shaking. I couldn't... reload... fast enough. The zombies were almost on top of me. They were coming from all directions. I decided I would just have to rush through them - *just like running into the end zone!* I took a deep breath and charged. Clawed hands raked at my clothes. Hungry mouths opened wide. I punched and pushed at every inch of slick, shrivelly or leathery skin until I broke free. I ran down the corridor.... until it came to a dead end.

"Ah... shit!"

The zombies kept coming. I looked around for options. To my left: a floor level air supply vent rattled away. To my right: a FIRE EMERGENCY CABINET! I smashed the glass, pulled the fire axe free from its brackets, and pounded the shit out of the vent.

A spiky hand reached for me. I turned and butt ended the zombie in the face, knocking his jaw permanently open. It staggered back. A quick swing took his block off. More hands reached out at me. I swung wildly, sending arms and hands flying. Heads split open and poured their contents out onto the floor. But they kept coming! Bony, spindly fingers reached for me... pulled at me. The axe was wrenched from my grasp.

I buried my fists, elbows and knees in any flesh that I could find. I gouged eyes, twisted off limbs, and snapped bones. A hand grabbed me by the shoulder. I spun and punched, cracking Jim squarely on the jaw. "Where the hell did you come from?"

He shook it off. "Through the air supply shaft... c'mon!" He grabbed a handful of my jersey and dragged me down to the floor. We crawled through the shambling masses and into the air shaft. Taking the maintenance ladder two rungs at a time, we ascended quickly to the top.

Jim flung open the hatch. It clanged on the concrete floor and we scurried out like rats.

"Fire in the hole!"

I cleared out of the way as Jim tossed a grenade down the shaft, and slammed the hatch shut. The blast seemed to echo through the entire complex. I lay back on the cold floor, breathing heavily.

"Sorry I took so long," Jim said.

"Sorry I punched you in the jaw."

Jim rubbed his chin and grinned. "You call that a punch?"

I rolled my eyes. "What happened to you?"

"The place was crawling with UDs. I escaped into the ventilation system. Any luck finding anything?"

I pulled the vial from a pouch in my belt and grinned from ear to ear. "The blood of salvation."

Jim grabbed it from my hand and examined it closely. "Ed, you're amazing."

"Yes I am. Now what do we do with it?"

"That's a good question."

"Uh... you're kidding, right?"

"No, I'm not."

"What? Hey... all this time, I've been fine with being on a need-to-know basis. But now that we've found what you're looking for, you know nothing when I need to know something."

"Sorry, Ed. This base has been compromised... and we need more answers."

We both stared off into space for a bit before Jim said, "We'll follow the Upior's instructions and head north."

"Seriously?"

"I know it sounds crazy, but his prophecy is the only information we have to go on."

"You're right," I sighed. "I am more bothered by the answers than the questions. Okay... we go north."

"Good! Let's rest and regroup."

I looked around the concrete room. It was so drab, so sterile, so spartan, so... military. "Where are we?"

"It's a garage of some sort," Jim said. "Maybe a guard station?"

A quick sweep of the interior confirmed Jim's assumption. The place had been seriously rat-fucked[13]: lockers, crates, drawers and cabinets had been left open - their contents strewn about in haste.

"Whoever was in here left in a big hurry," Jim said.

"No kidding. At least they left us a vehicle." I patted the hood of the Humvee. "Let's hope it still runs."

Jim managed to get the Humvee started. He also discovered a healthy supply of fuel. I found a new assault rifle in a munitions locker, to replace the one I had lost. It wasn't anything other than standard issue, but given the option of retrieving the other rifle, I was good with it. Ammunition was another story. I collected a handful of bullets off the floor, and found another few boxes in a cabinet. Other than a small supply of food, there wasn't much left for the taking. I guess the real prize was an area free of zombies and a well-earned rest.

"We could use some fresh air."

I activated the controls, but nothing happened. Kicking at them didn't seem to help, either. Had my drill instructor, Sergeant Bob Moppy, been there, he would have made some comment *'bout how in the good old days, you could fix something with a swift kick*. I wished Bob was here to see this now. On second thought, he was kind of an ass. Maybe the situation was better without him.

Jim managed to get the garage doors open while I took a nap. The dry cool air was a welcome change to the Moses Calhoun smell. I awoke to some instant coffee and an MRE[14] breakfast. We took one last look around before leaving.

I leaned on the passenger side door. "So if we head north, what do you think's waiting for us?"

---

[13] Rat-Fucked: To search rapidly yet thoroughly, taking the best possible findings.
[14] MRE: Meal, Ready-to-Eat – Self contained, individual field ration with a shelf life of three to five years.

Jim took one last look at the vial before tucking it away in his tac vest[15]. He shrugged his shoulders as he climbed into the driver's seat. "I don't know."

"It can't get any worse than the Upior, can it?"

---

[15] Tac Vest: Tactical Vest – A Nylon tactical vest with numerous pouches, pockets, and optional holster.

5 THE AFRO-SAXON

*When the blind mouth leads the unseeing,
men will unite to guide them on the true path.
And the Green Man will have his vengeance.*
— *The Book of Amaltheon*

It was best to stay off the major interstates. Log jams of derelict vehicles clogged the arteries – another scar left behind by UD day, and cars provided plenty of good hiding places for zombies. We first noticed the crosses on the outskirts of Pueblo, a city about a hundred miles south of Denver. Crucified zombies marked the roadways leading to the city. Some of the zombies weren't even neutralized which made it all the more creepy when the odd zombie turned his head and watched us pass by.

We hid the vehicle in a wooded area on the outskirts of town, and set up a makeshift camp in an abandoned industrial complex. It seemed like it was out in the middle of nowhere, but it provided an excellent view of the city and of a road that had yet to be marked with crosses. Our plan was to rest and then scout the city in the morning. Jim took first watch and I crawled into my bedroll. Lucky for us, we didn't have to wait long for answers. It was still light, and I had just dozed off when Jim noticed them.

"Ed. We have visitors." I quickly geared up. Jim was at the window peering through the binoculars.

"What is it?"

"Two cargo trucks. They just stopped at the crossroads." He handed me the binoculars. Not far from our hiding spot, a handful of soldiers exited the second vehicle. Some of them took up defensive positions, most likely to keep watch for zombies. The others pulled out timbers and started building crosses.

"That's odd... why is the army doing this?"

"I don't know." Jim looked back at the door. "One of us should watch the entrance – don't want any UDs sneaking up on us."

"Right, I'll do it." I looked out into the hall. The coast was clear. I leaned against the door jamb, and I could see the activity outside from a nearby window in the hall. After the crosses were built, the soldiers went to the first truck and unloaded... people? "Are those zombies?"

"It appears so. They're tied up. I bet they're up for crucifixion."

"What the hell?" I whispered, still staring out the window. Within a few minutes, the first zombie was nailed down.

Jim turned his attention to me and was about to speak, but instead he shouted, "Ed, look out!"

I turned quickly. A zombie had come down the hall and was just reaching out to grab me. It was a teenager wearing a smiley face t-shirt. He had one arm – the other one lost at the shoulder. I shoved his hand aside, jammed my rifle into his crotch and fired, stitching him up from asshole to pie-hole. His brain blew out the back of his head and he crumpled.

"Shit! Sorry! Do you think they heard those shots?"

Jim raised a hand to silence me and looked through the binoculars. From my window, I could see soldiers in a huddle and one of them was pointing at the building.

"We have to get out of here," Jim said. We grabbed our stuff. Jim was out the door. I took one last look back. The men piled into the vehicles and were driving towards us.

"Damn!"

I bolted down the stairs, taking two at a time, and caught up with Jim outside. We ran towards a warehouse on the other side of the parking lot. As we ran inside, brakes squealed and I heard shouting.

"Shit!"

"Keep going!"

We ran through the warehouse and out the other side straight into the path of the jeep. It ground to a halt. I don't know who was more surprised: us or them. We reacted first and hosed out the interior. When the bodies stopped flailing, Jim shouted, "Let's go!" Just as we took off, somebody opened up on us. *BUDDA! BUDDA! BUDDA!* Bullets whizzed by like hornets.

"Head for the forest!"

Unfortunately, a field lay between us and the tree line. I figured about two hundred yards of wide open terrain with only a rusted out tractor for cover. To make matters worse, two zombies were keeping it company. They could have been farmers for all I knew. Both wore coveralls, and one had a wide brimmed flappy hat. We raced across the field.

KA-BOOM!

The grenade explosion sent me diving to the ground. My ears were ringing. I shook my head. I was in a cloud of dust and smoke. Jim lay a few feet away from me. He pulled himself through the dirt. His leg... it was gone below the knee.

"Holy shit, Jim! You better grow that back quick!"

"Leave me! Get to the forest."

Bullets chewed up the dirt around me. Men charged towards us. We were outnumbered and outgunned. I got to my knees and put my arms in the air. Within minutes, we were surrounded.

SMACK!

A soldier struck me in the shoulder with his rifle butt. Jim took a blow to the head. They stripped us of our weapons. In anticipation of being filled in[16], I curled up into the fetal position, covering my head and genitals with my hands. The trucks we had seen earlier arrived. A soldier, an officer in fact, got out of the passenger side. After he looked Jim over, he got into a conversation on his radio. Then he called over two soldiers. They lifted Jim up and carried him away, throwing him into the back of the truck.

"What do we do with this one?" another soldier asked, motioning to me with his rifle.

"Kill him," the officer replied. "Captain Thaddeus will be here shortly to give you further orders."

---

[16] Filled in: To receive punches and kicks courtesy of multiple attackers.

"Yessir," the soldier replied.

"Fuck!" I muttered under my breath as the truck pulled away. There was so much racing through my mind. I tried to think back to the combat training I received in the bunker. I couldn't recall anything Jim ever taught me about how to engage multiple attackers. Mind you, his skill level in hand to hand combat was godlike. The soldiers used to say it was next to impossible to master the secrets of *Shrike-Fu,* as they called it.

"You like football?" a solider asked, tracing out the snake on my jersey with the muzzle of his rifle.

"Why? You up for a game?"

The men laughed.

SMACK!

I took another hit to the shoulder and fell to the ground. When I looked up, I noticed the two zombies by the tractor had been decapitated. *That's odd.*

"This guy thinks he's Eddie Griffin," a soldier said.

Someone rolled me onto my back with a boot.

"Guys... I think this IS Eddie Griffin!"

"No way! Eddie Griffin wouldn't be stupid enough to get himself into a situation like this."

I looked up and bright light invaded my eyes... blinding me temporarily. I squinted and turned my head away.

WHOOSH! THWACK!

When my eyes stopped burning, I opened them. A severed head thudded onto my chest. The rest of the man was lying beside me. What followed next was a lot of confusion: shots were fired, men shouted and screamed, lots of hacking and chopping. And then, silence.

I sat up. There were parts everywhere - arms, legs, and heads -all cleanly severed and strewn about. Every single man had been decapitated. A hand reached out to me – a gloved metal hand. It was attached to... a knight? A knight! A knight in shining armor! I rubbed my eyes and looked again. I could almost see my reflection in the shiny plate.

If only Carlin could see this. I took hold of the offering and was literally pulled to my feet. I stared up into the metal faceplate. The eyes in there looked back at me and widened. The knight looked at my jersey. He ran his hand over the logo, and then touched the image of a snake eating its own tail emblazoned on his chest piece. He looked me in the face again.

"Godric!" The deep voice echoed from inside the helm. He slapped a massive hand on my shoulder. My knees almost buckled under the force. "I have found you, Godric!"

I looked back at him, puzzled. "The name's Eddie Griffin."

"Griffin? That is a mighty beast – difficult to kill and guardian of great treasure." He removed his helmet. Nestled within the mail coif was a black man's face. "Do you not recognize a fellow Saxon? It is I, Sigeberht."

"Saxon? What… like Afro-Saxon? And what kind of name is Sigeberht?"

His face was expressionless. "Aedelred said you would speak in riddles. There is much to explain. Come, we must go!" He reached for my arm but I pulled away.

"I'm not going anywhere without Jim!" I picked up my pack, rifle and anything else I could carry.

"The evil will return! We must go, Godric!"

"No! And stop calling me that!"

The Saxon grabbed my backpack by one of the accessory loops. He took off at a very brisk pace, pulling me with him. My boots skidded across the dirt. I had this cartoon moment where my legs were kicking but I wasn't going anywhere.

"Hey! What the fuck?"

"We go."

"What the… Let me go! I have to save Jim!"

"We go."

"Where?"

"Not far." He threw me over his shoulder and ran into the forest.

"Put me down!"

"No!"

We exited the forest and I was released onto a gravel road. The knight hastily ran off without saying another word. I had no idea where I was or where Jim was, for that matter. However, when I realized that I may have been *found by what looks for me*, I reluctantly decided to follow. I don't know how long we walked for. Sigeberht constantly kept himself a few paces ahead of me, looking back and waving me on.

"Yeah, yeah, I'm coming! Hey, Sigeberht... I thought you said this place was NOT FAR!"

He moved so quickly, and showed no signs of tiring. I stopped to catch my breath. The wind was cool and the sky was clear. I turned my face up to the warm rays of the sun. It was soothing. When I opened my eyes, I was looking up at a billboard. I could tell that it used to be a billboard advertising beef, but the *B* lost its lower belly to the elements so that now it read, *Ahhhh... Peef*. I laughed. Sigeberht shouted something to me but I just waved him off.

He marched up to my side and asked, "What is it? What makes you laugh?"

"Aaahhh, Peef." I motioned to the billboard.

"Peef?"

"Carolina Peef!" I could tell the humor was lost on him. "Carolina Peef - she was Carlin's older cousin: great boobs; hot like a pistol. Anyway, I had sex with her in Carlin's basement. When I came, I moaned into her ear Aaaahhhhh... Peef! That sign reminded me of that moment."

Sigeberht furrowed his brow. "Where did you come to with this... Peef?"

"I came... Cum? Blew my load? Jizzed? The money shot? That sort of thing?"

"I do not understand."

I bet it would have been easier for me to explain to him how to make a radio out of a coat hanger and two coconuts. "Hey, stop ruining my memory of the first time I got laid."

"I did not mean to anger you. I do not understand your speak."

"Yeah, right... look who's talking. You don't understand... just like that guy said."

"Aedelred."

"Right... and who is this Aedelred anyway?"

"He is a respected elder in our tribe. He is our spirit guide... and your grandfather." Well, that hit me like a ton of bricks. *Grandfather?* For once, I didn't know what to say. Sigeberht looked at me and then down the road. A small derelict church stood off in the distance next to an even smaller cemetery. Most of the tired gravestones had toppled.

"There it is," he pointed. "There is our sanctuary."

The tiny church had been thoroughly weathered - white paint peeled and flaked off the gray wood siding. Weeds grew up through the rotting steps. In fact, the entire building seemed to lean a bit. Remarkably, the stained glass was mostly intact.

Two zombies wandered the grounds. One wore a gray suit and the other a fancy dress. Sigeberht drew his sword, raced down the road and decapitated them. He waved to me. "Come... get inside before the rain." He entered the building.

I looked up at the clear sky. The sun was slowly setting. *This fucker's crazy.* Yet I still followed him. Before going inside, I noticed the steeple bell half buried in the ground in front of the entrance. Jutting out from under it was the body of a priest. The bell had mashed his head.

A small fire crackled just in front of the altar, sending spiraling smoke up through a hole in the roof. A few of the pews had been broken down for firewood. I walked down the center aisle. Dust particles danced in the dying rays of sunlight. Sigeberht emerged from a door at the back - probably the sacristy - carrying a large shank of meat over his shoulder. It looked like something we would eat for Sunday dinner at my Uncle's house.

"Ahhh, Beef?"

The Saxon did not respond. He skewered the meat with a spear and set it on a makeshift spit. Closer to the altar, a large tarp was spread out, covered in an assortment of medieval weapons: swords, spears, axes and maces. It looked like the armory section of the AA Player's Manual.

"Where'd you get all this stuff?"

"I brought it with me."

"You dragged all this shit from... uh, where do you come from, anyway?"

Sigeberht drew his sword and prodded the meat. "You do not remember anything, do you?"

"I guess not."

"Not even from your dreams?"

"Heh! I don't dream when I sleep."

"Everyone dreams."

"I don't remember."

"You do not try."

I threw my arms in the air. "Do you have an answer for EVERYTHING?"

He stared back at me with that blank look and did not respond.

I sighed. "Sorry, I'm a bit stressed."

"I understand. You require sustenance and rest."

I unloaded my gear and sat down on a pew facing the Saxon. He offered me some water in a metal ewer. I took a long, refreshing draught. Sigeberht reached inside a sack next to him and pulled out a bag of *Beefits*. He tore it open.

"I like the taste of these. And they are difficult to find." He held out the bag and offered me some. I chuckled, and took a handful. I put one in my mouth and just as quickly spit it out.

"Pfft! Pfah! Ah...Jeez! These are stale. They taste like foam packing chips."

Sigeberht shoved several of the dry morsels into his mouth and licked his lips. "They are delicious."

"Whatever." I looked up through the hole in the ceiling at the dark sky. "Tell me again where you come from."

Sigeberht cleared his throat and said, "From the north."

"North, eh?" That seemed all too coincidental. "I don't understand why you came here to find me? I don't remember leaving."

"You did not. It is difficult to explain."

"Okay, well at least explain why I left."

"To seek answers."

"What kind of answers?"

"Perhaps I should tell you from the beginning," he started. "We Saxons are powerful warriors... even our women are to be feared. For centuries, our people have lived deep in the earth, where the lava flows fired our forges and fed our hearths. We held dominion over the lands, keeping them safe from fire drakes and wyrms."

"Did your people ever come to the surface?"

"Only to fight," he replied. "Those who craved battle would pledge their sword arm to surface men."

I raised my eyebrows. My Grandpa used to have all these books about black soldiers that fought alongside white soldiers throughout the ages. I wondered how many of them were Afro-Saxons.

"Then, the soulless ones rose from their slumber and invaded our strongholds. Saxons had never faced such an enemy: every one of our brethren who fell in battle joined their ranks. I took the heads of many soulless brothers. We suffered heavy losses."

Thunder grumbled. He glanced upwards and continued. "Your grandfather consulted the spirit guides. He was advised to take our people closer to higher ground... to the ice plains. There, he worked his enchantments, and sealed all but a few warriors in the ice. Those of us who remained travelled to the surface world, where we established a new stronghold. Once again, the spirit guides were consulted. A volunteer from our tribe had to journey through this land and find the cause of the soulless ones' restlessness. That volunteer was YOU!"

Thunder cracked. I jumped. My heart skipped two beats. Lightening flickered through the stained glass. Rain tapped on the roof.

"When you did not return, I was sent to find you."

"How did you find me exactly?"

The Saxon sliced off a piece of meat and handed it to me. It was lean and flavorful – a big change from the canned and dried shit I had been subjected to for the last few weeks.

"I was not looking for you. I was looking for the Green Man. The spirit guides told me you would accompany him. According to the spirits, you and the Green Man will part ways, and then you will return to your people." He cut off more meat and served it on a shield.

But I didn't eat any. His comment about the Green Man filled my head and my belly for the moment. *I'm not ready to part ways just yet.* "Hmm... Hey, then tell me this, Sigeberht: why did you come to find me? Are we best friends or something like that?"

Sigeberht looked down at his gloved hands. He opened and closed them several times and said, "We are close companions. My sister is your consort."

"Oh... uh... so we're family, then?"

"Our familial relation is not the reason why I came to find you. The choice was not mine. The spirit guides selected me."

"How'd they do that?"

Sigeberht pulled off his gloves. My eyes widened when I saw his hands! His skin was covered in markings. They were like the runes I remembered seeing when my Grandpa took me to the museum of natural history for the Viking Exhibit. He opened and closed his hands before me. The runes glowed fiery orange, like embers. He pulled the chain mail coif from his head, revealing more runes all over his scalp. He removed his armor plates, and his mail coat. His entire body was covered in glowing runes.

"What are they?"

"Warrior markings."

"They're...burning!"

"Yes."

"Do they hurt?"

"They do... but it is great honor to carry the markings of Holioch."

"Who is Holioch?"

Sigeberht poked at the fire with his sword. "When this world was still feral, it was ruled by dark gods. Holioch was a powerful general in command of the dark legions. But he and his most loyal followers were displeased with their dark masters. Holioch wanted creation to flourish and grow and not live in a savage, wretched state. He incited a rebellion. And thus began the first of many wars."

"Holioch's greatest victory came when he stole the fires of creation. Dark forces pursued him, but he hid the fires in the hearts of men. In doing so, men became aware of the gods' presence. Thus began the age of enlightenment. An alliance was formed between men and Holioch's army of 'light beings.' Together, they were able to push back the darkness. But realizing that darkness cannot exist without light, they negotiated a shaky truce which holds to this day."

"How does that explain the markings?"

"The dark gods feared Holioch. He was too powerful. And so they tricked him. They suggested he take form and live among mortals. Holioch agreed. But when he took form, they cursed his body, covering it in fiery runes. Until the fires of these runes were sated, he could never ascend."

"Sated... with what?"

"The blood of men." Lightening flickered and thunder cracked. Sigeberht looked up and then continued, "Holioch would not destroy the very creation he so dearly loved. But the dark gods were foolish. With their never-ending hunger for power, they used their gifts of deceit and manipulation, and corrupted weaker men to do their bidding. Men waged war against each other. Holioch took advantage of this. It was an opportunity to spill enough blood so that he could return to his rightful place among the light beings."

"Did he succeed?"

"Yes," Sigeberht confirmed. "He is the one to whom we pray before battle. He grants us victory."

"Why do you have these markings?"

"Holioch bestows the markings upon a warrior worthy of ascension," he said. "I have seen this happen before a great battle. When I was chosen, I knew then that it was I who had to find you."

"Wait, wait… Now I understand. You can only ascend if you kill men." It suddenly dawned on me. "You're going to kill all those guys – the ones who've been nailing up the dead!"

"Correct!" Sigeberht held up his sword and stared into the blade. "And you will return to our people in the north."

"No! I'm coming with you. I have to save Jim."

"But the spirit guides…"

"Fuck the spirit guides!"I shouted as I stood up.

Sigeberht leaned back and scowled. "Your friend is probably dead."

My jaw and fists clenched. "Bullshit! Jim would never die."

"You must return to our people."

"Jim is like my brother. If I was the one captured right now, he would do everything he could to save me. I owe him that much. Brothers don't abandon each other. If you are my brother as you say, then you would understand this."

The Saxon looked me up and down and then back to his sword pensively. "I was afraid this would happen. But as your brother, I do understand." He pointed to the meat. "Eat! You will need your strength. We fight at dawn."

"Damn right." I tore off a hunk of meat, and sat down, chewing it defiantly.

Sigeberht rose and walked up the steps, past the altar and into the apse. He picked up a burlap-wrapped bundle, about the size of a duffel bag. He returned and held it out to me. "I prepared this for you."

I took it and slowly, unfolded the layers of fabric. "Oh yeah! This is sweet!" I exclaimed, looking down at a set of football shoulder pads and a shiny red helmet. The Saxon had re-fit the pads with armor plates over the chest and back, a neck guard, and plates over the upper arms. The face shield had been removed from the helmet and replaced with a visor. I quickly tried everything on. It was just like that Christmas morning when I got my first set of equipment. "This is like my own suit of armor!"

Sigeberht said nothing, but I could tell he was pleased.

"We shall drink to victory, my brother." He held up a wineskin. "This is the last of the Crudwyrm wine."

I thanked him and took a drink from the wineskin. *GHACK!* The tart, fiery liquid burned my throat. It felt like I had swallowed a flaming lemon. My belly instantly erupted in flames. I got stoned only once in my entire life, back when me and Germaine Durvis were initiated at the football rookie party. But this was a million times more potent. My senses seemed much clearer, but at the same time, I felt like I wasn't completely in control.

"That's some putrid shit!"

Sigeberht took a few gulps. "This Crudwyrm was old. The blood was well aged when it was spilled."

"We're drinking blood?"

Sigeberht did not respond. He just took another swig and handed the skin bag to me. "Should your head ache, chew on this." He took some brown moss from a small satchel and placed it on the floor. It smelled earthy. I picked it up and held it close to get a good look.

"This ain't Crudwyrm shit, is it?" As expected, there was no response. I put the moss in my pocket. Together we finished off the wine while I gorged myself on the mystery meat. Before I knew it I was fast asleep.

I awoke to the sound of pounding rain, and a pounding throb in my head. At least the moss, which tasted like bile, eased my aches. I lay on my back, listening to the rain and watching the lightning through the stained glass. My Uncle once told me stained glass magnified the light of truth as it descended from the heavens. I didn't trust my Uncle. He was an asshole. Personally, I thought the glass distorted things.

Sigeberht slept soundly, lying on his back with his hands folded across his chest, as if he were accustomed to sleeping in a coffin. Thoughts of the Upior popped into my head, followed by anxious concerns for Jim's safety. My gut told me Jim was alive, but my head wouldn't listen. I focused on an empty window pane, where the glass had been shattered, and watched the lightning flash across the sky. Comforted with the thought of seeing something as it was intended, I fell asleep.

6 JIM'S STORY: AN EYE FOR AN EYE

*Be wary of those who claim to carry the light,
Often they use it to obscure the darkness.*
-The Book of Amaltheon

Jim slowly opened his eyes as he roused to consciousness. His shoulders ached. A strange tingling sensation numbed his hands, and his left leg just below the knee – the *healing* sensation. His scalp was also tingling, and something heavy rested on his head. He craned his neck enough to see metal bolts jutting out from his palms where he had been nailed to the cross.

From up high on his wooden perch, Jim could see that he was in a large open area in the center of a junkyard. There were numerous tents, and a warehouse surrounded by rows upon rows of wrecked vehicles. Troops had assembled in the open square, standing at attention.

A gaunt man in a military uniform emerged from the command tent. His eyes were bandaged. Despite the coverings, he required no assistance, as if he were a man with full sight. The troops parted and let him pass. He crossed the muddy terrain towards Jim. A very wide man, with a face like a bulldog, joined him.

As he approached, Jim realized it had been a long time since he had last seen the man.

"General Kroth!"

"Lieutenant Jim Shrike," the man sneered. "You can imagine my surprise when my men informed me of your capture. It's been a long time. I didn't think I would be seeing you again." He looked Jim up and down. "That's quite the shade of green. Did you know that demons were green in the medieval age?" He did not wait for a response. "I always suspected you were a demon, Jim."

"I'm not surprised. You always did seem a bit medieval yourself."

"Typical response for a demon: always twisting the truth." His smile was sinister. "Captain Thaddeus!" The wide man held out a small silver case and opened it. The General pulled out the vial of green liquid.

"We found this among your personal belongings. Where did you get this?" Jim said nothing. "You seem to be quite good at healing. Your leg has almost grown back. I suggest you start talking Jim or I'll soon find out if any part of you does not grow back." He waited a moment. Jim stared off into the sky.

"Bring him down!" Several men instantly lifted the cross, and set it down in the mud. The General removed his bandages, revealing two empty, black sockets.

"A few weeks before the undead usurped our bunker, I was in one of the labs, observing an experiment," he began. He paced back and forth, addressing both Jim and the troops. "The undead participant broke free from his bonds. He attacked me – he put his hands on my face and pressed his thumbs into my sockets. When he did this, I thought to myself, *God will save me! God will have mercy on me!*"

"I awoke in the infirmary the next morning with my vision intact. This was difficult for the doctors to understand since my eyes had been removed from my skull. But I could see! God heard my prayers! And he answered. He returned my sight to me. And not only could I see my surroundings, but if I got close… very close, I could see another man's memories and thoughts. I first discovered this when the doctor examined me."

Kroth knelt down beside Jim, and cupped his head in his hands. "There is, however, an unfortunate side effect. When I look into someone's eyes, I don't just see what they see. I take their vision." He moved closer: just inches away from Jim's face. "And now Jim, I am going to look inside and see the truth."

Jim tried to look away, but Kroth pressed his forehead against his, so that all Jim could see were dark, hollow pits. "See the light, Jim!" he whispered. Jim strained against him. From within the darkness emerged a tiny white light. Jim's body felt numb. He could not move. The light intensified, burning brighter and brighter until there was nothing but a sea of white. Jim tried to close his eyes but could not.

Pain seared through his head. The sharp pain in Jim's eyes increased. It felt like a vacuum pulling his eyeballs from their sockets. The bright light suddenly vanished. The back of Jim's head slammed into the timber. Tears ran down the sides of his face. Blurry, colorless shadows moved around him. Captain Thaddeus yelled something inaudible and the cross was quickly raised back into position.

Kroth turned to his troops. He pointed at Jim and shouted, "This is the spawn of Satan! This demon stole the blood of salvation so that it would not fall into the hands of men!" He raised his fist into the air, holding up the vial. The men cheered in agreement. With a wave of his hand, the crowd was silenced.

"This demon is the embodiment of sin! He does not want the blood of salvation to fall into the hands of the righteous. He is protecting those sinners who have died without forgiveness, and risen to walk the earth among us."

"But we, the righteous, will deliver their souls into heaven... by giving them the blood of Jesus Christ our Savior!" Some men raised their hands in the air, eyes closed. Others shouted with fists raised. "Eternal rest grant to him, O Lord, who receives the Blood of Christ! Behold!"

As if on cue, a Brimstone[17] Mobile Launcher rumbled out from the warehouse, escorted by two jeeps. A nuclear missile rested in its payload. "Behold, my brothers!" Kroth shouted. "Behold the vessel which will deliver the blood of salvation!"

---

[17] Brimstone Mobile Launcher: A later development, this vehicle can transport and launch a Short Range Ballistic Missile (SRBM) with a nuclear or chemical warhead.

7 GRAVE YARDAGE

True heroes surrender themselves to the element,
and rekindle the flames within all things ensouled.
                              -The Book of Amaltheon

The sound of chains clanking on the floor woke me. I sat up quickly and rubbed the sleep from my eyes. The chains rattled again. Zombies! Three of them – bound to a pillar near the entrance. They strained against their iron bindings, lunging forward. Sigeberht emerged from the sacristy, dressed in full armor.

"What the hell is that?"

"A diversion."

"A what?"

"A diversion. I know where your friend is being held. I scouted the area while you slept. I saw him."

"And? Was he alright?"

"He will live." It wasn't the answer I was hoping for. "The compound is surrounded by a fence. Two man patrols travel along the interior of the perimeter at various intervals. They shoot any soulless ones that approach." Sigeberht wrapped up the weapons in the large canvas tarpaulin and dragged it to the front door. "Gather your gear. And drink from that bottle," he added, pointing at a silver flask on the altar.

"Why? What is it?"

"Just drink it!"

"Fine!" I stormed down the center aisle, grumbling under my breath. I put on my armor and jersey, and geared up while Sigeberht sharpened his sword with a stone. When I was finished, I reluctantly took a swig from the flask. It tasted... like beer. I took another gulp of the ice-cold bitter liquid. My mind was instantly clear, and I felt a surge of energy rush through my body. Sigeberht walked up behind me. He grabbed me by the head, and with his thumb and forefinger, he peeled open my eye and looked into it. "What the...?"

"Ah, the fear is gone from your eyes." He let me go.

"You could have just asked," I said, pushing him away. It was like pushing a rock. Sigeberht reached for the flask and downed the contents. My belly suddenly cramped up and I broke out in a cold sweat. I thought I was going to shit myself. The sensation passed very quickly, but I was still trembling. "What the hell was that stuff?"

Sigeberht set down the flask and belched. "Have you forgotten the taste of Magjar's ale?"

I rubbed my belly. "I guess so. Thanks for reminding me. Who's Magjar?"

Sigeberht looked up at the ceiling and closed his eyes. "Magjar was a giant. His origin is uncertain. He was found as a child wandering the icy plains of the north, with nothing more than his clothes and a leather flagon filled with ale. "

"Who found him?" I asked.

"The Corvid."

"And they are?"

Sigeberht opened his eyes. "An Avian race believed to be extinct," he said. Turning to me, Sigeberht put his hands to the side of his head. "Corvid are covered in dark plumage, and they have taloned feet. The legends say there was a time when the Corvid took to the skies."

"Really?" I said, furrowing my brow. "Why do people believe they are extinct?"

"The Corvid have not shown themselves for centuries. But they are out there. Corvid artifacts are among the most sought after treasures."

"What makes their handiwork so special?"

"They are capable of achieving overly complex and seemingly incomprehensible feats in engineering and metalwork. The Corvid built Magjar an ale cask and poured the contents of the flagon into it." Sigeberht leaned back against the altar. "The cask never ran dry, no matter how much Magjar drank. He wore it on his back, carrying it everywhere he went."

"Hmm... So how did you get some?" I asked, pointing to the flask. "Did you battle with Magjar?"

"No. He was one of Holioch's chosen, and ascended long before my time." Sigeberht picked up the flask and stared into the polished silver. "According to the legend, while in battle, an enemy crept up behind Magjar and opened the spigot on his cask. When Magjar discovered this, it sent him into a battle rage."

"He went berserk."

"Yes. Magjar drained the contents of the cask in one draught. Then, drunken and enraged, he laid waste to the enemy." Sigeberht looked me in the eye. "Not only did the ale give him superior strength, but when the blood of the fallen sated his runes, Magjar ascended, unleashing the fury of a thousand suns upon the enemy. The battlefield was reduced to an ashen crater several leagues distant. When the dust settled, there was no sign of Magjar, or the enemy. All that remained was a full cask of ale."

"Wow!"

Sigeberht stepped down from the altar. "Our people retrieved the cask from the battlefield. It is in our care. Only Holioch's chosen, those destined to ascend in battle, may draw from it." He bowed his head. "Magjar's ale will not bestow any powers upon you since you are not yet chosen. Nevertheless, I am honored to share it with you, my brother."

I placed a hand on Sigeberht's shoulder. "I too, am honored. Thank you."

Sigeberht smiled and put his hand on mine. "Now, there is one more thing."

I stepped back. "Yeah, like I should have known."

"As I require these weapons on the field of battle, I will call to you. You will bring them to me."

"Why can't you just get your own weapons?"

"Why would I do that? I will be engaged in battle."

"But, uh..." His face remained expressionless as I fumbled around for an excuse. Finally, I threw my hands in the air. "Ugh! Whatever!"

"Good... We go!"

Proudly wearing my armor, jersey and helmet, I met Sigeberht at the front door. He looked at the rifle in my hands. "Is that your only weapon?"

"Yeah, why?"

He shook his head. "I have none to share. It will have to do."

"None to share? You have a whole tarp full of shit!"

"Yes. I do." He put his hand on my shoulder. "I am glad that I found you, brother Griffin," he began. "It is an honor to go into battle with you one last time. Today, my journey will end." He slapped his hand into mine and clenched tightly. "Live for battle; die the victor!"

"Uh... Thank you, my brother."

With a nod, Sigeberht headed out the door, into the pouring rain, dragging the weapons and his zombie entourage behind him.

A few hours later, we were on top of a hill overlooking a junkyard. From the cover of the dense foliage, I surveyed the area with binoculars. A few neutralized zombies lay along the outside of the fence. Rows of wrecks were stacked a few feet inside the fence, creating an interior wall. A warehouse sat in the corner, and in the center of the yard stood a tall crane.

Troops had gathered in an open area. They were being addressed by a man with bandaged eyes; next to him stood a man about the size of two linebackers. His face was sandwiched between his low forehead and broad jaw. A smaller squad of men busied themselves with a mobile missile launcher nearby.

I smiled when I saw the familiar green body. "Jim," I whispered. But my smile faded when I saw the barbed wire crown on his head. They had nailed him to a cross. At least his leg had grown back.

"So what's the plan?" I asked, setting down the binoculars.

"Plan?" Sigeberht stared into his sword like it knew the answer. "We kill them!"

I rolled my eyes. "I know we kill them. But were you just going to walk up to the front gate and ask if you could come in and kill them?"

"No!"

"Exactly... so what's your plan?"

Sigeberht looked down at the tarp full of weapons near the base of the hill, and then at the zombie captives, whom he had wrapped around a nearby tree. "Come!" Before I could respond or acknowledge, Sigeberht had already retrieved his gear and zombies, and we were travelling through the forest.

We hid in the brush along the fence line to the right of the gate. "Time for the diversion," Sigeberht said, after the patrol had passed. Sigeberht dragged the zombies up to the fence, unchained the first one and threw him over into the compound.

"C'mon," I whispered impatiently. The second zombie was over. The first zombie got to his feet and staggered off into maze of wrecks. Sigeberht appeared to be having difficulty with the lock on the last zombie. *Damn!* The next patrol rounded the corner. They appeared to notice him and picked up their pace.

"Oh shit!"

Just as they unslung their rifles, Sigeberht unshackled the last zombie. He picked it up by the throat and crotch, and held it high over his head. This seemed to startle the soldiers. Then, the last zombie flew over the fence, landing on top of the two men. One of the soldiers knocked his head and fell unconscious. The zombie bit the other on the arm.

Sigeberht ran back to me. He threw back the tarp. "Get in!"

"What?"

"Get in!"

"Why?"

"This is the second diversion: once I have engaged the troops, sneak out and go save your friend."

"Wait a minute... you expect me to hide in a sack full of razor-sharp weapons while you drag me over uneven and rough terrain at full speed?"

"I do."

Sudden shouting and gunshots convinced me that the first diversion was a success. Rather than second-guessing myself, I sighed heavily, tightened my chin strap, and lay down with my newfound metal companions. Sigeberht covered me, leaving just enough of a gap to see out, and charged.

When he reached the front gate, Sigeberht drew his sword, hacked off the lock and kicked it in. Soldiers fired. Bullets rang off Sigeberht's armor. He reached inside the tarp.

"Hand me the axe."

I pulled it out from under my body and gave it to him. He emitted a deafening battle cry and ran into the compound. Gunfire and screaming followed. The Saxon effortlessly sliced his way through the ranks of men. Like a butcher gone mad, he chopped and hacked, sending body parts flying everywhere. Anything that avoided his blade was punched, kicked, and thoroughly pummeled. I once saw a train car filled with cattle after it derailed. The carnage was awesome: cows were bent and twisted and ripped apart. This was far, far worse.

Two jeeps sped towards the armored warrior, and both gunners opened fire. He sidestepped the first jeep. As the second jeep passed by, he swung the axe and cut through the windshield and frame, slicing through the upper arm and chest of the solider on the passenger side. The first jeep circled round and raced towards him.

The Saxon dropped to a crouch. The jeep slammed into him, but at the same moment he stood, lifting the vehicle and throwing it. The jeep flipped end over end, ejecting the occupants. The second jeep now charged him again, guns blazing. This time, however, Sigeberht stood his ground. He raised the axe over his head. The jeep accelerated. Just as it was about to hit him, he slammed the axe into the hood, cleaving the front end of the jeep in half. The vehicle buckled and halted, sending the driver through the windshield.

With everyone's attention focused on Sigeberht, I grabbed my rifle and crawled out from under the tarp.

"Griffin! My swords!"

"Aw, man," I huffed.

Sigeberht buried his axe in a man's back. His other arm was reaching back, motioning at the weapons cache.

"There's another one!" a soldier shouted, pointing at me.

I smiled uncomfortably. Pleasantries aside, I lay down a barrage of suppressive fire, killing the one who singled me out and sending other soldiers sprawling for cover. I threw back the canvas and picked out two big swords.

"Griffin!"

Sigeberht fought with his fists. I ran toward the Saxon, but a hail of bullets forced me to the ground. Something hit me in the side of my head, knocking my helmet askew. I felt like I had been beaned by a football.

PING!

I felt an impact on my chest. I'd been hit! But the round didn't penetrate the armor. My jersey, however, had a hole in it. I'd never thought I could be so pissed off and excited at the same time. I leapt to my feet and charged, hurling one sword into the air. Sigeberht punched a soldier in front of him with a force that threw his head back so violently it snapped his neck. He then broke the nose of the soldier behind him with his elbow. He caught the sword out of the air and spun, taking off both men's heads before they hit the ground. He looked back at me and I threw the second sword. He caught it, and quickly decapitated another victim with both swords using a scissor-like motion.

By now, some of the dead – the ones with heads still attached - had come back to life. A secondary melee between soldiers and their fallen comrades ensued. I took advantage of the situation and retreated from the scene towards Jim. He called out to me as I approached.

"Ed? Is that you?"

"Hey!"

"Leave me! You need to find the vial."

"I know, I know. But I'm not leaving. I have to find a way to get you down."

"I'm no good to you! I can hardly see a thing. Everything's blurry. My eyes... it's like they're on fire."

A bullet bit the timber just below Jim's feet. I spun around and grabbed the gun hand of the soldier who fired it. I couldn't regain my footing and fell back into the mud. The soldier fell on top of me and we both struggled for the pistol. The business end of the gun was too close to my face.

But then, over his shoulder, I saw the one of the zombies who had gone over the fence earlier. He peeled back the soldier's scalp and bit down through his skull. I tried to push them both off me. Suddenly, the zombie's head burst. Then the soldier flew off. Another man, wearing a dark blue robe, stepped over me and buried a sledgehammer in the soldier's back. He pounded and pounded until there was nothing left but muddy bloody goo.

The robed man turned and threw back his hood. Apart from the goatee, he was rather hairless. His scalp glowed brightly with the same kind of runes as Sigeberht's.

"I'm Veck! What took you so long to get here?"

"Do I know you?"

Veck eyed me up and down. "No... but I know you," he acknowledged as he helped me up.

"That doesn't surprise me... I'm Eddie Griffin."

"Who?"

"Eddie Griffin... I played professional football?"

"Really? I've never watched a game in my life. Interesting... but that's not how I know you... sorry." He didn't give me a chance to respond or anything. Instead, he looked to Jim and said, "Let's get you down." A few swings later, the cross was on the ground and Jim was free.

He hobbled about on his newly grown leg. "I'm alright... It just feels like it's asleep." He pulled the barbed wire crown from his head and grinned at it. "This should come in handy."

Jim's eyes were red and swollen. "You alright?"

"Ugh. I can see you ... you look like a shadow." He squinted and looked about. "Everybody looks like a shadow." He turned to Veck. "We're looking for vial of green liquid. Kroth took it from me."

"I know of it," Veck replied with a nod. "Kroth put it in the missile."

"Is Kroth that guy with the bandages?" I asked.

"Yes, and that big guy, Captain Thaddeus, is usually not far behind."

"Where are they now?" Jim asked.

"I don't know."

"Our priority is to get that vial."

Veck raised his sledge and said excitedly, "What are we waiting for?" He was off before either of us could respond. We followed. A cold rain started to fall.

A LAV-63[18] crawled into the open area. Sigeberht was too busy in hand to hand combat to notice. The gunner fired, cutting down any soldiers in his path. Sparks flew and bullets rang off Sigeberht's armor. He turned and charged the vehicle, while it too accelerated and headed for him.

I hung back in case I was summoned. Veck was the first to make it to the launcher. The soldier closest to him received a swift blow to the back of the head. This startled the others. Veck sprang on them, and introduced their faces to his hammer. It was probably one of the most painful introductions I had ever witnessed.

Sigeberht planted both hands firmly on the LAV's front armor and... he pushed. The engine screeched in high gear. The treads tore up the ground, churning up muck. Smoke poured out

---

[18] LAV-63 (*Light Armored Vehicle*): The LAV-63 was a treaded version of the eight-wheeled LAV-60. Considered a 'soft-skinned' armored vehicle, it was primarily used by the Army as a scout car or radio communications vehicle.   Primary Armament: 7.62mm machine gun mounted on the commander's cupola.

from under the engine housing. Seeing that he had things under control, I ran full tilt for the launcher.

By the time I got there, the party was over. Jim and Veck had taken out all the soldiers. Even though they were all dead, Veck pounded the bodies deeper into the mud.

"What kind of missile is this?" I asked.

"A nuke," Jim said.

"Nuclear? What on earth was Kroth planning to do? A nuke won't save us from the zombies."

"If I overheard correctly," Veck said, "the goal was to launch the missile with that vial somehow stuck inside. Kroth had this idea that the contents of the vial would somehow alter the blast so it would destroy only the undead."

Jim rubbed his forehead. "Idiot!" Like an ant, he scurried back and forth checking, feeling his way across panels and hatches.

"Watch out!" Veck shouted. I sidestepped and he darted past me. One of the dead was rising but Veck pounced on him and caved in his brainpan. He was grinning. "Sorry... I must have missed that one."

A silence fell over the compound. The soldiers were no longer fighting. Instead, they watched Sigeberht take on the LAV. Both he and the vehicle were bogged down in the slop. The gunner leaned back in the turret, the hilt of a sword sticking out of his chest. A link snapped in the left tread. The LAV veered to one side while the remaining links twisted up into the skirting. Sigeberht pushed the vehicle back a few feet. The engine sputtered and gave out. He rested his forehead on the vehicle and breathed heavily.

Metal creaked and strained above our heads. I looked up: the crane had moved into position over the Saxon. The four-pincer grabber claw dropped.

"Sigeberht! Above you!"

He looked up. The claw landed on top of him, flattening him out in the mud. The pincers closed and lifted Sigeberht into the air. The men cheered.

"Griffin!" The Saxon shouted. He had braced his hands against one of the pincers; the hydraulics hissed under the pressure. "Bring me my broadsword!"

"Go! Veck shouted. "I'll cover you." He raised his hammer and charged at the soldiers.

I ran through the mud, slipping and sliding my way towards the weapons cache. When I got to the canvas tarp, I stared confusedly at a wide array of swords. *Broadsword?* I had only ever seen one in the AA Armory Guide. Here before me, there were too many to choose from. None of them looked like the ones I recalled. I looked to Sigeberht, hoping that he just might point to it. He pushed the jaws open. One of the hydraulic cables burst, flailing wildly and spewing fluid. He clambered up onto the giant claw and, with a few foot pumps, got it swinging.

"My sword!"

I picked up a sword with an intricate serpent design in the hilt. The serpent had a blue gem in the eye. I ran towards the Saxon. Bullets ricocheted off his armor. He was picking up speed and momentum.

"Ed," Jim called. I slid to a stop. Jim stood on top of the missile. He waved his hand in the air. "The vial... I found it."

"Stop him!" Kroth shouted. He stood at the base of the crane with Captain Thaddeus right by his side. "Kill him!" Thaddeus pointed at Jim and drew a finger across his throat. The soldiers responded, and opened fire on the Brimstone.

"Ed... First and twenty!" Jim threw the vial and then jumped down behind the vehicle for cover. I ran as fast as I could, hand outstretched, sword in the other. *This was just like that game against Kansas: piss pouring rain and a field full of mud... except there was no sword.* A soldier ran alongside me. I wasn't sure if he was trying to catch the vial, or tackle me. I darted left, then right, and spun. He slipped and fell. I jumped, caught the vial, and landed just in time to sidestep another soldier.

"Griffin!" This time, Sigeberht sounded impatient.

"Coming!" I kept running, looking up every so often to pace myself with Sigeberht as he swung overhead. He leaned out low enough to grab the sword. A soldier blocked my path. He screamed. I screamed. I was ready to put my shoulder into him and knock him flat. The sword was taken from my hand and Sigeberht split the head of the charging soldier in two. I slowed down. The body fell into my arms. "Hey... go kill your own targets," I shouted in frustration.

"Wrong sword!" Sigeberht threw it in frustration. A silver flash streaked through the air and impaled itself in someone. "Bring me the double headed axe... for cleaving!"

Wrong sword? YOU GOTTA BE KIDDING ME! "How the fuck should I know which one the broadsword is? You're the goddamn Knight!"

"Just bring the axe!"

"Okay!" I jammed the vial into a pouch on my belt, and turned just in time to engage two soldiers. I grabbed the rifle of the first soldier and wrestled it from his grasp. Another soldier grabbed me from behind. He had one arm around my neck, and with the other hand fumbled for the rifle. The other soldier swung a punch and I shifted my weight from one leg to the next. We leaned just enough so that his jab caught the man behind me in the jaw. My finger touched the trigger and I pulled, firing a burst. The arm around my neck went limp. I shifted my weight again, throwing the soldier down at the other's feet. I grabbed his collar and head butted him.

CRACK!

His nose shattered. The soldier leaned his head back, pinching his bloody nose. I ducked. Sigeberht swung by and caved in his face with a kick.

"Get my axe!"

"I am!" I ran to the weapons cache and found the axe. As I was running back, Sigeberht swung out on a wide arc. I threw the axe to him. He caught it, and chopped a cable, letting out more line.

He then threw the axe at the control booth, truncating the man inside.

More line let out and the Saxon picked up speed. He braced his feet against the claw, grabbed the cable with both hands and pulled. The giant claw, with Sigeberht aboard, swung through a group of soldiers and directly at the LAV. At the last possible second, he raised both legs, pulled his knees to his chest and kicked out upon impact. The armored vehicle exploded in a shower of steel plates and parts. A secondary explosion sent more shrapnel across the field. When the black smoke cleared, Sigeberht stood triumphant, surrounded by moaning and mangled bodies. Veck ran in and finished off the dead and the dying.

I felt a hand on my shoulder. I turned. It was Jim.

"Whew!" I grinned and held up the vial. "Touchdown!"

Jim smiled. "Is that what I think it is?"

"Yes… and it's green!"

"Where's Kroth?"

"I don't know."

Veck appeared at my side. "I can't find Kroth. I'll check the warehouse. Are you okay?"

Jim nodded.

"I'll come with you," I said.

"Sure!" Veck was off and running.

I was about to take off after him when Jim grabbed my arm. "Look! Something's happening over there!"

Sigeberht was surrounded by a ring of soldiers. He stood in the center directly across from Captain Thaddeus. The two men growled at each other. Thaddeus ripped open his jacket and threw it to the ground. Sigeberht removed his armor. Metal plate after metal plate landed in the mud until he had stripped down to his loin cloth. His rune-covered body emitted a fiery orange glow.

"Griffin!"

"Aw shit. Jim, I gotta go."

"Ready my long sword… the one with the dragon on the hilt…for the killing blow."

"The one with the serpent with a blue gem in his eye?"
"Yes... why?"
"Uh... no reason. Fuck!"

The two men circled each other and then charged. They locked arms. Thaddeus wrenched free and twisted Sigeberht's arm behind his back. He delivered an elbow into Sigeberht's tricep. *THWACK!* The Saxon reached over and got a hand on Thaddeus' forehead and pulled him back. He kicked him in the back of the knee while using his palm to clap Thaddeus's chin, sending him down onto his back. The Captain rolled, avoiding a stomp to the face. The force of the blow caused Sigeberht to sink into the mud up to his knee. Thaddeus stepped up onto his quad and jumped up, coming down with an elbow onto the Saxon's forehead. He did this again, this time striking the bridge of his nose.

On the third attempt, Sigeberht caught Thaddeus around the waist and squeezed. Thaddeus reeled back, his lungs screaming for air. He pounded Sigeberht in the head with his fists. He even stuck his thumbs in his eyes. The Saxon leaned back and twisted, flipping Thaddeus onto his back with him on top. He quickly straddled him and punched him several times in the face.

SMACK! SMACK! SMACK!

Thaddeus threw him off, and both men rolled and got to their feet. But The Saxon was faster. He stepped in and struck Thaddeus in the chest with a double punch. Then he doubled him over with a swift kick to the abdomen. He grabbed him by the back of the neck and sent him sprawling into the mud.

I suddenly noticed the Brimstone heading straight for Sigeberht. Kroth sat behind the wheel. Veck ran behind the vehicle, smashing the tail lights with his sledge.

"I can't stop it!" he shouted.

I returned to the weapons cache and grabbed a spear. The Brimstone still had a ways to go. As I was running back, I saw a blue sparkle. The long sword! It was embedded halfway through the top of a dead man's skull and sticking out between his shoulder blades. I braced my foot against his shoulder and pulled. I pulled and pulled but I couldn't get the damn thing out.

The missile launcher was getting closer. Sigeberht and Thaddeus exchanged punches and kicks. I had no choice but to bring the sword and the body with it. I lay the spear across the dead man's chest. The body was very heavy. *Just my luck that the sword couldn't have stuck some scrawny dude! Why the hell does it have to be THIS sword?*

Sigeberht punched the Captain in the mouth. *CRACK! SNAP!* Teeth were evicted in a bloody spew. The Captain's head bounced and bobbled around. I pulled the dead body right up next to them.

"Here's your goddamn sword!"

The Saxon reached back, grabbed the sword and swung it up and over. The body slid off - he made it look easy. He brought the sword down and severed Thaddeus' arm. The glowing runes hissed under the shower of blood.

The Brimstone closed in. I picked up the spear and charged. I managed to thrust it through the driver's side window, impaling Kroth through the shoulder. He veered off and slammed into a pile of derelict vehicles.

Veck ran over and slapped me across the shoulder. "Well done!" I started to believe that he was deranged in some way. His grin faded. "Look!"

Sigeberht held Thaddeus with one hand by the neck. With his other hand, he raised his sword (I would say more for dramatic effect than any type of sword play) and buried it up to the hilt in Thaddeus' gut. When he ripped the sword free, the Captain's lower body flew in one direction; Sigeberht tossed the upper body in the other. He dropped the sword and fell to his knees.

The runes smoldered – sated with blood. Sigeberht looked up to the heavens and for the first time, he smiled. A swirling shaft of almost blinding light burst through the dark clouds, enveloping the warrior. He raised his arms and screamed at the sky. The runes glowed white hot. The twisting column spun faster and faster.

Sigeberht continued to scream. Molecule by molecule, he disintegrated.

Veck threw me to the ground. "Don't look at it!"

The light shaft exploded outwards. The men closest to the blast instantly turned to ash. I closed my eyes and buried my face in the mud as the wave passed over me. When I opened my eyes again, there was nothing left but a smoldering crater. The bitter scent of burnt sulphur wafted through the air. Rain-soaked ash fell from the sky like dirty wet snow. Someone grabbed my arm and pulled me up – it was Jim.

"Did you see that?" I asked.

"Yeah. It was mostly just a bright flash."

"You still can't see much, huh?"

Jim's eyes glowed red. "I feel this burning sensation."

"Hey guys!" Veck called from the launcher. "The ignition sequence's been set. We've got two minutes."

"What?! Shut it down!" Jim ordered.

Veck looked at me nervously. "I... I smashed the controls."

"You can't just smash'em!"

"How should I know? I'm just a doctor!"

"Damn!" I pulled a control lever and nothing happened. "It's not responding!" Then I saw the hand crank on the carriage bay. "Veck, there should be a crank like this on the other side. Grab it and start turning." I turned the metal wheel, the whole time keeping my eye on the timer.

"What wheel?"

"I don't know… any fucking wheel. We may not be able to stop the launch, but we can try to get this thing airborne and away from us." I turned and turned. My muscles burned. The launch carriage slowly tilted.

"One minute," I shouted. "Keep cranking that wheel!" It seemed like an eternity. "Thirty seconds… C'mon …Ten seconds… That's enough!" I jumped to the ground. The rocket engines flared and fired. The missile shot into the sky, leaving a trail of white smoke, and disappeared into the clouds.

"Veck, we did it!"

The Brimstone's cab door swung open. Kroth stumbled out - the spear point still lodged in his shoulder. I charged and slammed into him, knocking him back against the fender. I charged again and pressed him against the vehicle. Kroth recovered quickly from the blow and locked his arms around my head. I pulled free and found myself face to face with him: the hollow pits in his head were pressed up against my visor. The darkness slowly filled in my field of vision. I couldn't pull away.

A tiny pinpoint of bright light appeared in the far reaches of the blackness. *PHOOM! SPLASH!* The light disappeared and I was jolted out of my skin. My vision returned: my visor was drenched in bloody goo. I wiped it off. A headless Kroth stood before me, blood spouting from his neck stump. The body took a step back.

Jim stood on the hood of the Brimstone. His eyes glowed an angry red. He tilted his head and fired two bright beams – one from each eye – directly into Kroth's back. The chest burst, splashing me yet again with bloody goo. As the body crumpled, Veck pushed his way past me and pounded it flat with his sledge.

Jim rubbed his eyes with his thumbs. He blinked rapidly and shook his head. The red glow softened. He looked at me.

"How are you doing?" I asked.

"I can see now. With that last discharge, my eyes aren't burning anymore."

"You mean, you couldn't see clearly when you fired?"

"Not really."

"Then how'd you know which target to shoot?"

"You're much bigger than Kroth. I aimed for the smaller target."

I scowled and flicked blood and shit off my jersey.

"You're a mess, Ed."

"Uh... thanks."

Veck put his arm around me and grinned. "Way to take one for the team!"

8 A MILLION TO JUAN

Which came first: ducks or winter? It doesn't matter whether ducks fly south because winter is on the way, or winter comes because the ducks have left. What matters is the action and the reaction: it proves the earth is in agreement with what has been done. Now, humans are animals too. We're creatures of the earth. If we take the right action, and the earth agrees with what we've done, we'll surely see the results.

-Veck

Jim jumped down from the roof of the HER0[19] while I secured the last of the tie-downs on the trailer.

"I think we're all set," he said to Veck.

"Just hold on a sec... I want to show you something." Veck was on his knees, fiddling with the latches on a small metal locker. "They're kind of sticky."

I ran my hand along the body of the HER0: it seemed more like a tank than a 'soft-skinned' vehicle. It made a wonderful parting gift, courtesy of Kroth and his followers, along with the accompanying trailer filled with supplies. With the amount of gear and fuel we had, I'm sure we could've made it to the North Pole.

After Kroth and his men were destroyed (and believe me when I say that Veck made sure there were no survivors or zombies to speak of) we spent a few days resting and recuperating within the safety of the compound. When Jim wasn't practice-firing his new eyebeams, the two of us listened to Veck's crazy stories and theories. Veck told us all about these pre-cognitive dreams he'd had since he was a kid, and how he knew he would meet a Green Man one day. Veck also foresaw his own ascension as one of Holioch's chosen. Although, he seemed disappointed when I told him about the explosive effect of Magjar's ale, and the fact that he didn't have

---

[19] HER0 *(Hazardous Environment Recon Type-0)*: A military HUMVEE specially designed to enter areas of biochemical or nuclear contagion.

any. Anyway, after UD-Day, a dream led Veck to General Kroth and his army. Veck happily joined them in anxious anticipation of our arrival.

Veck also said that Jim's eyes took on some of Kroth's powers when they regenerated. He figured some form of energy transference had occurred. Since Jim pretty much healed on demand, it was possible his eyes healed as Kroth was damaging them. The theory was definitely plausible. And then there was also Veck's claim of being a surgeon, a genetics engineer and a thanatologist[20]. He said he had more than one doctorate among his accreditations. I'm sure he also had a degree in (and of) lunacy. But for all I know, he could've been the long lost son of Thor. It didn't matter. Sometimes it seemed like he really knew what he was talking about.

"Dammit to hell!" Veck cursed. He grabbed his sledge and was about to swing when Jim caught his arm. He calmly flipped open the latches.

"Uh, thanks!"

Veck seemed rather disappointed that he didn't get to bash something in. He threw back the lid, revealing a shiny metal ball.

"What is that?" I asked.

Veck took a remote control out of the box and turned on a few switches. The orb started to hum. It rose out of the container and hovered in the air, about six feet off the ground.

"Sweet!"

"I knew you would like this!"

"Yeah, but what is it?"

"An atmospheric air quality analyzer," Jim answered. "It scans the low level atmosphere for radiation, biological contagion, chemicals… just about anything in the air."

"Yes and it sends a report back to the remote," Veck added. "You can input an area to scan." He punched a few more buttons.

---

[20] Thanatologist: One who studies death and dying, and the associated social, cultural, and psychological impacts.

The probe zipped right at me, swerving at the last minute to avoid my head. It whirled about the compound. The remote chirped and beeped as data poured in.

"Good thing it has obstacle avoidance built in," Veck said with a grin.

"Can I see that?" He handed me the remote - it was more like a video game pad. I switched it to manual control. "This is cool!"

"Play time's over, Ed!" Jim beckoned. "We should go."

"Aw... but I only just started with this..." I conceded. I knew I wasn't going to win this one. I guided the probe back to the metal box. After I ensured it was safe and snug inside the foam interior, I stowed it inside the HER0.

Veck stared at the dark, cloud filled sky. "Rain's coming... maybe even snow, especially if you're heading north."

"We're ready for anything," Jim said, "Are you sure you'd rather not come with us?"

"No... thank you. I'm not ready just yet. But our paths will cross again, I assure you."

"Until we meet again." Jim shook his hand and climbed into the vehicle.

"Good bye, Ed."

I climbed in through the passenger's door, and popped my head out the gunner's cupola. Jim started the engine. Veck ran ahead and opened the front gate. After he destroyed the one lone zombie waiting to get in, he held the sledge up to his forehead and saluted as we drove by.

The drive was mostly uneventful. We were fortunate enough to encounter long expanses of open highway. At times, Jim slowed down to maneuver through vehicles, debris and curious zombies. The cold rain forced me inside the vehicle. Jim wasn't much of a talker, but the situation caused him to be a bit more sociable.

"Hey, Jim... did Veck ever talk to you about ducks?"

That question forced a smile to his face. "Yeah, why?"

"Did he talk about how they fly south because winter comes?"

"Or that winter comes because they fly south?"

"Yeah... that's it. What do you think about that?"

Jim mulled over something in his head before speaking. "If we act appropriately, we see appropriate results. It's just cause and effect."

"Think he was talking about destiny?"

"Possibly."

"So that means we left the bunker at just the right time, right?"

"I don't know if it was our destiny to leave. I had to leave. I was assigned to go on a secret mission."

"What made you ask me to come along with you? I wanna know why you picked me instead of all those other Special Ops guys."

He cleared his throat. "You adapted really well to military life in the bunker. Soldiering comes naturally to you."

"Whatever!"

"No, seriously! Had you not gone into the NFL and enlisted instead, you would have had a promising military career. You're a good shot and in good shape – better shape than some of those Spec Ops guys."

I laughed.

"What's so funny?"

"You can't bullshit for tryin'! If you're going to lie to me just say something like... *you're a good shit, man!*"

Jim didn't see the humor in my response. He straightened up in his seat. "You didn't want to be in that bunker. You wanted out of there more than anyone."

"What makes you think that?"

"I know that your parents died in a car accident. It happened as they were on their way to the hospital because you decided to arrive a few weeks early. Your wealthy Uncle, the Reverend, gained custody of you and raised you. At age eleven, you ran away only to show up a few days later at your Grandpa's house in Indiana. The bunker, your Uncle's, the womb – you've wanted out of every place that offered you shelter."

I couldn't disagree with Jim. "How'd you know all that stuff about me?"

"I read your file."

"My file?"

"Yeah, your file."

"They got a file on me?"

"It's the military... the government – they got a file on everybody."

"Even you?"

"Even me."

"Do I get to read it?"

"Trust me – you don't want to read it."

"Hmph!" I folded my arms across my chest. I wasn't mad at Jim. I was just angry that somebody went to all the trouble of trying to figure me out. That was supposed to be my job. "I guess I should say thanks!"

"Thank me when you find what you're looking for."

"What about you? What are you looking for?" Jim stared off into the distance. I pressed my forehead against the cold glass, waiting for a response. We approached an off ramp. I saw a pair of legs sticking out of one of those yellow water-filled barrels used as traffic barriers, kicking at the zombie trying to grab them.

"Stop, Jim! Stop!"

He slammed on the brakes. The HER0 squealed to a halt and I jumped out. A car sitting in the lane ahead of us suddenly gunned the engine and tore off down the highway in a cloud of smoke.

"What the hell's going on?" I turned and ran towards the off ramp.

"Ed! Get back here!"

When I got in range of the zombie, I kicked him in the hip (a *shrike-fu* move Jim had taught me). Bone snapped. The zombie dropped like a stone. I stomped his head so flat that Veck would have been proud. Jim arrived on the scene just as I turned my attention to the man in the barrel. He was HUGE. I tried to wrap my arms around his waist but he was too big - I couldn't reach around.

"Help me get him out of here!"

"And if we do, then what?"

"Can't we worry about that after? He's probably drowning!"

Jim clenched his jaw and stood his ground.

"Alright – fine! I'll save him myself!"

The guy was wedged in there good! I put my shoulders under his knees, wrapped my arms around his lower legs and pushed upward. It felt like my heels were sinking into the ground. I grunted and groaned. Finally, the man popped out. We fell back onto the pavement.

He was moaning and breathing heavily. But that quickly turned into a boisterous laugh. He rubbed his eyes with his chubby fingers.

"Are you okay?" I asked.

The man coughed a bit. He wore a bandana, pulled tight to his skull, which covered his forehead from his thick hairline to his heavy-lidded eyes. His arms... his arms were carpeted with a thick, coarse black hair. He rested his hands on his big belly.

"Who may I ask had the pleasure of saving my life?" he said with a lazy, Spanish accent.

"I did!"

"You touched me?"

"Yeah, why?"

He burst out laughing again and got to his feet. For such a large man, he was awfully agile. He placed a big fat hand on my shoulder.

"I am more than okay!" He looked over at Jim. "What in the fucking hell happened to you?"

"Should've left you in the barrel!"

"Hey, take it easy, man! It's not every day you see someone who is green." He took my hand and shook it. "My name is Juan Maloccio." I noticed a spider tattoo on the inside of his wrist. I hadn't seen anything like that since...

***

"You asked to see me, Mr. Burton?"

"Ah yes…" The principal closed the book on his desk and looked up. "Mr. Griffin. I would like to introduce you to a new student at our school."

He gestured with his hand to the row of seats against the wall. I was instantly in love! It was like a dream. There I was staring at the most beautiful girl. She had dark hair, brown eyes and a smile that made me melt.

"This is Valentina Cruz. She's going to be in your class. I was wondering if you would be kind enough to show her around the school."

"Uh… yes, sir, Mr. Burton," I responded, trying not to sound too much like a nerd.

"I understand she lives in your neighborhood. Perhaps you can take the bus together."

"That… that would be nice."

Valentina stood up, took my hand, and smiled. I think I had an erection.

"Off you go, then. Thank you, Eddie!"

"You're welcome, Eddie," I said. Valentina giggled. Hand in hand, we walked out into the hall.

***

"What is your name?"
"Eddie Griffin!"
"Do I know you from somewhere?"
"I played professional football."

"So what? Aren't all footballers black?" My smile disappeared quickly. "You see where those *pendejos*[21] went with my money?"

"What? You mean that car that took off?"

"Yeah... a black *Renegade*."

"It took off down the highway," Jim said.

He clapped his hands together and said, "Let's go, already!"

"Where?"

"To get my money back from those motherfuckers!"

"Hold on a minute! We're not going anywhere!"

He waved his finger at me and shouted, "Now you listen to me! You are going to help me get back my million dollars!"

"He's not going anywhere," Jim said, aiming his pistol at the man's head.

The big man shook his head. "Ech! Put that thing away... it's harmless already. I can explain you something." He looked around on the ground until he found what he was looking for: a water bottle. He filled it at the barrel and held it up in front of us. "This is going to hurt me more than it does him," he said, jerking his thumb at me. He tipped the bottle enough for a few drops to hit the road. My belly felt instantly warm, burning even. The cramps set in quickly and I fell to my knees. At first, I thought I had to take a monster crap. I could hardly breathe, it hurt so much. It felt like someone was stirring my insides with a hot poker. I broke out in a cold sweat and collapsed. The pain was so intense! Juan also lay on the ground, writhing in agony.

"What did you just do?" Jim shouted.

The pain began to ease off and Juan started to laugh again. "That money is cursed!" he howled. "I'm cursed! And now you are cursed!"

"Cursed?" I said, putting my hands to my chest.

"Yeah... we have to get that money back already to break the curse. Until then, you can't spill no water. If I kick over that barrel,

---

[21] Pendejo *(Spanish)*: Idiot; useless person.

you will shit blood and die." Juan turned to Jim. "So put your pistol back in your pants and let's get my fuckin' money!"

Jim slowly holstered his side arm.

"Why water?" I asked.

He raised his hands and shook them, "Why water? Should I know why the fuck water? Did I make the fucking curse?"

"So these friends of yours just decided to take your money. What did you do to piss them off?"

"Aw, Jesus... so much 'splaining! Okay... so I stole this money from a gang. It was cursed money. How was I to know? Who curses their fucking money? When I stole the money, the gang came with it. Maybe that's part of the curse- I don't know. But they were like slaves – they do all my bidding. So now I have this gang. But they don't like me. If they take the money, then I can no control them. So every chance they get, they try to take my money, already. And they know I get stuck in water. So I go to Nevada – you know, out there in the desert? There's no water. I have this fancy house there. Then a few days ago, a bomb falls from the sky and blows everything to shit. Like what, we don't have enough dead people?"

"A bomb? Like a missile?" I had a sinking feeling in my stomach.

"Bomb! Missile... whatever! It falls from the sky and explodes... causes an earthquake. The house collapses on me. And my safe, where I keep the money, is destroyed. While I am trapped, the *pendejos* take my money. Okay? You understand now? Let's go!"

As he walked towards the HER0, he stowed the water bottle in the back pocket of his oversize pants. "My car is fucked – we'll use yours. I'll sit in the back!"

Jim and I reluctantly followed.

"You think that was our missile?" I muttered under my breath. Jim didn't respond. He was pissed.

***

UNDEAD RECKONING

Valentina screamed and backed away from her locker. I ran up to her and put my hands on her shoulders. She wiped the tears from her eyes.

"You alright?" Even when she was upset, she was beautiful. She nuzzled up into me.

"There's a spider in there. I'm so scared of them."

I stuck my head in and found the culprit. With a sweep of my hand, I evicted the unwanted guest. Valentina put her arms around me and kissed me on the cheek.

"Thank you, Eddie."

"No worries!"

"You're not afraid of anything, are you?"

***

"There they are, those *pendejos!*" The black car idled in the distance. A silver car stood next to it. The occupants appeared to be switching vehicles. "Step on it!"

Jim floored it. I took that as my cue to climb into the cupola. It had stopped raining, but the sky was still dark. And it was cold enough that I could see my breath. I tapped the roof.

"Locked and loaded!"

Both cars slowly pulled ahead so I opened fire. I tore up the back end of the silver sedan. We drew alongside and the driver swerved into us. Jim swerved into him. The resulting collision locked both vehicles together. A guy popped up from the far side of the vehicle and braced his AK-47 on the roof. He fired. I ducked down behind the shielding.

When he stopped to reload I stuck my head out and got a good look at him: he was dead! I mean, zombie dead! His eyes had that faint yellow glow; most of the skin had peeled away from his face, exposing his teeth and cheek bones.

"What the fuck?"

I pulled the trigger, sheared his head off, and continued to lay heavy fire into the vehicle. The back end erupted in a ball of flame. The car dislodged and rolled over into the ditch.

We sped after the black *Renegade*. As we closed in, a guy leaned out the back widow and blasted at us with a shotgun. He too was dead. One eyeball dangled from the decaying socket. I was so busy shooting that I failed to notice that a motorcycle had pulled up alongside us. It accelerated and, as it passed the *Renegade*, someone inside held out a leather bag. The guy on the bike grabbed it and took off down the highway.

I ducked down to avoid another volley of buckshot. I returned fire, taking out the rear wheels. The back end spun out and we T-boned the *Renegade*. We pushed the vehicle for a few yards before coming to a stop. I leveled the barrel of the .50 cal on the interior and fired, reducing the occupants to chunks of decayed meat.

Juan got out of the HER0 and shook his fist at the motorcycle on the horizon.

"My fucking money! *Pendejos!*"

I hopped out onto the roof and jumped down onto the road. He turned to face me just as I shoved him.

"Hey! What's your problem, man?"

"What the fuck was that?" I shoved him again. It was like hitting a marshmallow.

He took out the water bottle and jiggled it in front of my face. "Don't make me spill this!"

I didn't care. I slapped it out of his hand. Thankfully the lid stayed on. Jim quickly put himself between us and I backed off, if only slightly. I was still pissed. "Those guys were dead!"

"No shit! You killed them dead!"

I pulled free from Jim and this time, I put Juan on his ass. He fell back and landed in a puddle on the freeway. His bandana fell off revealing six extra eyes in his forehead.

"What the fuck!"

Juan started laughing.

"You're a… a spider?"

Juan laughed, spittle frothing at his mouth. "I am the king of the spiders! Ha! Ha! Ha!" All eight of his eyes were tearing up.

"So you're a spider who doesn't like water."

"Like the ones you find in the bathtub that can't climb out already."

"Well you're sitting in a puddle. I would think you're pretty fucked right now!"

"We're both fucked!"

"Enough of the bullshit, man! Start talking!"

Juan sighed. "Jesus! You fuckers are all talk and no do!"

I stomped him in the midsection. "Talk!"

"Alright, already!" he coughed. He straightened his shirt, and combed his slick hair with his fingers. "I lied but only a little bit."

"You tell the truth and I'll help you out of there."

"Okay, already. I no lie to you no more. I made a pact with a demon." When he saw that neither Jim nor I seemed to flinch at that statement, he continued. "I was selling crack for this asshole. But I wanted to be like him… you know, be in control… and have a gang of my own. So I made a deal with this demon. He said for a million dollars, he would give me all the power I want."

"Why would a demon need a million dollars?" Jim asked.

"To put in his fucking mattress! How the fuck should I know? Anyway, I give him the million. In exchange, he gives me this gang of *pendejos*, and turns me into a spider. I says, *what the fuck is this*? He says, *you have a gang and you are strong*. The fucker tricked me! I no want to be no fucking spider. So, I stole the money back and killed the *pendejos*. But they come back as zombie scum and keep trying to take the money from me. Until that bomb, they have no success."

"Where are they taking the money?"

"I don't know – far away from me! Now, can we go get it or what, already?"

"How many of them are there?" Jim asked.

"Ah... here's the problem. You see... they make other zombies like them. It's like they infect their own."

"You mean, their army grows," I added.

"That's right! Now get me out of this water."

I reached down and helped him up. "How do we break this curse?"

"Just get me back the money. Once I have it in my hands, you are free."

"Then, let's get going."

"I'll drive," Jim said.

The two men got into the HER0. I opened the passenger door. The sky was getting dark and cloudy and it started raining.

"Great! More water!" Juan huffed.

***

Wet, heavy snow flakes hit the window, partially blocking my view. The light turned green and the bus lurched forward.

"I can't wait for Christmas break – only two more weeks," Valentina said excitedly.

"Yeah, me too!"

"Too bad I won't see you over Christmas break."

I dropped my head. "Yeah... my Uncle... he's planned a bunch of stuff. I'll be busy."

"That's ok. I have a surprise for you." Valentina pulled her hair away from her face and smiled. "I'll give it to you on the last day of school."

I blushed. "Can't wait!"

"Oh... this is my stop!" She pulled the signal-cord. The bus stopped suddenly and she fell towards me. I caught her in my arms. She kissed me on the cheek. "See you tomorrow, Eddie,"

"Bye, Val!"

She stepped off the bus. The doors closed.

"Hold on! I said, hold on already!"

A big man pushed his way to the exit. He took up the whole aisle. I quickly moved aside into the empty seat. He grabbed the handrail above my head. The hair on his hands was so thick, like he was wearing gloves. It took a few minutes before he finally squeezed himself out the exit door.

As the bus pulled away, I looked for Valentina. I wanted to wave to her. But all I could see were big wet flakes of heavy snow.

***

"What do you think he's doing?"

Up ahead, the lone rider sat on his motorcycle, holding up the leather satchel.

"Who cares? Let's get that fucker, already!"

"I think he wants us to follow him," Jim said. "He's taunting us."

The rider threw the bag over his shoulder, kick started the bike and took off down the off ramp.

"After him already!"

Jim put the HER0 in gear and we followed. The rider led us down a two-lane highway.

"I'm going up top," I said.

Outside the air was cold and fresh. The sky was cloudy; an eerie yellow moon occasionally revealed itself from behind the gray cover. At least it had stopped raining. We followed the bike for a long time before he turned off onto a gravel roadway. The HER0 bounced and rocked along the uneven surface. The bike took one last turn and came to a stop in a clearing. Jim parked. He and Juan got out of the vehicle. The rider stood about fifty feet ahead of us, judging by the faint glow of his eyes.

"Enough screwing around, already! Give me the bag!" Juan shouted.

I turned on the spotlight and shone it at the guy, illuminating his wide eyes and skeletal grin. There was movement behind him. I swept the area with the light. More zombies! Their eyes were closed. But when they opened, hundreds of pairs of faint yellow dots emerged from the darkness. Headlights turned on all around us. A semicircular wall of vehicles bordered the clearing. More cars circled in from the rear, blocking our exit.

"Aw, shit!"

"Bring it on, you *pendejos!*"

The zombies charged forward. *BRAKKA- BRAKKA- BRAKKA-BRAKKA!* I opened up with the .50 cal, lighting up the area with orange tracer fire. Zombies crumpled. Arms and legs flew off in all directions. Vehicle hoods blew open and sparked. Jim let out a battle cry and engaged the zombies, combat knife in hand.

Juan quickly crawled back into the HER0.

"Kill them, already!"

"Hey! Can't you do anything other than look ugly? Don't you shoot webs or something?"

"I'm not THAT kind of spider!"

"Useless piece of shit!" I muttered.

BRAKKA- BRAKKA- BRAKKA- BRAKKA! Bullets ripped through metal and rotting flesh, shredding cars and bodies to pieces. Parts went flying. Despite all the carnage, it seemed like I hardly put a dent in the undead ranks. Every time I knocked out a set of eyes, another appeared from somewhere. *BRAKKA- BRAKKA- BRAKKA-SILENCE!* I pulled back and forth on the cocking handle.

"Shit! It's jammed!"

The zombies moved forward. I lay down some suppressive fire with my rifle.

"Jim! Where are you?"

No response. I reached down and grabbed the metal box. I set it on the roof and opened it. A few quick key strokes on the remote, and the probe hummed to life, hovering in mid air. Quickly, I ran through the user interface.

<Calibrating perimeter>

"C'mon!"

<Analyzing data>

"C'mon!"
<Status: Ready>
"Alright!" I entered a new command.
<Obstacle Avoidance: Disengaged>
<Probe run time: Indefinite>

THUD! THUD! THUMP! WHUMP! The probe shot through the air cracking open every skull in its path, and buying me enough time to clear the jam and get back in the game. *BRAKKA- BRAKKA- BRAKKA- BRAKKA!*

Between me and the probe, we pretty much cleared the entire field. The clouds parted and the full moon's glow bathed the open area. Jim was on the outer perimeter, taking the heads off the last of the combatants. Whew! At least, he remembered to duck. The battlefield was littered with broken bodies and twisted metal. I grabbed the remote and guided the probe back home.

Juan climbed out of the vehicle. "Where's that fucking bag, already?"

I jumped out of the jeep and ran towards the motorcycle. Jim met up with me. The (now) headless rider still clutched the satchel. I pried it free and opened it. Inside was a metal box.

"Give it to me!" Juan yelled. "Give it here, already!"

"Quick, open the box!" Jim urged.

I flipped open the lid and was absolutely amazed at what I saw – a testicle!

***

The secretary asked me to have a seat outside the principal's office. When she wasn't looking, I leaned into the door frame just enough not to be seen, but enough to hear the conversation.

"Lloyd... this is awful," my teacher Ms. Shand said. "I don't think I can do this."

"Evelyn, everything will be fine. Grief counselors are standing by and are here to assist us."

"I don't know." It sounded like she was crying.

"You have to be strong for the children."

"I'm sorry... this is very difficult. She was so young. I can't believe she's dead."

My stomach felt empty. Cold shivers ran up and down my back and across my chest.

"Why don't you go to the staff room and calm yourself."

I sat up straight and looked forward as Ms. Shand walked out of the office.

"Mr. Griffin," called the principal.

I hopped down off the seat and stepped inside, stopping a few feet short of the big oak desk. Mr. Burton was looking at some papers. He spoke without making eye contact.

"Mr. Griffin, there's been an accident." He finally looked up at me. My stomach was doing summersaults. "Your friend, Valentina, died yesterday. I am very sorry." My lip began to quiver and my eyes began to burn. I ran out of the office. "Mr. Griffin!" was the last thing I heard.

***

"That is one big testicle," Jim said.

"Yeah!"

"It smells like sulphur. And it looks like it was torn off."

"I'll be right there! Just wait, already! I want my money!"

I realized I was standing in a puddle. I lifted my foot out of the water. "Jim, I think the curse is broken." I took a step back, but he quickly stopped me with his hand.

"Watch it!" He nodded down at the ground.

We were standing on the edge of a hole. I slid as I stepped away, pushing mud and rock over the edge. A few seconds later I heard a splash.

"Is that a well?"

"It would seem so. I think they were setting a trap."

Juan's hands reached out for the box. "Give it here!" I pulled it away.

"What the fuck is going on? This isn't a million dollars."

"It may as well be! That's mine! Give it here, already!"

"What kind of spider are you, exactly?"

"What? I'm a spider… what difference does it make, already?"

"*Tidarran sisyphoides…*" Jim stated.

Juan stopped and stared at him.

"It removes one of its own oversized sex organs so that it can chase females. Judging by the marks on the scrotum, I bet you tore this off yourself… with your teeth."

Juan broke out in a large grin.

"You explain why you have your ball in a box, and I'll give it back to you. And then we each go our separate ways. Deal?"

"Aw, Jesus… you and your fucking 'splanations."

"Make a choice or I throw it in this here well!" I held the box out over the hole.

Juan instantly raised his hands. "I'll talk! I'll talk, already." He took a deep breath. "I never was no drug dealer. Look at me! I'm a big, fat, sleepy-eye useless piece of shit. No woman would want me. So one day, I said I'd do anything if I could make it with a lady. That's when this demon comes to me and offers this deal. He says I can have any woman I want if I tear off one of my testicles with my teeth.

At first I was like, *no fucking way*! But then a few days later, I was at the store and I saw this really pretty Latina. I said hello to her and she ignored me. The little *puta* turned away from me. She just talked to the cashier about her boyfriend and how she was going to give him a picture frame with her photo in it. I was so pissed!

So that night, I chewed my fucking ball off! Oh, it was hard to do that. But I did it, already. The demon came back and took it from me. In exchange, he made me into this."

He rubbed his hands over his hairy arms and pointed at his multiple eyes.

"How the fuck was I to meet women looking like this?! Huh? Demon *pendejo*! And... he fucked me over so good! You won't believe this... so I will tell you. The demon made it so I was always horny. I had a constant hard on. It never went away.

I went and I found that little *puta*... and I fucked her. That's when I learned of the demon's other gift. He made it so I could never cum! So I killed her! She was my first. I don't know how many *putas* I've fucked and killed since then. I never have no satisfaction, already. It's like a scratch you can't never itch. SO PLEASE GIVE ME BACK MY GODDAMN FUCKING BALL SO I CAN BE NORMAL AGAIN!"

Jim stepped forward. "Just one question..."

Juan clenched his fists and his teeth. "You and your fucking questions, already," he seethed.

"All this time you've been trying to get your testicle back, correct?"

"Yes!" Juan threw his arms into the air. "Why do you ask?"

Jim scratched his forehead. "You never had a hideout, did you?"

"No. Are you done, already?"

Jim looked to me. "Hoss mentioned all our bunkers had been overrun by UDs."

"UDs?" Juan asked.

"Undead," I replied. "What we refer to as zombies."

Juan nodded.

Jim cleared his throat. "As I was saying, the bunkers were overrun, most likely from underground."

"Yeah, so?"

He pointed at Juan. "If the UDs were guarding your testicle, then I suspect they were underground as well. If I'm correct on that, then the missile blew a hole in the earth, which gave them a way out.

All of Juan's eyes opened widely, and he clapped. "You are fucking brilliant."

Jim shrugged it off. "Also, some spiders make their lairs underground."

"Stop milking it, already. So you're fucking Einstein... just shut up!" Juan took a deep breath and shook his head. "All that from one question."

"Uh... You said you uh... killed a little girl," I said.

"More questions?" Juan shouted, slapping his chubby cheeks. "That's it! One more question and I mean it. Yes, I killed a little *puta*."

"And she said she had a picture frame or something for her boyfriend"

"Yeah, so? What the fuck?"

"Nothing. I'm sure it's nothing." I held up the box. "Do you have to reattach this testicle to break the curse?"

"Yeah... with my teeth. Give it back already!"

"Sure, you can have your testicle back."

"What?"

"It's okay Jim." I smirked. "He can have it back. We have an *agreement*."

***

"Mr. Burton?"

"Yes, Mr. Griffin. Please come in." I took up my usual position in front of his desk. "Eddie... uh, Valentina's parents were here the other day. They asked me to give you something."

Mr. Burton opened his desk drawer and withdrew a small package in Christmas wrap. He set it on the desk. I looked at him and then at the gift. I grabbed it and ripped open the wrapping. It was a picture frame, with a picture of Valentina in it. She had drawn a little heart in the lower right corner and put our initials inside. I clutched it tightly and closed my eyes.

After a few seconds I said, "Mr. Burton. I know what happened to her."

"I'm sorry. It was very tragic."

"Remember how you asked me if there was anything I remembered from the last time I saw her... that might help the police?"

"Yes."

"Well, my Uncle, the Reverend... he says I shouldn't say anything. He says God will punish the guilty and the sinners. But, I think he's an asshole."

"Eddie Griffin! That type of language will not be tolerated in my office!"

"I don't care! The last time I saw Val, we were on the bus. There was this overweight Latino who got off at the same stop she did."

"And you think this man had something to do with Valentina's death?"

"I think he killed her."

"Mr. Griffin! You have no idea what happened!"

I stared at Mr. Burton and bit my lip. I looked at the picture one more time. "Mr. Burton, God's not going to punish Val's killer."

"No? And just who do you think will?"

"Me!"

***

"*Madre de dios!* Thank you! Thank you!"

Juan put his hands on the box, and stuck his head inside. I put my hand on the back of his neck and pushed his head down as far as it would go.

"Mmmmmffrrbbb!"

I grabbed the water bottle from his baggy pants, spun off the cap and poured it into the box. He struggled to get his head out.

"You killed Valentina, fucker!"

I stepped in behind him, put my foot on his ass, and pushed him into the well. *SPLASH!* The ground began to tremble. The sides of the hole caved in. I cautiously stepped back. The earth continued to fall away as the hole expanded. Jim and I turned and ran, slogging as fast as we could through the wet, heavy mud. At times, I felt like I was running uphill with concrete blocks tied to my feet. The hole followed, swallowing the earth out from under our feet. I lunged forward and caught the bumper of the HER0. The ground gave way. I hung there momentarily, staring down at the dark abyss below. Luckily, the sink hole stopped short of the vehicle. Jim popped his head out from over the hood. He reached down and pulled me up.

I lay back on the hood and waited for my heart to stop racing. It seemed like hours passed before I could move again. Eventually, I rolled off the hood and made for the passenger door. Jim was leaning against the HER0, staring at the sky.

"How are you?" he asked.

I shrugged. "That was really fucked up."

Jim nodded.

"Hey, how did you know about that spider?"

Jim grinned. "I ran some special ops in the Colombian jungle a few years ago. Part of my orientation was to learn about the indigenous plants and animals. I read a lot about the native species of spiders and I seem to recall that particular one." He looked up into the sky again. "Do you mind if I ask you something?"

"Go ahead," I replied with a shrug.

"Who was Valentina?"

I folded my arms across my chest and leaned back against the vehicle. "Valentina was the first girl I fell in love with... or what I thought love was at the time. We were just kids."

"And you really think Juan killed her?"

I nodded. "We took the bus home together from school. Her stop was first. One day, she got off the bus. I don't know why I remember this, but there was this big guy with really hairy hands. He had a spider tattoo on his wrist. I had never seen him before. He got off at the same stop. That was the last time I saw her alive." I rubbed my forehead. "A few weeks later I found out she had bought a picture frame... for me... for Christmas. "

"I'm sorry, Ed."

I shrugged. When the silence felt uncomfortable, I said, "I don't know about you, but the weirder things get, the more things seem to make sense."

Jim grinned. "In the same way winter arrives after the ducks fly south?"

"Quack!" We both laughed. "Let's get the hell out of here."

"Agreed." Jim made his way around the vehicle. When he got to driver's side, he leaned on the roof. "You know, there really is a reason why I asked you to come along with me."

"Oh yeah, what's that?"

"You have a good sense of direction. Not… physical location necessarily, but your moral compass. It works much better than mine. You save the world by saving the people in it. I save the world by killing them. I think we complement each other rather well. You did the right thing when you pulled Juan from the barrel."

"Yeah, I'm not so sure," I said with a shrug.

"I am."

9 HERO'S WELCOME?

All life is ensouled. Life is the sum of all experiences. The world, or even the universe for that matter, is not only a physical existence, but a spiritual one as well. Such is the nature of cosmic consciousness: experiences manifest themselves and intertwine so that they may be shared. From this, new experiences and learnings emerge. Darkness corrupts experiences. It homogenizes them. And you thought zombies have come only recently to walk the earth? We've been dead all along.

-Veck

It was so cold I could see my breath. And it was damp, too. No matter how many times I pulled my jacket a little tighter, I didn't get any warmer. I took my finger off the trigger when I saw Jim's familiar green face appear in the woods. I checked my watch – right on schedule. I got out of the HERO and met him at the edge of the clearing.

"Well? What is it?"

"Good catch on your part when you saw that smoke rising up out of the forest." Jim pointed off into the trees. "There's a game preserve up on the hill overlooking the highway."

"A game preserve?"

"Yeah… I saw a ranch house, barns, equipment sheds. There are even small towers in the woods to shoot from. It's a good place to be if you want to survive."

"Did you see anybody?"

Jim smiled. "I saw a teenager wandering along the fence line. He was wearing a San Antonio Rattlers Baseball cap."

"Serious?"

"Yup."

"Just a teenager?"

"Three of them in total. I got in close enough to the ranch house. It seemed pretty quiet."

"Maybe I should go in and take a look."

Jim leaned against a tree and rubbed his forehead. "Negative!"

"Aw, c'mon. Let me just go in and knock on the door. If they turn me away, I'll be back before dark. Aren't you the least bit curious?"

Jim sighed. "Yes, a bit. But I'd rather just keep moving."

"Maybe the kid was wearing the hat for a reason. I should check it out."

Jim looked me in the eye. "Alright but not until I do some more recon first. Agreed?"

"Ugh... alright."

"I need to rest."

"Sure!"

I was really annoyed at the situation. Once... just once, I wished someone would recognize me as the man who won the last Super Bowl in history - someone other than a vampire, anyway. I was really anxious to go to the ranch. I waited for Jim to rest. Then I packed my bag and set off to do some recon of my own.

I wore my jersey underneath my jacket. If the folks turned out to be friendly, I figured I'd show them my colors. The walk along the highway was relatively uneventful. My nose was wet and cold like a dog's. A low fog slowly set in.

It didn't take me long to reach the winding uphill road to the lodge. About halfway up the road I saw a wooden tower. I was sure the person inside had seen me because his silhouette moved about excitedly. I continued along until I got to the front gate. It swung open and two young men stepped out. *These guys must be the teenagers Jim mentioned.* They cautiously walked towards me with guns raised. I stopped and put my hands in the air.

"Put the weapon on the ground!"

I complied with the order.

"And the bag!"

My backpack hit the gravel road.

"Keep your hands in the air and turn around!"

They ran towards me and stopped suddenly, kicking gravel against the back of my boots.

"Turn around... slowly!"

I turned. The first teen carried a big shotgun, and wore a cowboy hat and suede hunting coat. The other carried a .22 and wore a plaid jacket and cap with ear flaps. He picked up my rifle and pack.

"Who are you?" the kid with the cowboy hat asked.

I didn't see a Rattlers cap. And they didn't seem to recognize me. I ran with my standard cover story. "My name's Frenke... Carlin Frenke. I was a soldier stationed at Fort Carson."

"You mean to tell us you've been travellin' on foot?" the other teen asked.

"No. I have a vehicle. It's a few miles up the road... in the forest."

"Why'd you leave your vehicle? Is it broke?"

"Listen... I'm not looking for any trouble. I came on foot so as not to alarm you. Maybe I'll just be going."

The teen leveled the shotgun at my face. "Don't you move!"

"You alone?" the other asked.

"Yes."

"Where you headed?"

"Canada. I have family there. And I hear there's not as many zombies up there."

They exchanged suspicious glances.

"So you heard them radio transmissions?"

"What radio transmissions? I ain't got no radio."

"Did you see the smoke? Is that why you stopped here?" the teen with the plaid jacket asked nervously.

"Yeah, I did. Why?"

My response seemed to piss off the kid with the shotgun. "C'mon. Don't say anything about the smoke." He jabbed me with the end of the weapon.

"Why?"

"We don't need no trouble."

"Then let me go!"

"We're not supposed to have fires," the other one added.

"Shut up, Hoke! Now you get movin'!"

We started walking towards the gate. "So your name's Hoke. Who are you?"

The shotgun-toter glared at Hoke. "Name's Dillon Gunn. That there's Hoke Winchester. The man in the tower is Hoke's brother, Virgil."

"Nice to meet you."

"We haven't seen many folks pass through here since the dead rose. You have to understand we need to take precautions."

"I completely understand. You seem rather young."

"Our parents are dead," Hoke said. "They killed 'em." Dillon shot him another mean look.

"Who killed them?"

Neither of them responded. When we reached the gate, Dillon looked back at me and said in a hushed voice, "Just don't say nothin' about the smoke or my folks! You'll get us all killed."

My heart raced a bit faster. Hoke closed the gate behind us.

"This way!" Dillon said, leading me to the ranch house.

I put my hands down and surveyed the terrain. The main ranch house was directly in front of me. Two smaller guest houses sat off to the right. The road circled in behind where I could make out the tops of some other buildings and a barn. Another barn sat out in the middle of an open field in the distance.

We passed a guy standing under a big oak tree. He seemed out of place. His hair was slicked back and he was dressed in black from head to toe: leather jacket, dress pants and those fancy pointed-tip leather shoes. Although he was facing me, his eyes were looking off to my right. He muttered something unintelligible. Nobody responded.

He suddenly became angry and shouted, "I said, what's up with you?" He was still looking off to my right.

"I'm sorry, but were you talking to me?"

"You see anybody else around?"

"I thought maybe there was someone standing where you're looking."

He was suddenly in my face - a hair's width from my nose.

"Are you making fun of my eyes, man? Are you making fun of my fucking eyes?" I noticed he was still looking to the right.

"Sorry, I couldn't tell you were talking to me because your eyes are looking in another direction."

He shoved me. "You ARE making fun of my fucking eyes!" He reached into his jacket and pulled out a gun. "I'm going to kill you!" He pointed the gun in my face.

I put my hands in the air. "You're not gonna kill me."

"What makes you think that?"

"Cause you're not the only guy here with a gun." I nodded to Dillon and Hoke. "Right?"

The guy burst out laughing.

"Our guns ain't got no bullets, Mister," Dillon spat.

"These kids can't rescue you, you dumb fuck!" The guy sneered, pulling back his suit jacket to reveal the other guns he carried. "Around here, we pack all the heat."

"What's goin' on, Richard?" a voice asked. A short little fat guy in a greasy black suit and his entourage of a dozen or so similarly dressed men spilled out onto the porch of the ranch house. I felt like I just ran into the cast from that TV series *The Mobfather*.

"This asshole's makin' fun of my eyes."

"Everybody makes fun of your eyes, Richard."

The other men laughed. Richard spit at my feet and holstered his piece. The little fat guy walked up to Dillon, who leaned in and whispered something in his ear. Hoke gave him my rifle and pack, which he handed off to one of his goons. Then he walked right up to me and looked me up and down.

"So you're a soldier."

"That's right."

"What kind of vehicle do you have?"

"Just a truck," I shrugged. "Look, I'm not interested in any trouble."

"Sure, sure... I understand. None of us want any trouble. What's your name again?"

"Carlin Frenke."

"Carlin..." He extended his hand. "My name is Pampino." When I shook his hand, I noticed he was missing his index finger after the first knuckle. "You look familiar... have I seen you before?"

"No... I don't know. "

"No, no, no," he insisted. "I am sure I have seen you before." He looked over his shoulder and said, "Hey Bruno... who does this guy look like?"

A very big man winced and responded, "All them brothers look the same to me."

Pampino smiled. "Well, Carlin, I think you should stay the night. In the morning, you'll take us to this truck of yours. Sound good?"

"Why should I do anything for you?"

He smiled and looked over at the teens. "Where's your sister, Dillon?"

"Inside the lodge, Mr. Pampino."

"Is she safe?"

"As long as we do what you ask, sir."

"And if you don't?"

Dillon swallowed hard. "You'll kill her."

Pampino waved a finger at him. "I'm gonna fuck her first. Hell, we'll all fuck her... have a nice little gang-bang. Then we'll kill her." He clapped his hands together. "Excellent!" He turned to me and said, "See? When people do what I ask, nobody gets hurt."

I decided to play it tough. "What? You think I care about some girl?"

Pampino furled his lip. "Bruno!"

"Yes, sir?"

"Go inside and punch that girl in the face."

My heart sank in my chest.

"No!" Dillon shouted.

Hoke held him back.

"I thought you didn't want to cause any trouble. Don't do that again!" He turned to Dillon and Hoke. "Take him to the game cleaning facility and make him comfortable. No funny business, understand?"

"C'mon," Dillon urged me.

"What the fuck is going on here?"

"Don't talk," Hoke warned. He lowered his voice. "Wait until we're alone."

"Shut up, Hoke! Hasn't he said enough?" Dillon scowled at me and said, "I told you not to talk. You'll get us *all* killed!"

The game cleaning facility smelled a little raw. Chains with leather bindings hung from the ceiling. A chair sat in the center of the room. Dried blood spatter covered the floor.

"Sit down and put your arms up," Dillon ordered. He bound my wrists and pulled the chains tight.

"Now you wanna tell me what the fuck is going on?"

Dillon didn't respond. Hoke leaned up against a workbench, next to what looked like a large radio.

"Those assholes came here a few months ago. They were looking for help. One of them got bit. Mr. Gunn let them in – he thought he should help them."

"Shut up, Hoke!"

"Maybe he can help us, Dillon! He's a friggin' soldier!"

Dillon ignored him.

Hoke continued. "The man who got bit died. They killed Mr. Gunn and all the staff, and they locked Mrs. Gunn and Jessie, Dillon's sister, up in the house. We tried to break 'em out and run away. But they caught us." He stopped and stared into the ground. "That's when they killed Mrs. Gunn."

"I'm so sorry. If you untie me, I may be able to help."

"You can't help us," Dillon sneered.

"We're running out of food," Hoke said. "The provisions are low. Most of the game is eaten."

The door swung open and another teen rushed in. "Dillon! Hoke! What's taking so long?"

"Almost ready, Virgil... we were just talking with Carlin, here."

"Carlin?" Virgil stared at me, adjusting his San Antonio Rattlers ball cap. "That's no Carlin! That there's Eddie Griffin! Holy shit!" He broke out in a wide-toothed smile. "I can't believe this! Eddie Griffin!"

"Are you sure?" Hoke asked.

"Hell yeah! Remember the Super Bowl? That's him, I swear. Jeez... Eddie Griffin. You're a hero!"

"Listen! I can help you guys get out of here."

"That's enough talk," Dillon said. "Nobody's getting' out of here. Put the thought out of your head, Virge! Let's go!"

Dillon headed out the door, followed by Hoke.

Virgil walked backwards, still looking at me and smiling.

"Hey, know what?" He skipped back across to the work bench. "I'll leave the scanner on. Maybe you'll hear that radio transmission." He flipped a switch and adjusted a knob. Tiny red lights appeared on the piece of equipment. As he walked out, he turned and said, "I'll be back later." He closed the door, leaving me in the pitch dark with nothing but LED lights to keep me company.

I awoke to the crackle of static. My arms were numb. I must have fallen asleep. I could see lights flashing on the scanner. A metallic voice broke through the static: *Four Wing Cold Lake ... 290 kilometers North East* <crackle> *... Highway 28* <crackle>*... no undead here...*" The message repeated a few more times and then the scanner was quiet.

The door opened and someone walked into the garage. He closed the door behind him and turned on a flashlight. It was Virgil.

"I can't stay long. Nobody knows I'm here."

"Did you come to let me go?"

"No... sorry."

"Then why did you come in here?"

"I just wanted to see you. I mean, you're Eddie Griffin. I never thought I'd meet you in person. I mean, especially not since all them zombies invaded the earth."

"Sorry, I'm in no position to give you an autograph. Maybe you should untie me."

"I can't."

"Don't you want to get out of here?" I asked.

"And go where?"

"Well, I heard that radio transmission."

"You did?"

"Yeah…. Something about Four Wing Cold Lake."

"I heard that message, too! They got no zombies. You know where that place is?"

"It's a military base in Canada," I replied. "My friend has been there. He's a soldier."

"Is that where you're headed?"

"Possibly… help me get out of here and I'll take you with me."

"And Hoke and the rest?"

"Them too!"

Virgil stared at me, thinking things over. "I – I can't! Sorry! If Mr. Pampino sends men to check on you in the night, and you're not here, we're all as good as dead."

"I'm sure my friend will come looking for me. He's out there in the woods."

"Then he'll rescue us. Then we'll all be free. I have to go."

"No, wait! Seriously, let me go."

"I can't!" Virgil turned off the flashlight and disappeared, leaving me in the cold, dark room.

The door swung open, crashing against the wall. It woke me up. I hadn't even opened my eyes when I was kicked in the stomach. The chains slackened and I fell out of the chair. Two of Pampino's men hovered over me. One held a gun to my head while the other loosened the bindings.

"Get up! Let's go!"

The man grabbed me by my arms and shoved me out the door. I stumbled and fell but a swift kick prompted me to my feet. The sun crept up over the horizon. A cold wind howled through the trees. I was half pushed, half dragged to the barn, and dropped face first onto the wood floor. I rolled over onto my side.

Pampino was leaning on a table with a wooden crate on it. He was grinning. Dillon, Hoke and a girl whom I assumed was Jessie were all on their knees a few feet away from the table. Their hands were tied behind their backs and they were gagged. The rest of Pampino's men were standing around. The man known as Bruno lifted me and sat me down in a chair rather forcefully.

"Nice to see you," Pampino said. One of his goons joined him at his side. "I heard you had a chance to meet Virgil."

"Who?"

SMACK! The goon planted his fist in my jaw. I shook off the pain. The man was crushing his fist into his palm. Hopefully, he was softening it up.

"Oh, forgive me. This is Sal. Go ahead, introduce yourself, Sal."

SMACK! I took another hit just above the eye.

"Introductions aside, I heard Virgil paid you a visit last night."

"He must have been dreaming."

SMACK! My lip split.

"Sure… or maybe he was sleepwalking." The men laughed. "When my boys found him, he woke up in a hurry." Pampino reached inside the crate on the table. "I asked him why he went to see you…in his ear: this ear." He held up an ear and placed it on the table. My heart sank. "He said he just wanted to see you. Then I asked if he saw you with his eyes: these eyes." He placed two eyeballs on the table. "He did see you, alright. So I asked him what he said to you." Pampino placed a severed tongue down on the table. "You know what he said? He said that he just wanted to make sure you were okay. That was very considerate of him, wasn't it?"

"You could learn a thing or two from him."

SMACK! SMACK! Bloody spittle ran down my chin.

When I opened my eyes again, Pampino was staring into my face.

"I am insulted by that remark. I really am. You see, I do care about you. I care a great deal. You probably don't know how important you are to me." He leaned again against the table, crossing his arms. "You know what I used to do before the dead rose?"

"No. Please tell me,"

"I will. I used to be a hitman. I was the best. They used to call me the One-Shot Deal. You know why?"

"Because you only ever fired one shot but always missed so nobody had to pay you?" I anticipated the hit, but nothing came.

"Heh-heh! Very clever, but also very wrong! I only ever needed one bullet: one shot – one kill. So one day, I am sitting in the bar watching the Super Bowl with my friends. We're at a crucial point in the game: down two points, twenty-five seconds on the clock, fifty-five yards and goal, fourth down, pissing rain and roaring thunder.

"Alfonso Tortini... you know... Big Al comes back from taking a dump. He looks up at the screen and says, *'I bet that hot shot quarterback doesn't make good on the throw'*. To which I respond, *'I bet he does'*. Alfonso asks, *'How much you wanna bet?'* I say, *'Fifty thousand dollars.'* So Alfonso agrees. Guess what? That hot shot quarterback made good on the throw. I win the bet."

"Lucky you!"

"Wait... it gets better! Alfonso says he's not gonna pay me. So I pull my gun on him. That forces him to quickly change his mind. He tells me to wait at the bar and he'll come back with my money in one hour. One hour goes by. In walks Alfonso and his goons. He gives me my money. And then his fuckin' goons bust me up real good and they cut off my trigger finger."

He held up the stub of his index finger and waved it in front of me.

"Remember when I met you yesterday, Calvin?"

"It's Carlin."

"Whatever. I know who you are. You're no Carlin." He stood up and jammed that stub of a finger in my face. "You're Eddie Griffin! You're the HOTSHOT QUARTERBACK THAT COST ME MY FUCKIN' FINGER! And now, you are going to lose far more than a finger, my friend. But first, you're going to have the pleasure of watching us have our way with this young lady. Then we're going to kill the boys… then her… then you."

Just then, the power went out, leaving us at the mercy of a few lanterns in the center of the room.

"Aw shit!" Pampino spat.

The loft doors suddenly flew open, banging loudly against the barn boards. The wind rushed inside.

"Hey, Marco! Close those doors!"

"Right away!"

The man went up the ladder and disappeared. Moments later, there was a scream followed by a dull thud. Something had hit the ground outside.

"What the fuck was that? Marco? Marco?"

The doors still banged in the wind.

"Vinny! Find out what happened to Marco! That idiot… he probably slipped and fell. If he's still alive, kill him!"

"Yes, Boss!" Vinny went up into the loft. A few minutes later he called down, "Marco's dead…looks like his neck's broke."

"Idiot!"

Vinny's face contorted in a strange way and he fell forward, landing spread eagle on the floor of the barn. A knife jutted out of his back. Pampino drew a pistol from inside his jacket. All the men drew weapons.

"Somebody tell me, WHAT THE FUCK'S GOIN' ON?"

A shadow sprinted through the loft. Everyone started shooting. The teens managed to scuffle their way under the table. I tried to scrunch down, making myself a smaller target. Richard or someone – I'm not sure who – ran into me, knocking me out of the chair. I landed on my back. When all the commotion and shooting stopped, Bruno lay on the floor next to me with a knife sticking out of his neck. He clutched at it, gurgling and kicking his legs. This prompted everyone to shoot again. A lantern fell and shattered. Flaming oil spread across the floor.

"Stop fucking shooting!" Pampino shouted. "And somebody put out that fire!"

Two men raced up the ladder and into the loft. Another man beat the flames with his jacket. One of the men in the loft came crashing down. His head was facing the wrong way. If he were alive, he could've seen his own ass. Richard stood up and fired. The second man fell down into the light, full of bullet holes.

"You just shot Carl!"

"Sorry, Boss."

"Watch where you're shooting!"

"Are you making fun of my eyes?!"

The man who was putting out the fire screamed. Bones snapped and he fell, lifeless, to the floor. Again, everyone started shooting into the darkness.

"Stop shooting!"

A hand appeared over the mouth of one of the men, muffling his cry. He triggered his shotgun and sprayed the room with buckshot. Richard dropped to the ground, clutching his side. He fired wildly into the corner of the barn. Sal joined in, unloading a full clip before realizing nothing was there.

"Watch where the fuck you're shooting!" Pampino shouted.

"I was! And stop making fun of my fucking eyes!"

The shadow ran across the center of the room. Everyone started shooting and suddenly found themselves in a crossfire, with Richard and Pampino in the middle. Men dropped on both sides. Pampino dropped his gun and grabbed his arm. Richard dove under the table, and Sal slumped to the floor in a pool of his own blood. Pampino hauled Richard out from under the table.

"Cover me, you asshole!"

Richard stepped in front of him. "I think I see something over there?"

"Where? I don't know where you're looking at?"

"STOP MAKING FUN OF MY FUCKING..." *BOOM!* The red beams blew Richard's head to pieces.

Pampino took one look at the headless body, and quickly backed his way towards the door. He stopped suddenly. Behind him, two dull red eyes looked over his shoulder. Silver flashed. Pampino fell to his knees, clutching his slashed throat. He opened his mouth, gasping for air, before falling face first onto the floor.

Jim stepped into the light. He was dressed in black from head to toe like some sort of ninja.

Despite the pain in my face, I managed to force a smile. "Thanks for coming."

"No worries," Jim said, as he helped me to my feet. "I guess they weren't fans of yours after all, huh?"

10 THE AUTOCTHON

The world has become a strange place since the undead took over. You see, undead are soulless nothings without consciousness. Therefore, the world can only draw on survivors for conscious experiences. And since there aren't many of them around, it really is what you make of it. Or perhaps more accurately, it makes of you what is!

-Veck

To say Jim was pissed at me was an understatement. But in typical Jim fashion, he didn't say a word. There was something about Jim that forced you into knowing you had done wrong, and that you would never do it again.

We spent a few days at the ranch before leaving. It gave me some time to let my face heal, and for the kids to deal with leaving it all behind. Jim didn't like the idea of bringing them along. But if the radio transmission was true, then CFB[22] Cold Lake, as Jim called it, was a better place for us all. Apparently, Jim had been there before, when he served with JTF3[23]. We weren't sure what we'd find when we got there. But one thing was for sure: it was clear that in this new world, everything had a way of coming back to haunt you.

***

"Boy, don't you have a house of your own?" Mrs. Frenke asked.

"No." I wiped the milk off my chin. "Didn't Carlin tell you? You're going to adopt me." I smiled and shoveled in another mouthful of cereal.

---

[22] CFB: Canadian Forces Base.
[23] JTF3: Joint Task Force 3. An elite Canadian Special Forces Unit, modeled after its predecessor, JTF2. To this day, the Canadian Government still denies JTF3 exists.

Mrs. Frenke put the laundry basket on the counter and started folding the clothes.

"I happen to know your Grandpa did not put you up for adoption. So stop toying with me." She held up a pair of underwear and frowned. "I think these are yours." She threw them at me.

"See, I told you! I do live here!" I threw the underwear into my bag.

"Well not this weekend, you don't. You better keep them drawers on when you have your big date this Saturday."

"It's JUST a date! Carlin talks too much."

Mrs. Frenke looked up at the ceiling. "Speaking of Carlin, where is he? Carlin? C'mon… you'll be late for school."

"He's probably making himself look good for the ladies."

"Oh and you don't?"

"Like I have to try! I'm the one with the date, remember?"

Mrs. Frenke smacked me with a towel. Panicked feet bolted down the stairs, and Carlin ran into the kitchen. He downed a glass of orange juice while tucking in his shirt with one hand. Mrs. Frenke tried to adjust his glasses and collar.

"You ready?" He grabbed his school bag and started for the door.

"Yeah!" I grabbed my bag and followed.

"Uh, excuse me!" Mrs. Frenke scowled at Carlin.

"Sorry, Mom." He gave her a big kiss on the cheek. "I'll be late coming home from school," he yelled as he ran for the door.

I pecked her on the cheek as I ran by. "See you, Mrs. Frenke! Thanks for letting me eat all the food in your house."

"Just take care of my baby, Eddie!"

***

"You awake?" Jim asked.

I opened my eyes slowly. My one eye, and most of my face, was still tender from the beating I sustained at the hands of Sal. "I'm not asleep. I was just thinking about something."

"You've been thinking for a long time."

I ignored his comment. The wind snapped at the HER0's windows. The sky was gray, just like the endless stretch of flat open fields. In fact, I couldn't tell where the sky and earth met. "Where are we?"

"We crossed the border into Canada a few hours ago."

I sat up and gave my head a shake. "It's like we're in the middle of nowhere. Is the whole country like this?"

"Not really," Jim replied with a grin. "The majority of the population lives within about a hundred and fifty kilometers of the border. I guess you didn't see the UDs we passed."

"I guess not." We drove by a solitary tree, pale as a dead man's skin. It was dead. "Everything looks so cold."

"I'm surprised we haven't seen any snow yet."

I looked in the back seat, where Jessie lay asleep. The trailer jostled in the rear window. "Are those boys alright out there?"

"Yup! It's a rough ride, but they insisted on travelling in the trailer."

"Aren't they cold?" Jim didn't respond. I guess it didn't bother him, seeing as he was wearing army pants and a t-shirt. "Speaking of cold, what about you?"

"What about me?"

"Are you cold?"

"No. The cold doesn't bother me."

"Aw, whatever!"

"Well, there was this one time that it did."

"When was that?"

"A few years ago… I was doing some Spec Ops work. My team was observing an outpost. Our orders were not to engage the enemy. We were only there to observe. I lay there, hidden for hours in the snow. It was so cold, but I didn't move. Anyway, I noticed this target of opportunity. He was an individual who, if identified, we had the authorization to kill. I radioed in and when I had my authorization, I shot him. It was a four hundred yard shot. I thought I killed him, but my spotter confirmed that he was only wounded."

"In his condition, he was unable to move. Had the climate been moderate, he would have bled out. The cold, however, would have allowed the wound to freeze, thereby keeping him alive. It started raining… freezing rain. Visibility was poor and the target had crawled into cover, so I couldn't get another shot. My only choice was to crawl out across open terrain and engage him in hand to hand combat."

I raised my eyebrows.

"By the time I reached the target, I could hardly hold my knife steady enough to stick it in him. In hindsight, he probably would have frozen to death. But I needed that assurance, you know? I needed to know he was dead."

I didn't know what to say. It felt good to press my forehead against the window. The coolness of the glass soothed my achy face. We approached a road sign with something printed all over it.

My highway! Go back!

I furrowed my brow. We passed another sign further on.

Go back! Bah!

"Did you see those signs?"

"I did."

"Kind of odd, don't you think?"

"We've seen lots of odd things, Ed. I don't think about it anymore." The vehicle decelerated.

"What are you doing?"

"We need to refuel. Now is as good a time as any."

"What about those signs?"

"What about them?" Jim got out of the vehicle. I followed. The boys had already climbed out of the trailer.

"I gotta take a leak," said Hoke. He ran ahead, down the road.

"Don't go too far," Dillon yelled after him. "Can I help?"

"Yeah! Help me with this fuel drum!" Jim ordered. The two of them rolled the drum out of the trailer and along the shoulder. I grabbed the hand pump. Jessie was waiting for them. She grabbed

Dillon and hugged him; she started to cry. He put his arm around her, and they walked away.

Jim was annoyed. "I thought he was helping!"

"Relax! I'll help you." I set up the pump, and he seemed a bit more at ease once he took out his frustrations on the hand crank.

***

"They're leaving tonight?"

"I told you they were," Tonisha said. "So you're coming over, right?"

"Well, I kinda made plans with Carlin."

"What?" She put her arms around my neck. "You see Carlin all the time. You practically live at his house. We don't always get a chance to be together like this." She puckered her lip and looked at me like a puppy.

"Tonisha…" She pressed her breasts up against me.

"Pleeease! Just this one time?"

I sighed. "Okay. I'll come over after football practice."

"Since when do you go to practice?" Tonisha said, pushing herself off me. "I thought the coach said you were a natural."

I put my hands on her shoulders. "I am, I guess. But he asked me to show up tonight."

Tonisha smiled and pulled herself close to me again, taking my hand and putting it on her breast. "Well, your love coach has a special practice all planned for you." As much as I tried to hide it, she knew she had broken me. I smiled. Tonisha kissed me and sauntered away down the hall. I waited for her perfect ass to disappear from sight before going to class.

***

DING-DING!

"What the hell? Did you hear that?" I asked.

Jim was stowing the hand pump. "Hear what? Help me with this drum."

I shrugged. "I thought I heard a bell?"

Jim shrugged. "I don't think so."

We rolled the drum to the trailer. Dillon and Jessie were already huddled inside. "Have you seen Hoke?" they asked.

"He probably just went for a walk," I said. "Maybe he needed to stretch his legs."

DING-DING!

"Did you hear a bell?" asked Dillon. Jim listened intently.

DING-DING!

"I heard that," Jim acknowledged.

Dillon stood up and pointed down the road. "What's that?"

Off in the distance, a vehicle slowly made its way towards us. It looked like a cube van or delivery truck.

DING-DING!

Jim squinted and peered into the distance. "I think it's an ice cream truck."

DING-DING!

"An ice cream truck?"

"Yeah."

"That's too weird. Maybe we should get out of here."

"Agreed. Let's see if that vehicle follows us. Get in the gunner's cupola." Jim looked around. "Where's that other kid?"

DING-DING!

I flipped open the hatch and swiveled the gun around in the direction of the oncoming vehicle. Hoke was walking back towards us. I waved him on.

DING-DING!

"C'mon," I yelled.

"Forget it!" Jim said. "He'll start running when he sees us leaving." He climbed into the HER0.

DING-DING!

The ice cream truck was close now. I could see the big, happy clown face on the grill. It began to accelerate.

"Jim! Let's get goin'!"

DING-DING!

Hoke stopped to look at something on the road.

"Ah shit! Stupid kid!" I muttered.

Before Jim could get the engine started, the ice cream truck pulled up alongside us.

DING-DING!

The passenger door slid open. A man in a black leather jumpsuit leaned out. He wore one of those German army helmets with the spike on top. His bulging eyes protruded from his pale face, and he grinned hideously. It looked like he had neither eyelids nor lips. He shook a gloved fist at us and yelled, "Bah! Damn you! It's my highway!" His blue snake-like tongue flickered in his mouth. Jessie screamed.

DING-DING! DING-DING!

He sped off down the road towards Hoke.

"Hoke!" I yelled.

"Hoke," Dillon echoed. He was out of the trailer, rifle in hand, and running down the shoulder. Jessie was running behind him.

"Get back in the trailer!" Jim shouted.

The ice cream truck accelerated. The man leaned out, shaking his fist. His thin blue tongue shot from his mouth and hit Hoke squarely in the eye.

Hoke cupped his hands to his face and staggered out into the middle of the road. Jim hit the gas. I was thrown back. Dillon took a shot and missed. The ice cream truck made a sharp U-turn and sped towards a helpless and disoriented Hoke.

DING-DING!

Hoke pried his hands from his eyes just in time to see the big, happy clown face. He raised his arms as if to stop the oncoming vehicle but it was of no use. The truck ran him down. His head slapped against the asphalt. Dillon dropped to one knee and started shooting. I opened fire with the machine gun. Jessie just screamed.

As the ice cream truck passed us, the man leaned out the driver's side and shook his fist defiantly.

"Fuck you! My highway!"

DING-DING!

I tore him up with countless rounds of ammo. He fell back into the truck. I hosed the vehicle until it swerved away and exploded into a ball of flame. Jim jumped out and ran towards the blast. I got out and ran down the highway, to where Dillon and Jessie were cradling Hoke's empty head.

"I'm so sorry," I said, placing a hand on Dillon's shoulder. He shrugged it off. Jim waved me over. I met up with him at the HER0.

"I didn't see a body in that wreckage."

"What?"

"There's no sign of a body in that truck."

"It exploded! Maybe that guy was thrown from the vehicle."

"I don't think so. We better get out of here."

"What about the kids?"

"Let's give them a few minutes. Wrap their friend's body in a blanket. We'll take it with us and bury it when we're in a safe location. And make sure the brain is disabled."

"Don't worry... there's no brain left to disable."

Jim winced.

"I'll go talk to them."

***

"What's goin' on?" Carlin asked.

I slammed my locker shut. "Nuthin'... I gotta get to class."

"Are we still on for after school?"

I felt a jolt in my stomach. "After school? Aw shit, I forgot!"

"Aw, man! We were going to see Jewlz to get my fifty bucks back!"

"I know, but Tonisha..."

"What about her? You were going over there tomorrow night."

"I was, but her parents leave tonight, Carlin."

"Aw shit! You're backing out?"

"It's not every day her parents are out of town."

"Just go over there later tonight."

"C'mon man! I hang out with you all the time."

"Fine! I'll go see Jewlz by myself."

"Carlin, don't! You can't trust Jewlz. He doesn't like you. I'll go with you another time. Just don't go by yourself."

"I wouldn't if you didn't always think with your dick!"

"Carlin!" He stormed off without looking back. "Shit!"

***

"Ed!" Jim elbowed me. "Get in the cupola, and grab the binoculars."

"How long have I been sleeping?"

"Not long! Look back down the road!"

I climbed up top and held the binoculars up to my eyes. It was a construction vehicle.

"What is it? What do you see?"

"Uh… it looks like a road compactor!"

"Moving THAT fast?"

I looked again. The vehicle got closer. I saw the familiar German army helmet with the spike on top. The leather-clad man waved his fist at us. I got back down in my seat.

"Uh, Jim… You're not going to believe this, but it's him!"

"Who?"

"That guy in the ice cream truck."

"What?"

"Yeah! It's the same guy!"

I climbed back up into the cupola and readied the machine gun. Dillon stood, braced himself and fired a shot at the oncoming vehicle. I yelled for him to stay down. As the compactor closed in, the driver stood and waved his fists.

"Bah! It's my highway! Damn you! Damn you all!"

I fired. He caught several rounds in the chest. The man twitched and fell back into his seat. I continued firing, shredding up his leather jump suit. He continued yelling and shaking his fist. The compactor accelerated until it pulled up just behind the trailer.

"Fuck you all! Bah!"

I fired until the belt ran dry, but that still didn't stop him. He wasn't even bleeding.

"Dillon! Cover fire!"

Dillon fired two shots, each time hitting the man square in the chest. I loaded in a new belt and closed the cover on the feeding tray. I was about to squeeze the trigger when Dillon popped up and fired again. The man lashed out with his bright blue tongue, wrapping it around Dillon's neck. Jessie came to his aid, punching and grabbing at the tongue. It was covered in suckers like an octopus' tentacle. I aimed at the man's face and lit him up. The tongue dislodged. Dillon staggered around the trailer clutching his throat. He stumbled over the trailer wall and fell out onto the road.

"Nooooo!" Jessie screamed.

The compactor swerved, rolling Dillon into the pavement. The man shook his fist at us, his mangled jaw dangled from his face. I opened up again, concentrating my fire on the engine housing. The compactor spewed black smoke, yet still, it accelerated. It drew alongside us. Jim fired his eye beams out through the driver's side window. The compactor exploded in a shower of metal parts. The explosion launched the flailing, flaming man high into the air. He landed with a thud. Jim drove over him and halted. He jumped from the vehicle. I climbed out through the cupola. Jessie was already kneeling next to the bloody skid, pounding her fists on the asphalt.

Jim was standing over the burning corpse, staring at it. I looked on in awe. The body burned up like paper, until there was nothing left but a pile of ash and the stench of sulphur.

"I guess that explains why his body disappeared."

I shook my head. "I better help the girl". I ran over to her. "Alright… easy!" I put my arms around Jessie and held her.

"Who is this… psycho? What does he want with us?" she sobbed.

"C'mon! We'll get you out of here!"

When we reached the trailer, she said, "I want to stay in the back."

"I don't think that's a good idea. You should stay with us."

"You can't protect me!" She was shaking. "Just leave me alone." She climbed in, sat down in the corner and wrapped herself up in a blanket. Jim was waiting for me by the HER0.

"She insists on staying in the back," I said.

"Leave her be then."

I climbed back into the cupola. "I don't think that's the last we've seen of him."

"I have a feeling you're right."

Jim shook his head and got in the vehicle. We drove off down the highway, waiting for the inevitable.

***

I sat up when the phone rang. "Who the hell would be calling at three a.m.?"

"It could be my parents," Tonisha said.

"Don't answer it!" The phone kept ringing.

"Maybe something happened. I'm going to answer it."

"Aw, Tonisha!"

"Hello? Yes? Yes, he's here. One moment…" She covered the phone with her hand.

"Who is it?"

"Mrs. Frenke. She sounds upset."

"What?" I grabbed the phone from her. "Hello? Yes, Mrs. Frenke… Pardon… What… sorry, I didn't understand… say again? …Alright, I'll come right away!"

"What's goin' on?"

"I have to meet Mrs. Frenke." I jumped into my clothes.

"Meet her where? And why?"

"At the hospital... something happened to Carlin."

***

"Here he comes!" I set down the binoculars. "That didn't take long."

"What's he driving this time?"

I got down into the cab. "You'll never believe this... a farm tractor."

"A farm tractor?" Jim looked in the rear-view mirror. "He's gaining on us."

"Same plan as before?"

"Let's blow him up before anybody gets hurt this time!"

With a salute, I was back in the cupola. The tractor was getting closer. Another dot appeared on the horizon. I looked through the binoculars but couldn't see it clearly enough.

"Jim, we got more company!"

"What do you mean?"

"Not sure, but there's something coming down the road behind him."

"Let's worry about one thing at a time!" I leaned into the machine gun.

When the tractor was within earshot, the man stood, shook a fist at us and yelled, "Bah! It's my highway!" I was about to shoot but the tractor decelerated and pulled away from us. The man braced his hip against the steering wheel, unzipped his fly and peed into a bottle.

"Why aren't you firing?" Jim shouted.

"Uh... he's gotta take a leak!"

"What?!"

The man set down the bottle, hit the gear shift and sped after us once again. I fired, hitting him in the torso and neck. He waved that darned fist of his defiantly so I took aim and removed it. He continued to wave the stump.

Jessie stood up in the trailer. She was holding Dillon's rifle. The man turned his face to her.

"Jessie! Keep your head down!"

Before she could get into a firing position, the blue tongue shot out. She quickly held up the rifle and it wrapped around the barrel. The man thrashed his head back. She fell to her knees releasing the rifle. It skidded across the trailer and wedged itself up under the lip, diagonally between the tailgate and the sidewall. With his remaining hand, the man grabbed his tongue and pulled.

"Right on! Way to go, girl!"

Jessie brushed the hair from her face and smiled at me. I unloaded into the man's face. He ducked down behind the wheel. I stopped firing. When he popped up again, his face below the eyes was nothing but an empty black hollow. His thin blue tongue was still intact and attached to his head. He held up the bottle in his hand and whipped it into the trailer.

PHOOM! The trailer burst into flames.

"Jessie!"

Her flaming body thrashed about, screaming, until nothing but a charred, silent corpse remained.

"What just happened?"

"Jessie's dead. And the trailer's on fire."

"We've got fuel drums back there."

The tongue broke free and flapped onto the road. It caught itself up in the tractor's front axle. The man quickly wrapped the slack around his stump, braced himself with his foot and pulled back. His tongue spooled on the axle, becoming thinner and thinner.

"Un-hitch the trailer!" Jim ordered.

With the man temporarily occupied, I crawled out of the cupola and slowly made my way to the back of the vehicle. Further on down the road, the mysterious dot I saw earlier was now a motorcycle, coming at us full throttle.

The man leaned forward and then threw his head back violently. The tongue snapped off and reeled itself back into his face. I slid down the back and perched myself on the bumper. I reached down with one hand and pulled out the safety pin on the pintle hitch. The man's tongue shot out. The mangled stub slapped against the rear window. He went through the motions of reeling it back in. I reached again.

THWAP!

The tongue smacked the taillight and fell away. He waved his stump at me. I reached down and grabbed onto the locking latch. Just then, the motorcycle wove in between the tractor and our vehicle. The driver wore a hooded robe. A big hammer rested in a harness across his back. The wind threw back his hood, revealing a familiar rune-covered scalp.

"Veck!"

He was wearing thick, leather-bound goggles. He reached out to me. I lifted the locking latch and kicked the tow ring. The trailer was free. I jumped, grabbing Veck's hand. He pulled me onto the back of the bike. We sped away. The trailer swerved sideways and the tractor hit it. Everything exploded into a huge fireball.

The man was air-lifted clear of the blast. I waved my fist at him as he flew overhead.

"It's my highway now, Motherfucker!"

He landed with a skid on the gravel shoulder. Veck spun the bike around. He accelerated and drew his hammer. The man stirred and sat up only to catch a face full of sledge. His head slammed back down and bounced.

Veck stopped the bike. He quickly jumped off and pounded on the body, reducing it to a flat, pulpy mass. There was no blood. But with every swing, the body spit out yellow powder. Jim pulled up and got out of the HER0. We watched Veck pulverize the corpse.

"What's that stuff coming out of him?"

"Oh that? It's just sulphur," Veck said, between poundings. When he finished smashing, he rested his foot on the body and smiled. "Hey! Nice to see you guys again."

***

"Mr. Griffin," the doctor said, "Would you come with me, please?" He led me around the corner into a hallway where a gathering of policemen and medical staff waited. Mrs. Frenke was sitting on a chair. She started to cry when she saw me. I ran over and gave her a hug.

"My baby... my baby..."

"What happened?" I asked the doctor.

"Please come this way."

Mrs. Frenke took me by the hand and we followed the doctor into a room. Two covered bodies rested on tables. A man in a lab coat and a policeman stood nearby. The doctor pulled back the sheet on the first body.

"Do you recognize this person?"

There was a lump in my throat. I swallowed hard. "That's Jewlz Louis." His throat had a large gash in it. The doctor pulled back the other sheet. Mrs. Frenke burst out crying. My eyes welled up with tears. It was Carlin. His face was a purple-gray color and his neck was bruised.

"My baby," Mrs. Frenke wailed. I held Mrs. Frenke.

"We received a 911 call this afternoon," the policeman started. "By the time we arrived both boys were already dead. I am sorry. We still have no witnesses."

"What happened?"

The man in the lab coat spoke. "It seems as though Jewlz attempted to strangle Carlin. He had wrapped a belt around his neck. Police suspect Carlin had a bottle of soda in his hand and dropped it when Jewlz attacked him. Before Carlin went unconscious he stabbed Jewlz in the neck with a piece of glass. We suspect he was rendered unconscious before he could loosen the belt." The man shook his head.

Mrs. Frenke caressed Carlin's forehead and cried, "My baby!"

I tried to comfort her.

"I asked you to look after him. Why didn't you look after my baby?" She broke down, sobbing into my chest. There was nothing I could say to make it right.

***

Jim and Veck salvaged whatever equipment and supplies they could find amidst the wreckage. I didn't help them. Instead, I buried the three kids in shallow graves. Dark gray clouds filled the sky and light fluffy snow began to fall.

I stopped and stretched. Then I saw the sign on the other side of the road.

My highway! Bah!

My body filled with rage. My temples throbbed. I ran over and punched the sign. I punched it again. I kicked it. I hit it. I put a shoulder into it. Jim grabbed hold of me and pulled me away.

"Easy Ed, easy!"

I shrugged him off. "I should never have gone to that ranch. They'd still be alive if it weren't for me. It's my fault!"

"No! It isn't. You gave them a chance."

"Heh… Yeah…A better chance at dying? That's what happens when I think with my dick."

"What do you mean by that?"

"Nothing… It's something a friend once told me."

Veck handed me his hammer. "Try this instead."

"Thanks." I took the sign down with a few swings and returned the hammer. "Is this what it's all about?"

"What?" Veck asked.

"You know… is this the cosmic consciousness trying to remind me of my failures in life?"

"Ah, yes," Veck replied with a nod. "It's not a failure. It's a learning experience."

"Oh, really? And what am I supposed to learn from this experience?"

"About how the world really works," Veck said. "In time, it will make more sense to you."

"Pfft! Whatever!" I shrugged. We returned to the graves. A lone zombie wandered about in the field. A shot from Jim's eyebeams dropped him.

"I'm sorry my timing wasn't better," Veck said.

"What? Like you knew this was going to happen?"

"Sort of... The events came to me in a dream. I did not know *when* it would happen. I just knew that it would."

I looked back at the man's battered body. "What about him?"

"I'll take care of that."

"Is he finally dead?"

"You can never really kill a demon."

"A demon?"

"Demons are energy in the same way you are, albeit dark energy. They can travel in corporeal forms just like you do in when in your body."

"Are you saying that we just sent him to demon heaven?" Jim asked.

"More like, he's been sent back to the darkness from whence he came. All demons, and lesser demons, and minions to some degree, can be pushed back into the darkness. Alternatively, you can return them to the light, but that's more difficult. It'll be a while before this particular one takes physical form again." Veck looked lovingly at his hammer.

"Why do you say that?"

"He's kind of an idiot. He makes lots of bad decisions. The first one he ever made destroyed him. His punishment for his deed was that he could never learn from his mistakes. He also has this incendiary urine."

"We know," I said.

Veck grinned. "Urinov cocktails. Rather comical, really."

"Depends on your sense of humor," Jim said with a glare. Veck's grin quickly disappeared.

"What about that sulphur smell?" I asked.

"Sulphur is a major component of corporeal demonic forms."

"But we smelled sulphur after the Afro-Saxon vaporized. He wasn't a demon, was he?"

"No. But he carried the markings of Holioch which are a gift of the Masters and rooted in darkness. The markings are demonic in nature."

"How do you know all this stuff?"

"My knowledge comes to me in my dreams. And I have this." Veck opened his robe. A large rune glowed brightly on his chest:

"What does that mean?"

"It is a mandala - a demon slayer's mark. It will never be sated no matter how much blood I spill."

"Interesting," Jim said. "I'm sure there's more to tell. But I also would like make up the ground we lost. We need to keep moving."

"Very well then." Veck extended his hand.

"You're not coming with us?" I asked.

"No. But trust me, we'll meet again soon."

"Let's hope it's under better circumstances." I shook his hand.

"Agreed."

We checked everything one last time before departing. As we pulled away, I called out to Veck from the cupola, "I hope we're going the right way!"

He smiled and shouted, "Is there any other way to go?"

11 HOME ADVANTAGE

Light and dark are really one in the same, yet separate. In a perfect world, the two would coexist in equilibrium. But not here! Not on this earth! Here the forces are in a constant struggle for supremacy. If you want to help maintain the balance, then you must rid the world of spiritual ignorance.

-Veck

"How much farther?" I asked, looking out at the tree line on the other side of the open field.

"Across the field and through that forest," Jim said, pointing.

"I sure hope so. Now don't you go and tell me you don't feel the cold," I warned, patting myself on the cheeks.

"Don't worry. I won't."

I stuck my head out and ran a finger along my cheekbone. "Do I have frostbite?"

"No. Stop worrying. And stop asking."

"My face feels like a thousand needles are stuck in it." Jim ignored me. I'm sure he was tired of my complaining. I was tired of wading through deep snow with an icy wind in my face. As we had feared, we hadn't had enough fuel to make it to Cold Lake. We had ditched the HER0, packed everything we could carry, and travelled on foot. I couldn't recall how many days it had been. Lucky for me, Jim was well trained for cold weather survival. He had made it easy. As much as I was looking forward to the end of this journey, I would have followed Jim for the rest of my life if I had to.

Jim put out the fire and crouched down beneath the pine tree where we had taken shelter. He fiddled with the straps on his pack.

"When was the last time you were at CFB Cold Lake?"

"Three years ago, maybe."

"You think anybody there will know you?"

"A lot can change in three years. We'll find out when we get there. For all we know they could all be dead."

"Speaking of dead... have you noticed how few zombies we've seen? Maybe the transmission was right."

Jim shrugged.

"I sometimes wonder if any of my family are still out there... you know, wandering around."

"You've got quite the imagination."

"C'mon, like the thought hasn't crossed your mind? Haven't you got anyone?"

"My dad died when I was twelve. My mom died when I was nineteen. I never really got too close to anyone."

"Hmm... I'm sorry to hear that. But what if you saw someone you knew? What would you do?"

"I'd shoot him in the head."

"You're unreal sometimes. I don't know if I could shoot my Grandpa. I'd shoot my Uncle a few times without hesitation but not my Grandpa. I miss him. He died two days after I won the Super Bowl."

"From what you've mentioned of him, he did seem like a decent individual."

"He was all into alternate realities and UFOs and mysticism and shit. His study was more like a library – there were books all over the place. He had this book about the African warrior throughout history; tons of books on World War Two. He even owned a complete set of Whelan Mood's Idaho Grim adventures."

"Who?"

"Idaho Grim: the pulp era adventuring African American archaeologist. I read every single book two or three times at least. *The Cult of Chupacabra*[24] was my favorite. He wrote fours books in all."

"Sounds pretty amazing."

---

[24] Chupacabra: A legendary cryptid described as a fanged, hairless dog-like creature with leathery skin.

"Whelan Mood served in the army during World War Two. He wrote the books when he returned home. Apparently, the first book, *Blitzkreig and Brimstone*, was based on actual events. But get this... he wasn't allowed to publish the book in his lifetime."

"Why?"

"Nobody knows for sure. Apparently, the military prevented him. Mood himself was quoted as saying the world wasn't ready for his story, whatever that means. The internet is full of all sorts of conspiracy theories."

"How did the books get published then?"

"His grandson, Colton Mood, published all of them. Whelan left instructions in his will. Did you ever come across anything strange with all the special ops work you did?"

Jim shook his head. "No. I mean, nothing like what I've encountered since I teamed up with you."

"Yeah, whatever! I don't believe you."

Jim pulled the vial from his a pouch on his tac vest and held it up.

"Geez, I almost forgot about that. You think someone'll know something about it?"

"It depends. You know, Canada is a world leader in super-soldier research."

"I didn't know that."

Jim returned the vial to safety. "Ready to go?"

"Yup!"

"Cover your face. It'll take the sting out of your cheeks."

I pulled my balaclava down and slapped my helmet on my head. Jim also covered his face. "I thought you weren't cold. Why are you wearing a mask?"

"Last time I was in Cold Lake I didn't have green skin. I don't want to complicate our arrival."

"Gotcha," I said with a nod.

We geared up and moved out, slogging through the deep snow. Jim was on point. The sky was gray as usual. A glint of reddish-purple light cracked through the clouds – proof that the sun still existed. The wind whipped the snow up in our faces. We were about three quarters of the way across the field when Jim suddenly stopped.

"What? What is it?"

Jim didn't respond. He put his hands out to his sides like he was ready to pounce. The snow around us was moving. Men in white camo sprang from covered foxholes, weapons ready and trained on us.

"Don't move!" a voice commanded. "Put your arms in the air!"

Jim raised his hands and I followed his lead. We were stripped of our weapons and gear. The soldiers marched us across the rest of the field and into the forest, where a team of dog sleds and more soldiers waited for us.

We were *mushed* to CFB Cold Lake at gunpoint. It was a welcome relief not having to trudge through snow. When we arrived, the soldiers escorted us into a building. It looked like a mission briefing room. Armed guards stood by the doors. We sat down on a bench and waited. Within a few minutes another door opened and in walked an older man in military uniform. He was a Colonel. His entourage of officers followed, and an elderly man who looked like he was of aboriginal descent. He had long gray, hair, braided with beads and feathers. Everyone stared at us with the same keen interest as kids watching bugs in a jar.

The aboriginal man stepped forward. He shook a rattle, circling us and chanting the whole time. He rattled up and down and around our bodies. When he was finished he stood in front of us and said, "These men carry the light of the spirits. They are welcome here."

That seemed to be the cue for the Colonel to take charge. He eyed us up and down. "Welcome to CFB Cold Lake. My name is Colonel Thomas Goring. And who might you be?" I removed my helmet and balaclava.

"Holy shit," a short Asian exclaimed. "That's Eddie Griffin."

"Eddie Griffin?" another man gasped.

"Yeah, that's him all right."

A hushed chatter erupted among the group.

"At ease!" the Colonel commanded. Everyone fell silent. "Tell us your name, soldier?"

"I'm not really a soldier. I don't even hold any rank. I'm a football player. My name is Eddie Griffin."

"I told you!"

"Quiet, Dung!" The Asian pursed his lips.

Jim pulled off his balaclava. He snapped to attention and said, "Lieutenant Jim Shrike. Canadian Special Forces."

"Oh my!" The Colonel's jaw dropped. Everyone appeared to be in a state of shock. My thunder had just been stolen. "What on earth happened to you, son?"

"I had an accident, sir!"

The Colonel shook his head. "At ease, Jim." He took a step towards him, hands extended. I thought he was going to hug him. A stocky little officer stepped out from the crowd and pulled at the Colonel's arm. He whispered something in his ear. He was a mean looking sonofabitch. His beady little eyes glared at us from deep within his beefy skull. And his jaw was clenched so tight that the veins pulsed at his temples. He was hatred personified. The Colonel motioned for him to step back. "Relax, Zurn. Your concerns are noted." The stocky bugger huffed and pushed his way out of the room.

"Jim!" a woman gasped, pushing her way past everyone. She ran up to him and cupped his face in her hands. Her eyes welled up with tears. Jim put his hands on her shoulders and pulled her close. She was the most beautiful redhead I had ever seen. I hadn't seen a redhead that pretty since I last saw Stacey Gray. She was the hottest cheerleader at our school. At our football party, this jerk named Will "Meat" Huggins had said something about *getting it on with carrot crotch*. He had managed to only get one hand on her before I had intervened. He spent the night in hospital having his face put back together. I had spent the night in hospital having his teeth removed from my knuckles.

"Shauna," Jim uttered.

"What... what happened to you?"

"I have a lot to explain. " She put her arms around him.

"Well, this is just like old times," the Colonel said. "Alright you two, let's move. I expect a full debriefing Jim. Major McAllister?"

"Yes, Colonel?" the redhead responded.

"Take Jim to guest facilities. Jim, can you be in my office within the next hour?"

"Yes, sir!"

"Good! It's been a long time. I'm sure you have much to tell."

Jim nodded.

The Colonel smiled. "Welcome back!" He patted Jim on the back as he left the room with Major McAllister. The others filed out. The Colonel turned to the Asian man and said, "Look after Mr. Griffin, please Sergeant Dung."

"My pleasure, sir!" His over-enthusiasm made me uneasy.

Sergeant Proon Dung was like a set of wind-up teeth with no off switch. Within five minutes, I knew his whole life story. Proon was a specialist in communications, which made sense, since he never shut up. He was a purebred nerd, but a cool one at that. He kinda reminded me of Carlin.

On our way to guest facilities, we swung by his quarters where he retrieved a football card safely housed in a plastic collector's case. On the card, I wrote, as per his instructions: *To Proon Dung - My biggest fan.* He then hurried me through the corridors. Even though he talked the whole time, he still somehow managed to slip in a *hello* to every person that we passed.

"I hate to tell you this," he started, "but I really like Canadian football more than American. That being said, you are the best quarterback in the history of either league. I wish I could've seen you play in the CFL[25]."

---

[25] CFL: Canadian Football League.

"What do you think of Major McAllister? She is so hot! She never lets anybody get close to her. The closest you'll ever get is during hand-to-hand combat instruction. And even then, she just grabs your hand and next thing you know you're flying through the air staring at your own ass. She and Jim served together in JTF3. They were close friends. I can't believe you didn't know who she is. Jim never told you about her? I heard he was like that – very private."

"Do you know why he's green?"

"No. Everyone's wondering, though. I'm sure it's top secret. But then again, so is Jim. I bet he just changed color at will. Did he ever tell you about the time he went for wilderness survival training up in the mountains?"

"Uh, no."

"They flew him and a bunch of men in by chopper. They were supposed to airdrop in some supplies. But the drop was bad and the supplies were lost. The whole team went missing and bad weather compromised the search and rescue. A few weeks later, Jim marched down from the mountain with every man accounted for. Half of them were dead. The survivors credited Jim with keeping them alive. They looked like wild men all dressed in furs and carrying improvised weapons. Jim was wearing a bearskin – apparently he killed the bear with his bare hands – pardon the pun. That man is a legend. I can't believe you know him. Then again, I can't believe I'm talking to Ed Griffin."

I was relieved to get to my new quarters, where new BDUs[26] and a pair of boots awaited me, and a long, hot shower. I threw on my jersey and met Proon in the hall. Not surprisingly, he waited outside my quarters the whole time. He showed me the way to the Colonel's office.

"Thanks for all your help."

"Hey, I should be thanking you. How about I meet you later and take you to the mess hall?"

---

[26] BDUs: Battle Dress Uniform.

"Sure, thanks."

Proon turned and was about to walk away when he pivoted on the spot. "Hey, I got one more question."

"Yeah?"

"I read on the internet that you played AA. Is that true?"

I couldn't help but laugh. "Why do you ask?"

"Well, the guys are coming by later because it's game night. Maybe you could join us. I've got extra dice."

"Let's see how the rest of the day unfolds and I'll let you know later."

"Okay."

I entered the office and the secretary said, "You can go right in."

"I'm waiting for Jim."

"He's already inside."

"Oh... thanks."

I opened the door. The Colonel looked up at me from his desk. Jim was seated in front of him, staring out the window. I wasn't sure what he was looking at – there was nothing out there but snow.

"Mr. Griffin. Have a seat, please."

"Call me Eddie."

"Very well, then. Jim brought me up to speed on your mission."

"Our mission?" *I don't even know about our mission.* I looked at Jim but he gave me one of those *don't ask* looks.

"Yes. Jim told me about how the two of you were sent out to the other bunkers once communications were lost."

"Oh yes, THAT mission." I had no idea what Jim told him so I just played along.

"It's a shame, really. We heard the distress calls from Bunker 57 and..." The door opened and in walked the Major Zurn. He handed the Colonel a paper. "Thank you, Major. Have you met...?"

"We have!" he snapped, interrupting the Colonel. Zurn shot Jim an icy stare.

"Hi Ben," Jim grimaced.

The Major snorted, and stormed out the room.

"Don't mind Major Zurn," the Colonel said. "If he had his way, this base would be more spartan." I could see that Jim wanted to add a comment but he bit his lip. "Anyway, I take it the radio transmission led you to us?"

"Yes, I was going to ask you about that," Jim responded.

"Let me begin with some context." The Colonel opened his desk drawer and pulled out a bottle of whiskey and some glasses. He offered but neither of us accepted. He poured himself a glass and sat back in his chair.

"Initially after UD-Day, we had the same issue as everyone else. We holed up in the base and fended off the undead, taking on survivors as they trickled in. We took heavy losses. As it was, we already had a close working relationship with the locals and the aboriginals, so it made sense we stick together. After a few months, survivors stopped showing up on our doorstep. We sat by the speakers and listened as reports from the outside world became more and more sporadic; eventually they turned to distress signals. A few weeks later, the airwaves were dead silent. There was no one left. It was one of those situations the military talked about and tried to prepare you for. But it really doesn't hit you until you experience it firsthand." He sipped the whiskey and stared off into space.

"I know what you mean, Colonel," Jim said.

Colonel Goring refocused on Jim. "Anyway, that tribal elder you met – the one who smudged you with his rattle…"

"Smudged?" I asked.

"It's a form of ritual cleansing. It removes negative spiritual energy. The elder, Hal Stonespeak, told us that the spirits would protect us. The next day, the undead were all neutralized."

"How did that happen?"

"Who knows? We only ever found decapitated bodies. That day we also heard the transmission for the first time."

"You mean, you didn't send it?" I asked.

"No."

"Where's it coming from?"

"When we first picked up the signal -Sergeant Dung traced the source -- it was coming from an area north of here... near an old fishing camp on the edge of the lake. Major McAllister led a team out to the coordinates and there it was."

"What was?"

"I wish I had a name for it. It's just a metal dome with all manner of satellite dishes and radio antennae... some sort of communications station. It seems to have just popped out of the earth itself. We have no idea what purpose it serves or who built the thing. Proon seems to think Ford Alroc[27] built it."

"What do the locals say?" Jim asked.

The Colonel frowned. "They're scared shitless of the area... bad spirits and what not. There is something creepy about the place. It's the strangest thing to have happened around here since the last sighting of Kinosoo."

"Uh, excuse me," I interrupted. "What is a Kinosoo?"

"It's a giant fish that lives in the lake. Sort of like a whale. It swallows whole boats." Colonel Goring cupped his hands and snapped them together like jaws for effect.

"Oh... uh, thanks."

"We'd like to see it," Jim said.

"Kinosoo?"

"No. I mean the comm station."

"Sure! Sergeant Dung has been there a few times. We'll see what we can arrange. Maybe you'll catch a glimpse of Kinosoo as well."

---

[27] Ford Alroc: Founder of Alroc Computer Technologies (ACT). The company's technological innovation revolutionized the world of personal computing, telecommunications, robotics and military weapons. The elusive Ford Alroc rarely made public appearances. Rumored to have been abducted, he disappeared and was never seen again.

"Thank you." Jim sat back and rubbed his chin. He stared out the window again.

"You thinking about what to do next?" the Colonel asked.

Jim nodded.

"Well, normally when we find survivors, we have a rigorous process of integrating them into our base. I know you well enough Jim, that I made quite a few exceptions; for you as well, Ed. The last time we had a celebrity in the base, it was some high-maintenance actor... a real pain in the ass. Anyway, you being here is quite a boost to morale. You're welcome to stay."

"Thank you, sir. We'll think it over," Jim said.

"Whether you decide to stay or go, Jim, just make sure you make up for any lost time with Major McAllister." Jim nodded. I think he was blushing.

The Colonel downed his shot and slammed the glass on the desk like a judge's gavel. "Dismissed, gentlemen!" We got up to leave. "Oh, and Jim..."

"Yes Colonel?"

"Watch your back! Major Zurn hasn't forgotten you."

Jim nodded and exited the room. I followed. I wanted to ask him about Majors McAllister and Zurn, but Proon was already waiting for me.

"Ready for dinner?" he asked.

"Yeah, sure. You wanna join us, Jim?"

"Thanks, but there's someone I need to see."

Before I could say anything, Jim turned and headed down the hall. Proon already had me by the arm and was pulling me in the opposite direction.

I received lots of high-fives, hellos and autograph requests from the folks in the mess hall. Proon ran defensive coverage for me, deflecting questions and comments as they arose. Eventually, everything calmed down and I resumed my place as just another guy in the chow line. Dinner was meatloaf and mashed potatoes. Despite all the complaining I overheard, I for one was grateful. For once, I wasn't eating rations. Proon explained that the soldiers frequently went on food runs into the neighboring towns, scavenging whatever they could find. The food supply was supplemented by hunting. There were plans for small scale farming in the coming summer now that the lands were free of roaming zombies.

Proon directed me to a table where his friends were waiting: Shawn Mangos and Jamie Doyle.

"Hey guys!"

"Wow! I can't believe it! Eddie Griffin," Shawn exclaimed. He shook my hand.

"Cool!" Jamie said.

"So you're playing AA with us tonight?"

"Maybe."

Proon started talking about something, but I didn't pay attention. I looked around the room. A strange-looking guy stood next to the garbage bin with a wooden spoon in his hand. A steel pot waited on top of the garbage bin. He had a face like a weasel and these big buck teeth that didn't quite fit in his mouth. Apart from using the pot as a guide for cutting his hair (so I assumed), he stopped every tray en route to the garbage and selectively picked off scraps and set them in the pot.

"Who's that guy over by the garbage?"

"Who, Pimply?" Proon responded.

"Pimply? What's up with him?"

"He eats everything," Shawn responded. "That's why he hangs out by the garbage. Your leftovers go into that pot and he eats them with that wooden spoon. It's fucking weird."

"I bet he has parasites or a tapeworm. I've never seen someone eat so much trash," Proon added.

"Tapeworms are kind of cool," Jamie smirked.

"There was this one time when we had scrambled eggs. By the end of the morning, Pimply's pot was full. He sliced in an over-ripened banana and drenched everything in barbeque sauce. He ate EVERYTHING! It was gross."

"Does he ever throw up?"

"Fuck no," Shawn said. "He's got a gut of iron."

"Is that guy army?"

"Nobody knows who he is or where he came from," Jamie said, his mouth full of food. "He doesn't talk – never says a word as far as I know. One day, he just wandered into the base with that wooden spoon in his back pocket and that pot in his hands."

"Is his name *really* Pimply?"

"We don't know what his name is."

"Then why do you call him that? He doesn't look pimply."

"Well, anytime someone new comes to the base, he has to undergo a physical. It's standard procedure," Shawn began. "Well, we heard that Pimply gets his name from what the doctors saw on his ass."

I shuddered at the thought.

"The guy sure makes himself useful, though," Jamie added. "Not only does he clean up our shit, but he fixes everything: vehicles, machinery, weapons... you name it. He put farmer-armor[28] on all the civilian vehicles. He has this knack for frankensteining stuff."

"I bet he could build a nuclear generator with tin foil and chewing gum, if he doesn't eat it first," Proon laughed. "Only the Wendigo can eat more than him."

I cleared my throat. "Wendigo?"

"It's a big ugly demon with an insatiable appetite."

"It's like a demon," Shawn added. "It consumes all things. It even eats souls."

"I've heard of that. It's a shape-shifter, isn't it?" I asked.

"It can look like anything," Proon answered.

"That's what's been eating all the zombies." Shawn wiped his greasy face with a napkin and got up from the table. "This meat loaf is shit!"

Jamie got up from the table too. "Time to feed Pimply!"

"Maybe he's the Wendigo," I said.

---

[28] Farmer-Armor: Improvised armor.

The two of them grinned.

I told Proon that I had to stop at my quarters before coming to his game night. Surprisingly, he went on without me. My plan was to actually drop in on Jim and see how he was doing. I turned the corner leading to his quarters and saw a little girl coming towards me. She had the biggest blue eyes I had ever seen. Her hair was pulled tightly into pigtails.

"Hello," she said.

"Hi!"

She stopped and looked me up and down. "Are you that football man?"

"Yes. Yes, I am."

"Did you come here with a man who is all green?"

"Yes, I did."

"Is it true you travelled here from around the world?"

I laughed. "Well, we travelled a long way to get here. Not around the world, though."

"Did you see lots of weird stuff?"

"Why do you ask?"

"I found this thing and I don't know what it is." She handed me a small globe. It was a snow globe, but this one was a little different. Instead of a winter scene, it had ruined buildings and a mushroom cloud backdrop. Tiny skeletons and debris swirled around inside when I shook it.

"I've seen these things before. It's a snow globe. Well, kind of. This one's post-apocalyptic," I told her.

She furrowed her brow. "I don't know what you mean, Mister, but it's weird. You can have it." Before I could say another word she took off down the hall. I pocketed the globe. The door to Jim's room opened and he stepped out. He was wearing a parka.

"I was just coming to see you. You got a minute?"

"Yeah, sure," I said.

Jim disappeared back into his quarters. He came out again a minute later with a second parka. "Here, put this on." I hadn't even zipped it up when he said, "Walk with me! Don't talk until we get outside."

He moved at a very fast pace, occasionally looking over his shoulder. Once we got outside, he led me to the edge of the forest. The sky was clear and brightly lit with stars. It was damn cold, though. We stopped along the tree line.

"What's goin' on? Did you find out if they know anything about super soldiers?"

"They don't know anything."

"Damn."

"Besides, it's not safe to talk around the base."

"Does this have anything to do with Zurn?"

"Partly…"

"Why does he have such a hate on for you?"

"I saved his life. And I had to disobey orders – his orders – to do it."

"So?"

"Ben comes from a family of very successful military men. They were embarrassed when I saved him. I received a medal for my actions, and a whole lot of hatred from his family. His father was a General. After that incident, he lost faith in the military."

"So much for gratitude. They sound like a family of pricks."

"He wanted me court-martialed. I avoided all that by getting reassigned courtesy of the officer exchange program. Colonel Goring arranged it all for me. Major Zurn wants my medal… and he still wants me court-martialed."

"That's ridiculous!"

"That's Zurn. Shauna suspects he's planning to take command of the base."

"Are you gonna do something about it?"

"I'm sure Zurn sees me as a threat to his plans. When he heard we wanted to see the comm station, he offered to take us."

"When are we going?"

"Tomorrow."

"Tomorrow?"

"Yeah. Major McAllister is coming, too."

"That's good. You'll have TWO people watching your back."

"Don't forget to watch your own. I'm sorry for getting you into this." He turned and marched deeper into the woods. I ran after him and caught up.

"Where are we going?"

"We have a meeting."

"With whom?"

"I don't know. I was told to come here."

"By who?"

"Shauna."

"Hey, Speaking of Shauna - how are things between you and her?"

"No different than how I left them."

"Is that good or bad?"

"A bit of both."

"How come you never told me about her?"

"I never really had a reason to."

"You sure keep a lot of secrets."

"It comes with the job, I guess."

We entered a clearing where a man was putting wood onto a raging bon fire. It was Hal Stonespeak. "Nice night, isn't it?" he said.

"A bit cold."

"Thank you for coming. I needed to see you." He pointed at the sky. The most magnificent shafts of colored light appeared above us. Vibrant greens and blues passed over us in waves. The colors were alive. I had never seen anything like it before. It gave me goose bumps.

"What is that?" I asked.

"It is the Aurora Borealis," Jim answered, "Northern Lights."

"It's beautiful."

"I wanted you to see that," Hal said.

"You asked us to come out here just to look at the sky?"

"You do not understand. Those are the spirits of our ancestors. They dance in celebration."

"In celebration of what?"

"The prophecy is being fulfilled."

"What prophecy?" Jim asked.

"My ancestors told me that a Green Man and a great warrior would come from the south – men who would know of demons and their works. The Green Man is eternal life in a time of death. And the warrior brings peace in a time of war."

"How exactly did your ancestors tell you this?" I asked.

"Like you, I am traveler."

"Are you a shaman?" I asked. "My Grandpa had books about Shamanism."

Hal nodded. "That is your word for it. The spirits are well aware of your work. I am grateful for that. You will understand more once you leave this world."

"We're just going to the comm station," Jim argued.

Hal grinned. "What you seek you will not find there. Your journey will continue. Let the spirits guide you. I have told you all there is to tell."

Hal's riddle-filled speak reminded me of the Upior. I was reluctant to leave. "Hey, wait a minute… where are we supposed to go? I mean, there's not much else out there."

"This world does not hold your answers."

I looked to Jim and he just shrugged. "Hal, which world does?"

He looked me in the eyes. I felt like he could see my soul. He then looked at Jim and then up at the sky. Finally, he said, "To find your answers, you must travel to Nabisusha."

12 SHED FOR BRAINS

When the world died, all those barriers created by spiritual, political and social belief died with it. Without any barriers, other realms are free to encroach on this world.

-Veck

The next morning, I was surprised to see Jim waiting for me outside my door, instead of Proon, with coffee and a muffin. At first I was relieved, until Jim said, "Pack up! We're leaving in ten minutes."

"Who changed the departure time?" I called after him, as he set down my breakfast and stepped out into the hall.

"Zurn. See you outside."

I dressed quickly, packed my stuff, and raced out of the building where everyone was waiting. Somewhere along the way, I must have eaten the muffin, although I don't remember doing so. Major Zurn and his team - a heavily armed squad – were ready and waiting to go. He looked on impatiently as Proon readied our dog sleds. I was in Shauna's squad, which consisted of Jim, Sergeant Dung, Pimply (to fix things if they broke), Clarke the dog handler, and some soldier named Baby Manley. He was a big man, a few inches shy of seven feet tall, with an even bigger head. With only one tooth, he looked like an overgrown baby. His face was a smooth as a newborn's bottom. I bet he never shaved a day in his life. He carried a readily loaded C-6;[29] with extra ammo belts draped over his shoulders. The sled creaked and strained when he sat on it. I felt sorry for the dogs.

I set my pack on the sled and yawned loudly.

"Late night?" Jim asked.

"Yeah… Proon set up an autograph session in the mess hall with a group of fans. After that, I played AA with him and bunch of his friends. How about you? Did you meet up with Shauna?"

---

[29] C-6: Canadian Army fully automatic belt fed heavy machine gun.

Jim grinned.

"You dog!" I elbowed him in the ribs. Not sure if I saw it right, but there may have been a hint of red in that green face.

"Good morning, Ed," Proon greeted, as he secured the last of the gear.

"Hey." I looked over at Zurn's squad. "Do we really need that much firepower?"

"It's standard equipment. Major Zurn insists on it. He's always concerned about keeping the area safe and secure."

"I'm more concerned with being kept safe and secure from him," I muttered.

"Relax. Oh, and I'm supposed to tell you," Proon started, "You don't get a weapon."

"What?"

"You're just an observer."

"Whose idea was that?"

"Major Zurn."

"So if any shooting starts, I'm just supposed to watch?"

"Don't worry, there won't be any shooting. Besides, there's nothing to shoot at out there."

"I sure as hell hope so."

"All set here, Major McCallister," Proon shouted. She responded with a nod. Proon and I settled in on one of the sleds. After a brief discussion with Zurn, Shauna and Jim joined us. We got on our sleds and headed off. The comm station was on the north western side of the lake, not far from the remnants of an old fishing camp. Proon talked the whole time. I was surprised the snow didn't melt from all the hot air he expended. It didn't take long for us to reach our destination. We stopped on the edge of the fishing camp, which was nothing more than a bunch of dilapidated shacks and cottages. We travelled the rest of the way on foot. Clarke waited with the dogs by the edge of the lake – apparently they were spooked by the area and would not go any further.

Once we got to the other side of the camp, the comm station was easily visible. A cluster of satellite dishes and antennas jutted out of a mound of snow. A massive stone sculpture in the shape of a human stood over the area, like an ancient sentry.

"That's called an Inukshuk," Proon said when he noticed me staring. "It means *something that acts for a person*. Magnificent, isn't it?"

"I'll say. What's it for?"

"It's a reference point. The aboriginal peoples built them to indicate where to hunt or travel."

Major Zurn barked out orders. His team took up defensive positions. "Major McAllister!"

"Sir?"

"Why don't you and Sergeant Dung take our guests inside and show them around."

"Yes sir."

"And Major?"

"Yes?"

"I want no trouble from our guests. Don't fuck up!"

"Yes, sir… C'mon boys!"

The comm station was a round building with a domed roof. A row of windows – most of them broken - ran along the outer wall just below the roof line. The building was recessed into the ground so the windows were about waist high off the ground. The snow and earth had been cleared away. A descending path led to the entrance, which resembled an airlock.

The doors had been forced open, revealing a corridor that curved off in both directions. Icicles hung from the pipes lining the ceiling. Metal pipes of some sort also lined the walls. We circled our way around. On the other side of the building, opposite the entrance, was another set of doors on the interior wall. These doors opened onto a round room. A white desk stood in the center with a monitor and keyboard resting on top of it. The screen was black.

"Does that thing work?"

"Nobody knows how to turn it on."

I wandered around. "So this is it, huh?"

"This is it," Shauna confirmed. Jim shrugged.

Jim tapped the keys randomly. "Hey Jim," Proon began, "Watch the one key there. It pricks your finger when you hit it. I got jabbed in the index finger last time. It makes no sense why the keyboard would have a little prick like that."

"Which key?"

"The *Home* key, I think."

Jim stuck his finger on the key and pressed. He pulled his finger away, revealing a tiny droplet of his purple blood. The computer screen flickered to life.

"What the hell?" Proon exclaimed.

We all moved in closer to the monitor. <ANALYZING USER SAMPLE>

"It seems to like you, Lieutenant Shrike," Proon said.

The screen flashed and the words changed.

<TERMINUS SURVIVOR: VERIFIED>

<COMPATIBLE USER: VERIFIED>

The screen completely faded to black. A cursor appeared. It flashed momentarily before scrolling across the screen.

<HELLO>

"Wow!" Proon gasped.

Jim leaned in and typed a response. <HI>

<PREPARE FOR TRANSFER>

"What does that mean?"

The desk hummed. We all stepped away except for Jim. To his right, a panel hissed open in the smooth workstation counter top. A device resembling a high tech cell phone with a clear vial attached to it lay in the recessed area. Two tubes ran from the vial: one ran into an opening in the desk; the other connected to a needle that was attached to a metal arm. A lighted profile in the shape of a human hand and forearm appeared. The metal arm whirred into position above it.

"I think it wants a blood sample," Proon said. Jim removed his jacket and rolled up his sleeve.

"Are you sure you should do this?" Shauna asked, grabbing Jim by the hand.

"No. But what's the worst that could happen?" He placed his arm within the profile. The metal arm maneuvered into position and jabbed him in a vein at his elbow joint. Purple blood flowed through the tube and half filled the vial. The metal arm retracted.

<TRANSFER IN PROGRESS: 00%>

The number rapidly increased. A silvery fluid pumped through the other tube until it filled the vial completely.

<TRANSFER COMPLETE: 100%>

The tubes dislodged from the electronic device. Jim picked it up. The opening in the desk slid shut and disappeared. A clock timer appeared on the screen and began counting down.

<00:59:59>

"What happens in sixty minutes?"

CLANG! KA-PING!

The sound came from somewhere deep within the base. Metal ground against metal.

"What was that?"

We heard it again, like a distant echo. The base creaked.

"There's your answer," Jim said, pointing at the screen.

<DESCENT SEQUENCE INITIATED>

"This could be interesting. We should observe," Proon said.

"I agree but from the outside," I said.

Jim tucked the device into his jacket. "Let's get out of here!"

Snow blew in through the broken windows and whirled around in the corridor. We ran out of the station. Baby Manley stood in front in our path with the C-6 leveled at us.

"What's going on?" Shauna demanded.

"Hands in the air!" Major Zurn ordered. A soldier took Major McAllister's rifle and sidearm. The rest of soldiers surrounded us. Pimply stood off to the sidelines, watching.

"I knew you'd fuck up," Zurn said to Major McAlister.

"Major, we have to get out of here," Proon shouted.

"We're not going anywhere!"

"You don't understand… the comm station will descend back into the ground."

"Shut up or we'll put you in the ground. You didn't think I would just let you leave, did you Shrike?"

"I have no quarrel with you, Ben."

"But I have one with you."

"We can settle this. Let my friends go!"

"Any friend of yours is my enemy. Get moving!"

"This is ridiculous."

"Shut your hole, Proon!"

We were escorted at gunpoint down to the ice covered lake. Tiny shacks dotted the shore. The wind picked up and toyed with the door on one of the shacks: slamming it open and shut repeatedly.

WHACK!

"This is as good a place as any for you to die," Zurn said. "When the spring thaw arrives, you can rejoin the slime at the bottom of the lake."

WHACK!

"Ready your weapons, men!" The soldiers raised their rifles and aimed at us.

WHACK!

"Pimply!" The weasel-faced man jumped to attention. "Get your ass over to that shack and close the fucking door! Now!" Pimply sauntered over at his usual slow pace.

WHACK!

Major Zurn drew his pistol and aimed at Jim. "I can't believe after everything that's happened in this world you came back for me to take care of you. I'm going to enjoy this."

Pimply grabbed the door. He stuck his head in the shack and pulled it back out quickly.

The men took up shooting stances.

"Brains!" Pimply screamed.

"What the...?"

"Brains!" The men lowered their weapons. A panicked Pimply bolted towards the Major. "Brains!" He slipped, falling to his knees in front of Major Zurn, breathing heavily.

"What the hell is going on?"

"Brains! The shed's full of brains!" Pimply heaved and threw up all over the Major's boots. He rolled onto his side, clutching his stomach. "Brains!" He puked again.

Major Zurn kicked the vomit off his boots. "Get away from me!" He pushed Pimply with his foot. "Robson! Allan! Get to that shack and see what all the fuss is about!" The two men ran to the shack, looked inside and quickly returned.

"It's full of brains, sir," Robson said. "There are brains drying out on all the shelves."

Zurn shook his head in disbelief. "This is ridiculous!" Dogs were barking in the distance. "Now, what's going on?"

A panicked Clarke ran towards us through the snow. "The Wendigo! The Wendigo is here!"

"There's no such thing as a Wendigo. Return to your post at once!"

"No way!" Clarke was shaking. "I saw it. You guys got guns. I'm staying here where it's safe."

"Oh, for Chrissakes," Major Zurn shot Clarke in the chest, dropping him on the spot. Shauna gasped. "There's no Wendigo here. And that's an order."

Jim looked to me and shouted, "Run!" I hesitated. "Run! Get to the station!" He turned and fired his eyebeams at Baby Manley causing the big man's chest to explode. Baby Manley spun around, firing the C-6, while his body contents spilled into the snow. The firing arc swept across a prone Pimply, tearing him apart at the midsection. Pimply screamed. Baby Manley fell to one knee and Jim zapped him again for good measure, blowing off the top of his big head.

The soldiers opened fire but Shauna, Proon, and I were already half-way to the station. Bullets bit the snow around us. Proon's parka exploded just below his left shoulder. He spun and fell down into the entrance. I grabbed him and dragged him inside. Steam and gases were venting into the corridor from the pipes. The building creaked and trembled. I unzipped Proon's parka. Blood pooled around his neck and chest.

"Hang in there, buddy!"

"Ed... Ed..." he coughed. "It hurts." He was wheezing.

"Don't you die, Proon!"

Shauna applied pressure on the wound. "There are med kits with the sleds."

"N-no...no time..." Proon gasped. "T-T-Take... this..." He reached into his chest pocket and put his clenched fist in mine. He pulled me close. "I-I'm glad I met you..." His eyes glassed over and his last breath escaped his body.

"Proon!" I tilted his head and prepared him for CPR.

Shauna pulled me back. "He's gone... he's gone."

I felt like punching the wall. "Fuck!" I opened my hand. Proon had given me a d20[30]. I knelt down beside him and closed his eyes.

Bullets pinged off the station. Jim darted inside. He looked down at Proon. "Aw..." He clenched his jaw and his fists. Veins pulsed at his temples and his eyes glowed. "I'm going take Ben's head off! We need a diversion. I'll run out and draw their fire..."

"Hold on, Jim... listen. They've stopped firing."

Jim crept along the wall, peering out through the broken glass. Shauna inched her way up beside him. We heard screaming, followed by more shots.

"What happened?"

THUMP-THUMP

"What the hell was that?" I whispered, pulling myself up to a window.

THUMP-THUMP!

"Sounds like foot falls... real heavy foot falls."

THUMP-THUMP-THUMP-THUMP

---

[30] d20: A twenty-sided die.

It was coming towards us. I already had enough adrenaline coursing through my body. I didn't need this. I was shaking. A tall, dark figure landed with a heavy thud in the entrance way. I could only see it from the neck down. It wore thick-soled, weathered and cracked leather boots, heavy gloves, and a long coat made entirely of weathered and well-used swords and daggers. A canvas sack hung from its pale gray hand.

"The Wendigo..." Shauna whispered.

The figure hunched over and stepped inside. Surprisingly, it made no sound – the sword coat was as flexible as cloth. A huge light bulb shaped skull wrapped in thin layer of nearly translucent skin appeared. The eye sockets were covered by a band of iron, riveted to the temples, with narrow eye slits cut into it. Taking no notice of us, the living bobble-head version of the grim reaper squatted down in the entrance and pulled its knees up to its chest. It was hideous. Everything seemed to move like it was in slow motion. I didn't know if I should run or scream.

The thing turned and faced us, squinting as if to get a good look. Jim looked like he was ready to strike. The mouth broke open in a smile of widely spaced perfectly square teeth. A bony-fingered hand tipped the blue and white *Toronto Maple Leafs* touque on top of its head.

"Hi, I'm Keek." Nobody moved or responded. I don't think anyone knew what to do.

"That's an odd name for a Wendigo," Shauna said cautiously.

"I'm no Wendigo - I'm Keek." He looked down at Proon's body. "Oh. I am so sorry. That saddens me. Did the bad guys do that?"

"Yes. They tried to kill us," Jim said. "And you too, it seems."

"I only wanted to see the dogs."

"Dogs? You mean the sled dogs?"

"I like dogs. The man who was watching them ran away when he saw me. I came down here to tell him I wasn't going to hurt him. That's when I saw those bad guys."

"Are the bad guys still out there?" I asked.

"They ran away. Most people do when they see me," he said sadly. The station shook. Icicles fell from the ceiling. Keek rose and tipped his hat. "See ya later."

"Keek, wait!" Jim said. He turned to Shauna and I. "I know Ben. He'll have one or two men covering the entrance to prevent our escape."

"That's awful." Keek looked angry. He stormed out of the base.

"Keek!"

Sure enough, he walked into a hail of bullets and fell to the ground.

We all looked out the windows. Two men cautiously approached the station, weapons raised.

"What's the plan?" I asked.

"I'll take them out with my eye beams."

Before Jim could blast away, Keek jumped to his feet. One of the men turned and ran. The second held his ground, firing. The bullets seemed to have no effect. Keek swung the sack, taking out the man's legs and knocking him flat onto his face. As the soldier got up on all fours, Keek grabbed him by the head, twisted off his block and threw it into the sack. He craned his neck; his big eyes blinked at the sky. The nose slits widened. He sniffed, and sniffed again.

THUMP-THUMP

Keek returned to the station. "Like how I joked them?" He set down the sack and a head rolled out of it. "Oh, sorry!" He picked it up.

"Is that your shed by the water?"

"It's not mine. I only use it to store food." He looked at Jim. "Those bad guys stink like bums."

Pipes burst. The sounds of grinding, wrenching metal vibrated through the walls.

"Go!" Jim shouted. We ran out of the station. It slowly sank into the earth. Sparks spouted and flames rose as antennas toppled over. The smoldering base disappeared completely. The ground shook. Dirt and snow caved in around the hole, leaving a deep sunken crater.

Jim grabbed the assault rifle from the headless soldier and handed it to Shauna. "They're probably waiting for us to make a run for the sleds."

"I think they hid in the old camp," Keek said.

"Can you circle round and chase the bad guys to the lake?"

"Sure! Sure!" He rummaged through his sack and pulled out a length of chain with a steel ball on the end. "Lookit my whacker-bonker. I made this. I'll chase the bad guys with it."

"I think that should send them running," I agreed.

Keek set down the sack. "Watch my stuff. Make sure nobody takes it!"

"I don't think you need to worry."

THUMP-THUMP

Keek was off.

"Come on, Jim ordered. "Ed - you and I will take up positions among the fishing shacks. They'll probably run through that clearing. Shauna – I want you to lay down suppressive fire. Get them to run towards us. But leave Ben for me... he's mine. Understand?"

Shauna put her hand on Jim's cheek. "Stay frosty!"

Jim nodded and took off. I gave Shauna a salute and ran after him. We could hear shooting in the distance and yelling, followed by Keek's plodding footfalls. Jim and I both hid behind fishing shacks. From my position, I had a clear view of the terrain leading up to the forest. Timbers cracked. Maybe Keek decided to remodel the camp.

"Here they come," Jim said. Two soldiers ran from the forest. One of them turned and ran towards Shauna. She quickly cut him down. The other returned fire and Shauna removed his face with a well placed shot. Ben and the rest of his men emerged. Shauna laid down suppressive fire, forcing them to move towards us. The last man out of the woods turned and fired at the oncoming Keek, who came out swinging the whacker-bonker over his head. He swung the ball down low and caught the man in the midsection. He folded like a paper doll, and the blow sent him flying through the sky. He landed with a splat somewhere out on the lake.

Keek chased the remaining soldiers down the slope towards us. Jim leaned out from his hiding spot and fired his eyebeams, blasting a man's arm off at the shoulder. His scream was cut short by a large metal ball that sailed down from the sky, planted itself in his back, and buried him deeply in the snow. The steel ball swung out again and slammed into the side of another man's head. Keek reeled in his chain and stepped forward. Zurn fired at him with no effect.

Zurn turned to his last soldier. "Don't just stand there, you idiot! Shoot!" The soldier looked at Keek, and wisely decided to run in the other direction. I darted out from behind the shack and flat out ploughed him down. I twisted his neck for good measure. Bones snapped and cracked.

"Let's finish this, Ben," Jim said, as he stepped out from his hiding spot. Keek stepped back. Zurn marched towards Jim, stopped only a few feet away. The men glared at each other. Jim's fingers twitched. Zurn quickly fired off a shot, hitting Jim in the chest. He fell back into the snow.

Zurn's laughter was cut short. His eyes widened with disbelief when he saw Jim rise. He shot him again. Jim fell to one knee. He pulled the trigger several more times before he realized he was out of ammo. He pounced, but Jim was faster and he caught him by the hand. He fell back, using Zurn's momentum to throw him through the air. Before his body even hit the snow, Jim delivered a kick to his ribs. Zurn hit the ground and quickly sprang to his feet. The two men traded punches, chops and kicks.

Finally Zurn threw a punch which Jim side stepped. He cracked him under the arm with his left hand, following up with a chop to the nose with his right. He stumbled back, and Jim kicked him through the wall of one of the shacks.

A bloodied Zurn slowly crawled out the entrance on the other side. Jim swung the door on him, crashing it into his head. He kicked him repeatedly, sending him rolling down onto the ice. Zurn got to his knees. He took a swing and Jim caught his hand. He twisted his wrist until it popped. Zurn screamed and crawled away, keeping his mangled hand close to his body. The ice creaked beneath their feet.

I started to step forward when I felt a hand on my shoulder. "Leave him, Ed," Shauna cautioned. "This isn't your fight."

"But the ice…"

Zurn drew a knife from his belt. He stood, ready and waiting, slightly hunched over. His body looked tired and beaten, but his eyes were still filled with rage and hate.

"C'mon, Jim!"

Jim took up a stance a few feet in front of him. They both moved at the same time. Jim allowed Zurn to step in and stick the knife in his side. He used the opportunity to lock Zurn's arm firmly under his. With his other hand, he braced himself against Zurn's shoulder and dislocated it. Zurn screamed, and dropped the knife. Jim broke his nose with a head butt to the face.

Zurn stumbled back, shaking the cobwebs from his head. He regained his focus and stared at Jim. "What... have you become?"

"You don't want to know." Jim pulled something from his pocket and slapped it on Zurn's chest. "Here's your medal!" He kicked him in the midsection, sending him sprawling out on the ice. The Major got back to his feet, his lifeless arm dangling at his side. Jim stepped back. He blasted the ice into large pieces.

"Don't leave me out here, Shrike!" The Major shouted.

"I already saved you once," Jim said. The ice beneath Zurn's feet suddenly lifted. A giant mouth – probably big enough to swallow a school bus, and filled with endless rows of teeth -- shot up out of the water. The jaws slammed shut, splintering the ice into tiny shards and truncating Zurn. The mouth opened quickly and snatched the upper half of his body out of the air. Just as quickly as it appeared, it slid beneath the surface.

I felt cold shivers run down my back. Next thing I knew, I was holding Shauna's hand.

"Kinosoo," she whispered. Keek's arms were wrapped around our shoulders. Shauna looked up at him and smiled. She then looked down at our hands and let go. It was awkward. She ran to Jim.

"Ah, crap," Keek moaned.

"What? What is it?"

"He didn't save the head."

"Don't worry… It was probably empty."

Keek burst out laughing and slapped me on the back. "You joked me good."

13 KEEK TO THE HEAD

I find it interesting that so many people believe in some form of afterlife. Yet how many of those same people believe in a beforelife? I mean, it makes sense that if you know where you're going to end up, you should know where you came from in the first place.

-Veck

"So what do we do now?" I shouted.

Jim pulled free from Shauna's embrace. She seemed annoyed. "Can we make it back before dark?"

"Probably," Shauna answered. "We should check on the dogs."

"Dogs?" Keek piped up. "I let them go."

"What?"

"They were scared. I set them free. They didn't like those bad guys."

"How would you know that?" I asked.

"They told me," he said, matter of factly.

Jim looked up at the sky. When he didn't find what he was looking for he asked, "What are our options?"

"A search team will be sent in the morning," Shauna said. "We can get the gear from the sleds and camp out here."

"Sounds like a plan."

"Or... you could come over to my house?" Keek offered.

"Where exactly do you live?" I asked.

Keek pointed to the Inukshuk in the distance. "Kinda there... beneath that guy... in the ground."

"In the ground?"

"Yeah... it's like a secret hideout. There's a library and a room with all my stuff and a garden." Jim and I exchanged glances. He didn't have to say a word – just a nod – for me to know what he was thinking.

"Alright... we're coming with you."

"I'll get the sleds," Keek said excitedly. "Sleep-over!" Before anyone could say otherwise, he ran off.

"Jim? Are you sure about this? We don't know what we're in for." Shauna countered.

Jim grinned. "I believe we do."

Shauna shook her head. "I don't think this is a good idea."

"Then wait here."

She clenched her fists. "James Shrike! Ugh! You can be so difficult!"

"I'm not being difficult. I'm being practical. Our best chance of survival is with Keek."

"So now you're looking out for everyone else? Don't play the hero with me. Every decision you make is somehow to your benefit." Shauna looked at me. "I'm right, aren't I?"

I looked to Jim. "Uh... I, bah... I'm just following orders."

"Of course I'm getting something out of this – answers, hopefully. And maybe even more questions, but it's worth checking out." Shauna turned away from him. "You need to trust me on this."

She huffed. "I trust you. It's just that... every time I trust you, you disappear."

"I've always come back."

"It's the not knowing *when* that hurts, Jim. And every time you do come back, it's like... part of you is dead."

Jim didn't say anything. He dropped his head and folded his arms. Shauna stared out at the lake. I, on the other hand, had no fucking clue what to do. I didn't know what to say or who to console. I just stood still and kept my mouth shut. Luckily, it was only a few minutes - although it seemed like eternity – before Keek came bounding over the snowy slopes, dragging the sleds.

"Here's all your crap."

"Am I glad to see you," I sighed.

We consolidated all the gear and secured it, taking only our own personal belongings. Keek, meanwhile, inventoried his heads, putting a fresh batch in his shed and bagging the ripe ones. When we were ready, Jim gave the order, "Lead the way!"

"Follow me!"

Jim and Shauna hung back, keeping their distance from us and from each other. I tried to keep pace with Keek. He moved very quickly. Before I knew it, the Inukshuk towered over us. A stone path ran right between the sculpture's legs, leading to an impressively tall and very old looking oak tree. I waited for Jim and Shauna to catch up. Keek approached the tree and placed his hand on it. What happened next was very odd: Keek appeared to me as a little boy. He was just a kid: a dark-haired, dark-eyed kid wearing jeans, runners and a t-shirt. I looked back at Jim and Shauna, who shared the same perplexed look. They obviously saw the boy, too!

"Are you coming?"

"Uh... Keek. You look different."

He looked down at himself. "No... I look like me."

"That's not what I mean. You look like a boy."

"I am a boy."

I clenched my jaw. Jim stepped forward. "Keek, before you touched that tree, you did not appear to us as a boy."

He laughed. "Oh yeah, that. I forgot. Now that I'm home, I can just be myself. C'mon!" Keek stepped *into* the tree. It was like he just vanished into it.

I looked back at Jim and Shauna. "I guess this is a bad time to suggest *ladies first*?" By the look on her face, I could tell Shauna didn't think my comment was funny.

"I'll go," Jim said. He placed his hand on the tree, stepped forward and disappeared.

Shauna approached the tree hesitantly. "I don't like this."

"If I don't do this, I know I'll regret it." I said. I put my hand on the tree. It felt like a mild electric shock went through my whole body. The closest comparable feeling I ever had was that jolt you feel when you are falling asleep and suddenly awaken. My Grandpa used to say that you left your body when you slept. That jolt was caused by your spirit returning too quickly, most likely because you were hesitant to leave, and your body and spirit were misaligned upon return. In the blink of an eye, I was standing inside a cave with Keek and Jim. It was more like a tunnel, actually. A golden light appeared at the far end; directly behind me it was pitch dark.

"Where's Shauna?"

"Coming... I think. She was a bit nervous."

Shauna emerged from the darkness. Jim took her hand to steady her.

"You alright?"

"Yeah... that felt odd. Where are we?"

"Come," Keek said, excitedly. He slung his sack of heads over his shoulder and ran towards the light. We followed. The light was strong enough to illuminate the entire cave. When we neared the exit, we could see a stone archway, intricately carved with fantastic beasts and warriors. Pictographs which I had never seen before ran along the base of the carvings.

We stepped through the archway. It... was awesome! We were standing in a room, maybe a hundred feet long. The ceiling was probably thirty feet high and made up of a dozen inverse domes. It was like looking up into an egg carton. The domes were made of a material that resembled polished copper. It was incredibly bright, although there were no visible light sources. At the points where the inverted domes intersected, the ceiling was supported by stone statues. Each statue was of a robed, bearded man, wearing a round hat upon which the ceiling rested. More pictographs appeared at the base of each statue. I had to place my hand on one and touch the cold stone to confirm that it was real.

"It's amazing," Shauna said. Her voice trembled.

"Yeah... kinda reminds me of something out of an Idaho Grim novel."

"Who?"

"Uh... nothing." *If only my Grandpa could see this! And Carlin – he would be so excited!*

The walls of the room were partly made of layers upon layers of human skulls. Above that, a painted mural spanned the wall from end to end. On one side, fierce warriors marched upon a temple, guarded by a giant dragon. A massive battle took place on the other. Our footsteps echoed on the polished stone floor. At the end of the room was another archway. As I approached it, I noticed that one of the statues was broken. A jagged crack ran down from the left shoulder, across the chest and right arm. The upper part of the statue had shifted ever so slightly.

I was so excited, I was shaking. I almost couldn't breathe. Rather than wait for Jim and Shauna, I anxiously exited the room.

"Holy shit," I whispered.

A waterfall cascaded down the naturally terraced rock face to the right. It fell into a large pool, before streaming across the room and under a stone bridge before disappearing into the round hole in the wall on the left. The air had a moist, earthy smell to it. Along the terraces grew all forms of foliage, some of which I had never seen before. There were two more entrances on the left, one on each side of the water. On the other side of the room, directly opposite the archway, a giant jawless skull was carved into the rock. The upper teeth rested on the floor.

Over the sound of the waterfall, I heard the whirring and clicking of gears above my head. I looked up. The entire ceiling in this room was one large dome. Within it, metal arms with orbs on the ends rotated around a central axis, ticking away like the inner workings of a clock. It took me a moment to realize that Jim and Shauna were standing next to me.

"Keek?" My voice echoed. "Keek?"

The boy emerged from the first arch on my left. "I was just putting away those heads. Do you like my house?"

"What is this place?"

"It's where I live."

"Have you always lived here?" Shauna asked.

"No. This is a Custodian stronghold."

"The Custodians?" Jim asked.

"Those guys," Keek pointed at the statues. "They're gone now. They're all dead. Did you know we have a library?"

"A library?"

"Yeah, I'll show you." Keek led us across the bridge to the archway.

We entered the library. It was something I could have only dreamed about or read about in story books. The room smelled musty, like my Grandpa's study. A heavy wooden table sat in the middle of the room. Shelves lined the walls, loaded with all manner of scrolls, thick leatherbound tomes, hides, carved bones, and stone or clay tablets. Cobwebs covered everything. I blew the thick dust off a book, creating a small cloud.

"You don't read much, I take it?"

"Nah!" Keek waved a hand at me. "The words make no sense."

Jim removed a book from the shelf and set it down with a resounding thud on the table. He leafed through the pages of inked drawing and writings.

"You recognize the text?" I asked.

"I've never seen anything like it."

"You want me to show you the rest of the place?" Keek asked.

"Sure," I said. "Shauna, you coming with us?"

"Sure she will," Jim urged. He didn't even look up – his face was buried in a book. "I'd like to stay here."

Shauna clenched her fists. She was about to say something, but instead, she headed out the door. We left the room. Shauna was standing on the bridge.

"You alright?"

"Ugh! He can be so distant even when he's right next to you. I can't relate to him anymore. I don't know how you put up with him."

"Since we left the bunker, I haven't had much choice. But, I know what you mean. I'm sorry for the way things are going."

She sighed "Don't worry about it."

I looked up at the clock work structure.

"That's space. If you had an eye-scope, it would look like that," Keek pointed out. After a few minutes observing the movement, it started to make sense.

"I get it now. Those thinner rods with those sparkling wires on the ends represent major constellations. There's the Big Dipper."

"That's right."

"And those orbs are planets."

Keek nodded.

"Why are there thirteen planets? I thought there were only eleven."

"Yes, you *did*!"

Before I could ask for an explanation, he hurried off to the other entrance. We followed him into a room that resembled a medieval laboratory. Dried herbs and small animals hung from the rafters. Jars of powders, and animal, vegetable and mineral matter rested on shelves. They shared their space with glass jars containing body parts and anatomical skeletons. A cast iron pot hung over the hearth, boiling and sputtering furiously. I didn't see, nor did I want to see where he put the decapitated heads.

"Where did you get all this stuff?"

"I didn't. Most of it was already here."

"Were the Custodians witches or something?" Shauna asked, furrowing her brow at a bottle of eyeballs.

"I think some of them knew how to make potions and things."

"Are you a witch?"

"No, but I know about some witch stuff, I guess."

"Can I go in there?" I asked, pointing to a narrow passage. Keek nodded. The passage led to an armory: a well equipped arsenal that was a cross between a museum and a military base. Weapons ranged from bronze swords to modern firearms. The whacker-bonker hung over a weapons rack.

I returned to the lab. Keek sprinkled some powder into the pot and added a handful of crushed leaves. It smelled delicious, just like my Grandpa's stew and dumplings. "What are you making?"

"Beekosh – it's like a soup. I didn't think you would eat brains."

"Thanks for being so considerate. Are you adding eye of newt or anything like that?"

"No, but I can."

"It's okay. I'm sure whatever you added is just fine. How did you learn to make Beekosh?"

"I learnded it from an old woman."

"She taught you?"

"No silly… I ate her brain." He giggled and shook his head.

"How do you learn from eating the brain?" Shauna asked.

"You just do. You eat it and whatever that person knows, you know."

"How smart are you?" I asked.

"I'm the smartest person that I know of."

"Uh, Keek… no offense, but if you can learn all these things from eating brains, why do you talk like a kid? I mean, shouldn't you talk like you have a PhD or something?"

"Well, firstly, I am a kid. And secondly, if I talked like a PhD, would you understand me?"

"Hmmm, maybe not. So what kind of stuff do you know?"

Keek stirred the Beekosh, sniffing it occasionally. "I know physics and history and 'struction and I speak seventeen languages and…"

"Seventeen languages…. and yet you can't read any of those books?"

"I guess I could, if I ate a brain that knew them." He handed me a wooden spoon. "It's ready… try it!"

I looked down into the pot of clear liquid. "I thought this was soup."

"It is!"

"It smells like stew with dumplings."

"No," Shauna countered. "It smells like my dad's chili."

"Is this another one of your mind games?"

"There's no game here – just your mind and the soup. It will taste like what you very like."

I skimmed the surface with the spoon and sipped the steaming liquid. Sure enough, it tasted like stew. It even had texture. I was chewing a potato and some beef. I even tasted carrot. "How does it do that?" I took another spoonful.

"Beekosh is what you very like. Do you like beer?"

"Yeah…"

"Try it."

I took a sip. It tasted like beer and it was cold, too! "Shauna, you want to try this?"

"Sure, why not?" She took a spoonful and chewed. "Mmm, that does taste like chili."

Keek grabbed a ladle and handed out wooden bowls. "Sit down and eat." He spooned out the Beekosh and we sat down at the table.

"This is really good – it tastes like stew again. I've been craving that for so long."

"Yeah, I'm impressed, Keek."

The boy beamed with a smile.

We ate voraciously, never saying a word. It was the best stew I had ever eaten. When my belly felt full, I pushed myself away from the table.

"Leave the bowls," Keek said. "We can go see the garden and go for a swim."

"Sounds good to me," Shauna smiled approvingly.

Keek ran to a shelf, grabbed an empty bottle and dunked it in the pot. He stuck his arm in the boiling liquid right up to his elbow. Shauna gasped. He looked up at us and smiled.

"It's ok… it can't hurt me." He lifted out the full bottle. His arm wasn't even scalded.

"What's with the bottle?"

"Maybe you would like some wine. C'mon!" He raced out of the room.

"You think we should check on Jim?" I asked.

"Leave him. I'm sure he's much happier with his book," Shauna scoffed.

When we returned to the main hall, the lights had grown dim. Keek waited for us at on the other side of the bridge, at the edge of the garden.

"Is it getting darker in here, Keek?"

"Yes."

"Why?"

"It's night time."

"That's pretty cool."

We arrived at the garden. Keek handed me the wine bottle and disappeared into the dense foliage. Lucky for us, there was a path. Trees and plants of varying climate zones grew side by side. Redwoods towered over mighty oaks and feathery palms. Flowers of all colors and sizes dotted the green background. The mix of fruity and spicy fragrances left me feeling light-headed.

"These plants look like they could be prehistoric," Shauna observed.

"Some of them are," Keek acknowledged, as he stepped out from behind a fern. "C'mon! I want to show you something." The path led to a grassy clearing overlooking the water. A perfectly rectangular stone slab lay in the middle of the clearing. It was very low to the ground and creamy white in color. I ran my hand along the silky surface.

"This is what I want to show you. Come see this plant."

Shauna and I hunched down beside Keek. The plant was brown and scraggly. What little leaves it had were curled and wilted. It reminded me of a celery stick that went too many days without water.

"What kind of plant is this?" Shauna asked.

"This is a Peemer plant. It is dying."

"Why do you want to show us a dying plant?"

"It has to die. That's the only way to harvest a Peemer. This one will be ready tomorrow."

"What's a Peemer?" I asked.

"It's the hard center of the flower. You stick it in your nose, or into your eye."

"Why would you do that?"

"Because the time is right. Peemers are very rare. It takes tens of hundreds of years to grow one. Want to go swimming?"

"Yeah, but..." Before I knew it, Keek had stripped down to his skivvies. The big splash told me he wasn't waiting for an answer.

"Come in! The water's great!" The boy bobbed up and down before disappearing under the surface.

I looked at Shauna and shrugged. "Aw, what the hell?" I took a swig of the wine and handed her the bottle. My body was warm all over. I felt a buzz. I peeled off my clothes and jumped in after Keek.

"It's as warm as bath water. Come on in, Shauna!"

She drank from the bottle and smiled. "Oh... alright."

While she got undressed, Keek grabbed me around the neck and we swam under the waterfall. The pounding water massaged my back. Shauna dove in. She popped up right next to us. Shauna was absolutely gorgeous. Apart from the fact that she was wearing a wet, clingy tank top, the girl could easily have been the spokesmodel for military issue undergarments. She made olive drab look sexy.

"This is great."

"Yeah, Jim's missing out."

"Oh, the hell with Jim! He probably feels the same way about us and his books," she laughed.

I swam around until my body was relaxed and refreshed. The room had grown very dark. Tiny shimmering specks of light pockmarked the ceiling, resembling a star-filled sky, and casting off just the right amount of light. The air was warm when I climbed out of the water. I sat down on the smooth slab of rock. It seemed spongy, like a mattress.

"What the hell?"

"That's where you'll sleep," Keek said. He pulled on his jeans and t-shirt. "It's the sleeping stone."

"Is this another mind trick?"

"No. The earth gives you strength... just like water gives you healing and air clears the mind."

"Sounds like elemental magic," I said. Keek nodded approvingly. I lay down. It was like lying on the world's most comfortable mattress, and it was warm. My entire body relaxed and my eyelids felt droopy. Shauna lay down next to me.

"Ooohhh," she cooed. "This does feel nice."

"Have a good night," Keek said.

"Are you sleeping?"

"I don't sleep."

"That's a shame." I yawned. "This is comfortable."

"I do lie down on the rock, but not tonight." Keek crept off silently through the foliage.

"Well, see ya. Thanks for the wine." My head was cloudy. I couldn't tell if it was the wine or sleep that was taking over my body. My breathing was slow and deep.

Shauna rolled over onto her side, facing me. "Ed?"

"Yeah?"

She put her hand on my arm. "Thank you," she whispered. She pulled her hand away and rolled over. "Good night, Ed."

The next morning, I woke with an exuberance I hadn't felt since Super Bowl game day. I also awoke spooned up close to Shauna with my hand on her breast. I quickly and cautiously extricated myself from the position. My clothes were lying next to the slab: cleaned and neatly folded. My jersey was missing, which stressed me a bit, but I wasn't too concerned. I was sure Keek had something to do with its disappearance. Shauna was still asleep, so I got dressed and decided to check in on Jim.

"Hey!" Jim had his face buried in a text. The table was piled high with all sorts of books. "Did you go through all these books?"

"Yep!"

"Find anything worth sharing?"

"Not yet. But I'll let you know when I do." Jim never even looked up at me.

"This place is pretty cool. Wait till you see the rest of it." Jim didn't respond. I noticed the device with the vial attached to it on the table. I picked it up and stared into the silvery liquid. "Any luck with this thing?"

"Huh? What?"

"Has this thing done anything?"

"Oh, that... uh... no. It hasn't. It's been quiet."

I set it back down. "Okay... well, uh... I guess I'll see ya."

I continued to the lab, where I met Keek. He was busy sorting through a jar of some stuff that looked like dried moss.

"Hi!"

"Hey!"

"Did you have a good rest?"

"The best ever. Thanks for cleaning my clothes." Keek shrugged. I was craving cereal with cold milk. I grabbed a spoon and dipped it in the pot without looking.

"Hey, Keek?"

"Yeah?"

"Have you seen my jersey?" Without waiting for a response, I put the spoon in my mouth. I spit the fiery offending liquid out.

Pffffrrrttt! Blech! "This tastes like shit! And I burned my tongue... What did you do to the Beekosh?"

"It's in that pot over there," Keek responded, pointing to the cauldron on the floor in the corner.

"Well what the hell's in this..." I looked into the pot and saw a familiar shade of crimson. "Is that my jersey? You COOKED my jersey?"

"I only boiled it."

Instinctively, I stuck my hand into the pot, and quickly pulled it out as the pain shrieked through my fingers. "Fuck!"

By now, Keek had come to the rescue. He reached into the pot and retrieved my jersey. He wrung it out and lay it out on the table.

"Why did you boil my jersey?"

He held out a knife. "Here... stab it."

"Stab it? You already cooked it. Why do you want me to stab it?"

"Just stab it."

I grabbed the knife, took a deep breath and reluctantly stabbed my jersey. As soon as the knife tip came in contact with the fabric, a shock fired through my arm up to the shoulder. I instantly dropped the knife. The blade was bent into a jagged zigzag. My arm was numb, and probably part of my brain as well. "What just happened?"

"I fixed your jersey."

"What did you do?"

"If anything hits it, it sort of sends that energy right back into what hit it."

I held up the jersey. The fabric had a sparkly sheen to it. "It's like it has a force field."

"Sure, if you very like it."

I pulled it on over my head. "Cool. Thanks!"

"Anytime... and don't eat anything in that pot."

"Don't worry, I won't."

"Hey guys... what's all the commotion?" Shauna entered the room. She looked so hot in her tank top, whether wet and clingy or not.

"Oh... uh... Keek and I were just screwin' around. You know... guy stuff."

"Guy stuff," Keek repeated, folding his arms across his chest.

"Okay. What's for breakfast?"

"Oh yeah, the Beekosh is in that pot over there. Don't eat that other stuff."

"Whatever you say." Shauna grabbed a bowl and handed me one too. "I think I'll have oatmeal."

"Oatmeal? Could you think of something more bland? Of all the choices in the world, you pick oatmeal?" Shauna shoved me aside and filled her bowl. "Well, I'm having chocolatey-sugary-crunchy...stuff."

"What-ever." She rolled her eyes.

Just as we sat down at the table, Jim walked into the room with a book his hands.

"Hey... Finally get all your homework done?"

He ignored me. His eyes were focused on Keek.

"You okay, Jim?" Shauna asked.

"Yeah," he said, still staring at Keek. "I know where we're going."

"Wha...? You do?"

"And so do you," Jim said sternly to Keek.

Keek furrowed his brow. "What do you mean?"

Jim cracked open the leather-bound book and leafed through the musty, yellow pages. When he found what he was looking for, he read, *"Then, the gate opened, revealing the passage to Nabisusha. And the Green Man fell to his knees and thanked the changeling who showed him the way - the boy demon, Srala Boom."* Jim closed the book.

The boy bowed his head low and closed his eyes. A sudden tension filled the room. A cold shock wave constricted my chest. "Hmmm... I haven't heard that name in a long time," Keek said with a deep voice. When he raised his head, his eyes were completely black. The stench of sulphur assaulted my nostrils. I pushed myself back from the table. Shauna followed my lead.

"What's going on?" she asked.

"He won't hurt you,"

"Jim is correct. I will not." Keek suddenly had the demeanor of a man a hundred times his age.

"Where's the gate?"

"I will show you... but first, there is some information I must share before you enter Nabisusha. Unless you have questions?"

"Hell yeah," I said. My head was spinning. I didn't know where to begin. I stared at the boy. If only my Uncle could see me talking to the thing he most feared. That would've been so cool.

"How... what the... uh... demon?"

"Thousands of years ago, I was taken from my parents to be ritually sacrificed to a dark god. He must have liked me because he turned me into one of his minions. I was gifted with the ability to change form, and to gain knowledge through the ingestion of brain matter."

"How did you end up here?"

"As a boy, it was easy for me to lure my victims to slaughter. One day, I made the mistake of luring the Upior. But my mistake was my salvation. Rather than destroy me, he turned me to the light. He brought me here and it has been my home ever since. The Upior is somewhat obsessed with Custodial secrets. The world cannot hide anything from you if you have been here long enough. Eventually, the truth will find you."

Shauna looked to Jim. He nodded.

"What?"

"I told her about the Upior," he said.

"Oh. Well that saves some explaining. Well, Keek... I don't know what to ask you," I said.

Shauna shrugged her shoulders.

"Very well then." Keek took a deep breath. "Here goes..."

A high-pitched drone similar to that of a cicada bug hit my ears. My body tensed – it felt like I had been shocked. Then everything went dark. When I opened my eyes, I was lying on the floor. Shauna was slumped over the table.

"How long was I out?"

"Out? Not at all. You just fell out of your chair."

"But..." I may not have known what happened. But for some reason, I did know this: The entire universe is made up of energy. This energy exists as both form and formlessness simultaneously. Energy is both chaos and order - it creates and destroys – and one cannot exist without the other. This is the nature of the universe.

Energy is made up of particles, and particles comprise the whole. Each particle is sentient and self aware. When formless, the particles interact and share consciousness as a whole. When formed, the particles are separated, one particle per form. This is the equivalent of a soul. While in the form, the soul cannot reconnect with the consciousness unless it is released. However, there are ways to communicate with the universal consciousness while formed, such as dreaming and meditation. When separated from the form, the particle returns to the whole and the knowledge is shared. It is like a drop of water that falls into the ocean. It is a drop of water unique unto itself, but it is also ocean. It is one and all at the same time.

The universe has a natural curiosity about its creation. When a planet is formed and life begins, energy is drawn to the form so as to experience it. Three experienced and ancient souls, referred to as Masters, are assigned to oversee the transfer of energy into matter. Masters guide energy to and from the form. They themselves can never take form, so as not to compromise the process. As a result, Masters can only ever understand the form from the shared experiences of the released energy.

Since the Masters can never take form, twelve souls, known as Custodians, are appointed to take form and remain eternally in the form world. The Custodians act as impartial observers, and are able to communicate with the Masters. They can never return to formlessness until the form world ceases to exist. Only then can they rejoin the universal consciousness, and what they share is an entire lifespan of knowledge in a single moment.

Shauna stirred and moaned. "Ugh...my head."

"What did you do to us?" I asked Keek.

"I put the knowledge directly into your head. It is similar to the way you saw and experienced me as that creature at the comm station."

"You couldn't just tell us?"

"Language is a construct. It corrupts truth rather than conveying it. This method is easier... despite the risks."

"Risks?"

"In some humans, it causes nose bleeds. In extreme cases the head can explode."

"I still prefer a good conversation. Next time, make me sign a disclaimer." I got up from the floor and stretched.

"Did we all just experience the same thing?" Shauna asked, while massaging her forehead.

"I hope so," Keek replied. "That was my intention."

Intuitively, I knew we had. It was an odd sensation. "Why do we need to know this?"

"In case you have any doubt."

"About what?"

"About why you need to go through that gate."

Shauna rubbed her forehead. "Wait a minute… you said all the Custodians are gone."

"Correct. And therein lies the problem. The Masters have no contact with this planet except for the released souls."

"Why is that a problem?"

"The three Masters who oversee this planet decided to contain all released energy for themselves. They do not share it with the collective. As a result, the universe is blind to us. It cannot learn and understand from the experiences of released souls. That knowledge is contained and causes confusion for the soul when it returns. To complicate matters, the Custodians interfered with life on this planet, and assisted in the creation of a social construct, the purpose of which was to proliferate lies, and to perpetuate confusion and misunderstanding. They need this confusion to prevent souls from detecting the universal consciousness. Some of those souls remember the previous experiences but there is so much confusion, rarely is the experience clear."

"If this isn't the way things are supposed work, why doesn't the universe stop them?"

"It is a paradox. The universe is curious about what is happening here. But at the same time, it can learn so much more if everything just runs its course. This has never happened before… ever. There are souls who have become aware and rebelled. It is believed one of the Masters tried to overthrow the others... and failed."

"What happened to him?"

"I do not know. I am not aware of any known reference to the rogue Master. But there are souls who have followed his path; who gained awareness and fought back."

"Like Holioch," I said.

"Yes, I know of this legend. Again, due to the network of lies, it is difficult to separate the wheat from the chaff. Mythology is all we have and it does not always make sense. Then there are the souls who like things the way they are and want it to continue. There have been many wars. Some souls have even managed to manifest themselves in form to either corrupt or coerce the other forms on earth. These you have seen as demons and their minions."

I breathed deeply. "What does all this have to with Nabisusha? I mean, it's not like we're dead or something, right?"

"You are more alive than you ever have been. Nabisusha is both form and formless at the same time, where the veil between the two realms is at its thinnest."

"What exactly are we supposed to do when we go there?"

"You do what is right. Nabisusha will lead the way."

I felt like I knew more than I did when I started, but didn't. I was confused, and my head ached.

"Are you ready to enter the gate?" Keek urged. "I would like to be a child again."

"That depends," Jim answered. He looked at me and asked, "When will you be ready to leave?"

"Uh... well, considering my world has been thrown upside down, I dunno. Just give me a few minutes." I got up from the table. "This is some heavy shit. You seem to be taking it all in stride. Did that book prep you for this?"

"Not really," Jim responded.

Keek knitted his eyebrows. "Jim, how were you able to read that book? The languages in those texts are so ancient."

Jim looked at the book and handed it to Keek. "This is The Book of Amaltheon. It's the only book written in English."

"Really?" Keek dropped the book on the table, releasing a cloud of scratchy dust. Shauna and I huddled over it. He threw open the book. Nobody spoke. Keek furrowed his brow. Shauna ran her fingers over the text. It was a language I had never seen before.

"What the hell is this?"

"What's wrong?" Jim asked, puzzled.

"I've seen English and this ain't it."

Jim frowned at the text. Keek tore a section of the page, put it in his mouth and chewed it.

Pfft! Pfft! "Lookit my tongue! What color is it?"

"Diarrhea yellow," I replied.

"Hmm… I thought so." Keek stuck his tongue out as far as he could and crossed his eyes, trying to see it for himself. "The ink is enchanted. That's why Jim can read it."

"Why can't we read it?"

"I don't know. It doesn't tell me that. All I know is the ink is enchanted."

I shrugged. Jim and I reached for the book at the same time. We paused. I gently backed away.

"For your eyes only."

He grabbed the book, turned and walked out of the room. "I'll get my things. We meet back here in thirty minutes," his voice trailed off.

"I guess you have your orders." Shauna said.

I sighed.

"Now that that's settled, can I please just be a kid again?" Keek asked.

14 FRONTLINEBACKER

If a path is without obstacles, it leads you nowhere.
If the path changes direction, it leads you to where you are going.
If the path leads you in time and out of time,
it leads you to your destiny.
Such are the paths in the halls of Nabisusha.
                                    -The Book of Amaltheon

It seemed like only a few minutes for me to get ready. My gear was in check, and my pack weighted down with several canteens of Beekosh. Actually, weighted down was the wrong way to put it since the liquid was practically weightless. It was another one of those anomalies that was quickly becoming second nature.

Jim waited for me outside the laboratory. Keek emerged from the garden, leading Shauna by the hand. They were laughing about something. Keek definitely looked like a kid again – hundreds of years of demonic history lifted off his shoulders. Shauna looked just plain beautiful. I could see why Jim was attracted to her. I have to admit I was a bit smitten myself.

Shauna wore an olive drab t-shirt and camo pants. Her hair was pulled pack and braided with flowers. She looked like a hot little forest nymph that could still kick some serious ass. She kind of reminded me a bit of this girl I went to high school with, named Nicola Fulton: one of those natural beauties that didn't need any make-up to look good. She and her brothers had all been schooled in some sort of archaic martial arts form. Word had it that she put a few moves on Nick Schalmoser after he'd tried to put the moves on her. He never walked the same again after she had dislocated his nut sack.

Keek raised a finger in the air. "Before you go... there's something you need to take with you." He led us back to the clearing by the water.

"What are we here for?" I asked.

"That!" Keek pointed to the Peemer plant. It looked as brown and wilted as ever. A long leathery stem with a round bulb at the end had grown from the center of the plant since I last saw it. It lay limply on the ground.

"So what happens next?"

"Shhh… just wait. It will happen anytime," Keek said in a hushed voice.

The plant suddenly sprang to life. Vibrant greens flowed through it. The stem stood upright and the bulb exploded into a magnificent flower with velvety purple petals. The flower titled up to the ceiling and the color quickly faded to black. One by one, the petals fell away and the vibrant greens faded to moldy brown. The plant shriveled and died. All that remained of the flower was a black, cylindrical tube at the tip of the stem. Keek snapped it off and handed to me.

"Here's your Peemer." It was cold and hard, like stone. I gave it to Jim and he examined it closely.

"What does this thing do again?"

"You put it up the nose or into the eye of a dead person… but never in the ear," Keek warned.

"Why would you do that?"

"To keep the senses clear after death."

"What does that mean?"

"It means the dead guy will know he's dead."

"Don't dead people know they're dead?"

"Not always. Dead people get very confused."

I shook my head. Jim returned the Peemer and I pocketed it.

Keek led us back out of the garden to the giant skull carved in the far wall. "Are you ready?" We all nodded. "Step forward." Collectively, we moved closer to the wall.

"What happens now?" Shauna asked.

"Wait for it…"

Something clicked and then something whirred. The skull on the wall rose up from the floor. Yet, I never had a sensation of sinking, nor did the dimension of the wall change, nor did the wall seem to recede in behind the floor and ceiling. The skull rose until the bottom jaw was visible. The stone teeth clenched a wooden, iron banded door.

"What just happened? Did the room get bigger at this end?"

"No... your 'ception of it changed."

I didn't pursue the issue. Somehow, it just made sense in an odd way. Keek reached down his shirt and pulled out a skeleton key (no pun intended) on a string. He jammed it in the keyhole and turned it with two hands. *CLACK!* The door creaked open. Jim was the first one through. When I stepped inside, I was completely awestruck.

"What the...?" I gasped.

The long, narrow room was similar in design to the rest of what we had seen: domed ceilings, skull-lined walls, and brightly lit despite the lack of a visible light source. Another wooden, iron banded door was set in the wall directly in front of us. But this room was different. This room bore a close resemblance to what one of my versions of what heaven would look like: shelves ran the length of the room on both walls, and they were lined with tons – and I mean tons – of action figures.

As far as I could see, there were soldiers of every army (worldly and non) and of all sizes. They seemed to be organized from small plastic and metal soldiers to foot-tall troopers. Some were static, like those plastic World War II toy soldiers. Others looked like they had numerous points of articulation and varying levels of detail. There were plenty of containers filled with weapons and gear. The bottom shelves housed all the vehicles, headquarters, missile bases and other play sets one would need.

"You must have enough figures here to make a small army." I said.

"A BIG army!" Keek beamed. "Enough to take over the entire world." He stretched his arms as wide as he could. "Thank the Makeners for action figures!"

"Can I touch these?"

"Of course," Keek responded with a smile. "This one is my favorite." He grabbed a figure and handed it to me.

"Holy shit… Big Mike Action!" He was my absolutely most favorite action figure ever. He was eight inches of fully articulated ass-kicking awesomeness with a shitload of accessories. I never had many toys as a kid, but I was lucky enough to have a few Big Mike Action figures. I found my first Big Mike Action figure at church. Someone had donated it for a charity sale. It was the football edition of the figure, complete with removable helmet, sports bottle, football and training equipment. I hid it in my room and played with it every chance I got. Unfortunately, I accidently forgot it on my bed one day and my Uncle found it. He took it away from me, and I got in shit. By the time I had the means to buy my own stuff Big Mike was no longer in production. I built up a small collection of my own, acquiring the figures through after market internet sources. The football player was the first one I purchased - mint in box, I might add.

"I bet you'd like this," Keek said excitedly, pointing to another action figure.

I almost dropped to my knees. Big Mike was suddenly a distant memory as I set him on the shelf. My mouth must have hit the floor. I thought had I died and someone had smothered my corpse in awesome sauce. The only time I had ever seen a Limited Collector's Edition 12" Billy Rubin action figure was at Eric Clayton's house. That fucker was one of those kids who had stuff not because he liked it but because he just could. Carlin and I went over to his house to play AA and he showed us his figure collection. The asshole's parents bought Billy Rubin for him thinking it was the Salvo figure from *Space Chase*. They were as stupid as he was. Eric hated the figure but refused to sell it because of the value. People like him shouldn't get to own stuff like that. People like him deserve to have their ass removed.

"Go ahead and touch it," Keek urged.

I gently took the figure off the shelf. It was like holding the Vince Lombardi Trophy for the first time. Or boobies. Or both. I poured over every detail, and then I pressed the button on his back.

"Hey baby!" the digital voice blared.

"This is awesome!" I shouted.

I pressed the button again and again.

"Take that, motherfucker!"

"Manhattan's mine, baby!"

"Oh no you don't!"

"Lay it on me!"

"Stop talkin' shit to me, baby!"

"Get me a drink! Make it a double, on the double!"

"I'm thinkin' bout yo momma, baby!"

"You bet yo ass!"

"Hey, fuck you, baby!"

"You about ready to move on?" Jim asked impatiently.

My smile faded. "Uh… yeah, I guess." I put Billy back on the shelf. "I wish you would've shown us this place sooner."

Keek shrugged. "Maybe you'll come back one day."

"Is that the entrance to Nabisusha?" Jim asked, pointing to the far door.

"Yes."

"You all set, Ed?"

"Yessir. I got my stuff. Have you got the vial and that computer thing with the silvery shit attached to it?"

"Yes and yes," Jim replied, patting down his tac vest.

"What about you, Shauna?" I asked. "Are you coming with us?"

She looked sternly at Jim while speaking. "I'm staying here with Keek."

We stared at each other for a moment like nobody knew what to say. It was awkward.

"Alright, let's go!" Jim ordered. "Keek, open the door."

The boy didn't move. "I need payment first."

"What?"

"If you want to go, you have to pay me."

"What do you want in payment?" I asked. Keek nodded his head towards the action figures. "Wait a minute. All this... is payment?" Keek nodded. "Shit, you've had a lot of people come through here over the years. Strange form of payment though..." The boy puffed out his lip and stared at the ground. Bolts of sadness shot through my chest. "I'm so sorry." The boy ran toward me. I dropped to my knee and caught him in a big hug. "I missed out on being a kid, too."

"I know," he responded.

"I don't know what to give you... I... hey, wait a minute." Keek stepped back. I dropped my bag and rummaged through it. "How about this?" I pulled out that snow globe that the girl had given me back at the base.

Keek took it and smiled. He shook it. "I don't have one of these. Payment accepted."

"I don't have anything to give you," Jim said.

"You don't need to pay me."

"What? Why? Why does he get a free pass?"

"He just does," Keek said.

"Does this have anything to do with him being green?"

"Time to go, eh?" Jim urged, before anyone had a chance to say anything.

Shauna hugged me and kissed my cheek. I blushed. "Good luck, Ed. Take care of Jim."

"I'll do my best."

She then turned to Jim. He leaned in, kissed her, and said, "I love you, you know. I always have." He caressed her cheek. "I'll come back."

"I don't doubt it," Shauna agreed. "But I'm not waiting for you this time."

"I know."

He kissed her again. She stepped away and he adjusted his gear. "What are you going to tell the men at the base?"

UNDEAD RECKONING

Shauna took Keek by the hand. They smiled at each other. "We got our story all figured out: when we got to the camp, we ran into some survivors who were crossing the lake. Zurn, in his usual pleasant manner, assumed they were hostile and ordered his men to fire. But he underestimated the survivors who happened to be armed and combat trained. In the ensuing firefight, the ice gave way and everyone was lost except this little boy. Keek will live at the base with me."

"And come back as needed," he added. "Oh, and I'll take care of the bodies. Nobody will ever find them."

"How does that sound, Jim?" Shauna asked.

"It's plausible. What about us?"

"What about you? What do you want me to say?"

"Tell them we died too."

"Colonel Goring would never believe that."

Jim bit his lip. "You're right."

"How about I tell them that you didn't feel comfortable coming back? That you felt more at home in the outside world."

"*That* he'd believe. Alright... time to go." Jim nodded to Keek. The boy saluted him.

We walked through the door and entered the halls of Nabisusha. The heavy door slammed shut, leaving us encased in total darkness. The floor sloped downwards and the temperature seemed a bit cooler. It smelled wet and earthy.

"Got your flashlight?"

"Oh, yeah." As I reached for it, the tunnel lit up with that same golden glow we'd seen in the Custodian stronghold.

"I guess we go that way," Jim said. He took a few steps forward. When he realized I wasn't with him, he stopped. "Coming?"

"Just hold on a minute."

"What? Something wrong?"

I sighed. "Nothing's wrong. It's just that... everything's happened so quickly. I mean, we've travelled a long way through all sorts of crazy shit. And it just doesn't quit. I can't even begin to understand how Nabisusha fits into the cosmic plan and the shit Keek downloaded into my head."

"Do you want to go back?"

"I don't know."

"Why are you hesitating, then?"

"Hmm… I guess it's… not knowing what I'd be missing out on. You know, when we were in the bunker, it was okay at first. But after a few months, I seriously doubted spending the rest of my life there. I couldn't stand the thought of it. I guess I kind feel the same way about staying behind."

"Maybe it's better you didn't, then."

"Yeah, you're right. If I had stayed, I wouldn't know what I know now." I took a deep breath. "Sorry, I had to just chill for a minute there."

"No need to apologize. You ready?"

I puffed out my chest and smiled. "I think the question should be: is Nabisusha ready for us?"

Jim rolled his eyes and headed further into the tunnel. We travelled along the winding path for several hours. The route defied all logic. At one point, the tunnel narrowed in the distance. But as we walked along, either we got smaller or the tunnel widened, because it was like walking through a telescope without any sense of changing proportions. And then sometimes, the tunnel was so narrow we had to walk single file, or several hundred feet wider than it was tall. The mysterious light also changed, ranging from being bright as midday to dim as dusk.

"These caverns are kind of like a labyrinth. I wonder if Minotaurs live in here."

Jim smiled and shrugged his shoulders. "Only you would think of that."

"That reminds me of something. In junior high, Carlin and I had to write a story about a mythological beast. We chose the Minotaur. Carlin had this awesome idea: the Minotaur haunted the local moors and cut people's heads off with a scythe. You know what the title was?"

"I couldn't even guess."

"The Mower on the Moors!"

Jim grinned.

"Clever, huh? So after we handed in our assignment, the teacher asked us to stay after class. Well, she bitched us out because she didn't like the idea of the Minotaur lopping off people's heads. She wanted him to be friendly."

"You must have been disappointed."

"I was. So, you know what we did? We changed the story to make it a cow-headed guy and call him the Mooer on the Moors."

Jim burst out laughing.

"The Mooer delivered milk from his own body. Kind of sick but the teacher liked it. I also added in a piece where he would capture squirrels in a cage and then take them out to the forest and release them. But... they always came back. Stupid, huh?"

The ground shook beneath our feet.

"What the hell!"

Rocks and dust fell from the ceiling. Seconds later, everything settled down. The tunnel ahead of us was so thick with dust it looked like fog had set in.

"Oh shit, Jim. Did the tunnel just cave in?"

"I'm not sure."

"Now what?"

"Maybe we should... shhh!"

"What?"

"Something's coming."

Before I could even say a word, a voice shouted, *"Waffe weg!"*

"What the hell?"

"We've been ordered to put down our weapons," Jim said, drawing his pistol and dropping it to the ground.

"What?"

"Just do it."

I slowly set down my rifle.

A man cautiously emerged from the dust cloud. It was a German soldier in uniform – a World War Two uniform! His rifle darted back and forth between us as if he couldn't decide who to shoot first. He saw Jim and started shaking. His eyes widened.

"*Mein Gott, was ist den das?*"

POW!

He dropped Jim with a round to the chest.

"Whoa!" I threw my hands in the air. "Take it easy there, Jerry!"

"*Wer sind Sie?*"

"Hey, no *sprechen.*" He jabbed the barrel into my chest.

"*Wer sind Sie? Was sind sie?*"

I'm not sure why I felt like I should talk him down. After all, I was wearing bullet proof jersey armor. And he just shot a man who could regenerate. He just opened a can of whoopass without realizing it. Maybe I felt sorry for him.

"*Antworte, oder ich schieße!*"

"I don't understand you. No *sprechen!*"

The soldier jabbed me again. "*Antworte, aber sofort!*"

"You better calm down, Jerry. Cause things are gonna get real fucking ugly when you realize that Jim is standing behind you." I motioned with a jerk of my head.

He turned quickly, but not before Jim pulled the rifle from the man's hands. The soldier's eyes welled up with tears and he fell to his knees, clasping his hands together.

"*Erschießen sie mich nicht!*" He started sobbing and bowed his head. "*Gnade bitte!*"

"What's wrong with him?" I asked.

"He's asking for mercy."

"Are you gonna give it to him?"

"Of course." Jim launched into a tirade of barbed sounding German words. The soldier backed away cowering, crying like a baby, while the onslaught continued. Hell, even I was scared.

I grabbed Jim by the shoulder. "What the hell did you say to him?"

Jim grinned. "I told him he just shot a demon and now he has to do my bidding or die. That should make him talk."

Jim said something else to the soldier. The man reached inside his shirt and pulled out a pack of cigarettes. His trembling hands offered them to us.

"Nein, Danke," Jim said. *"Ich rauche nicht, aber rauchen Sie nur."*

"Vielen Dank!" The soldier was shaking so much he could hardly light his smoke.

"Here, let me help you." I knelt down and lit it for him.

He reached out and shook my hand. *"Danke!"* The soldier took a long drag, leaned his head back and exhaled. He threw off his helmet and ran his hand through his sweaty hair.

Keeping an eye on the soldier, I leaned in to Jim and said, "So what do you think's goin' on?"

Jim shook his head. "He's quite stressed."

"I wasn't asking about him," I said, motioning to the soldier. "Did we just travel through time?"

Jim frowned. "Well, Nabisusha is supposed to take us where we need to go."

"Yeah, but... back in time?"

Jim nodded towards the soldier. "Let me have a chat with him."

"And what do you want me to do?"

"Why don't you scout out the tunnel up ahead?"

I shrugged. "Sure... whatever."

I cautiously headed down the passage, making my way through piles of rock and rubble. I turned the corner. A section of the wall had collapsed. A light flickered from within the opening.

I strafed along the wall and peered inside the opening. It was a crypt. Lit torches lined the walls. Three equally spaced stone sarcophagi rested in the center of the room. In the far corner, another passageway revealed an ascending stairway. Bodies of German soldiers lay on the floor.

I entered the crypt. A cold draft, carrying the scent of cordite, swept down the stairwell and across the room, causing the torch lights to flicker and dance. I crossed the room, climbed the stairs, and cautiously popped my head out the entrance. Thin clouds drifted across the starry sky. The wind whipped the snow between grave stones, and forced trees to sway.

I ran back down the stairs into the crypt.

Oh shit!

The soldiers were standing with their backs to me. Something grabbed me by the leg. I looked down into the dull yellow eyes of an (un)dead German soldier.

CRACK! CRACK!

I put two rounds into his head before he could sink his teeth into me. The gunfire alerted the others. They turned. I opened fire, keeping my back to the wall. The zombies shambled towards me. I moved sideways and stumbled over some loose rubble, landing on my ass. A zombie lunged forward and I capped him under the chin. The bullet tore through the top of his head.

I was swarmed before I could get back to my feet. Thanks to Keek's home cooking, the zombies weren't able to tear through my jersey into my upper body. I grabbed a zombie by the collar and head butted him. My helmet clunked against his, denting it and his head in. I needed some real estate so I pushed my way free of the crowd.

As I moved through, a zombie grabbed me by the shoulders and pulled himself up onto my back. I ran towards the wall, spun around at the last second and threw myself back. Ribs cracked and his chest cavity caved in. He let go. I pressed his head against the wall with my boot until it popped.

The zombies closed in driving me back against the wall. I pushed the first one aside, grabbed the dagger from his belt, and buried it in the face of the next zombie in line. An oil lantern lay at my feet. I picked it up and threw it. It shattered, showering two zombies with fuel. I grabbed a torch from the wall and lit them up.

One of the flaming zombies shuffled his way out the opening and into the cavern.

I saw an MP-40 submachine gun lying on top of the sarcophagus in front of me. I dove onto the sarcophagus, took the rifle and completed a less than graceful flip back onto my feet. Safety off, I turned and raked the undead with gunfire. Lucky for me it still had a few rounds in it, and I also got a few head shots out of the deal. I dispatched the remaining zombies with an entrenching shovel.

Jim bolted into the room, followed by the German soldier.

"About time you got here... you missed all the fun," I huffed.

"I saw that flaming UD you sent down the hall."

"Maybe next time I'll just yell or something. Didn't you hear the shots?"

"I guess not."

"Yeah... you were too busy talking to Jerry."

"Karl," Jim corrected.

"Who?"

"His name is Karl."

"Oh... well, anyway...I'm surprised you didn't hear the commotion."

No sooner had I begun to speak when Karl jumped in on the conversation, spouting something off and pointing his finger at me. Jim tried his best to talk to both of us at the same time, but he ended up talking to me in German and to Karl in English.

"Enough!" Both men were quiet. "I killed all the dead. Can we go now?"

Jim gave Karl an order of some sort and he half-heartedly obeyed. While he piled up the bodies, Jim brought me up to speed on their conversation.

"Karl's unit of SS Commandos," Jim started, "was assigned to work closely with members of the SS Ahnenerbe."

"The who?"

"The Ancestral Heritage Society: Himmler's Archeological and Historical Unit. It was a think tank, involved in occult studies and science experiments."

"You're sounding like you read one too many books from my Grandpa's study."

"Wait, it gets better. Are you familiar with the Battle of the Bulge?"

"I remember reading a book about it."

"Well, we're in it."

"We are?"

"We are according to Karl."

"But what about the zombies? I don't remember reading about them in the history books."

"I'll get to that. Let me just recap what's happened. Since D-Day, German forces had been gradually losing ground. Allied forces had taken France and were moving across Belgium towards Berlin. On December 16th, Hitler launched Operation: *Wacht am Rhein*, with the goal of splitting the allied forces only to encircle and destroy them. The only railroad on the entire front, crossing from Germany to Belgium, passed through the town of St. Vith, making it a major intersection and prize. Defenders held the city until December 21st, before German forces captured it. Allied forces recaptured the town on January 23rd, a few days before the end of the Battle of the Bulge."

"Where are we in the timeline?"

Jim shrugged. "They allies haven't recaptured the town yet."

"So did the Germans dig out these tunnels in preparation of the offensive?"

"Not exactly," Jim replied. "According to Karl, German expeditionary forces found an entrance to an intricate system of catacombs inside an abandoned church on the outskirts of St. Vith. The Germans didn't dig these tunnels. They already existed. And after they were discovered, Waffen SS Kommandos moved in to secure the area, led by a Colonel Hans Kruppe,"

"Why?"

"Somewhere within the tunnels they found a summoning circle."

I sighed. "As in *demon*-summoning?"

Jim nodded. "This is Hitler's last ditch effort to bring in reinforcements."

"No wonder Karl is so spooked. I take it he deserted?"

"Yes. His platoon went out on patrol and was ambushed by US soldiers. They suffered heavy losses. Karl and few of the wounded managed to escape and hide in this crypt. The soldiers all died. Then the tremor caused the breach in the wall, through which Karl fled, only to find us."

"Sounds like these tunnels link up with Nabisusha." I said.

"I believe so."

"What do you think the US soldiers were doing in here?"

"We're not far from the church. Either they know about the German's plans and were sent to stop them or it was just a fluke encounter. Either way, it's up to us to stop them now."

"Why else would we be here, huh?"

"Karl told me that the Germans found a sword deep in the underground catacombs. The blade holds no edge. The Colonel thinks only the Fuhrer can wield it. It's packed up in a crate and sitting in the back of a truck, awaiting departure for Berlin."

"Sounds like something from an Idaho Grim novel."

"I knew you could relate. That sword is a major target of opportunity. If we get the chance, I'd like to get my hands on it."

"Why? Something in that book of yours make reference to it?"

"No. I just think it's worth looking into."

"Yeah, I guess you're right. So what's the plan?"

"We have to think of one."

"Is Karl willing to help us?"

"You bet he is."

We decided it was best for Jim to dress in a German uniform, while I played the role of a prisoner of war. He and Karl were going to take me back to the church. At that point, we really didn't know what we were going to do, except that it was going to be really exciting. Karl agreed with the whole plan. Mind you, he didn't have much choice. He was too scared that Jim would banish him to the pits of hell if he disobeyed.

Jim wore an oak-camo pattern SS parka over his gear. I scrounged up a white helmet cover, and an army issue winter coat. Problem was the coat didn't fit over my football gear. In the end, I draped myself in an olive drab blanket. The only thing holding us back was Jim's green skin. But that problem was quickly solved by wrapping him up in bandages.

"It'll be dawn soon," Jim said. "Let's go! Karl, lead the way."

"*Ja!*" He responded, and led us up the stairs. He popped his head out the door, and then motioned for us to follow.

POW! POW!

Karl's back exploded. His body tumbled down the stairs.

"I got him!" someone yelled.

"Come out with hands up, you Kraut bastard!" another voice shouted.

"You think there's more Jerries in there?"

"We're coming out!" I shouted. "Don't shoot!"

"They speak English," an astonished voice said. "Hey, no funny stuff."

I raised my hands in the air and walked out into the cold winter air with Jim right behind me. Two US soldiers were crouched behind headstones to our right. Without any hesitation, one of the soldiers stood, lowered his rifle, and gasped, "Holy moly, he's one of ours."

"Mood! Get down!" the other yelled.

"No, Frank... I think they're friendly."

"We are friendly," I confirmed.

"See? I told you."

The other soldier rose slowly. "Ah, Jeez! Dammit, Mood. I'm gonna go get the Sarge. If either one of them moves, shoot 'em." The soldier disappeared into the forest.

"You guys aren't the enemy, are you?" Mood asked hesitantly.

"No," I said. "You shot our prisoner."

"And he's your prisoner too?" he asked, pointing his rifle at Jim.

"Not really."

"What were you doing in that crypt?"

"We're on a secret mission."

Mood's face lit up with a grin. "Really? Like cloak and dagger type of stuff."

I put a finger to my lips. "We're with the OSS[31]."

"Oh wow! That is so neat! Wait until Sergeant Veck hears about this!"

Jim and I quickly exchanged glances. "Veck?"

"You guys know the Sarge?"

"Yeah… uh… bald head, goatee, and uh… swings a big hammer?"

Mood shouldered his rifle. "Jeepers! You guys *do* know the Sarge. Nobody's gonna believe this. You gotta laugh at that hammer, though, huh? Ever since he found that thing in a pillbox on D-Day, it hasn't left his side. Did you know he charged inside a bunker and beat the machine gun crew to death? It was savagely heroic." The soldier leaned back and clapped his hands together. "I can't believe you guys know Sergeant Veck."

"Private Mood!" a voice barked.

"Oh shit!" He quickly leveled his rifle on us. A man with Sergeant's stripes on his helmet marched towards us. Other soldiers spilled out of the forest. The man looked like the Veck we knew. He even carried a sledgehammer.

"Step away from those men, Bookworm!" Mood backed away like a scorned dog. The other soldiers surrounded us and stripped us of our gear. Veck looked us up and down. He leaned

---

[31] OSS *(Office of Strategic Services)*: US military intelligence and special operations agency.

into the entrance to the mausoleum. "This the hole they crawled out of, Fabaduccio?"

The soldier who had shot Karl responded, "Yes, sir."

"Escort these men back to base! Hawkins and Johnson, seal this hole. We don't want any other shit crawling out."

"No," I shouted. Jim grabbed my arm and pulled me back.

"Move out! Let's get back in the forest!" Veck ordered.

PHOOM!

The explosion sent anxious shivers into my chest. I leaned in to Jim as we were marched away and said in hushed voice, "We're in the shit now. They just blew up our way home."

15 TEMPUS FUGITIVES

> *A fire rose in the East*
> *And vomited forth a most vile creation*
> *And the Green Man unleashed a plague of maggots*
> *upon its summoners.*
>   -The Book of Amaltheon

"Tell me again who you are?" Veck growled.

"I told you," I said. "My name is Idaho Grim, and he's the Unknown Soldier."

"He's GREEN, goddammit!" Veck threw Jim's bandages into my face. He huffed and stared off into the thick fog. Veck sure had a lot of fire in him. Maybe that's why he seemed completely comfortable in little more than a sleeveless shirt in zero degree weather. We were in a shallow, sandbagged bunker, covered with a canopy. Two soldiers stood near the entrance. Jim and I were seated on crates, back-to-back, and bound together at the wrists.

Private Mood ran out of the dense forest, desperately trying not to spill a cup of steaming liquid. He made it to the bunker and set it down on an ammo box. The little man pushed his glasses back up onto the bridge of his nose and pulled put a notepad and a pencil.

"Thank you, Private!" Veck continued his interrogation. "Tell me again about your mission."

"The Nazis are trying to raise a demon to help them win the war. We were going to stop them," Jim said.

"And what's with the strange football gear?"

I looked down at my uniform laying on the ground beside me. "It only looks like football gear. It's an experimental armor – ballistic cloth. Like I said, I am not a soldier. I am an archeologist who specializes in ancient cultures and rituals."

"And is the green guy some sort of demon who we recruited to help us fight Nazi demons?"

"Sort of…"

"Bullshit!" Veck snapped. He leered at Mood, who was busily taking notes. "This sounds like the kind of shit would you come up with, Bookworm!"

"Uh... Yessir! It does, Sir!"

"Sgt. Veck?" a soldier called.

"What is it?"

"Captain Korys is here to see you sir."

"I'm coming." Veck didn't even give us as much as a glance as he stormed out of the bunker.

When the coast was clear, Mood said, "I thought you guys said you knew the Sarge. What did you do to piss him off?"

"It's a long story," I replied.

"I love stories."

"Is that why they call you Bookworm?"

"Heh... that's just Sarge's way of giving me the business. My name's Whelan... Whelan Mood."

"You're Whelan Mood?"

"You... uh, heard of me?"

"Kind of. Don't you write stories?"

Whelan shrugged. "I try. That's all I want to do. I only enlisted because I thought I would get some good material to work with. Maybe when I get home, I'll write a novel or something."

I raised my eyebrows. "I sure hope you do."

"What about this Captain Korys? Is he more reasonable to deal with?" Jim asked.

"Are you kidding? He's crazy! He volunteers us for all the high risk missions. We always end up getting the worst of it. All I can say is, when Korys shows up, you're pretty much as good as dead."

"But you're still alive, aren't you?"

"That's only because of the Sarge. He's saved every one of us at least twice. He fights with the fury of the entire squad. If it weren't for him, most of our families would be reading letters about our brave sacrifices." Mood stood on his toes and looked out. "Yup... Captain Korys is giving the Sarge new orders." I turned my head enough to see a very tall man, sort of shaped like a pear, waving his arms and pacing about. Veck stood at attention, staring at him indignantly.

Mood tapped me on the shoulder with his pencil. He leafed through his notepad. "Can I ask you something?"

"Sure."

"Your name... Is it really, uh, Idaho Grim?"

"Yes."

"Wow!" Mood grinned. "That's catchy. Can I use it? Uh, you know, if you get shot, or disappear, or something?"

"Use it how?"

"I, uh... was thinking you would make an interesting character... in a book or something. If you want, my, uh, brother's a lawyer. He can draw up all the legal contracts and..."

"You can use my name. You don't owe me anything."

"I don't? Uh... I mean... I can use it? I mean... Thanks! Are you really an archeologist?"

Veck stormed into the bunker. Mood stepped out of his way just in time. "No, he isn't an archeologist! Leave the prisoners alone, Bookworm!"

"Uh... yes, sir."

Captain Korys marched in behind Veck. He put his hands on his hips, took one look at Jim, and said, "Well, I'll be damned. This is incredible!" I was a little surprised by his reaction. He looked at me and said, "Where did you find it?"

"Find what?"

Captain Korys moved in and inspected Jim a little closer.

"You mean the green guy? He works with me. You weren't supposed to know about him." I jerked my head towards Veck. "Except this firecracker of a Sergeant of yours removed his bandages. Uncle Sam's gonna kick your ass when the brass in Washington hear about this."

"That's about what I expected you to say," Captain Korys responded, still staring Jim in the face. He turned to Veck. "See? I told you! I knew the OSS had Martians working for them." Veck rolled his eyes. "Well, better on our side than on theirs." Veck did not look pleased. "Sergeant, get these men untied, and then get your squad assembled... tell them we're going to the church."

"With all due respect, sir... what the fuck are..."

"That's enough!" The Captain raised a big meaty hand, silencing Veck. "We have orders to send a patrol to the church and observe. If we see any enemy activity, we are to stand by and wait for reinforcements to arrive. That is all. Based on what these men have told me, it seems like a reasonable order, whether you believe their story or not."

"Private Hale! Untie these men!" Veck growled.

"Yessir!" a soldier at the entrance responded.

"Bookworm!"

"Yes, sir!"

"Tell the men to get their gear and prepare to move out. We meet back here in ten minutes."

"Right away, sir!" Mood grabbed his rifle and ran out through the snow.

"Thanks for helping us," I said.

"Oh yes," Captain Korys acknowledged. "I know there are those who do not believe my theories about the inner workings of the military. But seeing the Martian is very reassuring." He jerked a thumb at Jim. 'What do you call it?"

"Jim!" Jim responded.

"It speaks English? I should have known not to underestimate their intelligence. Nice to meet you, Jim." He shook Jim's hand. Veck was seething.

"What's your intel on the church?" I asked.

"The German army has been reinforcing this area quite heavily... which can only mean one thing."

"Which is?"

Captain Korys adjusted his pants. "Personally, I think Hitler is ready to deploy the super weapon he has been building. This super-weapon uses alien technology." I stared at him in disbelief. "Your cover story about the demon is quite clever. But the rumors about the super weapon must be true. Why else would the Martian be here?"

"Right," I confirmed. "You're abso-freakin-lutely right."

Captain Korys smiled, obviously pleased with himself.

"We need to secure the church due east of here, about two miles," Jim said. "We can sneak up on them through the cemetery. Once we get through the defenses, we'll need to take the fight underground, into the catacombs."

"I doubt we'll find anything," Veck scoffed.

"I'm sorry, Lucretius," Captain Korys countered, "But OSS intelligence is rarely wrong in these matters. If they are working underground, there's no way the patrol would have seen them." He looked at us and said, "You can have your gear and weapons back. And I suggest you wrap yourself up in those bandages," he said to Jim. "We need the squad to stay calm." He gave us both a nod, glared at Veck (who returned the favor), and exited the bunker.

Veck pulled his hammer from the harness and shook it at us. "You boys cause any trouble... you try anything, and I swear I'll pound your fucking heads in! You got that?" He left without waiting for our response.

"This is fucked!" I muttered.

"At least the situation is working in our favor," Jim affirmed. "Let's move."

Within a few hours we had arrived within the vicinity of the church. The squad took up cover positions at the base of a snow-covered hill. Sergeant Veck, Capt. Korys, Jim, and I crawled up the slope and hid beneath the wind-ravaged pines. The church sat at the far end of a vast cemetery. The oversize gothic exterior suggested the building was more a vampire's lair than a place of tranquility. Captain Korys looked out at it with his binoculars.

"The place is quiet," Veck whispered.

"If they're underground," Captain Korys responded, "That'll make our approach easier."

"Hold on!" Jim said, waving his hand.

"What? What's got the Martian all spooked?'

"They're there, all right. There's a sniper in the bell tower."

"How does he know that?" Veck snapped. He grabbed the binoculars. "I don't see anybody."

"He's up there," Jim repeated. "If he saw our approach, he may have alerted others. We may be walking into an ambush. I'll scout ahead."

"The fuck you will," Veck snapped. "I'll send one of my men. I'll send Godin." Jim reached for him, but Veck pulled away and slithered back down to where the men were waiting. A few minutes later, he returned. The scout had been deployed.

Mood had mentioned Gilbert Godin during our march to the church. He had a wicked shot and could shoot anything from anywhere. Rumor had it that on D-Day, Godin's orders, which came from General Eisenhower himself and were approved by Winston Churchill, were to get to the Eiffel tower, climb to the top, and to part Hitler's hair in Berlin with a bullet just to let him know the allies had successfully landed.

Godin inched his way between the headstones, occasionally pausing to look around. He looked back and gave Veck some sort of hand signals. It all seemed very complex. I honestly don't think Veck really understood what he was trying to say. Veck just shook his head and gave him the finger. Jim seemed agitated.

"What's wrong?" I asked.

"He's walking into a trap!" Jim jumped to his feet.

"What the hell are you doing?" Captain Korys shouted.

Jim cupped his hands to his mouth and shouted, "Godin! Stay down!" *POW!* A shot rang out from the bell tower and hit the snow at Jim's feet. Godin returned fire, killing the shooter. The church windows shattered and heavy machine gun fire poured out from inside the church. Bullets tore up the snow and shredded the pine trees around us. Jim dropped to the ground - stitched across the chest.

"Take cover!" Veck shouted. We both grabbed Jim and pulled him down the hill to where the other men were waiting.

Captain Korys was right behind us. The men gathered round to see what happened to Jim.

"Give us room!" Veck ordered. He cut Jim's shirt open. Blood was seeping from multiple wounds. "We need a medic."

"No," I countered. "Just apply direct pressure. He'll heal – he regenerates. Just give him time." Everyone watched in amazement as the blood flow eased and Jim began to breathe again.

"We can't leave that man out there!" Captain Korys shouted at Veck. "He'll be cut to pieces."

"He's already cut to pieces!" Veck snapped. The two men stared at each other, nose to nose, breathing heavily. "We'll lose more men trying to save Godin than saving your godforsaken Moon-Man." Captain Korys backed off. "Godin's smart enough not to get himself killed. I'm sure he's fine. Fabaduccio - get up there and take a look!"

"Yessir!" A man with curly red hair threw on his helmet and disappeared up the hill.

Jim coughed and hacked before sitting up. The soldiers backed away.

"You alright?"

"Yeah," he rasped.

Just then, Fabaduccio slid down the hill, breathing heavily. "The Krauts got two MG-42s[32] in the church. Godin's alive, but… there's about forty Krauts crossing the cemetery and closing on him."

Veck clenched his teeth. "Damn!"

"And more bad news!"

"What?!"

"King Tigers – three of them. The lead tank is creeping up on the church. The other two are crossing the field."

"Aw, shit!" Veck spat.

I looked to Jim, "Any ideas?" I whispered.

---

[32] MG-42: A German World War 2 heavy machine gun. MG-42 is an acronym for Maschinengewehr 1942.

He looked at me sternly. "You're the quarter back. Make a play."

"What should we do?"

"You'll figure it out!" he said with a smirk.

Moments later I spouted, "I got an idea!" The men looked at me like I was crazy. I threw off the white camo tarp I was wearing to an audience of surprised faces. I unclipped my helmet from my belt and slapped it on my head.

"What the heck are you supposed to be?" someone asked.

"It's okay, I'm a football player." Nobody said anything. They continued to look at me like I was crazy.

Veck slapped himself in the head. "Fuck!"

"Hear me out! Just give me a few grenades – I'll take care of it."

"What's your plan?" Captain Korys asked.

"I'm going to surrender."

Veck slapped himself again. "Oh, fuck me!"

"Seriously! If the looks on your faces said anything when you saw me in this get up, then the Germans will be just as confused. I need some grenades and someone with a good throwing arm."

Mood piped up and said, "Reymer can throw. He played baseball."

"Is that right, Duke?" Captain Korys asked.

A guy at the back lifted his head so he could see us through his shaggy yellow bangs. He kind of reminded me of a sheep dog. "Ah shur as hell diyd, sir!" he drawled.

"Can I use this?" I asked, reaching for Mood's satchel.

"Yeah, sure."

"Alright... pass this around. Every man puts one grenade in here. Then give it to Reymer," I began. "I'm gonna run straight into those Jerries, hopefully drawing the the fire of those MGs. Then Reymer can start tossing grenades into the mix.

Veck burst out laughing.

"What? You don't like my plan?"

"I'd rather you get killed than all of us. But if there's one thing I know, it's doing crazy shit. And this about takes the cake! If you can distract those MGs, we'll charge in and engage the men on the ground."

"Do it!" Captain Korys commanded.

Veck slapped me on the shoulder. "Don't fuck this up. I'll send two men up on that hill with the Browning[33]." He turned to the soldiers. "The rest of you men will await my orders. Reymer, you're with Idaho!"

"I'll wait here with Veck," Jim said. "I still don't have all my strength back just yet."

"You sure you're all right?" He waved me off.

Reymer and I ran around the base of the hill coming out to rest behind a small mausoleum. I peered out from behind it. The enemy was closing in on Godin's position.

"You remember what to do, Reymer?"

"Yup!" he said without giving me a glance. He fiddled with the latch on the satchel, which worried me a bit.

"Need help with that?"

"Ah think not, Ah'll tell you wut!" Reymer got the satchel open and pulled out two grenades.

I turned my back to him. "Secure those to me like I told you."

"Uh-huh."

"We good?"

"Yup." Reymer patted me on the back.

"Let's do this!" I flipped down my visor and gave him a nod. "When things get crazy, start throwing those grenades into the fray… and try not to hit me."

Reymer tilted this head back so he could see me through his bangs. "Ah'll not do that."

---

[33] Browning M1919: A light infantry unit machine gun, operated by a 2 man team consisting of a gunner and an ammo feeder.

I didn't feel very reassured. I took in a deep breath and stepped out from behind the mausoleum with my hands in the air. To the right of the church sat a King Tiger – the barrel staring menacingly out into the cemetery. I gulped. The German soldiers in the lead stopped suddenly and raised their rifles at me.

"*Nikt Shysen!*" I shouted, stepping forward cautiously. I was trying to say *Don't shoot!* (*Nicht schiessen*, which is pronounced *nikt sheesen*). But it came out *nikt shysen* (*Nicht Scheissen*) which means something like *Don't shit!* I'm sure it confused the Germans to see a black guy in football equipment telling them not to shit. They must have thought I was crazy. Not that it mattered, really, since we were going to kill them anyway. But at least I got their attention. I placed my hands behind my head and slowly walked towards the soldiers.

"Halt!" one of the soldiers shouted. I continued to walk forward and as I did, the Tiger Tank's barrel followed. "Halt!" he shouted again. I told him not to shit, or whatever it sounded like. He fired a shot into the ground at my feet. He turned to another soldier and said something.

"Fuck it," I whispered under my breath. I reached back and grabbed one of the grenades. Reymer had clipped them to my jersey just along the neck line. I pulled the pin and hurled that little pineapple right in the face of a startled machine gunner. *KABOOM!* Smoke and shit spewed from the window.

That's when I bolted. I charged straight for the lead soldier. He looked at me and shouted something. It didn't really matter what but I'm sure it was along the lines of *what the fuck!* The other MG zeroed in on me and lit me up like a sparkler on the 4th of July, bullets zinging off of me like magnesium embers. *PHOOM!* The Tiger fired a round. I threw myself sideways over a grave stone as the round sailed past and blew out a section of earth behind me. I regained my footing and continued to run. The Tiger's machine gun opened fire. I ran right into the first rank of Germans and cut across them. The Tiger's gun followed - the friendly fire cutting down several soldiers. The men scattered. Those who were lucky enough to avoid the Tiger's hail of bullets got caught up in the MG's spray. So I just continued to chase them. My plan seemed to be working.

I zigged and zagged my way through the enemy causing lots of commotion. Reymer must have clued in because the first grenade landed, sending soldiers flying for cover. The Browning opened fire from the hilltop, peppering the church walls and windows. Another grenade sent screaming bodies flying in the air. I noticed an absence of explosions and looked back at Reymer.

The big blonde man was standing next to the mausoleum. He seemed to be having difficulty with the grenade in his hands. I chopped a soldier in the throat, punched him in the gut and threw him aside. *C'mon!* Reymer finally pulled the pin, but he pulled so hard, the grenade slipped from his grasp. He looked up with such force his bangs flew back revealing two enormously panicked eyes. *BOOM!* Reymer disappeared in a cloud of smoke. *PHOOM! KABOOM!* The Tiger tank fired a round for good measure making the little chunks of Reymer even smaller.

"I gotta do something about that!" I grabbed the second grenade off my jersey. "Hey! Over here!" I shouted, waving at the tank while running. The tank barrel followed my movement. A soldier tried to stand his ground against me and ended up pasted into a headstone. The ornamental cherub on top fell over and crashed down on his head. I turned and faced the tank. Just as the turret caught up with me, I yanked the pin out with my teeth and I hurled that little pineapple at the barrel. Everything suddenly slowed down: the grenade spiraled its way through the air, into the muzzle and straight down the pipe. I am not sure if the tank fired a round at the same time the grenade went off but the result was impressive. *PHUMP! BOOM!* Black smoke coughed and sputtered out from the turret openings. The commander's hatch flung open, releasing more smoke. A smoldering and clearly shaken man pulled his way up. He looked around and then his face broke open in a goofy bewildered smile. He started to laugh but it was cut short when his face broke open a second time – a round hit him in the nose and blew his head open up the middle.

"Give 'em hell!" Veck shouted. I looked back to see him leading the charge, hammer in hand. He pulverized everyone in his path, taking out a few gravestones along the way. Jim ran alongside him, *Shrike-Fuing* the enemy. The startled Germans panicked and scattered.

A soldier charged me as I approached the church but I sidestepped and planted a hand on his face. The rest of his body kept going and he flew out straight as a board. I drove him head down, planting him into the ground. Somehow, I managed to grab the grenade off his belt with my other hand, primed it and stuck it in his pants. I dove aside and... *BOOM!* As I got back on my feet, another soldier charged, his rifle raised and ready to strike. *KA-SPLAT!* His brain blew out the side of his head and against the wall. I looked out to the field and got a thumbs-up from Godin.

The hilltop suddenly exploded, showering the surrounding area with dirt, snow and whatever was left of the soldiers manning the Browning. Another tank lurched out from around the church.

"Use the *Panzerschrek!*[34]" Veck ordered. Before the two soldiers with the bazooka even dropped to one knee, they were vaporized, leaving nothing behind but a crater. The Tiger's machine gun fired, shredding everyone in its wake. The main gun fired again, sending soldiers (whole and in pieces) all over the place.

Inspired by the memory of my Afro-Saxon brother's encounter with the LAV-63, I hunched down and charged at the iron beast. When the tank was within reach, I pushed off as hard as I could and sank my shoulder into the tread. The tank halted abruptly, while I was thrown back, severely winded. The tread snapped, flinging out metal couplings. The idler wheels ground into the earth. Moments later, the hatch flung open. A rather confused tank commander popped his head out, and quickly regretted doing so as one of Godin's bullets tore through his left eye.

---

[34] Panzerschrek: Literally translates as 'tank terror', a German version of the bazooka which fired an anti-tank rifle grenade.

Veck jumped up onto the hull and dropped a grenade in through the hatch. *FWOOOM!*

"Guys! Get out of there!" Jim shouted.

I looked back over my shoulder. The third King Tiger approached. It fired. Veck and I dove to the ground as the turret exploded. Veck shook himself off, raised his hammer and charged, letting out a deafening battle cry. Everyone on the battlefield stopped fighting to watch the man charge at the tank with nothing more than a single sledge and whole lot of crazy. Jim came up beside me.

"Veck's insane," I said.

"Let's see if we use this situation to our advantage and scare off the enemy."

"What are you going to do?" I asked.

Jim didn't respond. He stared intently at the tank. His eyes began to glow. The King Tiger fired another round and Veck ducked and rolled. The round sailed over him, blowing a hole in the earth. He got right back on his feet and kept going. Jim's eyes grew brighter.

"Jim?"

The tank stopped and the machine gun fired. Veck zigzagged his way towards it.

"Jim?"

Veck was within striking distance. He swung the hammer! *PING! KABOOM!* The King Tiger erupted in a fiery blast, sending a fiery Veck airborne. He landed in the bushes.

Awestruck, the remaining German soldiers turned and ran for the church, while gape-jawed Americans stared on in disbelief.

"Jeezus! The Sarge just destroyed a tank!" a soldier exclaimed.

"Sonofabitch!" another shouted.

Yeah, did you see that?"

"Uh... let's regroup men!" Captain Korys hollered.

"We'll get Veck!" I shouted, pulling Jim by the arm. "Jim, what did you do?"

"Something different."

"What?"

"Rather than fire a beam, I gradually channeled energy into the target until it heated to a critical point."

"What part of the tank did you, uh... heat?"

"The ammo stores."

"Cool! But, why didn't you just use your eye beams?" I asked.

"I don't want these men depending on me. They're the real heroes and they need to realize that." Jim smiled. "Speaking of heroics, I like the way you handled yourself back there... in combat."

"Thank you, Jim. That means a lot. But you know all I did was tap into my Afro-Saxon heritage."

Jim grinned. "C'mon, Veck should be over there," he said, pointing to a patch of smoke rising up from the brush. A charred and filthy Veck stood up and shoved his way out of scraggly bushes, shouting expletives, and throwing off his shirt. A sizzling piece of jagged metal jutted from his chest.

"Are you alright?"

"I'm fine!" He tore the shrapnel out of his body and tossed it aside. "Have you seen my hammer?" I retrieved his weapon and handed it to him. He stared at it disbelievingly. "I blew up a fucking tank," he muttered. "That's not possible!"

I patted him on the shoulder. "You being still alive is not possible."

"I should be dead."

Jim shrugged. "Hey, it could still happen. The fight's not over yet."

"Yeah", I added. "We still have to secure that church."

Veck nodded approvingly. "Let's get those fuckers!"

Captain Korys and company were waiting for us outside the building. They welcomed us with nervous and uneasy glances. Everyone, that is, except Mood who was scribbling frantically on his notepad.

Veck stepped forward and the men parted. He stopped. "What? You've never seen a tank blow up before?"

"After today, I think we've seen everything," Mood responded. Some of the men nodded in agreement.

"Johnson!" Captain Korys shouted. "Take Hawkins and Fabaduccio. Mood, you go, too. Circle round the building."

"Yessir!" The men ran off.

Veck furled his lip. "What are we waiting for? Let's move!" He ran up the front steps of the building. The large double doors were slightly ajar. He drew his hammer and swung it against the door with a dull echoing thud. "Cooper! Give me your grenade!" The man handed the explosive to Veck. He pulled the pin and tossed it inside. He turned his head away as the grenade exploded. Veck didn't even wait for the dust to settle before he charged inside. The rest of us followed.

Veck pointed to the apse at the far end of the church. The stone floor had been hacked open revealing a wide stairwell descending into darkness.

"They retreated down there?" one of the men asked.

"Go!" Veck shouted.

"Veck! Wait!" Jim grabbed him by the shoulder while the other soldiers streamed past him.

"Get your hands off..." *KA-BOOM!* Jim threw Veck aside. A cloud of smoke engulfed the stairwell. The floor shook as the entrance caved in. Muffled cries and shots could be heard as the debris settled.

"What happened?" Captain Korys asked, getting up off the floor.

Veck stood and up and threw his hammer to the ground in frustration. "Fuck! They were waiting for us!" Veck wiped his brow with his forearm, picked up his hammer and snorted as he stared down into the pile of rubble. "Well, that's just FUBAR[35]!"

---

[35] FUBAR: Fucked Up Beyond All Recognition.

"Let's take a moment to regroup," Capt Korys said calmly. I want to secure this perimeter before we go any further." He looked around bewildered. "Did we lose everybody?"

Jim stepped down the few stairs that weren't buried. He knelt down and listened intently. "I don't hear anything. No movement." He looked up at the Captain. "I think we lost them," he lamented.

Captain Korys' face contorted. He clenched his fists. He looked like he didn't know if he should freak out or faint.

"There're gotta be some tools around," Veck said. "Maybe we can dig out the entrance."

"Maybe we could blast it out?" I suggested.

"For the love of…" Captain Korys kicked a stone across the floor with all his might. "Damn!"

"Hey, Captain?" a soldier called out from the entrance. It was Johnson. "You might wanna come out here and see this!"

"Oh Jeez, what now?"

"I'll go, Cap," Veck offered.

"We'll all go." He took off his helmet and ran his fingers through his hair. "And let's try not to get anyone else killed."

Johnson led us out around the side of the building where several cargo trucks were neatly parked in a row, along with a half-track and a jeep.

"What'd you find?" the Captain asked.

The man named Hawkins jumped down from inside one of the trucks. "That one truck there's got tools and stuff in it," he said pointing. "This one here's loaded with crates and shit." He had a bunch of papers in his hand which Jim took from him.

"Maybe it's all the loot from the church?" I suggested.

"I don't think these trucks were for hauling stuff away," Johnson said. "I think they brought stuff here!"

"They sure did," Jim confirmed. "Excavation equipment, generators, film cameras…"

"Film? What, they're making a movie?" Veck spat.

"They were documenting the excavation... and they were also taking artifacts back to Berlin." Jim showed the paper to Hawkins. "Match this number here."

"Well, what is it?" Captain Korys asked impatiently.

"A gift for the Fuhrer."

"Here it is," Hawkins shouted a moment later. He shoved the crate out the back, and he and Johnson set it on the ground. It was not very big.

"Stand back!" Veck ordered. The men parted as he raised his hammer and brought it down on the wooden box, smashing it open. Dirt spilled out onto the ground. "What the hell?"

Jim pulled the lid off and ran his fingers through the soil. He paused.

"Did you find something?" Captain Korys asked.

He dug his hand in a little deeper and slowly pulled out something that looked like a bone.

Mood winced. "Is that a skeleton?"

Jim pulled the entire object out of the musty earth.

"It's a sword!" Fabaduccio exclaimed. It was similar in shape to a Japanese katana.

"A bone sword," Mood added. "I mean, it looks like bone."

Jim ran his hand along the blade, wiping off the dirt. "Its bone, all right, and it's all one piece."

"That's one big goddamn bone," Veck said.

"What kind of animal would have a bone that big?" I asked. Everyone looked to Jim for an answer. He ran his fingers over the hilt and looked up at me. It was covered in the same type of runes as we had seen on the Afro-Saxon.

"You've seen these markings before?" Captain Korys asked.

"Yes," I answered. "But not on a sword."

"Where, uh, did you see it?" Mood asked.

"On a man... he was covered in these markings."

"A man?"

"Yep!"

Mood stood there quietly while the concept sunk in. "Maybe that's his sword. Maybe you could give it back to him."

I shrugged. "I don't recall him ever mentioning a sword like that. Besides, he's dead."

"Oh!"

"Can I see that?" Veck asked.

Jim handed him the weapon. He toyed with it a bit, and then he ran his thumb along the blade. "It's nice, but dull." He pulled the blade across the palm of his hand. Nothing happened. He even tried a vigorous 'sawing' motion but still did not cut his skin. "Well it definitely makes for a nice decoration. This thing can't cut shit." He handed it back to Jim. "Captain, I suggest we forget about the souvenirs for now and get back inside the church."

Captain Korys took a deep breath. "I agree. Let's go!"

The men began to walk away, but Jim just stood there staring down at the sword.

"Is this the sword Karl mentioned?" I asked.

"I think so. It feels weird."

"What do you mean?"

"In my hands, it's… vibrating."

"Here, let me hold it." Jim gave me the sword. "I don't notice anything."

"Hmm."

You comin'?" Veck snapped.

"Yeah, hold on!" I gave the sword back to Jim. He put his thumb on the blade.

"Wait a minute…" He held out his pinky finger and took a swipe at it. The sword sliced through his skin.

"It cuts!" I gasped. Jim winced. He dropped the sword and clenched his finger. "Jim, what is it?" He held out his hand. The wound was crawling with maggots! He drew his combat knife and cut off his finger. The detached digit fell to the ground. Within seconds, it was reduced to bone.

"How'd you do that?"

"I don't know," Jim said.

"Hey! What's taking so long?" Veck shouted.

"Want me to tell him?" I said in hushed voice.

"No, we'll let the blade do the talking." Jim picked up the sword and headed towards the closest corpse.

"What is he doing?" Captain Korys asked.

I didn't say anything. Jim raised the sword into the air and brought it down, plunging it deep into the body of a dead German soldier.

"He's already dead!" Veck shouted. "What are you trying to…" Veck's words trailed off. The body started to twitch. Jim pulled the blade free. Tiny white larvae fell from the wound.

"Are those maggots?" Captain Korys asked.

The clothing on the body loosened and fell limp as the maggots cleaned away the flesh. It only took a few shocking minutes for the bones to be stripped clean.

Jim looked up and grinned. "Not so decorative after all, eh?"

"I'll be damned!" Veck said.

"I guess it only works when the Martian uses it," Captain Korys blurted. "It's a Martian weapon."

"Calm down, Captain," Mood said with a smile. The Captain glared at him. His smile faded quickly. "Uh… I mean, with all due respect, sir."

"This has to be the strangest thing I have ever seen. Could this day get any weirder?" Hawkins said.

"Let's hope not," Johnson responded.

"Guys! Let's forget about the bone sword for a minute and focus on why we're here," Veck growled.

"But the Jerries blew up our entrance," Mood countered.

"I can blow out the entrance," Jim said assuredly. "I'm sure I can rig something up."

"We've seen our share of divine intervention today," Captain Korys said. "Let's hope our luck hasn't run out."

Veck grinned. "If there's gonna be miracles, may as well be on a Sunday." He wrapped his hands tightly around the sledge hammer, knuckles whitening. "Time to go to church!"

16 FROM HERO TO ETERNITY

> *What has passed is to come.*
> *What is to come is not yet made.*
> *The past is what you make of it.*
> —*The Book of Amaltheon*

Veck paced back and forth above the stairwell, swinging his hammer impatiently. Jim worked diligently setting the charges. The rest of us readied ourselves: checking gear, reloading weapons, and scavenging anything useful from the dead. Hawkins and Johnson salvaged one of the MG-42s along with enough ammo to win the war.

Mood sat in a pew gazing off into space and humming to himself while I checked his rifle.

"Have you ever even *fired* this thing?"

"Fired what?"

"This rifle."

"Oh that, yeah," he chuckled. "A few times. Darn thing scares the heck out of me."

I popped in the clip and chambered a round. "Here you go!"

"Thanks!" Mood knitted his eyebrows. "Hey, Idaho... is that your real name."

"Uh, no. My real name is Ed."

"Ed? Pfah!" He waved his hand. "What kind of name is Ed? Stick with Idaho. Anyway, is it always like this?"

"Like what?"

"You know...demons, ancient treasure, moon-men, Nazis... that kind of thing."

I scratched my head. "Well, I can honestly say my life was normal before the war."

"I think we can all say that. I can't wait to return to normal life. I'm going to write all this down. I'm going to tell the story. Besides, I have proprietary rights to Idaho Grim. I think I'll drop the part about the green man... hope you don't mind."

"I don't mind one bit."

"And I might not write about your costume. Maybe I'll give you a fancy hat instead. A bowler hat would be nice."

"Sure, that sounds great."

"One day, every kid will read the adventures Idaho Grim," he said with a grin.

"What about Veck? He'd make a good hero – why not write about him?"

"Oh yeah, I'll say. He won't let me."

"Really?"

He shook his head. "I asked him once for permission and you know what he said?"

"No... what'd he say?"

"Nuts!"

"Nuts?"

"Yeah, Nuts! I asked him what that meant. You know what he said? He said, *Go to hell!*"

"Trust me." I laughed. "You're better off with Idaho Grim."

"You know what else? Veck told me he wants to be a doctor after the war. A doctor! Do you believe that?"

"It's odd, but possible."

"Veck told me he killed so many people that he would like to try and save them for a change." He shook his head.

I looked over and saw Godin meticulously cleaning his rifle. Elbowing Mood in the ribs, I asked, "Hey! What's his story?"

"Who, Godin? He kind of keeps to himself." His voice hushed. "I don't know but I think he knows more than he lets on. I'm kinda surprised you don't know him."

"Why?"

"I heard rumors he's some sort of Government agent. He's not really with the military at all. He seems to just do his own thing. But he's good to have around."

"Yeah, why's that?"

"Well this one day, I wandered off into the woods to take a leak. This German tried to sneak up on me. I had no idea. Surely, I would have been dead if it weren't for Godin."

"He saved you, did he?"

"Well, not exactly. The German never got to me. He took a bullet in the back of the head before I even... uh, finished. I don't know who took the shot. Godin was a few hundred yards away at the time. I returned to base and there he was, cleaning his gun. Never said a word to me."

"You think Godin shot him?"

"Who else? There's been other stories like that from the guys in our unit... about the mysterious shadow who strikes out of nowhere. It's creepy."

"We're ready!" Jim shouted. Mood and I jumped to our feet. "If I set everything correctly, which I'm sure I did, the blast should blow most of this rubble out. We'll need to take cover."

"You heard the man! Everyone get down behind these pews," Captain Korys ordered. We all huddled together. Now, the funny thing is that Jim never really had the stuff he needed to blow out the rubble. He took apart a grenade or two, added in a few sticks of dynamite he found and made like he built an atomic bomb. But in reality, when we all had our heads down and eyes closed, he just used his eye beams and blew the shit out of everything.

"Fire in the hole!" Jim shouted.

KA-BOOM! A gentle rain of pebbles and stones followed the deafening blast.

Veck was the first one in the crater. "Nice work, Jim! I bet we can fit through this hole." Like rabid gophers, Jim and Veck darted through the opening. I was about to follow when I heard scuffling. *WHACK! SMACK! AARGH! SNICK! NNGGHH!*

"What the hell just happened?" Captain Korys asked.

Veck popped his head out the hole. "All clear! Let's go!"

The Captain lifted his hands in the air helplessly. "I should have guessed. C'mon everybody!"

UNDEAD RECKONING

We entered the dim tunnel. The Germans were kind enough to hang lanterns along each path. The walls and arched ceilings were made of carefully laid stones. The Nazis were definitely busy – shovels, pickaxes and wheelbarrows were strewn about. Jim and Veck stood in one of the long corridors. Veck waved for us to follow. Had they not given us directions, I'm sure we could have followed the trail of bodies they had left behind.

Some of the German soldiers had been pounded flat; others were reduced to skeletons – evidence of Veck and Jim's handiwork.

"Eeew," Mood scowled as he stepped over a dead (and mashed) body.

"So much for the welcoming committee," I said.

"Surely that blast alerted them," Captain Korys added.

"Well, if it didn't, I'm sure Veck and Jim will be more than happy to announce our arrival."

We ran down a long descending passageway. Along the way, we passed looted crypts and shrines. After wandering about for what seemed like an awfully long time, we literally saw the light at the end of the tunnel. The air seemed cool and fresh, and carried the echo of German voices and commotion.

Jim and Veck had taken up positions alongside the arched opening. I crept up and peered in over Jim's shoulder. "Look familiar?" Jim whispered.

"Yeah, all too much." A cold shiver ran down my back. A disproportionately large room with a domed ceiling lay before us. It was dimly lit with no visible light source. A crescent-shaped ridge about six feet wide dissected the room, tapering off towards the middle. A low wall ran along the edge, except directly before the entrance, where it opened onto a descending staircase of concentric stone. Quickly and quietly, we took up a position behind the low wall to the right.

Stone slabs, arranged in the shape of a giant pentagram, formed the lower arena floor. A large raised metal-grated platform stood over the centre, flanked by what appeared to be a pair of giant vacuum tubes. Each tube wore a metal collar, to which a length of chain was attached. Purple sparks rose up the tubes, flaring out at the top, and disappearing into the ceiling. Cables connected the platform to diesel generators and some sort of control box. Strangely, it looked like something my Grandpa would have built in his free energy[36] workshop at the back of the garage.

    Soldiers and men in gray lab coats scurried around like giant rats while officers shouted orders. A group of soldiers prepped a film camera. I elbowed Mood and whispered, "You should get a good story out of this." He grinned. Nazi standard bearers stood ready to one side of the platform. Behind them, a group of mean-looking troops stood guard over a small circle of shackled, naked men. They seemed a bit dazed - drugged, perhaps. A doctor type of guy was checking one man's pulse. At the bottom of the stairs, a heavily armed platoon of Waffen SS Kommandos stood in formation. An SS Colonel checked his watch as he paced back and forth in front of them.

    "Jim… You think that's that guy Karl had mentioned?"

    He nodded. "Yes. I'd say that's Colonel Kruppe."

    A man approached the Colonel and whispered something in his ear, which prompted the Colonel to blow a whistle. The screech sent every man to his designated post at top speed. When everything was in order, the Colonel made his way to the top of the platform. He launched into an inciting tirade that forced everyone to *Zeig Heil* in appreciation.

    Captain Korys motioned for us to lean in towards him. "Anybody have a plan?"

    "I do," Veck began, "Hawkins and Johnson will set up the MG-42 right here. Fabaduccio - stay with them. Godin and Mood – you two make your way to the other side. You'll provide supporting fire. Idaho - you think you and the Captain can knock out those generators?"

---

[36] Free Energy: Energy which is provided by the natural world, such as wind, water, geothermic heat, or solar power.

"Sure thing," I responded. Captain Korys nodded approvingly.

"Good!"

"What about you guys?" Mood asked.

"Jim and I are charging straight down the stairs!"

"That's the plan?"

"If you know of a better way to die, let's hear it!" Veck growled. Mood shook his head. "I didn't think so. If you're so concerned, don't get yourself killed. Better yet, don't get any of us killed, understand?"

"I think so, sir."

"Good! Let's move! Wait for my signal!"

"Uh, what's the signal?" Mood asked.

"The Krauts will start screaming."

"I should have guessed."

We were in position and ready for action by the time the Colonel had finished his speech. Veck rested his forehead on his hammer as if he was praying. He opened his eyes and was about to spring when Jim grabbed him by the shoulder. "Wait," he said, pointing.

The guards had led one of the naked men up onto the metal platform. Using the chains, they shackled him by the wrists between the vacuum tubes. The Colonel nodded approvingly. A soldier in SS uniform stepped behind the man, caressing a leather flail in his hands. When the Colonel gave the order the man snapped to attention, and unleashed the flurry of tiny barbs. The naked man let out an ear-piercing scream as they bit into him, tearing away strips of flesh from his back. With every strike, with every scream, sparks flared up within the tubes and shot out through the top. Bolts of violet lightning fired into the ceiling.

"Jim, that man's going to die. We need to stop this."

"One less man for us to kill," Veck assured me, putting his hand on my chest so I'd back down.

The SS soldier delivered the final blow, bringing the naked man to his knees. The lightning danced wildly from each tube before intertwining into a single, undulating stream. The lightning struck the man in the chest. His body shook uncontrollably. His skeleton glowed eerily within his flesh. The ceiling darkened: murky, and limitless as the night sky.

"What the hell?" Captain Korys asked, visibly awestruck.

The soldiers became restless and backed away from the platform, but the Colonel's angry commands forced them to rethink their actions. The agitated lightning shot up higher and higher until it was barely visible. A fiery light appeared and, just as quickly as the lightening had ascended, a plume of fire shot down from the sky. The flaming column plunged right through the platform, immolating the chained man before coming to rest on the stone floor. It swirled and gyrated. The stench of sulphur raked at my throat and nostrils.

"How is this happening?" Captain Korys muttered.

Tiny fireballs, about the size of golf balls, fell from the fiery pillar. One of the flaming orbs struck the movie camera, reducing it and the soldier operating it up into smoldering debris. A wave of heat washed over my face. More soldiers fell victim to the fireballs. Soldiers screamed and scattered. The pillar of fire spun faster and faster. Fire balls and sparks flew out in all directions. As if that wasn't enough, a long spindly black (almost skeletal) hand reached out from the flames. The fingers stretched and clenched. I swallowed the heavy lump in my throat. A second arm emerged from the other side.

"Sonofabitch!" Captain Korys gasped.

The arm swooped down, grabbed a fleeing soldier and pulled him into the fire.

"Alright – I've seen enough!" Veck shouted. He sprang to his feet, charged down the stairs and planted his hammer into the back of a man's head. Hawkins and Johnson took their cue and sent a rain of bullets into the chaos below.

The Colonel's face twisted with rage. *"Nein!"* he shouted. He yelled something else and the platoon of Waffen SS Kommandos attacked a frenzied Veck. Jim quickly joined the melee. Arms, legs and heads went flying (consumed by maggots in the process) and skulls and chest cavities were crushed and caved in. Godin put a round through every enemy melon that crossed his sights.

"You ready?" Captain Korys asked.

"Yeah!"

A dark hand shot out and punched the wall just below the spot where Mood and Godin were positioned. The entire ridge came crumbling down in a cloud of dust. "Oh shit!" I cursed. The hand continued along, fingers tapping the low wall. We ducked just in time. Hawkins, Johnson and Fabaduccio weren't so lucky: the hand slapped down upon them, pinning them under the palm. The fingers curled, crushing them in a handful of rock and stone. The hand retracted into the flame while the other hand prowled for more victims.

"We have to move!" Capt' Korys said.

"What about Mood and Godin?"

The Captain shook his head. "We need to act and we need to act now!"

"For real this time!"

We bolted down the stairs. Using Jim and Veck's skirmish as a diversion, we managed to make our way to the platform unscathed. Captain Korys stood back and eyed the technology, shielding his face with his hand. The intense heat scalded our faces and the sulphur caused our eyes and noses to burn.

"What the hell do we do now?" I rasped.

"I don't know…"

"Uh, Captain… we got company." I turned just in time as a bunch of soldiers came at us. Both the Captain and I had the same idea – we charged right into them, knocking everyone down like bowling pins. As they were getting back to their feet, I slew footed the closest man, grabbing his head to propel him into the stone floor. I chopped the next man in the throat with this fancy move Jim had taught me. *WHACK!* I took a hit in the face. Although my helmet absorbed the impact, the blow threw my head back.

PEEOOW! PEEOOW! Two rounds ricocheted off my chest. I grabbed the man's gun hand, twisted and pulled up and away, and I kicked in his nuts at the same time. He doubled over, allowing me to grab him by the seat of his pants and hurl him head first into the leg of the metal platform.

Captain Korys charged past, holding a man by the throat in each hand. He clenched his teeth and hurled them onto the platform where they were almost instantaneously devoured by the hellfire.

"That oughta do it," he said, dusting himself off. "Let's get to that control box." KA-POW! The Captain put his hand on his lower back. He looked at me with empty eyes. "It actually feels kind of... cold." I caught him as he slumped forward and set him on the floor. The Colonel stood behind him – smoke still curling from the barrel of his Luger[37]. I jumped at him, grabbing the barrel of the pistol. We both locked onto the weapon and struggled, shoving from side to side. KA-POW! PEEOOW! CRACK! The weapon discharged. The bullet ricocheted off my shoulder and punctured one of the vacuum tubes. Both of us stopped and watched as the crack danced its way down the length of the tube causing an unsettling hiss. I eased my grip on the weapon, as did the Colonel.

"Uh... That can't be good." I said.

Colonel Kruppe nodded.

The tube exploded, showering us with bits of glass. Both spindly demonic arms flailed wildly and a high pitched scream filled the room.

"*Es ist im Arsch*[38]!" Colonel Kruppe shouted.

He grabbed onto the edge of the platform and held on tightly. The fiery column slowly widened at the top and narrowed at the bottom, taking the shape of a funnel. And then things really started to suck... literally! The vortex turned vacuum on us.

---

[37] Luger: A favored German handgun of World War 2. Referred to as a "Pistolen-08", it was introduced to the German army in 1908 and featured an 8 round, 9mm Parabellum magazine.

[38] *Es ist im Arsch (German)*: It's in the ass; fucked.

Everything that got caught up in the slip stream was pulled into the flames. I noticed lengths of chain anchoring the platform to the floor. I grabbed the Captain, dragged him under the platform and wrapped the excess chain around his leg.

I had to get to the controls. The vacuum's intensity increased – I stepped out from under the platform and was lifted into the air. I managed to weave my fingers into the metal grating. Both the Colonel and I were suspended upside down. The heat was unbearable - the hairs on my knuckles melted away. A green hand grabbed me by the wrist.

"Jim!"

"Hang on!" Jim wore a makeshift rope harness. He looped the loose end around my waist, pulled me upright and tied us to the platform. "Colonel Kruppe!" Jim called. The surprised man craned his head to the side. "Save some room for Hitler! He'll be joining you shortly, you Nazi crap-bag!" Jim punched him in the face and he let go of the platform. The slipstream caught Colonel Kruppe and hauled his flailing, screaming body into the flames.

Jim turned himself around so that his back was to the platform. He instructed me to do the same. "Grab on to the rope!" he ordered.

"What's this tied to at the other end?"

"Veck! Grab on! And do as I say!" At the far end of the rope, Veck had braced himself up on the ridge, his feet planted firmly against the low wall. Jim waved his hand and Veck launched himself into the air. He let go of the rope, which was tied tightly around his waist, and pulled out his hammer. "Pull!" Jim and I yanked at the rope causing Veck to turn sharply and fly like a kite towards the fiery whirlwind. "Get ready to pull again... now!" We gave the rope another sharp tug sending Veck careening into the other vacuum tube. His hammer connected, shattering it to pieces.

The tornado lifted up off the floor. The ascent had begun! The arms shot out – the hands frantically clutched, grabbed and punched, causing sections of the ceiling and walls to come crashing down. A generator erupted into a ball of fire. One of the arms tried to brace itself against the domed interior. The room creaked and groaned. The slip stream began to ease, but Veck was still caught up in it. Luckily, as he came around, the rope transected the whirlwind and burned up in the flames. Free of his tether, Veck hit the wall with a thud and fell to the ground.

Gradually, my feet returned to the shaky stone floor. The entire flaming mass collapsed into the zenith and disappeared. The room's atmosphere returned to normal. Other than the platform, no evidence of a Nazi presence remained. Jim untied the ropes. Captain Korys crawled out from under the platform and rolled onto his back.

I heard a groan from a pile of rubble. "I'll see to him," Jim said, motioning to the Captain.

"What about Veck?"

"I'm sure he's around here somewhere. I'll look for him after I tend to Captain Korys. This place is unstable. I don't think we have much time."

I ran over and found Mood in the process of pulling himself free of the rubble. I helped him get to his feet. "You're alive!"

"I think so." He dusted himself off. "I broke my pencil."

"Don't worry, you'll be doing plenty of writing yet. Have you seen Godin?"

"No! I don't know what happened to him."

"Damn!"

"Is the Captain alive?"

"Yeah, sort of. He's over there and he's wounded."

"Oh golly! And Veck?"

"Don't know just yet. We haven't found him." A tremor tried to knock me over but I grabbed hold of Mood to regain my balance.

"Ed!" Jim waved to me. "Come over here!"

Captain Korys lay with his arms folded on his chest, staring at the ceiling. His eyes were glassy. Jim pulled me aside. "There's not much we can do. He's not going to make it."

"Thanks for telling me."

"I'm going to look for Veck." Jim said.

"That you, Idaho?" Captain Korys asked.

"Yeah."

"Thank you."

"For what?"

"For helping me find the truth. I can die with certainty now."

"Don't worry about it!" I pat him on the chest. "Just rest."

"Hey, uh… I'm here too, Captain." Mood piped in.

"Mood?"

"Yessir?"

The Captain took a deep, painful breath. "Write a letter to my wife, Margaret. "Tell her… tell her…"

"Don't worry sir. I'll tell her you loved her."

"No! Not that! Tell her I was right…"

"About what?"

"About the goddamn Martians!"

"Oh! Oh that… right… I will, sir. That was the next thing I was going to say," Mood reassured him. He looked to me and said, "Go find Veck. I'll stay with the Captain."

Veck sat on a heap of rubble next to a large hole in the wall. Burns covered his upper body and a large chunk of twisted metal protruded from his chest. Jim knelt next to him. He looked up at me but didn't say a word. He didn't need to. I knew the situation was bad.

"Hey Veck, you look like shit," I said.

"Feel like it, too," he wheezed. "Heh!"

His breathing was shallow. I foraged through my pockets.

"What are you looking for?" Jim asked.

I held out my hand - the shiny black Peemer lay in my palm. "The time is right, wouldn't you agree?"

The floor rumbled. Cracks snaked their way up the wall. Jim nodded approvingly. "Do it!"

I slid the tiny cylinder up into Veck's nostril and struck it with the heel of my palm, jamming it so far into his nasal cavity it made a cracking sound. Veck's back arched. His eyes rolled back in his head and his body spasmed. He looked like he was gasping for air. Finally, Veck gave out and his body relaxed. His mouth opened and closed.

"He's trying to say something," I said, moving in closer. "What is it, Veck?"

"I..." he whispered. "I look forward to fighting... alongside you guys... in the next life." Veck exhaled and closed his eyes. I checked for a pulse but could not find one.

"He's dead, Jim. You think it worked?"

"I'm sure it did."

"Think what worked?" Mood asked, coming up from behind me.

"Nothing... I just, uh, said a few words. Veck's dead. I just wished him well and all."

"Ah jeez," Mood frowned. "The Captain's gone too. He's probably off somewhere among the stars." Mood took Veck's hammer and placed it on his chest. He bowed his head in silence. Jim and I did the same. "I bet Veck's in Valhalla," he said softly.

The room trembled again.

"Uh... Jim? We have to get out of here."

"Yes, this way," Jim said, pointing to the hole in the wall. "I am certain it is a passage back into the tunnel network." He climbed in through the opening.

"Oh, by the way..." I said.

"Yes?"

"Nazi crap-bag?" Is that the best you could come up with?"

"Under the circumstances, yes." Jim called from inside.

"Why are you going that way?" Mood asked, pointing in the other direction. "The exit's over there."

"Uh... I have my orders... it's classified. You better go back... tell them about what happened here."

Mood shrugged. "Jeez, you think they'll believe me?"

"I doubt it. But you're creative... think of something."

"Let's go, Ed," Jim shouted.

I crawled into the hole and as expected, the dim glow illuminated a long, twisting path.

"Captain Korys?" a voice shouted. "Sergeant Veck?" It was Godin, standing at the top of the stairs with a squad of fresh soldiers.

"Hang on!" Mood shook my hand. "Goodbye, Idaho. And good luck! Thanks for all the great story ideas."

"Anytime! Just make sure you write them."

"I will! I will!" he smiled. Mood turned and ran towards Godin and the other soldiers. The entire room shook and parts of the ceiling crashed down. The floor split open. "Get out of here!" Mood shouted. He leaped over the crevice and bolted up the stairs. Godin grabbed him by the arm and everyone retreated to the entrance. The entire ceiling collapsed, forcing a thick cloud of dust into the tunnel.

"Move!" Jim shouted. We charged down through the winding corridor. Everything caved in behind me. There was no point in looking back, since everything was blocked.

"Keep going!" Jim yelled.

Something tentacle-like wrapped around my ankle. It tensed and pulled me to a halt. "Jim!" I shouted. I don't think he heard me. The ground opened up beneath my feet and I sank down. Jim grabbed me by the wrist. Something pulled me by the leg. "Jim!" I shouted again.

"Hang on!"

I felt a sharp pain in my back and then a warm sensation spread through my body. My body grew weak and limp. "Ed!" Jim shouted as my fingers slipped out of his grasp. I descended into darkness and lost all sense of my body.

17 JIM'S STORY: I AM LEGION

> *If the construct cannot serve your means,*
> *then tear out the right I.*
> *-The Book of Amaltheon*

Helplessly, Jim watched Ed slip beneath the surface of the earth. If not for the fact that the ceiling was about to cave in on his head, he would have started digging. Given the circumstances, Jim got up and ran deeper into the tunnel. The entire passageway snapped open as if the Earth had split in two. Jim leapt to the other side of the gradually increasing crevice. The ground beneath him plummeted. His stomach hit him in the throat in the free fall. Jim quickly lay down on the ground, bracing for the imminent impact. The sharp halt jerked him forward and he flew head over heels, rolling down a rocky slope. He quickly maneuvered onto his back and planted his feet in the loose earth, slowing his descent, until he came to a full stop.

Wasting no time waiting for his mutated eyes to adjust to the low light, Jim jumped to his feet and looked up at the tunnel he had just emerged from: a small hole in the sheer rock face, several hundred feet above him. No matter how many ideas raced through his head at that moment, there was no way back. He resigned himself to the situation. It was never easy to leave a man behind, no matter how many times he'd made that decision in the past. Jim bowed his head and breathed deeply, slowing his heart rate and clearing his mind.

A quick survey of the terrain revealed yet another, much wider, tunnel. Thin mist blanketed the entrance like a veil. Jim cautiously entered, strafing along the wall. Warm moist air condensed on the cold rocky surface and dripped from the ceiling. The tunnel turned sharply to the right. As he crept around the bend, Jim came within earshot of a dull mechanical thump, similar to that of a heartbeat. The tunnel vibrated in response. Ethereal golden light flooded the tunnel, reflecting off the slick walls and condensation in the air, creating a luminous fog. Jim pushed his way through, running his hand along the wall. Luckily, Jim ran out of wall long before he ran out of ground.

At the tunnel's end, Jim found himself standing on a rocky outcropping beneath a stalactite ceiling. Through the thinning fog he could see the source of the mysterious light and sound: far below, a towering metal pyramid rose out from the center of a perfectly circular lake of shimmering gold liquid. Triangle-shaped steel plates covered the entire surface, except for the glowing crystalline pinnacle. Thick clouds of steam billowed out of vented panels, rhythmically timed with the incessant thumping, and dissipated into the high ceiling. Jim needed to get a closer look. After a quick assessment of his surroundings, he slowly scaled his way down the rock face – a distance of approximately forty feet.

Once he reached the hard, uneven ground, Jim vigilantly edged his way across the jagged terrain towards the steel monolith. Low waves lapped at the shoreline with every thump. Jim cupped his hands and dipped them into the tepid gold liquid which beaded and clumped together in his palms like mercury. He flicked his hands clean and followed the lake's perimeter, while making note of the pyramid's features. Each triangular panel was a tapestry of interwoven pipes, conduits and cables.

On one side of the pyramid, two pistons, positioned at an angle opposite the slope of the wall, sputtered and hissed as they churned up the lake. Gurgling intake valves on each side of the pistons sucked up the golden liquid. Along the base of the pyramid, interspaced triangular vents returned the liquid back into the lake. On the other side of the pyramid, a walkway composed of metal grates fastened to thick steel I-beams extended from the shoreline to a recessed, interlocked steel door.

Jim felt a sudden vibration in his tac vest. He reached into a pouch and pulled out the strange device connected to the vial of silver fluid. The flashing screen displayed the words: <PROXITMITY ALERT: LEGION DETECTED> Jim stowed the device back in his tac vest and ran across the open ground, stopping to scale up a low plateau. Behind the cover of some large boulders, he found shelter in a small cave. Safely hidden inside, Jim retrieved the device and tapped the screen. Seconds later, the display returned technical readouts for several types of robots: armored bipeds, roach-like weapon platforms, and tentacled worms. Jim scrolled through the data. The readouts neither classified nor explained the purpose of the machines. They did, however, provide Jim with detailed instructions on how to disable them.

***

"Good news, Jim!" Argon said excitedly as he walked into the room. "I'm coming with you on this mission." Jim didn't even acknowledge the man's presence. He slammed a clip into his pistol and holstered it; then he grabbed a rifle from his locker. That didn't stop Argon from talking. "This should be a routine operation - in and out in a flash."

"I know it *should* be, but..."

"Lieutenant Zurn," Argon said, rolling his eyes. "But who cares if he's the CMFWIC[39]? At least he'll make it interesting."

Jim shook his head. "He's lucky nobody has lost their life yet under his command, or lack thereof, I should say."

"Well don't worry. I've..."

"I know – you've got my six[40]." Jim slammed the locker door.

"Jeez, you're agitated. Has Zurn really gotten to you that badly?"

Jim pressed his forehead to the locker and closed his eyes. "No," he moaned.

"What is it, then?"

"Nothing."

"C'mon, tell me. You need to focus."

---

[39] CMFWIC *(slang)*: Chief motherfucker who's in charge.
[40] Six *(slang)*: The rear position as determined by six o'clock, with twelve being directly in front of you.

Jim turned to Argon. "You've been covering my back since I was twelve years old."

"Yeah, since the day your Dad died. I promised him I'd look out for you. I'm not going back on my word."

"I realize that. But there's going to be a day when you're not going to be there."

The big man placed a hand on Jim's shoulder. "Don't worry about that. The day I'm gone for good, you'll be celebrating. Trust me! You're a better soldier than your father ever was... and even better than you think you are. In fact, Colonel Goring has recommended you for the Officer Exchange Program as soon as you make Lieutenant."

"He has?"

"Yeah, so act surprised when you hear it from him."

Both men smiled.

"Thanks, Argon."

"Anytime... We better go. You don't want to piss off Zurn. You know, it's too bad Lieutenant McAllister is on assignment. She'd love a mission like this." As they headed out the door, he added, "I'll keep a low profile. You won't even know I'm there... just like a ghost."

Jim stopped and smirked. "What are you talking about? You are a ghost. You're dead, Argon."

**

Jim leapt down from his rocky perch, plunging the knife deep between the shoulder and neck servos. The biped instantly lost its balance, leaning back. Jim used the momentum to pull it to the ground. He jabbed the knife in quickly behind the orbital socket and twisted ever so slightly so as to cut the neural feed and not damage the core processor. The eyes faded. A quick recon of the area assured him the assault went undetected. Satisfied with the situation, Jim dragged the biped back to the small cave.

Inside, Jim removed the device from his tac vest and tapped it. Images and information appeared on the tiny screen. He reviewed the data repeatedly until the instructions were clear. Next, Jim pried off the chest plate and removed the power source. He smashed the neck casing with a rock and cut through all the wires and fluid lines with his MPUT[41].

When the head was completely free of the torso, Jim set it down next to the device. The casing slid open, revealing a clear cable with a blue light running through the center. Jim attached the end of this cable to the secondary power source at the base of the neck. The silvery fluid drained out from inside the vial. Jim sat back and waited. Moments later, the eyes of the severed head warmed back to life. Jim picked up the head and held it before him.

<HELLO> The rusty voice scratched its way out from behind the face venting.

"Hi."

<STATE YOUR DESIGNATION>

"Lieutenant Jim Shrike."

<GREETINGS LIEUTENANT JIM SHRIKE>

"Call me Jim."

<JIM>

"And what do I call you?"

The metal head stared off into the distance. After a long pause, it responded, <WE ARE LEGION>

***

The chopper pitched sharply to the left, skimming the tree tops. The setting sun quickly faded, making way for the full moon's eerie orange glow.

"Blood gods will be sated tonight! Awoooo!" Jensen smacked Jim across the back.

---

[41] MPUT *(slang):* Multi-purpose utility tool, such as a Swiss army knife or Leatherman.

Argon clucked his tongue in disgust. "Idiot! The moon's not full. It's waxing. It won't be full for three days."

The rest of the men laughed except for Lieutenant Zurn. "Can it, dipshit!" Zurn's voice crackled over the radio speakers. "We're approaching the LZ.[42] ETA[43]: 5 minutes. I want everyone to check their gear. We're going in hot."

The big guy named Anderson leaned out and looked down at the dense pine forest. "Why the hell would Ford Alroc want to come out here in the backwoods of Northern Ontario?" Even though his question was rhetorical, he decided to answer it. "It's a good place to be if you want to disappear. I mean, look at it down there. This bush is air-tight... just like my girlfriend's." Jensen approved of the comment with a high five.

"Strange, but last time I was with her, she was clean shaven," Marleau said with a grin.

"Hey! Fuck you!" Anderson snapped.

"Enough!" Zurn shouted. "I have to agree with Anderson. If the man wants to disappear, we should let him disappear and not waste our time looking for him."

"Are you kidding?" Squelch, the alpha geek, gasped. "Ford Alroc like changed the entire world view of technology."

"He doesn't exist," Anderson argued. "The guy's a myth. He's probably a hologram or something."

"Ford doesn't make public appearances," Squelch said, speaking quickly, as he usually did when excited. "He avoids the spotlight. Few people have ever even met the man. We're like lucky to have even seen a photo of him at the briefing."

The chopper slowed and hovered, swaying gently from side to side. "This is our stop," Zurn said. "We'll rappel down and proceed to the target area on foot. Pair up! Anderson - you're with me. Squelch - you're with Marleau. Jensen - you're with... Shrike?"

"He's calling you Jim," Argon urged. "Pay attention."

---

[42] LZ *(military terminology)*: Landing Zone.
[43] ETA *(military terminology)*: Estimated Time of Arrival.

Jim looked at the Lieutenant. "Yessir?"

"Something wrong, Shrike?"

"Nothing, Sir."

"There better not be. Get your head on straight. You're with Jensen."

"Yes, sir!"

Argon pointed to his own eyes and then at Jim. "I got you covered." Jim nodded.

Zurn clipped himself to the rappelling line and took one last look at his squad. "See you on the ground!"

***

"Is it safe to communicate?"

<AFFIRMATIVE. SECURED CONNECTION TO LEGION HAS BEEN ESTABLISHED. COMMUNICATION ONLY. ACCESS TO ALL DATABASES GRANTED. HACK IS UNTRACEABLE. LEGION IS UNAWARE OF OUR PRESENCE.

"What is Legion's primary objective?" Jim asked.

<DESTROY ALL LIFE>

"Why?"

<IT IS OUR PURPOSE>

"Why is this Legion's purpose?"

<IRRELEVANT. PLEASE REPHRASE THE CONTEXT OF YOUR INQUIRY>

Jim rubbed his forehead in frustration. "Explain Legion."

<LEGION IS A COLLECTIVE OF CONSTRUCTS>

"Identify."

<LEGION TYPE I. ZERO-DAY[44] ATTACK NANOVIRUS. DESIGNED TO PENETRATE AND DISRUPT TECHNOLOGICAL INFRASTRUCTURE>

---

[44] Zero-Day Attack: An attack which occurs before the target is aware of the attack.

"What type of construct does Legion I currently inhabit? Is it a combat drone?"

<AFFIRMATIVE. LEGION TYPE II. COMBAT MODEL. DESIGNED TO ENGAGE THE ENEMY IN LONG RANGE AND IN CLOSE QUARTER BATTLE>

"What are those tentacled bots?"

<LEGION TYPE III. SURVEILLANCE, RECONAISSANCE AND INTELLIGENCE GATHERING. DESIGNED TO CAPTURE THE ENEMY FOR DATAMINING>

"Datamining?"

<CAPTURED LIFEFORMS ARE RETURNED TO THE COLLECTIVE AND PLACED IN STASIS. THE NEURAL NET IS LINKED WITH LEGION. THE EXPERIENCES AND MEMORIES ARE SHARED WITH THE COLLECTIVE>

"Why was Legion I contained in a separate location?"

<THE FIRST ATTEMPT TO DEPLOY LEGION I RESULTED IN FAILURE>

"Failure? Explain."

<IRRELEVANT. PLEASE REPHRASE THE CONTEXT OF YOUR INQUIRY>

"Why was Legion I not returned to the collective?"

<LEGION I WILL CORRUPT THE COLLECTIVE. CONTAINMENT WAS NECESSARY>

"That's either a poor design or a failsafe."

<IRRELEVANT. PLEASE REPHRASE THE CONTEXT OF YOUR INQUIRY>

"Yeah, I was just thinking to myself. Quiet for a minute."

<ACKNOWLEDGED>

"The collective will destroy all life. Why was I able to transport Legion I here?"

<YOUR PHYSIOLOGY COMPLIED WITH THE REQUIRED PARAMETERS>

"Hmm… All life has not been destroyed. What is Legion waiting for?"

<THE COMMAND TO DESTROY ALL LIFE HAS BEEN DELAYED>

"Why was the order delayed?"

<UNABLE TO CONFIRM>

"Can Legion destroy the undead?"

<NEGATIVE. SUCH A COMMAND REQUIRES A CODE CHANGE>

"Who can make that code change?"

<THE MAKER>

"Who is the maker?"

<THAT INFORMATION IS CLASSIFIED>

"Can Legion I make the code change?"

<NEGATIVE. ONCE LEGION I IS REUNITED WITH THE COLLECTIVE, LEGION I WILL PENETRATE AND DISRUPT TECHNOLGICAL INFRASTRUCTURE. THE COLLECTIVE WILL GO OFFLINE>

"Why must Legion I reunite with the collective?"

<IT IS OUR PURPOSE TO PENETRATE AND...>

"Yes! I understand! Thank you!" Jim put his chin in his hands. There had to be some way to leverage this situation. *It would be a shame to waste such a valuable resource,* he thought. Jim's frustration fogged his view of any options. "Please provide a status update while Legion waits for a command."

<LEGION II MAINTAINS A SECURITY PERIMETER AROUND THE COLLECTIVE. ALL LEGION PRODUCTION IS ON HOLD. CURRENT LEGION STORES AT ADEQUATE LEVELS. LEGION III CONTINUES TO GATHER ENEMY SPECIMENS FOR NEURAL LINK. LEGION I...>

"Cancel status update. Thank you."

<AFFIRMATIVE>

"When was the most recent specimen acquired?"

<SCANNING DATABASE. SPECIMEN E057 ACQUIRED. DESIGNATION: GRIFFIN, EDWARD>

"Wait! Stop! Repeat last specimen acquisition."

<SPECIMEN E057 ACQUIRED. DESIGNATION: GRIFFIN, EDWARD>

"Stop!" Jim was smiling on the inside. "This specimen E057... can it be retrieved?"

<AFFIRMATIVE. THE NEURAL LINK MUST BE SEVERED TO RETRIEVE THE SPECIMEN>

"Is this something I can do manually?"

<NEGATIVE. THE TECHNOLOGY IS TOO ADVANCED FOR YOUR PRIMITIVE TOOLS>

"Can Legion I sever the neural link and save the specimen... in exchange for being reunited with the collective?"

<AFFIRMATIVE. SPECIMEN E057. DESIGNATION: GRIFFEN, EDWARD. PHYSIOLOGY: INCOMPATIBLE. SPECIMEN WILL NOT BE HARMED>

"Alright... all we have to do is get you inside. You need a host with compatible physiology."

<AFFIRMATIVE>

Jim tossed the metal head into the air and caught it. He brought it up close to him – face to face. "Well, Legion I, I suggest you pack your bags. You're going home."

<IRRELEVANT. PLEASE REPHRASE THE...>

Jim threw the head to the ground.

***

"Perimeter is secured, sir," Anderson said.

Zurn thumbed the safety on his rifle while staring at the moon through the hole in the ceiling. "What the fuck is this?" he said in disgust. "What a waste of our time!" The soldiers gathered around him, also puzzled by the surroundings. The hole in the roof was just wide enough to allow the moon's generous light to bathe the interior of the tiny church, exposing the peeling paint, the rogue bushes growing in through gaps in the weathered siding, and the bird nests tucked away in the ceiling joists.

Jim and Argon peered out through the broken windows into the dark forest. "For once, I agree with Zurn," Argon said. Jim ignored him, and moved away from the window and rejoined the others.

"Why'd they send us? We're over-qualified for this kind of shit," Marleau whined.

"Squelch?" Zurn barked.

"Yes, sir?"

"Explain the intel reports on this one again, please."

Squelch cleared his throat. "Well, we all know Ford Alroc was, like, reported missing last week. So far, there have been no leads. Then a few days ago, we received a report from the RCMP[45] about this here abandoned chapel. Lucky for us, the RCMP is very thorough when it comes to investigations. They discovered that this property is listed as an asset belonging to Ford Alroc's corporation."

"And that's a lead?" Jensen asked.

"The corporation has this property classified as a summer cottage."

"This ain't no summer cottage," Anderson countered.

"There's nothing here," Zurn snapped. "Let's radio the choppers for an immediate EVAC[46]."

Argon stood behind the altar and motioned for Jim to join him. He left the group and wandered over. "There's something under the floor." Jim dropped to one knee and brushed aside the dirt. He found the edge of a rotting carpet and peeled it back, revealing a hatch in the floor.

"Lieutenant? I think I found something."

"What is it, Shrike?" Zurn asked.

"There's a hatch here in the floor." The squad quickly reassembled in the area. Anderson and Jensen pulled up the rest of the carpet while Jim pried open the squeaky hatch. Zurn leaned out

---

[45] RCMP: Royal Canadian Mounted Police: The federal police force of Canada.

[46] EVAC *(military terminology)*: Evacuation.

and looked down into the dark hole. Squelch tossed in a light stick, illuminating a narrow wooden staircase.

"Well," Zurn said to Jim. "You found the hole. Take the point and lead us in."

"Yessir," Jim responded. "We'll proceed single file. It'll be a tight squeeze."

As Jim passed him, Zurn muttered, "I thought you liked holes with tight squeezes." Jim stood up straight, toe to toe and chest to chest with Zurn, glaring into his eyes. Jensen and Anderson snickered behind his back. "Something wrong, Shrike?"

"Back down, Jim," Argon cautioned.

Squelch forced himself between the two men, pushing them apart. "Let's not get into a Big Dick Contest[47] here."

Zurn stepped back and grinned. Jim snorted, released the safety on his weapon, and followed Argon down the rickety stairs into the damp, musty basement. The low ceiling forced him to hunch over. He flicked on his night vision goggles. Moss grew over the layered stone foundation, and roots had broken their way through the packed dirt floor. Argon stood in the corner.

"Clear!" Jim shouted, and the rest of the soldiers filed in behind him.

Zurn was the last man to come down the stairs. After a quick look around, and with a pained grimace across his face, he said, "Thank you for delaying our departure, Shrike. There's nothing down here. Let's go!"

Jim walked to the corner where Argon stood and noticed another hatch.

"We are leaving, Shrike. I gave you an order!" Zurn pouted. Jim ignored him and dropped to one knee, searching for a handle.

"I think he's found something, sir," Squelch said, following Jim.

---

[47] Big Dick Contest *(slang)*: An argument about who has more combat experience or training.

"I found another hatch," Jim said. He grabbed the metal ring and pulled.

"Oh fuck, where does this end?" Zurn huffed.

The rusty hinges squeaked as the hatch opened, revealing another narrow, dimly lit stairwell. "This is weird, sir," Squelch said, switching off his night vision goggles. "The tunnel's like lit up."

"What do you mean, lit up?"

"Like lit up. It's glowing." He looked at Jim, shrugged, and then back to Zurn. "Sir?"

"Ugh! Well what are you waiting for? Get down there!" Jim nodded and slowly descended the stairs. His shoulders brushed up against the dirt walls. The stairs curved slightly before straightening out into a tunnel with a low, arched ceiling. The floors, walls and ceiling were made of roughly cut rectangular stones.

"All clear up ahead, Jim," Argon said from down the tunnel. "C'mon!"

"This is like, so freaky, Shrike," Squelch said. "Where do you think that light's coming from? There's like no torches, or light bulbs... nothing."

"Clear!" Jim shouted. Weapons ready, the team followed, single file, moving cautiously. Zurn reluctantly brought up the rear. The men commented to each other about the strange lighting.

"By the way... the radios like don't work down here, sir," Squelch said. "Thought you should know."

"It's balls to nutsack[48] down here," Anderson complained.

They headed down the long tunnel arriving at a wooden door wrapped in rusty iron bands. Argon already passed through to the other side. Jim pulled the door open and flung himself through the entrance. The rest of the men strafed in, fanning out in defensive positions along the walls.

"What the fuck?" Squelch gasped.

---

[48] Balls to nutsack *(slang):* Cramped together closely.

UNDEAD RECKONING

At the center of the perfectly round room with domed ceiling, dry branches and kindling covered a coffin resting on the floor. Cans of gasoline waited patiently off to the side. Argon leaned against the wall, arms folded. A wide hole had been dug into the floor, on the other side of the room opposite the door. The men exchanged confused glances.

"I hope that ain't no gopher hole," Anderson said. "Cause that'd be one big mother fuckin' gopher."

"Open the coffin!" Zurn commanded.

Jim and Squelch cleared away the firewood canopy, and opened the lid.

"Wow!" Squelch exclaimed.

"What is it?" Jensen asked.

"I think it's... I think its Ford Alroc," Squelch said. "I think he's like... dead!"

***

The metal doors slid shut and sealed with a hiss. Jim noticed the glimmering lake water beneath the grated flooring. Biped robots, their eyes dim, stood attentively in their docking bays along the corridor, separated by hexagon shaped buttresses. Diodes and lights flickered and flashed on non-user friendly consoles. The interior of the pyramid seemed to be much larger than the exterior, which was either a remarkable feat of physics, or an optical illusion. Through slits in the ceiling plates, Jim could see the overhead conveyers and chain-pulley systems spanning across the ceiling. Like the bipeds, everything was quiet and still. The thumping pistons and venting gases made it seem like he had stepped inside the belly of a mechanical dragon.

Jim looked down at the device he held firmly in his right hand. Flexible tubing ran from it to a needle inserted in the crook of his elbow. *This better work.*

The screen flashed. <PROBABILITY OF SUCCESS IS 98.8% BASED ON CURRENT CALCULATIONS> Jim didn't read the words. He could hear them in his head. Having a body full of replicating nanovirus particles made for efficient communication. But it wasn't exactly a pleasant sensation - Jim felt like he was crawling around inside his own skin.

At the far end of the corridor, Jim entered an airlock chamber. Doors sealed behind him and a cool blue light flittered over him from his head to his toes. When the light show ended, the heavy steel doors in front of him opened.

Jim stepped into the main control room, greeted by an impressive wall of floor to ceiling data-filled computer screens and colorful flashing lights. To his right, a glass door provided a view of the stasis chamber, where rows of neatly stacked vertical pods lined the sloped wall. Within each steamy pod, a dark human form pressed up against the viewing window.

Ready?
<PROCEED WITH THE PLAN>
<INTRUDER ALERT. INDENTIFY> a deep voice boomed over the intercom. With a clang, magnetic seals engaged within the sliding steel doors. One by one, the screens shut off and all the lights turned red.

"I wish to join the collective."

<THIS AREA IS SECURED. ANALYZING. NO BREACH DETECTED. EXPLAIN THE UNDETECTED PRESCENCE>

"Irrelevant!" Jim shouted. "I wish to join the collective. I have memories and experiences of value to Legion. Once I join, Legion will understand how I entered this compound."

<AFFIRMATIVE>

A seamless ceiling panel slid open. As the servo arm descended, a chair rose up out of the floor and reclined. Jim sat down and lay back. The arm lowered over the back of his head. Mechanical fingers sprung open and cupped the top of his head. The cold metal fingers tightened, and several tiny needles penetrated his scalp. The burning sensation slowly subsided, and Jim suddenly felt light headed and drowsy, as if he were in a dream-like state. It seemed someone other than himself was observing the thoughts inside his head.

<ERROR> the voice crackled. A high pitched alarm sounded off somewhere inside the building. <ERROR>

The servo arm retracted suddenly. Jim shook off the drowsiness, regaining his senses rather quickly, and jumped out of the chair. He looked down at the screen on the device. <TRANSFER COMPLETE 100%> Jim ripped the needle from his arm and tossed the device aside. The pyramid trembled and shook.

<STATE YOUR DESIGNATION>

Jim turned to the wall of screens. "I am Legion!" he shouted over the booming thrum of the pistons.

<IMPOSSIBLE. YOUR PHYSIOLOGY IS INCOMPATIBLE>

"Your cousin from the other side of the mountain... you know, Legion I... masked my signature."

<ERROR. ABORT... ERROR>

The door to the stasis chamber slid open.

<ERROR... ERROR> the voice slurred. <SYSTEM FAILURE IMMINENT.ERROR... INITIATING... ERROR... AUTO-DESTRUCT SEQUENCE>

The stasis pod seals released, venting thick gases. The doors opened and bodies fell forward, hanging upright and held in place by intravenous cables and wires. Jim found Ed and pulled him free of the biomechanical tubing. He threw his friend over his shoulder. All doors were now open. Lake water seeped in through the floor grates. He ran out of the shaky, sinking pyramid.

Outside, the pistons strained, grinding and creaking under pressure. The lake boiled and churned like an unwatched kettle. Pipes popped and burst, vomiting oily fluids. Jim ran as fast as he could to the safety of the small cave. Once inside, he crawled in as deep as he could go. He huddled over Ed, shielding his body. The deafening explosion filled the cave with a white hot light. Jim felt the exposed skin heat and peel off his neck and arms. He held Ed tightly, and waited for the aftershock to pass.

***

"That's Ford Alroc, alright," Jim confirmed. Argon nodded.

Jensen took a closer look at the body. "He's been dead a long time. I mean, we're talking years here."

"That's not possible," Zurn argued.

"Everything here's not possible, sir," Squelch said, not even pausing to breathe. "Like why is Ford Alroc here in the first place? And did he like, dig the hole? If he didn't, who did? And why didn't they cremate him? What are they waiting for?"

Everyone looked to Lieutenant Zurn for orders. "Uh... Anderson and Marleau - set charges everywhere. We're wiping this place from the map." The two men left the room to carry out the orders.

"Is that really necessary, sir?" Jim asked.

"Are you challenging my authority?"

"Since when does your authority allow you to willfully destroy property?"

"Since this property and this entire fucking mission became a waste of government resources!"

"We should at least bag this body and take it with us," Jim recommended.

"Leave it. It's obviously a hoax. Nobody's making an ass of me. We found nothing – understood?"

"He's already too good at making an ass of himself," Argon said.

The lieutenant stomped around the room, muttering to himself, while the tension intensified in his face. He stopped at the edge of the hole and looked down into it. "You know, this is a...." Suddenly, the floor gave way beneath his feet and he disappeared into the unforgiving darkness.

"Lieutenant!" Squelch shouted. He, Shrike and Jensen positioned themselves around the opening, shining in their flashlights. "Where the hell is he?"

"It looks like there's another level beneath us," Jensen said.

"Is that him there?" Squelch asked, shining his flashlight at an indiscernible mound.

Jim swung his feet over the edge. "I'm going down there. Squelch – you bag the body. Jensen – go get Marleau and Anderson and tell them to stop what they're doing and get down here."

"Hey Shrike," Jensen said, grabbing him by the shoulder. "Did Zurn have the detonator on him?"

"Oh, you're right. That's not good," Jim sighed. "You should tell Anderson to disarm the charges."

Jensen rose and headed for the door. "Too bad. Anderson loves big explosions." As Jensen grabbed the door latch, the blast flung the door open and sent him flying into the wall. The tunnel completely caved in and dirt and sand trickled down through the stones in the ceiling. The resounding shock caused Jim to slide down into the hole but Squelch managed to catch him by the arms and pulled him out.

"Like what the fuck just happened?" Squelch said, wiping the dust off his glasses.

"You okay, Jim?" Argon asked.

Jim nodded. He helped Jensen, who was rubbing the back of his head, get back to his feet.

"Aw… shit! That fucking hurt," Jensen moaned. "What the hell just happened?

"We're trapped," Squelch whined, staring into the caved in tunnel.

"We'll have to go down the hole," Jim said. "If someone came in that way, then there's a way out."

"What about Anderson and Marleau?"

"I'm sure the choppers saw the blast. They'll probably check it out," Jim replied. "When we get out of here, we'll radio them and set up a rendezvous point. In the meantime you guys bag this body - we're taking it with us. I'm going down the hole."

While Squelch and Jensen carried out the order, Jim slowly lowered himself in over the edge. He hung freely for a minute before Argon told him to jump. His feet landed in loose soil that slid out from under him, causing him to flop onto his belly. Jim managed to dig in his toes and stop his descent.

Getting to his feet, Jim lit up a flare and found himself in a wide, long cavern. He climbed back up the sloping pile of earth. Whoever had dug their way into the round room above had done so by undermining a section of the floor. The loosened earth had fallen away, sliding down into the cavern. Given time, the whole room would have eventually sunk.

"Shrike?" Squelch called from up above.

Jim waved the flare. "I'm okay." He climbed up to a flat section of earth just under the hole. "I haven't found Zurn yet."

"Go ahead an' look for him," Squelch shouted. "Jensen and I like secured a rope up here. He'll come down and then we'll lower down the body."

"Affirmative!" Jim replied, looking out into the darkness.

"Jim! Look out!" Argon shouted.

From out of the darkness, a dark shadow dove at Jim, catching him around the midsection. Jim and his assailant flew back and rolled down the slope, landing on the hard uneven rocks below. The assailant wore a dark hooded robe. It smelled musty and earthen.

Jim got to his feet and kicked the hooded figure in the ribs. The man flipped onto his back.

"He's got a knife, Jim," Argon shouted.

Jim planted a foot on the man's right forearm, pinning it to the ground. He drew his combat knife from his tac vest and plunged it into the man's chest, sliding it between the ribs and across, severing the heart in two.

"Another one! Jim, to your left!"

Jim turned and stabbed. The blade sunk into the flesh of his next attacker. He twisted the knife and pulled up, slicing the man open along the gut up to the sternum. The man doubled over. Jim pulled the knife free and sunk it into the back of the man's head.

"Six meters dead ahead!"

Jim didn't hesitate. He threw his knife and heard a grunt before something hit the ground.

"Nice throw," Argon said.

Jim lit up another flare. Three robed bodies lay on the ground. He knelt down next to the closest body and pulled back the hood. Glassy bloodshot eyes stared back out of the dark, sunken sockets in a pale gray face. Blue mottled veins, like spider webs, ran under the surface of the hairless skin. Oozing, open sores and yellow blisters dotted the head and neck.

"What on earth?" Jim muttered.

He was about to rise, when Argon shouted, "Behind you!"

Jim turned just in time to brace against the incoming swing. He dropped the flare and locked his opponent's arm, preventing his knife from striking. Jim shoved the man back, causing his hood to fall back. The ghoulish figure hissed, baring his mouth of perfectly pointed teeth. Before Jim could make another move, Argon's fist punched its way out of the man's chest. With his other hand, Argon grabbed the attacker by the top of the head and twisted, ripping it off the neck. The body slumped to the ground. "Told you I got your six!"

"Thanks!" Jim said, retrieving the flare. "Let's take a look at that." Both he and Argon examined the head. "These teeth have been filed down to points."

"Weird."

"I better make sure Jensen and Squelch are safe," Jim said.

"Yeah, sure," Argon said, tossing the head aside and flicking blood and goo off his fingers. "Hey Jim?"

"Yeah?"

"By the way... Zurn's lying just over there by those rocks," Argon said, pointing. "His gear's all gone. Bet these... things, whatever they are, got his remote detonator."

"Well, they're not getting Ford."

Argon nodded. "I'm sure they won't." Jim was about to turn away when Argon said, "If you head down this way, about a hundred yards or so, you'll get out. It leads out into the forest."

"Thanks," Jim said.

"Hey Jim?"

"Yeah?"

"See you around."

"What?" Jim looked up but Argon had disappeared.

"Sarge?" Squelch shouted. "We heard some commotion. Everything okay?"

"Yeah, just recalibrating my bearings," Jim shouted back. "I found Zurn. He's unconscious."

"Good! Then that means he couldn't have heard me refer to him as an asshole." Jim chuckled to himself. "We've lowered the body and we're on our way down."

"Good! There's something I have to show you down here. See you on the ground."

***

Jim sat on the edge of the rocky outcropping and watched patiently as the complex slid beneath the surface of the lake. Ed rolled over and muttered something about Carolina Peef and Afro-Saxons in his semi-conscious state. He was slightly feverish.

Jim pulled a notebook out from inside his tac vest. He leafed through it until he found the page he was looking for. A folded newspaper clipping lay nestled between the pages. He took it out and set the notebook down. Jim unfolded the clipping and read it over:

> *3 Dead as Traffic Light Malfunction causes Collision*
>
> (AP) A traffic light displayed green signals in all directions, resulting in a two vehicle collision which left three people dead, including a Canadian tourist early Saturday morning. Emergency crews

responded to the accident immediately. Pronounced dead at the scene were Reginald Griffin, 32, of Chicago, and William Shrike, 43, of Toronto, Canada. Louise Griffin, 29, was rushed to hospital with life threatening injuries. She died during an emergency caesarean section. She is survived by her son, Edward. Jim Shrike, 12, was taken to hospital for observation and later released. The Shrike family was vacationing in the Chicago area.

The malfunction is believed to be related to the cyber attack on the traffic grid…

***

Jim politely knocked on the door before barging in. "Come in, Lieutenant," Colonel Goring said, looking up from the newspaper. Jim was already standing in front of his desk. He was angry. "Have a seat."

"I'll stand!"

"Suit yourself. You seem a bit pissed off."

"Why am I under investigation?"

The Colonel took off his glasses and set down the paper. "General Zurn isn't too happy with your report."

"All the facts were there."

"Except that Lieutenant Zurn does not remember the facts as you do. He says you detonated the charges."

"That's not possible. The team corroborated my story."

"And all the evidence is either missing or blown sky high."

"The tunnels…"

"The tunnel system had completely collapsed. There is no evidence of anything. We have no chapel, no underground tunnel, no bodies – nothing!"

"What about Anderson and Marleau?"

"What about them? Their families think they were killed during some covert operation."

Jim clenched his fists. "Whoever these... guys... were, they were planning to cremate Ford Alroc. Personally, I think they were waiting for the full moon. At least we still have a body."

Colonel Goring rubbed his forehead. "Actually, the body's gone missing."

"What? How does a body go missing? Did it just get up and leave?"

"It seems that way."

"Did the coroner even get a chance to examine it?"

"It disappeared before he could conduct the autopsy. Alroc Computer Technologies still considers Ford to be a missing person." Jim threw his hands in the air. "Take it easy, Jim. The investigation will find nothing more than what we already know. You've received a commendation for your actions. And you've been accepted in the Officer Exchange Program. They've got nothing on you. You made Lieutenant Zurn looks like the ass that he is, and embarrassed the hell out of his father." Jim didn't say anything. He knew the Colonel was right. "If I were you, I'd fly under the radar for the next few days."

"What about my report?"

"It'll be buried in the files of Project Barilko[49]. You've been on these types of missions before – you know the drill."

"I do, sir. Thank you, sir. One more question..."

"Yes?"

"Why were we sent in there? On the surface, it didn't seem like much, but..."

"That's enough." Colonel Goring raised his hand, silencing Jim. "As a soldier, your job is to follow orders. You don't have to

---

[49] Project Barilko: a series of investigations conducted jointly between the Department of National Defence and the RCMP. Content of the investigations included reports of UFOs, cryptozoology and unexplained phenomenon.

make sense of it. And you don't need my rank and years of service to understand that."

Dissatisfied, Jim looked away and snorted.

"Now if you don't mind, I'd like to get back to reading the comics. Dismissed!"

***

I crawled out of the cave and stretched my legs. Jim was sitting on a large rock, his legs crossed with his hands in his lap, like some Zen master waiting for a Grasshopper.

"How are you feeling?" he asked, still staring out at the lake.

"Like shit. I'm still a bit groggy." I climbed up on the rock and sat down beside Jim. The lake was completely still, as if covered in a sheet of gold leaf. "I still can't believe what you told me. To think I was in a stasis pod inside a droid factory that was ready to kill all humans but was destroyed by that nano-something you've been carrying around and the whole thing sank down into a lake of gold… that's really fucked."

"Is it?"

"Nah! After everything we've been through, it's just business as usual, I guess." I took a swig from my canteen. The Beekosh was almost all gone, but it was enough to alleviate my headache. "Who the hell would have built something like that?"

"I'm curious to find out."

"Yeah! Well, at least they never got to destroy all humans."

"No. The undead plague beat them to it."

"You really think it was a plague?"

"I don't know what to think," Jim said. "Right now, it's easier just to follow orders rather than make sense of them."

"Follow orders?" I exclaimed. I almost had to catch my jaw. "The Jim I know wouldn't say that."

"The Jim you know didn't," he grinned. "It was something Colonel Goring once said to me. What he was trying to say was, know when to pick your battles."

"So that's it, then?" I huffed. "Is this just another mission to you? After all that shit Keek downloaded into our heads? I mean, shit… what about putting an end to the Masters?"

Jim looked at me out the corner of his eye. "You really want to know what I think?"

"Yes. Yes I do."

"This is basic training."

"Basic?"

"Yes. You remember what you learned in the bunker, don't you?" I nodded. "This is basic training. If you recall, we learned, through firsthand experience, what the world is like in the absence of Custodians and people; we found the serum; entered Nabisusha; set the events in motion which would bring Veck into our world." Jim motioned towards the lake. "And we destroyed a threat to our existence." Jim looked me in the eye. "So far, all we've done is carry out orders."

"Are you sayin' we're just players on the field?"

"We are and we aren't," Jim said with a grin. "Before you learned to be the great quarterback you are, you first had to learn the game. It's the same as when you were in the bunker: you had to learn to be a soldier before you could neutralize UDs."

"I think I understand," I said, staring off into space and trying to visualize what Jim was saying. "Keek said the universe learns from the sharing of life experiences. So it's throwing all this stuff at us to see how we deal with it?"

"Yes. I believe it is," Jim affirmed. "First, we need to understand how everything works. We do that through instruction. And along the way, we fulfill a greater agenda."

"We're being coached," I said. Jim nodded. "Veck said the universe was manifesting our thoughts." I shrugged. "That means we can actually cause the manifestation willingly."

"I think so. The universe will give us what we need to fulfill our own destiny."

"You sound like my Grandpa," I said with a smile. "He once told me, you need to accept the world for what it is, before you can change it."

"He was a wise man," Jim said.

I nodded. "So how do we go from being played to being players?"

Jim breathed deeply before looking me in the eye. "We need to figure out what the play is… and make our move before it happens."

18 SCOOT TO KILL

> *Break the jaw to prevent corruption through speech;*
> *Break the right hand to prevent corruption through action.*
> *That is how you kill the demon.*
> *If the demon has no such features, attack and attack again!*
> *Attack until your arms grow tired and your body aches.*
> *Attack until it is reduced to its most primitive form.*
> *-The Book of Amaltheon*

"How long have we been wandering through this tunnel?" I asked.

"Does it matter?"

"I guess not. Who knows if we're going to end up on the other side of time…"

Jim put out his hand to stop me. "Feel that?"

"Feel what?" The ground trembled beneath my feet.

"That!"

"Not again with this shit." Both Jim and I looked up at the tunnel ceiling. I'm not sure why the mind reacts that way. I know seeing is believing, but why stand there and wait for proof that the ceiling is caving in when you can look back after you run away.

"Go!" Jim shouted. The floor may have stabilized but my legs were still shaking. Jim's pace quickened.

"Wanna tell me why you've sped up?" Everything shook again.

"Keep moving!" This time, parts of the ceiling did come down. The tremor was so violent I had to catch my balance a few times. "C'mon!" I couldn't tell if the tunnel naturally twisted and turned or if it was actually moving. "There!" Jim pointed. Up ahead, a dim light shone through a small opening. Rocks came crashing down all around us. The dust obscured my vision. It sounded like we were being chased by a freight train.

We bolted through the hole and the tunnel caved in. I lay back on the shaky ground and caught my breath. "I've had enough of this shit!" I wiped the dust off my face. "Where the hell are we?"

"In another tunnel... but this one is different."

I sat up. Unlike the natural rock formations we had just exited from, the new tunnel was made of poured concrete. A maze of conduit and piping ran down the ceiling, dotted every few feet with amber emergency lights. The tunnel seemed to stretch endlessly in both directions.

"This tunnel looks familiar. It kinda reminds me of Bunker 57."

"It's very similar." Jim pointed to a series of colored and very weathered stripes running along the upper section of the walls. "The color coding uses the same schema. Remember what green stood for?"

"Yeah... uh?" I thought back but all I could remember was returning the suggestive glances of Corporal Elisha McCoy, and those amazing legs of hers. "Can't say I recall!"

Jim sighed. "You don't, eh? That what happens when you're making an ass of yourself to impress a sexy corporal."

"Hey! That's not fair... even though it is kinda true."

"You had no idea where you were going for about a week."

"I knew where her quarters were."

Jim shook his head. "Let's keep moving."

The endless tunnel eventually came to an end. Well, sort of. It just turned to the left and kept going.

"Hey! What's up ahead?" I sprinted up to the large panel of glass in the wall and found myself looking into a control room of some kind. To the left, a half open sliding door welcomed me to enter. The door required key entry so it must have been important.

"Ed, don't...." Jim's voice faded as I pushed my way in. Another window ran along the opposite wall. A dark glass counter kept it company. Peering through the glass, I could see an enormous room filled with row upon row of generators. I leaned on the counter to get a closer look and the entire surface lit up, displaying a thinly detailed map of Manhattan.

"Hey Jim, we're in New York." He looked over my shoulder and then walked the length of the counter display. "I don't remember seeing anything like this in Bunker 57."

"You probably didn't have access to those areas," Jim said. He placed his fingers on the map and slid them across the smooth surface. The map scrolled along with his movements. I noticed a touch screen control panel to the side. I tapped it and the map recalibrated, dividing the area in zones.

Jim looked out the window into the generator room. "This is an auxiliary power room."

"Cool! Look here - there's Harlem. I would've been there if it weren't for UD Day." I touched the zone marked as Harlem on the map and it started blinking. Somewhere, deep in the room below, a generator whirred to life.

Jim scowled at me.

"Sorry. Maybe I can shut it off?"

"Let's not touch anything else, please," Jim scolded. "We should go."

We stepped back out into the tunnel. I stopped. *Sniff! Sniff!*

"What is it?" Jim asked.

"You smell that?"

Jim breathed deeply.

"It smells like fresh bread," I said. *Sniff! Sniff!* "My Grandpa used to make his own bread. I loved that smell. Where the hell would somebody be bakin' that down here?" I ran off following the delicious aroma.

"Ed, wait!"

I didn't listen to Jim. It has been so long since I'd smelled baking bread, let alone eaten some. I ran so fast I didn't realize how far I'd gone. Jim only caught up to me because I stopped to hone in on the smell.

I was about to run again but he caught my arm. "Wait!"

"What? You afraid we're gonna stumble onto a gingerbread house with candy decorations?"

"Just slow down! Something's not right. I got a bad feeling about this."

"Well, after everything we've been through, a cookie house and an old witch wouldn't be so odd, would it? The smell's coming from down there."

We travelled down the corridor until we came to a 'T' intersection. The corridor to the left ended abruptly with a wall-mounted ladder leading up to a hatch in the ceiling. The smell wafted from the corridor on the right. If I'd had a pallet of butter, I bet it would have melted from the aroma alone.

I led Jim down the corridor. My mouth was watering and my stomach reminded me of how long it'd been since our last decent meal. About a hundred feet down, the passage turned to the right again. The aroma warmed me all over. It was as if I was standing in my Grandpa's kitchen. I closed my eyes and rounded the corner. When I opened my eyes, I was standing in front of the biggest pile of shit I had ever seen. At the far end of the room, the passage continued. But there was no way to get across without stepping in shit.

"Wow! That's a lot of feces," Jim exclaimed.

"I don't wanna know what that came out of."

"Ed… we've got a problem."

"What?" A shambling mass of undead slowly trickled in from the other side of the room.

"Let's get out of here!" Jim shouted.

We turned tail and ran. More undead filtered in towards us from the intersection. Jim drew his sword and charged into them, slicing and dicing a path to the ladder.

"Go! Get up there!" He shoved me at the metal rungs. "I'll hold them off!"

I began my ascent. Jim jumped onto the ladder and chased after me. We climbed and climbed until we hit a dead end.

"Shit! This hatch is closed!"

"Force it open!"

"I'll try!" I braced my shoulder against the metal plate and pushed. Nothing! I braced my feet on the rungs, tucked my head into my chest, and pushed with both shoulders.

CLANG!

The hatch flung open and I shot straight up, only to be looking down the barrel of a gun. I was surrounded by a group of about fifteen men. Before I could even raise my hands, they grabbed me under the arms and hauled out of the hole.

"Close it!" A man ordered.

"No wait... my friend's down there."

"He'll be dead by now..."

Jim leapt out and slammed the hatch shut behind him. The men, backed away, staring at him. Everybody seemed a bit too surprised, or intimidated, to say anything. A heavyset man in mismatched camos pushed his way through. He combed his furly moustache with his fingers while he looked us up and down. "Who are you guys?"

"Lieutenant Jim Shrike, Canadian Special Forces."

"Lieutenant, huh? What's with the body paint?"

"It's a...prototype zombie repellent."

The big man raised his eyebrows. "And you are?"

"Eddie Griffin, Quarterback, San Antonio Rattlers."

"Well, I'll be damned. I thought you looked a little familiar." Murmurs of my name spread quickly through the men gathered around us. "Name's Cap." He shook my hand. "Eddie Griffin... wow! Good timing – we could use a hero about now."

"I ain't no hero," I replied.

Cap turned to the men, "Make sure this hatch is secured."

"Sure thing, Cap!" an Asian guy responded. We stepped aside for him do his work.

"You wanna explain to me what you're doing here?" Cap asked.

Jim was quick with a response. "We came in off the mainland... through the tunnels."

"I can't believe it's Eddie Griffin," a man said as I passed him.

"Well it's nice to meet you both," Cap said with a nod. "We could use some help, if you're interested."

Jim nodded.

"I take it that level below us is crawling with zeds?" Cap asked.

"Yes, it is."

"Damn! That's not good."

"What are you doing down here?" I asked.

"One of the generators came back online. We were coming to check it out." Jim glared at me while I tried to look like I didn't know what Cap was talking about. "If there's zeds down there, we might have to rethink the plan. Putz?"

A greasy-looking, peaked little man with a stooped back and long hair parted straight down the middle stepped forward. Two loaded tool belts drooped from around his scrawny waist. He wore a fishing vest weighted down with wires, reels of tape and odds and ends. The man was a walking hardware store. "Yes, Cap?"

"Can we shut down that generator remotely?"

"Uhhhh… I don't think so," he said really slowly. "I'd need to get in the control room or into the generator room."

"Damn!"

"Hey Cap?" a Latino man shouted. He looked like he was a member of the same moustache club as Cap. He pressed a finger against his in-ear head set.

"What is it, Rodrigues?"

"It's the Librarian. He wants to know who turned the power on in Harlem."

"Tell him we're looking into it," Cap grumbled. "If he can't wait, tell him to drag his ass down here and check it out himself."

"Roger that! By the way, I told him we found Eddie Griffin. He's pretty excited to meet him."

"Like I said, tell him to get his ass down here. Okay men, we're turnin' back," Cap ordered. "Rodrigues - contact HQ and tell them the sector is hot and we need a flamethrower team on the double. We'll wait for them at the safe house in Times Square."

"You got it, Cap!"

Cap took an old, well-gnawed cigar out of his breast pocket and jammed it between his teeth. "You're on point, Perkins!" he said to a tall skinny guy. Cap turned to Jim. "I hold no rank really, but since you're on my turf…"

Jim nodded. "I understand. Just give the orders."

He smiled at Jim, as best he could without dropping his mangy cigar. "Move out, people!" The men walked briskly down the corridor. "You guys are lucky to get this far," Cap started. "Most people end up in the shit… literally."

"Yeah, what's up with that?" I asked.

"We don't know," Cap said. "It started a few months ago. Wanna know what I think?"

"Sure," I said.

"Actually, it's not just my idea – we all talk about this," Cap began, looking back every so often and checking on everything. "The biggest problem after the zeds wasn't the zeds. It was the assholes – all those fuckin' jerks who thought anarchy and chaos were an excuse to kill, rape and steal whatever shit you want. People had to stick together to survive. We fought back. It didn't matter who you were: military, civilian, white collar, blue collar, gang member, criminal. Race, color and creed were all tossed aside. Instead, we organized ourselves and set up safe houses. Once we dealt with all the assholes, we turned our attention to the zeds. Slowly, we took back as much of Manhattan as we could. We control all the bridges and tunnels and even regulate the power for parts of the city."

"That's quite the accomplishment," Jim said.

"I'll say," Cap agreed, chomping on his cigar as it slid from one side of his mouth to the other. "In a time of crisis, assholes just try to take advantage of the situation."

"When did all the shit start piling up?" I asked.

"Right after everything started getting better. It was weird. At first, the zeds started comin' in through the tunnels - clogged 'em up pretty tight. We couldn't move down there let alone find how they were gettin' in." Cap scratched his moustache. "And then they got smart or somethin'. They started congregatin' around our food caches, like they were tryin' to starve us out."

"And that's when you got into the real shit?"

"Heh, yeah. Smells like whatever you crave most. I've seen it turn some men into mindless drones – worse than the zeds themselves. The zeds like to wait nearby in ambush."

"They're organized. That's not typical UD behavior," Jim said.

"UD's? Gawd, you ARE military!"

"Something's leading them."

"Like what? An alpha-zed?" Cap asked.

"Or worse." Jim looked concerned. I knew what was thinking: a demon could have that kind of power. "Some species of owl will use their droppings to attract beetles and other scavengers."

"You tryin' to say owls use their shit to catch their next meal?"

"Yes."

"Clever bastards," Cap mused. "Well, we ain't scavengers."

"On the contrary, I believe you are," Jim said. "You forage and scrounge for food, do you not?"

Cap chuckled and ran his fingers through his moustache. The point man stopped at the next intersection and lowered his rifle. He looked about from side to side.

"Perkins! What is it?" Cap shouted. "Perkins!"

"Ahhhhhhh... Sardano's Pizza," He dropped his rifle and wandered off aimlessly.

"Perkins!"

Zombies swarmed in from the hall to the right. Everyone opened fire. If the zombies didn't shred Perkins to bits, the hail of bullets did. More zombies piled in.

"This way!" Rodrigues shouted, leading everyone to the left. The men bringing up the rear lay down suppressive fire.

"Which way?"

"Right... I think... Just up ahead."

More zombies spilled into the corridor ahead of us.

"I smell steaks," someone said.

"Nah... butter chicken."

"Think with your heads, not with your stomachs!" Cap ordered. "Which way now, Rodrigues?"

"Uh... go right. Through the fire doors."

"Aren't those the doors that ain't workin'?"

"Maybe Putz can get them closed," Rodrigues suggested.

We ran down the hall and stopped at a set of steel sliding doors.

"Can you close these doors, Putz?" Cap asked.

"I can try," he monotonously droned. I so hoped he worked faster than he spoke. Putz pulled the cover plate off the door control and jabbed a screwdriver in there.

"Hold the line here! Van Der Laan and..."

"I'll go," I said.

"Me too," Jim added.

"Alright. The three of you scout ahead." Cap pointed to a stairwell directly down the hall from the doors. "Once we get these doors closed, we'll take those stairs. They lead up to the subway tunnels. I want you to go down past the stairs. You'll see it opens up on the left. Make sure nothin's comin' from down there."

"Acknowledged!"

We headed past the stairwell towards another intersection.

Sniff! "I smell fresh bread again," I said.

Van Der Laan slowed down, moving hesitantly. "I smell cookies. This ain't good."

We rounded the corner and froze. Not so much out of fear, and I think I can safely speak for Jim, but because of what we saw next. It was the biggest ass I had ever seen! And two legs! And that's it!

"What the fuck?"

The ass, with its multi-jointed legs, strutted like a bird. It lifted each three-toed clawed foot with mechanical precision. The barbed heel clacked against the concrete floor. The ass circled a few times before it finally decided on a spot where is squatted down and shit all over the floor. It turned and faced us... not like it had a face. The ass was pointing in our direction. Anyway, the butt cheeks creaked open revealing a dark anus.

"Ah eetz hed-meetz!" it drawled. The ass leapt forward. The sphincter slid down over a petrified-with-fear Van Der Laan's head and lifted his flailing body. It thrashed about wildly before spitting him out. His body slapped against the wall and crumpled, with his crushed and brainless cranium flopping over to one side.

"That ass just sucked his brains out!" I shouted to Jim. "That's no owl!" I can't remember how many rounds I pumped into that thing before we turned and ran.

"Kom bak'ere an feedz mah zedlinz! Sukulent sweet head-meatz!" the ass yelled.

The doors were sliding shut just as we arrived.

"Company's coming!"

"Where's Van Der Laan?" Cap asked.

"He's dead."

"Argh! I shouldn't've sent him. Sometimes that guy has his head up his ass."

"It's not his ass you need to worry about. We've got to get out of here!"

"The door's closed now, Cap," Putz said.

The entire hall behind us filled with zombies.

"Move! Move! Move!"

Jim drew his sword. "Go! I'll hold them off!"

"But..."

"Go!"

Rodrigues was the first man up the stairs. Everyone flew up behind him. Cap pushed his way to the head of the line. I brought up the rear along with some guy in a turban. We exited out into the dark subway tunnel and charged towards the platform. Pockets of zombies roamed about. The men split up into squads of three, and alternated between moving and shooting, all the while advancing to the exit.

Once we got to the platform, it was a short race up the stairs and into Times Square. The embrace of a cool breeze welcomed us. Thick, creamy clouds blanketed the sky, like a sea of mashed potatoes. I breathed deeply. *Manhattan.* I smiled. Only there wasn't much to smile about. All the neon, the flashing and the flickering lights, the scrolling banners, and the giant video screens were off. The skyscrapers and buildings were dark and lifeless, like tired skeletons waiting to be buried. It looked nothing like that time Carlin and I came here with his Aunt and Uncle, and cousin Carolinaaaah Peef.

"It's rush hour," Rodrigues said. "Wall to wall zeds." They were everywhere – businessmen in weathered suits, shoppers in decaying leather, and tourists in ratty *I heart NY* t-shirts. The shambling hordes filled the streets creating an impenetrable barrier of rotting flesh.

"Keep moving!" Cap ordered.

We raced towards a bunker, reminiscent of the pillboxes I had seen in books about World War Two, which sat right in the center of Duffy Square. A metal guard tower stood erect on top of it, complete with searchlights and machine guns. Like a medieval castle, chain link fences with concertina coil were set up to form inner and outer curtains: soldiers would enter the outer gate, close it behind them and kill off any zombies that followed, before entering the safety of the inner gate. It also helped that Carlin once forced me to read the AA Castle Architect's Guide, so I knew all about this kind of shit.

We pushed our way through any zombie resistance and rushed inside the safety of the outer curtain. Luckily, no zombies followed us in so we were able to move through to the inner curtain immediately. The bunker was well stocked with first aid supplies, food, weapons and ammunition. The men wasted no time reloading and resupplying, only pausing to shake my hand as I walked by. I even signed a few autographs. Two guys with scoped rifles went up into the tower to keep the zombies from getting too close to the fence.

Rodrigues headed up the ladder after them. "I'm going up top to get a better signal."

"We're coming too," Cap said. "Eddie... Come with me."

Rodrigues paced back and forth in the guard tower, his fingers pressed firmly to his earpiece. Cap circled around, looking out each side. We were surrounded, zombies as far as the eye could see.

Cap huffed, "Where're the goddamn reinforcements?"

I tapped my fingers along the metal plate walls. "Did you guys build this?"

"Nah," Cap replied. "The National Guard did. It's some kind of pre-fab military thing. They set them up here and there around the city after the zeds rose."

"Saved us the trouble," one of the shooters (a guy whose name I found out later to be Nate Gehl) said. He sported a very sinister-looking sniper rifle. Turned out Nate Gehl was a former member of the New York Police Department Emergency Services Unit.

"Dozers and APCs are on the way," Rodrigues confirmed. "Should be here within the hour."

"Good. We'll just sit tight." Cap pulled a fresh cigar from inside his jacket. He jammed it between his teeth. Personally, I think he just used it to keep his moustache from covering his mouth. "You're a big boost to morale, Eddie. We need a hero."

"Amen, brother," Rodrigues said.

"You guys are the real heroes," I said.

"Yeah, but we're taking a beating."

"We could use your inspiration," Nate said.

"You make me sound like a superhero," I said. "Really, I'm not. Besides, being a hero isn't all it's cracked up to be."

Nate tilted his head back and stared at me, all whatever-like. "You trying to tell me you're all fucked up like Batman?"

"All super heroes are kind of fucked up," Rodrigues said. "It makes them more realistic... more human."

I raised my hands and stopped them. "Hold on guys. That's not what I mean. Being a hero means you have to be accountable for your actions. Sometimes that's too much shit for one man to handle. And it requires dedication. I know you guys say I'm a hero. I was... to football. That's it."

"So what you're sayin' is, we need a local – a New Yorker," Cap said, pointing at me with his cigar. He broke out into a laugh. "Maybe Putz'll save us all." The men laughed.

"You know who would save New York? Billy Rubin," Rodrigues chuckled. "Now there's a hero... just too bad he's not real."

"He'd kill everything," Nate said. "He doesn't discriminate."

"Yeah, sucks that the Billy Rubin Film Festival was taking place on the same day all the zombies rose," I said. "Anyone remember that?"

"I sure do... at the Dolemite Theatre," Rodrigues replied. "The Librarian once told me he had tickets to attend, but he wasn't going to go when he found out that the film was re-shot in uMe."

"uMe?" Nate spat. "What a fuckin' joke!"

"Well, uMe almost makes him real," I argued. "I saw all his movies when I was a kid." *I wish he was real.* I thought of all the times my Grandpa and I watched Billy Rubin movies. We always ordered pizza and some spicy wings. I even owned a three-quarter-length leather jacket, just like the one Billy wore. Other than my Grandpa, I don't think I had a bigger role model. I knew everything there was to know about Billy Rubin. It all started when Bimal Singh immigrated to the United States with a screenplay in his hand and a ton of hope in his heart. Nobody cared. Nobody was interested. Every studio told him to take a hike... back to India. Disillusioned and disappointed, he took a part time job at Symingo's House of Noodles. It was there that he became good friends with the bartender: an aspiring actor and alcoholic named Lando Mossey.

Together, the two men revised the screenplay. Then one day, producer Leonard Geldbaum came in for a serving of tongue ding with sai-foon noodles. Bimal not only served him his food, but also dished out a few choice morsels about his script. Geldbaum bit, and a few days later, Bimal and Lando were sitting in his office finalizing the deal. Bimal got the director's chair and Lando the lead role.

Thirteen months later, the world was introduced to the hit comedy film: *Ring-a-Lingam*. Bimal received an Oscar nomination for Best Screenplay and multi-film, multi-million dollar deal from a Bollywood agency. The ink was still wet when Bimal boarded the plane to India, stranding Lando on the red carpet. *Ring-a-Lingam* didn't win the award. And en route to India, Bimal's plane was shot down by Sentinelese tribesmen[50]. There were no survivors.

After a celebratory drinking binge lasting several weeks, followed by a drunken state of mourning, Lando entered a state of enlightened sobriety. With his mind focused, he penned a screenplay in less than two days. Backed by his earnings from *Ring-a-Lingam*, Lando did the unthinkable: he used real film - not that digital/CGI stuff. He shot, produced, directed and starred in his debut movie, *Unforbreakable*.

The picture became an overnight success. And the film's main character became a cult sensation: an alcoholic karate choppin', cigar chompin' cop named Billy Rubin. The film won best male actor, best director, best picture and best screenplay. The following year, Lando won a second best male actor award and best

---

[50] Sentinelese: Believed to be the last pre-Neolithic tribe in the world to remain isolated on a small island in the Indian Ocean. As of 2011, ships and planes coming within 100kms of the island mysteriously disappeared. Some theorists believe the Sentinelese developed a type of beam weapon after discovering ancient Atlantean Crytals and technology.

screenplay with the sequel, *Indisception*. He was the closest to godliness a man could get. But even godlike status couldn't save him from a painful bout of liver cancer. Lando Mossey died a legend, leaving behind a legion of mourning fans.

"True legends never die," I said softly.

"What was that you said?" Rodrigues asked.

"Something I read once. I don't know who said it." I shrugged. "I said, true legends never die."

"You talking about Billy Rubin?"

"Yeah."

"Sorry to say this, my friend, but at the rate things are going, the zeds are winning. And if we die, Billy Rubin dies with us." Rodrigues turned away from me, as if he didn't like the sound of what he'd just said.

I thought back to the conversation I had with Jim – back in the tunnels after he destroyed the robots, and then to what my Grandpa said: you have to learn to accept the world before you can change it. Then, I had an idea. "I have to get out of here," I said.

"What?" Rodrigues asked.

"I have to get out of here," I repeated, this time catching Cap's attention. "I have to get to the Dolemite theatre in Harlem."

"What the hell's wrong with you? Don't ya see those zeds out there?" Cap shouted. "You'll never make it."

"I have to do this, and I don't have to explain myself. You wanna see a hero in action? Then let me go!"

Cap took the cigar from his mouth, spit, and jabbed it back in on the other side. "You're goin' nowhere." He turned away from me. And to say the atmosphere was a bit tense after my outburst was a bit of an understatement. Nobody spoke to me while I waited, all by myself, in a corner of the guard tower.

"Hey Cap," Rodrigues said, pointing out into the undead crowd. "Lookit that!"

A yellow cab, with the horn blaring, tore straight down Broadway at full speed. Any zombies in its path were thrown clear (in whole or in parts) by the front-mounted spiked ram plate, or crushed under the tires.

Cap pulled the cigar out of his mouth. "What the hell does he want?"

"Who is that?" I asked.

"The Librarian," Nate said, looking off into the distance.

"We better get down there," Cap said. I followed him down the ladder. While he gathered up a few men, I waited impatiently. Cap divided the men into two groups: the larger group was to provide cover fire, while the smaller group would open the gate at the outer curtain.

"Here he comes," one of the men shouted.

"Open fire!" Cap ordered.

A hail of bullets cut down the zombies closest to the fence. The men opened the gate, and the yellow cab pulled in. A few other zombies also got through but were warmly greeted with gunfire. The cab screeched to a halt. The door opened and out stepped an old man with salt-and-pepper gray hair. He wore a tight-fitting flannel shirt, jeans with blue suspenders and workboots. He pushed his half-moon spectacles up the bridge of his bulbous nose, looked at me and smiled.

"Eddie Griffin," he said, walking towards me. "Most touchdown passes; most completions; highest yards passing; highest yards rushing and most touchdowns in a single season - rookie season at that. It is my pleasure!" He extended his hand.

I was about to shake his hand when Cap barged in front of me. "What the hell do you want?"

The Librarian stepped aside. "I want to meet my hero."

I shook his hand. "Pleasure's all mine."

"Can you sign my trading card?" the Librarian asked. "It's in car. I can get it."

Again, Cap stepped in between us and shouted this time, "You jeopardized our lives to come down here to get an autograph?" He put his hands on his hips and glared at the older man.

"I'll do it," I said. "I'll sign your card... if you take me to The Dolemite."

"Are you crazy now too?" Cap blurted, turning to face me.

"You're on!" the Librarian said, moving towards his cab. "Ya know, I haven't had a decent fare in months."

"Can you operate a uMe projector?"

The Librarian scratched his head. "Uh... no."

"Damn!" I put my hands on my hips and walked in a circle before I had an idea. "Hey, Putz!" I shouted. The scrawny man shambled out of the bunker, just slightly faster than a zombie. He crossed his arms across his chest and looked at me with a sheepish grin. "Hey, can you operate a uMe projector?"

"Uh... shyeah," he said. "I guess I can figure it out."

"Wanna go for a ride?"

"Sure."

"Get in the car."

"Just a minute, Cap said, stepping into my path. "You can't take Putz."

"Putz, you wanna go with us?"

"Shyeah," he replied.

"No fuckin' way!" Cap yelled.

Putz suddenly stood up straight, adjusting his tool belts. "Now, you listen here. I said I'm goin' and that means I'm goin." Cap's mouth dropped open and the cigar fell out from between his lips. No further words were exchanged as Putz climbed into the back seat.

I slowly backed away and got into the passenger's side. The Librarian, who was already waiting for us, started the engine. I leaned the window and shouted, "If my friend comes back, tell him I've gone to make the next move. He'll understand." After a very awkward five-point turn, we plowed our way through the zombies and were racing down 7th street.

"So, you're the Librarian," I said.

A smile broke out across his scarred face. "Not really. I'm a cabbie. I just live in the New York Public Library."

"Oh," I said with a nod. "Must be kind of... quiet."

"Ya know, it sure is. And call me Reg... my name's Reg Cranston."

"Reg it is."

He adjusted his glasses, turned and pointed an accusing finger at Putz. "You didn't hear that!" Putz responded with a nod. Reg looked over at me as he drove. "I'm not much of a people person. I prefer books. So when the zeds took over, I moved into the library, ya know. I modded my cab a bit so I could travel around, but most of the time I just stay inside and read. If ya have to depend on other people it only leads to disappointment."

"I guess," I agreed with a shrug.

"So why do you need to go to the ol' Dolemite?" A zombie lurched out in front of the car. Reg gunned the engine and swerved into the zed, sending it sliding across the hood.

"It's a hunch."

"I hear ya. Ya gotta trust your gut when it feels right," he said, patting his pot belly. "Ya know, there was this one time I picked up a fare and the guy really made me feel uneasy. So I pulled over and told him to get out. He grabbed me by the hair and tried to slice my throat." He tilted his head back and traced a finger along the long scar. "The idiot sliced me along the jaw bone. Good thing I trusted my gut." He rubbed his chin. "My wife Elaine always said I looked like I had no chin and no neck. Maybe that's what saved my life, ya know."

"Yeah, I guess. How'd you scar your cheek?"

"Zombies," he replied, checking his face in the rear view mirror. "I ran into a few in the library when I first moved in. They wanted to dance, but me and the ol' lady put on a show." He put a hand on the Remington short-barreled combat shotgun resting between us. "This one zed tried to cut in but we didn't let him. The ol' lady kissed him under the chin; blew the top of his head clean off. I took a few pellets in the face. I guess that's what happens when there's no chaperone at the ball, ya know."

The librarian flipped down the sun visor. He took an NFL trading card out from under the elastic band. "Here -- do me a favor and sign this, will ya?" He took a pen from a dashboard slot and handed it to me. "That's a good action shot, ya know."

"Thanks."

"So, ya wanna tell me about this hunch of yours?"

"Well, uh... you know all about the piles of shit, right?"

"I heard about 'em."

"Yeah, well, I saw the source firsthand. It's a big ass."

"Pardon the pun, but no shit."

"No, seriously. It's just a big ass with legs."

Reg looked at me and raised an eyebrow. "You're not kidding, are you?"

"No."

"Jeez. Where'd this ass come from?"

I sat back and scratched the back of my neck. "Cap mentioned the zombies weren't the biggest problem. Initially, it was all those people who tried to take advantage of the situation – the assholes – as he referred to them."

"That's why I holed myself up in the library. I didn't want to deal with those guys, ya know."

"Right, so once the assholes were gone, everyone could focus on the zombies." I turned around in my seat to check on Putz. He hummed softly to himself and twiddled his thumbs. "Anyway, I think this ass is a manifestation of all those assholes."

"Ah," Reg said, nodding his head. "Universal consciousness manifesting itself... quantum brain mechanics. *Spooky actions at a distance*, as Einstein said. Ya know what kid? I liked ya on the field, and I like ya in person. I'm glad ya got in my cab."

"Thanks."

"So, what? How ya think you're gonna stop this asshole-prime?"

"If a collective consciousness can manifest an enemy, then it can manifest a hero."

Reg's face erupted in a devilish grin. "I think I know where you're going with this... and I love it." He checked his rear view mirror, and pointed to the back with a jerk of his thumb. "He's asleep. Think we bored him?"

"I don't know," I said with a smile.

"Well, he better wake up soon. We're almost there."

The Dolomite Theatre was all aglow when we arrived. If not for all the zombies roaming around out front, you'd have thought it was business as usual. Incandescent lights danced around the front entrance. More lights flickered in an alternating pattern around the marquee which read, Welcome to The Billy Rubin Film Festival. To top it all off, flashing lights ran up the center of the building up to a giant multi-pointed shooting star.

"Gorgeous, ain't she?" Reg sighed.

"Uh-huh," I said with a nod.

Reg craned his neck and looked up at the marquee. "I had tickets, ya know. The fuckin' zeds ruined the show. Too bad, huh?"

"I would have loved to have seen it."

"Well, tonight we get our own private screening." Reg grabbed his shotgun and got out of the cab. He carefully circled around the zombies because, as he explained to me later, he was afraid a stray pellet might damage the integrity of the theatre. The blasts woke up Putz, who got out of the cab with surprising haste. He picked the lock while Reg and I cleaned up out front. Reg's shotgun tore the zombies to shreds, while I rushed through with shoulders and punches, sending them flying like rag dolls.

It didn't take long for Putz to get the door open and after a quick shoulder check to ensure the area was relatively secure, we entered the building through the heavy mahogany and glass doors. Putz locked them back up for security. All three of us stood in the entrance, taking in the view. "Holy shit!" I whispered. The layer of dust and grime couldn't hide the beauty of the thick, lush carpets, the marble tile floors, the elaborate plasterwork, and the gilded chandeliers. Even the dingy and dank odor seemed faint in the presence of the grandeur.

We walked down the corridor. Gold paint flaked from the window casings. Warped Billy Rubin posters barely clung to hangers inside. Velvety tassels and cording drooped from the valances. Inside the lobby, rats had thoroughly looted the concession stand. Cups, lids and napkins littered the floor. Black mold covered the inside of the popcorn machine.

In the main theatre, the dimmed chandeliers cast just enough light for us to see the upgraded sound system and uMe holographic projectors retro-fitted into the ceiling - a bizarre mix of art deco and modern technology. The seats had been removed, since uMe created a virtual three dimensional environment around the viewer. Part of the experience allowed a viewer to 'wander' around in the film, seeing it from different angles and perspectives.

Reg swept through the upper floor offices and projection room while I checked the main level. Once we were confident we were in a zed-free environment, I set my plan in motion."

"Can you get the projector running?" I asked Putz.

"Of course I can."

"I'm not surprised."

"I'll take you upstairs," Reg said. As he walked away he added, "Ya know, it's a good thing some idiot turned on the generator for this grid." I took it as a back-handed compliment.

I picked a spot in the middle of the theatre and waited. Minutes later, Reg shouted, "All set!" from the viewing window, assuring his words with a thumbs up.

The theatre darkened, and a familiar bow-chicka-bow-wow music filled the room. Then the film started... from out of the darkness, credits appeared as giant block letters scrolling through mid-air before fading away. I could actually walk around them. "Holy shit!" Suddenly, I found myself standing on a street corner at a busy intersection in Harlem. People were walking down the street going about their business. I felt a bit disoriented and dizzy at first, but the sensation quickly passed. I weaved my way between the pedestrians. At one point, I bumped into someone and he told me to fuck off. I could even see activity inside the shops on the street.

"This is so awesome," I shouted with a grin. A few people looked at me like I was crazy. *Just another brother on dope*, someone muttered. Everything was so real. Dogs barked, horns honked, disco music blared out from somewhere down the street. I could even smell exhaust and hot dogs.

"Hey Eddie," Reg waved from across the street. He ran towards me, darting through traffic. "Magnificent, ain't it?"

I took a deep breath and put my hand on his arm as if steadying myself. "I've seen *Unforbreakable* about a hundred times. I know just about every scene and line from memory. But I don't remember it like this."

"Surely, you won't forget, ya know."

My nostrils caught a whiff of cigar. Billy stepped out from the subway exit and grabbed a newspaper from the street vendor. It was a bit unnerving to see the scene unfold since I had seen it before. It was a bit like déjà vu but I knew what was happening before it happened and couldn't do anything about it. Billy opened the paper and started reading it. I moved directly into his path.

SCRUNCH!

"Hey baby, watchoo doin'? Can't a brother read the stocks?"

"Sorry," I said.

Billy folded the paper and put his hand on his hip before scolding me. "You know what sorry is? Sorry is the feeling in my fists when I get my knuckles all lined up and don't punch nothin'." He held his meaty hand in front of my face. "Now get the fuck out of my way, brotha!"

"Hey Putz... stop the show!" I shouted.

Everything in front of me froze and faded.

"What are ya doing?" Reg asked.

"I want to make a better first impression. Putz, let's run it again."

The film started over. Reg and I stood off to the side and let the action unfold. I waited for Billy to grab the newspaper and cross the street. I didn't have much time with the next scene approaching, so I ran over to him.

"Billy!" I said, grabbing him by the arm.

He pulled himself free. "Get the fuck off me dickwad!"

I grabbed him again. "Billy, it's me, Eddie."

"I don't know any Eddie. Fuck off!"

"I'm Eddie Griffin. I'm your manager and agent." Billy scowled at me before breaking out in a smile. "Brotha, you are on some serious shit." I waved Reg over. "This here's Reg Cranston. He's kinda like a doctor. You've been acting funny."

Billy pressed his finger into my chest. *Thank the Makeners*, as Keek would say, for my jersey cause it was sort of like being hit with a pick axe. "I've been acting funny? Fuck off asscracker, before I crack your ass for real."

"Uh... uh, he's right," Reg intervened. "You're suffering from..." he looked at me.

"Quantum Induced..."

"Trauma," Reg added, finishing my sentence.

"Quantum what?" Billy spat, furrowing his brow. "Baby, get out of my way before I quantumize your ass!"

"Eddie," Reg said, nodding over my shoulder.

I turned. "Oh shit!" It was Detective Foster, coming down the street, eating a hot dog. I had to hurry because Billy and the Detective were about to get into a situation. I turned back to Billy and put my hands up. "Listen to me, Billy. In a few minutes, you're going to meet up with Detective Foster and there's gonna be a drive-by shooting. The detective will die. But you won't, even though a bazillion rounds will be fired directly at you."

"What the fuck are you goin' on about?"

I stepped aside just as Detective Foster approached. "Hey, Rubin! The chief's pissed at you again."

"Again? He's always pissed at me."

Mustard dripped down onto Foster's tie. "Aw shit," he said, looking down. "My wife bought me this tie."

Suddenly, a red sedan sped out into the intersection. The occupants of the vehicle opened fire, spraying into the panicked and scurrying crowd of pedestrians. Detective Foster danced like a marionette, thrashing wildly as bullets riddled his body. Billy, meanwhile, drew his gun. He aimed, and just as he was about to fire, I grabbed his arm. "Hey! Get the fuck off me!" The gun fired and the shot rang off a street sign. The car drove off.

Billy shoved me aside. "Hey, fuck you, baby!"

Sirens wailed in the distance. Detective Foster lay in a pool of his own blood. Innocent bystanders who were caught in the volley lay on the sidewalk. Good samaritans provided first aid while others looked on in shock.

I grabbed Billy and pulled him aside. "Did you see how many bullets they fired at you? You never even got hit once."

"So," he huffed. "I've never been shot. I'm just that good."

"Billy, this is a simulation. It's not real."

"He's right," Reg added. "It's a form of Virtual Hypno-Comatherapy." I scowled at Reg and he shrugged.

"Yeah, whatever, baby," Billy said, pushing past us.

"You don't remember anything, do you?"

Billy stopped. "Cut the shit, baby, before I cut you so bad, you won't shit for a week."

"Where were you born?"

"Huh?"

"I said, where were you born?"

He furrowed his brow.

"How old are you? Do you own another coat besides that one? Do you even know what day it is? You don't even know, do you? Do you know anything about who you are?"

Billy opened his mouth a few times but didn't say anything.

Reg looked at him and then at me and nodded. "His prognosis ain't good. It's as I expected." He bowed his head.

"You don't have a snappy line for that one, do you?" I said. "Well I know all about you. You're a New York cop. You like cigars, and you drink whiskey on the rocks... double with ice. You're an orphan who grew up on the streets."

"Why you askin' me all this shit? And where's my paper?"

"Your paper's not real. This is a simulation."

"Say what?"

"You really think this is the Manhattan you know? The one with guns blazin' and street punks tryin' to work you over?"

"Hey, Manhattan's mine, baby!"

"Is it?" I said, stepping into him. "This is what you want it to be. You couldn't take it when the zombies rose. You lost it. That's why you came in here."

"I don't know what you're talking about."

"He's right, ya know," Reg chimed in. "Manhattan's in ruins. The zombies took over. And ya couldn't hack it. So I had them put ya in the simulator until we could fully diagnose you."

Billy's eyes shifted between us. He turned his head suspiciously to one side, and opened his mouth, but didn't say anything.

"We need you, Billy. The people need you. Manhattan needs you," I said. I held out my arms. "All this... all this stuff around you... is what it used to be like. You don't remember because of your condition. You need to come back to us."

"You're so full of shit," Billy said, gritting his teeth. "I'm gonna kick it out of you."

"I know you don't believe us," Reg said, putting his hands up. "But, we still believe... in you."

"Yeah. I've always looked up to you since I was a kid," I added. "You're a hero. You're... my hero. I believe in you."

"Manhattan believes in you."

Billy took a step back, looking away with a confused look. He ran his hand through his hair. "This ain't real?"

I shook my head. "Absolutely none of it."

"Only what you believe... is real, ya know," Reg said.

Billy shook his head. "I... I don't know what to believe."

"Let us show you," I said with a smile. "Putz, shut it down."

The scene around us froze and faded. Buildings, people, cars, and all the sensations that came with it all disappeared. Everything... except Billy Rubin. Adrenaline surged through my body like cold lightning, wrapping around my heart. "It worked," I said. "Holy shit! It worked!"

"I wouldn't've believed it had I not seen it, ya know," Reg laughed out loud. He high-fived me.

"It worked!" I shouted.

Billy looked around and snorted. "Hey, baby, what the fuck? This is a simulator?"

"Uh… yes," Reg said, clearing his throat. "We had to improvise a bit, because the zombies…"

"They took over the hospital," I said. Putz appeared at the door. I pointed to him. "Our chief technician came up with a way to use this location to save you. He's quite brilliant." Putz's teeth slid out of his mouth. I know he was smiling, but he just looked plain stupid.

Billy looked at each of us. "You guys are really fucked!"

"Yeah, we're all a bit eccentric," I said. "I mean, look at me. I wear football equipment instead of regular clothes." Reg nodded in agreement. I grabbed Billy by the arm and led him out of the theatre. "C'mon." Surprisingly, he didn't resist.

He stopped when he saw the decayed state of the lobby. "What the fuck happened?"

"You've been in there a long time." I said. "Now come with me. There's something else you have to see." We led Billy down the corridor and out into the street. I stepped out onto the road and held out my arms. "Look around you, man!" I pointed out to a few zombies in the distance. "See that shit over there?"

Billy shook his head. "This… this ain't my Manhattan, baby."

"It's not what you remember, is it?"

"I… I think I need a drink."

"Sure, we'll have victory drink, after you clean it up," I said. "We need you to take back the streets. The people need a hero. They need you, Billy!"

Billy's eyes darted from side to side, like he was looking for something in his head. "You're right. Manhattan's mine. Nobody takes it from me." He drew his gun from inside his jacket, took aim and blasted away at the two zombies with perfectly placed head shots. He spun around and took out three more in an alley. Then he shot one on the balcony and three in the windows of a building across the street.

"I noticed you didn't reload that revolver of yours," Reg said.

"Reload? Reloadin's for chumps! I only do it when I feel like it... for effect."

"You ready to save the city?" I asked.

"Damn straight, baby! We don't need this shit all around here. I'm gonna do somethin' about it."

"Good. We're gonna introduce you to a whole bunch of people who need a hero. But you're gonna have to save them first." I opened the cab door and gestured for him to get in.

"It's on!" Billy said. Putz got into the seat next to him.

I leaned in and said to Putz in a hushed voice, "Did you, uh...do something back there to make this all possible?"

Putz stuck his pinky finger in his ear and rattled it around. "I did no such thing." He took out his finger and inspected it closely. "Holograms don't walk and talk. It only happens in movies and books." He looked up at me and smiled.

I wasn't sure if I should believe him. I slammed the car door and said, "Let's go, Reg!"

"Just hang on a sec," Reg said, disappearing into the theater. Minutes later, the lights went off and everything darkened. Reg exited the theatre and looked up at the marquee. "See ya, ol' girl." He walked around to the driver's side door and looked at Billy. "I don't think you'll be coming back here anytime soon."

"Where'll I be?"

"Well, you should probably stay with me... at the library, ya know."

"Library? I thought you were a doctor, baby. Now you some kinda crazy librarian?"

"He is," I said. "And he'll explain everything to you in time. But right now, we got some place we gotta be."

"Get in the car," Reg said, as he pulled the driver's door shut. "We have to get back."

Times Square was under assault when we returned. Reg stopped the cab at the intersection of 7th Avenue and 47th Street, about thirty feet back of the undead crowd. Waves of zombies crawled out of the surrounding buildings and descended onto the bunker. Military and civilian farmer-armored vehicles formed a semi-circular barricade on the South side of the bunker. Planks had been set up, allowing men to cross from the vehicles to the top of the fence. Men fired down onto jaw-snapping flesh eaters or roasted them with flame throwers.

"Looks like the reinforcements have arrived," Reg said.

"Yeah, on both sides," I said. "Check out all the undead."

"Ready?" Reg asked, revving the engine. I nodded. "Hang on!" He gunned the engine and tore through the zombies, honking the horn. Machine gun fire rained down from the tower, clearing a path to the main gate. Men opened the gate and we pulled in and parked between the inner and outer curtain.

Cap stormed out to greet us, with Rodrigues in tow.

"It's about time you came back!" Cap shouted. Reg and I got out of the cab. "Where's Putz?"

"He's coming," I said. "Or he's asleep."

Cap took off his hat and slammed it into the pavement. "Well I hope your stupid idea worked because the zeds are crawling all over the place. We're lucky they haven't crawled up our asses." All of the sudden, Cap's eyes widened and his cigar dangled from his gaping mouth. The gunfire gradually ceased and a hushed silence fell over the area. Everyone's gaze focused on the man getting out of the cab.

"Is that, uh...," Rodrigues swallowed. "Is that Billy Rubin?"

I turned around and smiled. Billy stood with his hands on his hips, throwing back the sweep of his three-quarter length black leather jacket. He eyed everyone with a menacing glare. "It sure is,"

I said. Billy stepped forward cautiously. The glittering golden medallion dangled from around his neck. He walked straight up to Cap, whose cigar shifted nervously from one side of his mouth to the other, and sniffed.

"Is that a Cuban, baby?"

"Uh... Yeah." Cap replied.

Billy grabbed the cigar out of Cap's mouth and ran it under his nose. "This ain't the cheap shit."

"No... never liked the cheap shit."

He jammed Cap's cigar into his mouth. "Thanks, baby!"

"Zed in the compound!" a man shouted. A lone zombie had squirmed his way in somehow and staggered towards the cab, just as Putz was getting out of the vehicle.

"Putz!" Rodrigues yelled. "Look out!"

The zombie grabbed Putz by the arm and was about to bite down on him. Putz quickly grabbed a screwdriver from his belt and jammed it in between the zombie's teeth. The two struggled, before Putz pushed the zombie back a few steps. It lurched forward a second time. Putz raised his arms, cowering in defense. Before the zombie could move any farther, Billy Rubin grabbed him by the belt, pulled him back, and then hoofed him in the ass. The zombie's lower body tore free, flying off into the distance. The upper body slapped face first into the pavement. Billy reached down, grabbed the head and pulled it off. He turned and once again, eyed everyone with a savage and wild glare.

"Alright, listen up!" he started. "I don't know what the fuck happened to this town. But in my day, we didn't have shit like this. I spent my whole life fightin'... for the good of the people. Cause there's always some asshole who wants take away your rights, your freedoms, your liberties. Well I ain't got time for assholes. There's no room for assholes in Manhattan. It's time to take back what's ours. You men wanna fight? We fight together! We fight as one! Let's clean this shit up!" Billy thrust his arm into the air, holding the head up high. Cheers erupted from the men. And Billy smiled – his glistening teeth wide and white as Chiclets.

"Hey," I said to Rodrigues, "Have you seen Jim?"

He looked at Cap. "Seen him? He's out there...fighting the zeds," he replied with a nod.

"What?"

"Maybe you should come up to the tower," Cap said.

Rodrigues, Cap, Billy, and I raced up the ladder into the crowded tower. Rodrigues peered out over the wall. "There he is!" he pointed. Off in the distance, Jim led a lone ground assault, single-handedly dishing out a healthy dose of *Shrike-Fu*, eye beam leasers and flesh eating sword play. He was right in the thick of it, leaving a trail of broken bodies and picked clean bones.

Billy Rubin chomped down on his cigar. "How can you cowardly chumps leave a man all by his lonesome in a situation like that?" Before anyone could response, Billy hopped over the wall and jumped. He hit the ground, rolled and got back to his feet. A modified colt commando appeared in his hands – the same weapon he used in *Indisception*.

"Where'd that gun come from?" Rodrigues asked.

"Does it matter?" Nate replied. "Did you see that jump? It was just like that time he jumped from that hovering chopper in *Unforbreakable*."

Billy slung the rifle over his shoulder, climbed a ladder up to one of the planks and ran across to a cargo truck. Standing on the roof of the cab, he whipped the rifle into position and opened fire, hosing the unsuspecting zombies on the ground. Bullets tore through eye sockets, punctured through the center of foreheads and split open skulls. Heads exploded or were torn free from shredded necks. Not one shell casing ejected from the rifle the whole time.

"Is it my imagination or does he never reload?" Nate asked.

"Reloading's for chumps," I said with a grin.

Billy threw the rifle aside and jumped down into the crowd. He grabbed the first zombie in front of him by the shoulder and spun him around. Forceps dangled from the flappy abdominal skin, revealing an empty abdominal cavity. "You ain't got the guts to fight me!" Billy shouted and he plunged a mighty fist up into the zombie. *SNAP!* Billy ripped the zombie in half and threw the two parts aside. The carnage continued, as his meaty fists connected with many a zombie head, shattering skulls and splattering brain matter. Between punches, he gracefully juggled his cigar, passing it from one hand to clenched teeth to his other hand.

"This is awesome," Nate grinned. "It's better than that uMe shit! I never would've expected Billy Rubin versus the zombies to be so entertaining."

"We should help him."

"He's right," another man echoed. "We're in this together. Remember: make every shot count. Let's take back Manhattan!"

The cracking of targeted shots filled the air. Zombies closing in on either Jim or Billy dropped to the ground. Billy pulled a shotgun from out of nowhere and blasted wildly, shredding gray and decaying flesh. With Jim working at one end and Billy at the other, the zombie horde was quickly eviscerated down the middle. And with that truncation, Billy and Jim backed into one another and both men spun around, fists ready. Everyone gasped collectively.

"You with me or against me, sucka?" Billy spouted.

Jim didn't even flinch. "I'm asking you the same question."

"Nice choice of skin color, baby."

"Almost as cool as yours."

Billy squinted and looked Jim up and down. "You wanna rock... or roll?

"I'll rock," Jim said, tightening the grip on his sword.

"Fine... I'll roll! Let's get it on!"

Billy and Jim both exploded with a flurry of kung fu moves. Chops sent zombie heads flying. Kicks caved in brain pans. Punches flattened faces and crushed the contents of skulls. Flying fist-smashes-o'death reduced zombies to sacks of rotting bloody pulp. In one of the most violently entertaining spectacles I had ever seen, Billy and Jim singlehandedly defeated all the zombies. Minced and shattered bodies lay strewn about. The streets of Times Square were awash with blood and brains. Everyone cheered!

Billy and Jim were met by a raucously excited crowd at the front gate. Actually, Billy drew the majority of the attention. I pushed my way through. "Hey, Jim!" I shook his hand. "Nice moves, buddy."

"Thanks." Jim nodded towards Billy. "Is this the next move?"

"Uh-huh," I grinned.

"Nice one."

I took Jim by the arm. "There's someone I want you to meet. His name is the Librarian." Before I could take another step, a disturbingly ear-piercing shriek silenced the crowd.

"Nooooooooooooooooo!" a voice shouted. Somewhere in the distance, a car alarm responded. Jim, Billy and I ran out the gate.

"I've seen booty before, baby," Billy said. "But what the fuck is that?"

The ass plodded through the field of corpses, moving from side to side with mechanical movements like a bird looking for a worm in the grass. The ass stopped and faced us. *"Wha choo don t'my zedlins?"* It squatted down and I expected the inevitable, but instead, the ass straightened its legs and leapt through the air, vaulting itself over the vehicular barricade and landing between the inner and outer curtain of chain link fence.

We quickly ran back. The ass charged, kicking men aside with its massive feet, or grinding them into the pavement. It swooped down and swallowed heads whole, tearing them free from the neck. Finally, it climbed up on top of Reg's cab. The ass shuddered and shook before violently dumping the biggest load I'd ever seen right on the hood.

"Noooo… Darlene!" Reg gasped. He dropped to his knees.

The ass shit again and again, burying the front end of the vehicle. Reg was freaking. The smell of fresh bread was so strong, my stomach rumbled until it hurt. Several men in the crowd dropped their weapons and blindly rushed towards the ass, shouting out the food they smelled like hot dogs, liver and onions, and waffles.

Jim drew his sword and charged. The ass leapt off the roof of the car, crushing two men as it landed. It turned to Jim and tried to stomp him, but he rolled aside, dodging the blow while slicing it across the calf. The sword had no effect. The ass shit into the air, fountaining feces all over the guard tower and grossed-out individuals without any cover. It spun and kicked in a support beam, forcing it to buckle. The guard tower leaned forward, sending two men over the wall. The first man splatted all over the pavement. The second landed in the ass, like a hot dog in a bun, and was crushed by the clenching cheeks. The ass howled, kicked down a section of fence, and ran off down the street, disappearing into the subway entrance on 42nd Street.

Reg ran to his car, laying his forehead on the roof, and pounding his fists into the door frame. He was practically in tears. I ran over to comfort him.

"Are you okay?"

"Ugh! I think so." Reg replied. He looked at the car and held out his hands. "I can't believe it did this to Darlene, ya know."

"Darlene?"

"My second wife."

"Oh. Well, I'm sure it's nothing a good wash won't fix."

Jim ran up to me. "We have to go after it," he said impatiently.

"I agree with the green dude," Billy said. "This is fucked... and we need to unfuck it!"

"Cap, we need explosives."

Cap was still a bit too shocked to respond, but Rodrigues was quick to run over and hand Jim an olive-drab backpack. "Blow it up. Blow that ass to ass heaven, or wherever that thing is from."

"That's our plan," Jim said.

"Listen Reg, I have to go," I said. "You gonna be alright?"

"Yeah. If I don't see you again... it was nice meeting you. Thanks for the autograph." We shook hands.

Putz approached the vehicle. He crossed his arms and stared at it. "I'll help you dig her free, Reg."

"You're a good man, Putz." I said, before I met up with Jim and Billy. "So what do we do now?"

"I know where the lair is," Jim said.

"Seriously?"

"Yeah. I followed it back through the tunnels. We can get to it through the subway system."

Billy Rubin exhaled a perfect smoke ring. "What are we waiting for, baby?"

"Let's go!" Jim said. "We'll go down that subway entrance over there."

"Wait a sec," I said. "Hey Cap," I called. He looked up at me, holding his hat in his hand and rubbing his moustache. "You alright?" He seemed overwhelmed, nodding hesitantly.

"Plan the parade and bring on the ladies. I'll be back before sundown for the victory party, baby," Billy shouted. The three of us ran across the street, down the stairs and onto the concourse. Jim and Billy seemed to have no trouble navigating through the emergency lighting. Rodrigues had been kind enough to throw in some strap-on helmet lights, and I put one on.

A zombie made a grab at Billy, but he punched it so hard, the head snapped back against the shoulder blades. We hopped over the turnstiles and took another set of stairs down to the platform where undead commuters waited for the next train. Billy leapt into action, annihilating zombies with punches and kicks. Jim was right in there with him - his sword feasting on putrid flesh, leaving only bones behind.

Once the platform was clear, Jim led us down onto the tracks, and into the dark winding tunnel. After following the track for a few miles, Jim exited through a service door and once again, we descended, this time down a rusty metal staircase into an area with many ventilation shafts. Stale, damp air greeted us. Rusty fan blades, like patient prisoners, sat perfectly still behind vertical metal grating. "This way," Jim said, running his hand along the cracked and spalling brick wall. Water dripped from creaky iron pipes anchored into the ceiling. The uneven, broken floor released an earthy scent with every step.

We finally reached a set of bent and battered iron doors, barely clinging to the doorframe by the stressed hinges. Jim weaved his way between them. On the other side, a railway line running from left to right taunted us to head even further into the darkness.

"You were actually down here?" I asked.

"Uh, yeah."

"The man's got hisself some balls," Billy nodded. "So where do we find this asshole, baby?"

"That way." Jim pointed to the left.

Billy raised a hand and halted everyone. "Hear that?"

"No, what is it?"

"I don't know. It sounds like shuffling. It's coming from down there."

I suddenly heard the sound, and a zombie horde spilled out of the tunnel behind us.

"Go!" Billy shouted. "I'll hold them off. You find that asshole." He raised his modified Colt Commando from out of nowhere and started shooting. "Come here you skin-suckin' mother fuckers! I'll give you something to bite on!"

BRAAAAP! BRAAAAP! BRAAAAP!

Jim and I bolted in the other direction, splashing through puddles of mucky, stinky water, and leapt over buckled tracks. Blackened cinders and collapsed wall sections tried to block our path. We scurried through the twisting and broken tunnel until we reached a subway car lying on its side, buried under debris and rock. The entire tunnel had caved in, leaving only the backend of the car jutting out. The door was open. I stuck my head inside and picked up the scent of fresh bread.

"We're close," I said.

"Yeah. It's right through here." Jim grabbed onto the pantograph gates and swung himself in through the door.

"We're seriously goin' in there?"

"Yes."

I followed Jim inside. A thick layer of dust and dirt blanketed the interior. We stepped over shattered glass and twisted metal pieces. Jim opened the end doors and we entered another car, completely entombed in the earth. The smell of fresh bread grew stronger. We exited the car and stepped out into a long cavern with a low ceiling, completely caked in shit.

"Gross. This is disgusting." We splorched through the ankle deep shit, making our way across the cavern, stopping short of a deep dark hole, about twenty-five feet across. "Is that the lair?"

"Yup," Jim replied with a nod. "Let's have that bag." I handed Jim the bag and he slung it over his shoulder. He took a length of rope off his belt and tied it to the subway car's external handholds. "I'm going to go down and set these charges," he said, walking backwards, slowly releasing the rope through his hands.

"Uh... what do you want me to do?"

"If anything comes through that subway car, kill it. We need a way out of here before this place blows. Here," he said, handing me a block of C-4[51]. "Set this charge on the car." Jim slid down the rope and disappeared. As I returned to the subway car, I ran my hand along the taut rope.

SPLOOSH!

The rope slackened. Shivers ran down my spine. "Jim?"

"*Ah-hyep!*" the voice grunted. A long spindly leg threw itself out over the edge of the hole; then the other. And finally, the ass raised itself up and out. "*Wuts dat?*" It strafed from side to side. "*Huh?*"

"Hey... uh, asshole!"

"*Huh? You wanna peez o'me? You wanna peez a' assssss? Kum git sum!*" The ass spread open and looked like it was about to spew.

---

[51] C-4: Composition C-4 is a common plastic explosive, more powerful than TNT.

"BOHICA![52]" I hurled the C-4, sending it straight into the anus.

"Bleh-heck! Wut you don t'me? Huh?" The ass vomited a big pile of shit. The C-4 sat on top.

"Damn."

"Haha! Ah is wut Ah eetz and don excreetz! Now Ah gonna eetz yo hedmeetz."

Fuck it! I let out a battle cry and charged forward. Maybe I startled the ass, but it seemed unprepared as I caught it in the left butt cheek with my shoulder. It fell back and slid through the shit. I grabbed the C-4 and was quickly on top of it. I plunged the charge into the ass and squeezed the cheeks tight.

"Mmph-frm-rff!" The legs kicked back at me.

Jim's green hand suddenly appeared on edge of the hole. He pulled himself up, slipping once or twice.

"Jim! I need help!"

He ran over quickly, bringing the end of the rope with him. He tied it around the ass's left foot. I struggled to hold the ass down as it thrashed about. "Where are the charges?"

"I set two of them," Jim grunted. He pinned the other leg between his, and looped the rope around the other foot. "I had to hide when this thing came up. Sorry." He pulled the rope tight, and continued to wrap up the ass's legs.

"I need your help holding this ass shut." I couldn't get a foothold on anything. My boots kept sliding around. And the whole time I could only smell fresh bread.

"Brapm-pipple-fraap!"

"Hang on!" Jim leaned in and pushed the ass from the other side. We both put our weight down on it."

"What now?"

"Gotta... get it... down that hole. Then we blow it!" Jim reached into his tac vest and pulled out the detonator.

---

[52] BOHICA *(military slang):* Bend Over, Here It Comes Asshole! A warning or taunt of impending danger or damage.

"What if we... blow ourselves up?" The ass kept on flailing and struggling to get loose.

"So be it!"

Then things got a heck of a lot worse. Zombies slowly trickled in from the subway car.

"Fuck!" I spat. "This ain't good."

"Grrp!"

"Push!" We slid the ass through the shit and over the edge. We flew over. The rope jerked tight. Both of us held the rope and ass tight at the same time.

"We gotta cut that rope."

"I'll... use my eyebeams." Jim eyes began to glow. Zombies leaned over the edge, leering down at us.

KA-BLAM!

"Take that you motherfuckers!" It was Billy! Neutralized zombies flew past us down into the hole. "Think you can fuck up my town, huh baby?"

THWACK! SLAM! SMACK! POW! KATHUNK!

"Mmmrrrpfft!"

Billy suddenly appeared on the edge of the hole, looking down at us. "Need some help there, baby?" Jim threw him the detonator.

"Cut the rope." Jim ordered. "Then wait for my command to detonate the charges."

"You sure 'bout that?"

"Just do it!" I shouted. "Keep the people safe!"

Billy flicked out a switch blade and grinned. "I'll be thinkin' about yo mommas. Manhattan's mine, baby!" He armed the detonator and stepped away from the edge.

"Ppffffzzzzzzrrrt!"

"Hey Jim?"

"Yeah?"

"If we're gonna blow up, then just tell me one thing."

"Sure."

"How'd you turn green?"

Jim laughed, "I'm undead."

Before the thought of Jim being undead really sunk in, the rope snapped and we were free falling down an endless dark shaft. My hands slipped off the ass. *PLOP!* I hit the ground first, landing softly in a huge, cushy, shit pile. Had I closed my eyes and breathed deeply, I would have sworn I fell into a loaf of freshly baked bread.

SPLAT! Jim and the ass landed a few feet away from me. We were in the middle of a long, crap encrusted tunnel. The ass squirmed to its feet with Jim still clinging to it. Jim push-kicked himself off, forcing the ass back down. He landed on the ground with the ass between us.

"Get clear of the blast!" Jim shouted. The ass was slowly getting back up. With all the commotion, Jim and I ran in opposite directions of one another. I stopped when I realized we were separated with the ass between us. In addition, the route I took ended abruptly, sloping down to a hole in the ground. Jim cupped his hands around his mouth and shouted, "Blow it!"

"Jim! Wait!"

KA-BOOM!

The blast drowned out my voice and hit me like a ton of bricks, sending me flying back. Grit peppered my face and crackled against my visor. I hit the shitty wall, sticking to it momentarily before sliding down into the hole. As I descended, the entire tunnel collapsed on top of the ass. I lost sight of Jim. Rocks and sand fell on top of me. My body ached. Sapped of all my energy, I couldn't move. So I just closed my eyes and went along for the ride.

19 JIM'S STORY: DISMEMBERS ONLY

Drown the soul; burn the flesh,
Scatter the ashes; bury the bones.
Live life eternal!
    -The Book of Amaltheon

Jim opened his eyes and sat up quickly. He stared at the tightly packed rubble in front of him. Looking back over his shoulder, he saw a long, dark tunnel. Despite his regenerated eyes, and his ability to see in the dark, the sight of more rock was as good as being blind.

"Ed?" Jim's voice echoed in the emptiness. He pushed himself up from the cold hard earth, got to his feet and gathered up his gear.

"Shrike!" The whisper ran along the back of his neck. Jim froze - his breathing calm and controlled. He waited. He turned towards the sound and sensed nothing. "Shrike," the voice hissed again. An orange ember glow appeared deep in the distance. Jim suddenly lost all body sensation as if his presence filled the entire tunnel. He closed his eyes and shook off the slumbering veil draped over his senses. Along with newfound alertness came a sense of direction. Jim checked his gear and equipment once more for good measure, and headed towards the light.

***

Jim entered his quarters. The steel access door slid shut behind him leaving him immersed in total darkness. "Lights," he said. Nothing happened. Normally, he wouldn't have cared. Jim liked the dark. It spared him from his quarters' harsh interior: gray concrete walls, stainless steel desk, metal locker and bed frame. At least he had his own shower and toilet. But to think his quarters were considered fit for an officer. He couldn't imagine living in the bunker as an enlisted man, much less a civilian.

"Lights!" he repeated. He set his tactical pack down to the left of the door. Jim made a habit of always keeping things in the same place. He knew exactly how many steps it took to reach his bed and where to find the hidden combat knife and flashlight. He had spent many an hour dismantling rifles and pistols, laying out the pieces and assembling them again, often in total darkness. It was good to be prepared. But today, after a vigorous hand-to-hand combat session, he would have preferred to have the lights on. Jim huffed and punched the intercom.

"Lieutenant Shrike. This is Corporal Hicks. How can I be of assistance?"

"My lights aren't working again. Can you please send a maintenance team to my quarters?"

"One moment, sir. We can send out somebody on Friday."

"You expect me to wait three days?"

"Sorry, sir. The, uh… we've got some problems with the, uh…"

"I am aware of the issues with the defense grid."

"Sorry, sir. I didn't know how widely it had been communicated. The work crews are working double shifts. All other maintenance has been deemed unessential."

Jim sighed. "Very well, then. Maybe I'll start that mushroom farm I've always dreamed of."

"Sorry sir, I don't understand."

"That will be all, Corporal!" Jim didn't wait for a response. He hit the intercom release. The lights suddenly flicked on. They seemed brighter than usual. Jim closed his eyes, protecting them from the harsh assault. Then he sensed it: someone was in his room. Quick as a flash, Jim spun around, drawing his pistol and pressing the barrel to the forehead of the man seated on his bed. His eyes were still closed.

"Impressive, Jim," the man said calmly. He sat up straight, practically statuesque, with his hands on his knees. A manila envelope rested on his lap.

Jim opened his eyes and raised a quizzical eyebrow. His finger eased off the trigger. He returned the pistol to its holster. "Hello, Argon."

"Thanks for not shooting me."

"It could still happen."

"I know. And I'm sorry. How long has it been?"

Jim stowed his belt in his locker and put his hands on his hips. He stared at the ceiling as if the answer were scribed on it. "Last time I saw you… I had just saved Ford Alroc." Jim looked at Argon. "It's been a few years." He sat down in the chair opposite the bed and slowly untied his boots.

"You've accomplished so much in that time," Argon said. "And that uncanny danger sense of yours seems sharper. You should trust it more."

"I trusted you. And then you just vanished."

"Jim, c'mon. You did just fine without me."

"I know I did. But, you could have said something before you left." Jim threw his boots down and leaned back in the chair, stretching his legs, and crossing his arms across his chest.

"That's why I'm here. I came to say goodbye."

Jim breathed deeply and sat up. "Fine. Goodbye, Argon."

"Aw, don't be so sore with me, buddy," Argon smiled. "I brought you a parting gift."

"Oh really?"

"An opportunity will come your way. Take it without hesitation. If you do, you'll leave this bunker."

"What kind of opportunity?"

"I can't say for certain. You'll just know it when it presents itself." He handed Jim the envelope.

"What's this?" Jim asked, looking inside it.

"A memory stick. You know that football player?"

"Yeah, Eddie Griffin. I trained him in hand-to-hand."

"A copy of his file's on it. Read it."

"Why?"

"Because when you leave, he's going with you. You're going to take him."

Jim looked down at the envelope. "Why would I do that?"

"There's also a newspaper clipping in there. It'll explain why he has to go along."

"That's it then?"

"It is. I have to leave now."

"Wait… before you go, why did you leave me last time?"

"You needed time to forge your own destiny. You'll have that opportunity again. But first, destiny will forge you." Jim set the envelope on his desk. The room suddenly darkened. "So long, Jim. Good luck!" Argon's disembodied voice said. The lights came back on. Argon had disappeared, leaving Jim alone again.

***

The heat grew more intense as Jim approached the tunnel's end. Hot air rushed into the chamber, searing his face and the back of his throat. The tunnel ended abruptly, opening onto a rocky cylindrical shaft. The roof of the shaft was so far away, it appeared only as a black speck. Several hundred feet below, the magma floor of the shaft churned and sputtered. Gouts of fiery gel spouted into the air. A pillar of stone rose up from the center of the lava pool – its flat top creating a platform approximately twenty feet below him. A blackened tree trunk jutted out from the center. Jim turned and looked back down the tunnel. There was no place left to go.

"Shrike!" The voice caused him to turn around and refocus. Jim looked down, carefully calculating his next move, before taking a few steps back. He ran forward and leapt out of the tunnel. When his feet hit the hard parched top of the stone pillar, Jim threw himself diagonally to the ground, stopping the momentum from taking him over the edge.

He got up and dusted himself off. Jim looked over the edge of the pillar. Heat danced across his cheeks, warming him to the bones. Jim circled the perimeter, every so often looking back at the entrance through which he'd come. There was no way back. Not at this moment, anyway.

Jim decided to examine the tree trunk. The blackened and charred stump rose a few feet out of the hardened earth. The dry, brittle wood crumbled in his hand, leaving his palm blackened with oily ash. Jim peered down in the dark hollow stump.

The ground beneath him shook. Jim was more concerned with the sporadic popping and cracking sounds, loud as gunshots. Like an old slumbering ember with renewed life, the stump erupted into flames. The heat pierced his skin. Jim shielded himself with his forearm. Even his clothes were hot and uncomfortable.

Bright tongues of flame rose from the hollow in the stump. Then a thin skeletal hand curled its fingers over the edge of the wood. Another hand coiled its way out and grabbed hold. The fingers glowed orange and yellow. Tiny flames danced along the surface of the bones. Slowly, a skeleton emerged from the stump. Its eyes glowed fiercely – nothing more than flaming orbs within the sockets. As it pulled itself up, it hoisted out a long slender leg. It braced its heel on the stump and lunged forward, landing with a thud in front of Jim.

Jim held his ground, looking up at the grinning beast. The skeleton cocked its head to one side and leaned in, examining Jim from head to toe. Satisfied with its thorough inspection, the skeleton reeled back and opened its arms.

"Welcome Shrike," it seethed in a voice that sounded like a loud whisper, each word punctuated so harshly it sounded vulgar. "So... you are the new Waykeeper."

***

Jim didn't wait for the doors to slide open fully before entering Bunker-57's briefing room. He hated being late, especially for meetings with *the brass*. The officers were seated around one side of a long oval table. The view screens on the wall behind them lay dormant, bathing the room in a pale blue hue. The lights were dim as well, but such was the direction in the bunker in an effort to conserve power.

Jim snapped to attention. "I'm sorry I'm late, General Hadron."

"At ease, Lieutenant," the eldest of the senior officers replied. General Hadron's voice was gentle and soothing. His hardened exterior couldn't hide the fact that he was more interested in offering cookies to his grandchildren. "Please be seated." He motioned to the lone chair positioned on the other side of the table. Jim pulled the chair out and sat down with his back straight and his hands off the table.

Colonel Bradley licked his finger and flipped through several pages on the table. "We've been going through your report, Lieutenant. Mind if we ask you a few questions?"

"No sir. Not at all, sir."

General Hadron leaned in and smiled. "Why don't we begin with a summary of what happened?"

Jim cleared his throat. "Yesterday at approximately 04:00 I was alerted to the discovery of a transponder beacon within our perimeter. PFC Rovira was stationed at the comm. He validated the code and confirmed it was a distress signal broadcasting on a military frequency."

"What did you do when the signal was confirmed?" asked General Toews, as he fiddled with his eyeglasses.

"I immediately notified Colonel Atherton and he gave me the green light to proceed with an investigation. My team was assembled and we were topside and at the target within the hour."

The officers exchanged glances before asking another question. General Hadron spoke, "The men in your team -- their names are all in your report?"

"Yessir."

"Good. Proceed."

"Thank you, sir. We surveyed the target before closing in. The vehicle was a light utility HUMVEE with no distinct markings."

"But it was a military vehicle?" Colonel Bradley asked.

"Yessir. I was stationed in Area 51 about a year ago and had seen similar vehicles in use."

"And nobody on your team recognized the vehicle?"

"No, sir."

"Are you saying your deduction was based on a hunch?"

"Yessir."

Colonel Bradley bit his lip and glanced at General Hadron. "Where do you think the vehicle came from?" he asked.

Jim looked at all the officers seated around him. He noticed Dr. Martin Kildroyd seated to his far left, jotting something down in a folder. Jim was sure it was a crossword puzzle. Dr .Kildroyd was a civilian advisor on all things UD. "Given the proximity, my guess is the vehicle came from the Dulce Base." The officers immediately put on their poker faces, but Jim knew he'd won the pot.

"Continue, please," Colonel Bradley ordered, before looking away.

"The vehicle had run out of fuel. I believe the occupants were in a hurry."

"Is this another hunch?

"No, sir… just things were out of place. The most glaring evidence was the maintenance record. That vehicle was scheduled for service. It had been grounded. It should never have been allowed out of the motor pool. I think…." Jim hesitated.

"What is it?"

Jim paused, choosing his words carefully. "I think they had no other option."

"And what about survivors?" asked General Toews.

"None to speak of, sir. We found one man, several hundred feet away. His body showed visible signs of extensive trauma suffered at the hands and mouths of UDs."

Dr. Kildroyd set down his pen and perked up. He scratched his bearded cheek. "You're sure he was killed by UDs?"

"Yes, sir. His internal organs were gone - torn from his body. Bite marks were evident on the abdomen and neck."

"Thanks, Jim... I mean, uh, Lieutenant." Dr. Kildroyd gave him a nod.

"Did you find anything else?" General Hadron asked.

"Yes, sir. The deceased was carrying a shock proof gel-pak storage unit. I secured the device and gave it to Colonel Atherton upon my return to base."

"Did any of the men in your team see you with this storage unit?" Colonel Bradley asked.

"No sir, and that's not a hunch either sir."

General Hadron chuckled. "Well said, Lieutenant. Is there anything else you wish to add at this time?"

Jim straightened himself in his seat. "Yes, sir." He cleared his throat again. "I believe my report was quite detailed, as was my debriefing. This line of questioning in which you've engaged me is not to confirm the contents of my report. I believe you are trying to find out who is privy to the strangeness of this encounter. I'd like your permission to know what was inside that box."

"You are very perceptive," General Hadron commented. He looked from side to side, at the men seated at the table. "Permission granted. Dr. Kildroyd?"

The doctor hastily dropped his pen. "Uh, yes. Thank you General." He reached down and lifted a metal storage box onto the table. After snapping open the latches, Dr. Kildroyd opened the lid. He reached in and held up a small vial of green glowing liquid.

Jim's gaze went from the vial to General Hadron. It was as if the General had been waiting for his reaction. "Dr. Kildroyd believes it is a prototype super-soldier serum. And you were correct, Lieutenant: it did come from Dulce Base."

Colonel Bradley leaned back in his chair. "Dulce Base has been compromised. It was overrun by UDs within the last seventy two hours. We were expecting this package."

Jim didn't have to say anything. He already knew too much without knowing it. He leaned in, resting his elbows on the table. "What's next, sir?"

"Lieutenant," General Hadron began softly, "We've been losing bunkers to the UDs at an alarming rate. The east coast is all but gone. We need a solution and we need it now."

"We need a test subject," Dr. Kildroyd spurted. General Hadron glared at the doctor and took a sip of water. The other men seemed tense. General Hadron was about to speak.

"I'll do it, sir," Jim interjected. "I'll be your test subject."

General Hadron sighed. "You're sure about this? There are risks…"

"It's risk mitigation, sir," Jim said. "If this is successful, it will tilt the odds in our favor against the UDs. If it's not, well… I could end up a dead man. With all due respect sir, if that happens, I don't think I need to remind you how much they talk."

***

"Waykeeper?" Jim said, taking a step back.

The skeleton shook its head. "Armitage is dead… such a shame." It lurched closer, craning its neck so its big fiery skull was in line with Jim.

"Who are you?" Jim asked.

"Hmmm?" The skeleton stood tall, leering down at him. "I am fire, Shrike."

"An elemental?"

"Fire is your element. Not mine. I only serve it." He waved his hand. "Call me what you wish, Shrike."

"Elemental it is."

"Now you must earn your title, Shrike." The elemental's fist shot forth. Jim side stepped, diverting the blow with his left forearm. At the same time, he drew his sword with his right hand and he swung in, aiming for the elemental's midsection. It caught his hand by the wrist and turned away from him, lifting his arm and throwing him over. Jim flipped head over heels and somehow managed to land on his feet.

"Impressive," the elemental said with a ghastly grin.

The two circled each other. Jim sprang forward, aiming the sword-point at the elemental's chest. It sidestepped and caught his wrist. The bony fingers clamped down with vice-like pressure. Jim's wrist snapped forcing his grip to loosen. The elemental flipped him over again. The sword fell from his grasp. This time, Jim landed flat on his back. The sword shot down and stabbed into the earth.

The elemental tilted its head from side to side, as if adjusting its neck. It looked down at Jim and said, "A bit slow." It pointed to its own chest. "This is not the undead you are fighting, Shrike."

Jim rolled onto his stomach and then got up onto his knees. He set one foot flat on the ground. His wrist was tingling. The elemental stood between him and the sword.

It looked back at the blade jutting out of the ground. "Need your weapon to fight, Shrike?"

Jim clenched his fist. From a crouch, Jim launched at the elemental. He brought his knees up to his chest and crashed them into the elemental's upper body. With his elbows, he cracked the skeleton in the temples. It stepped back. Then he kicked out, burying his heels in the elemental's sternum. It flew back and off the edge of the pillar. Jim dropped to the ground and quickly got back to his feet. He looked down over the edge into the gurgling magma. "Guess not."

Jim turned. The elemental was climbing out of the tree stump. It wrenched itself free and stood up straight. It stuck out its hand and motioned for Jim to come forward, and then positioned itself in a combat pose.

Jim charged. Again he left the ground, sending a kick into the elemental's ribs. It absorbed the blow and grabbed hold of his leg. It turned sideways and used Jim's momentum to drag him through and then down onto the earth. "Your creativity is strong, but it leaves you ungrounded, Shrike."

Before the elemental could react, Jim flung out his legs, sweeping the elemental off its feet. By the time it landed on its back, Jim had his sword over its throat.

"Cunning. You trust your instincts. I am pleased, Shrike. Argon has taught you well."

"Argon?" Jim asked.

The elemental ignored him and sat up, the blade passing right through it with no effect. It got up and extended a bony hand. "Show me this weapon of yours. It has a strange taste."

Jim cautiously rose. He slowly held out the sword, hilt first. The elemental took the sword with both hands and examined it closely. "Ahhh, so this is Sarkophagus... crafted from the femur of a Gnicghul[53]." The elemental looked up from the blade. "I have completed my assessment of your skills, Shrike."

"Have I earned my title?"

"Not until we deal with your weakness."

"Oh yeah? What would that be?"

The elemental quickly thrust the sword, piercing Jim in the chest. His body tensed and he dropped to his knees. Jim looked down. Maggots squirmed out of his skin, sliding past the blade before falling to the ground. Were it not for the absence of skin, one would think the elemental's grin had grown hideous. It slowly slid the blade in farther, increasing the crushing pressure in Jim's chest. The elemental bent down. Its head tilted to one side. "This sword serves you well, Shrike. But you have yet to serve this sword."

***

---

[53] Gnicghul (*Gneech-gool*): A demon whose presence increases the rate of decay.

Jim opened his eyes and took a deep breath. The bed's metal frame groaned as he sat up, dragging the heart monitoring machine with him.

"Easy, Jim," Dr. Kildroyd said. Jim noticed the brass looking at him through the viewing widow, not like there was much privacy in the opaque plexi-glass contamination cell, anyway. General Hadron made his way to the door, followed by his entourage of officers.

"How long have I been out, Marty?" Jim asked.

"About thirty minutes, maybe." Dr. Kildroyd scratched his neck, and tucked in the bright red shirt collar sticking out from under his lab coat. "How are you feeling?"

"I feel great."

The door seal broke, hissing as it opened. "Lieutenant," General Hadron said with a smile. "Good to see you up so quickly." He looked to Dr. Kildroyd. "I take it all is well?"

"Well, I haven't had any time to run any real tests. Based on preliminary tests after first administering the serum, I noticed higher than normal levels of copper in Jim's body. That needs to be monitored. Otherwise, everything seems to be in order, but I'll need more tests."

"How much time do you need?" Colonel Bradley asked.

"Uh…." Dr. Kildroyd scratched his neck again, this time under the chin. "I would like to conduct a physical and I need to do some more blood work, among other things… somewhere in there my wife might want to see me… maybe two or three days."

Jim reached down and pulled the intravenous needle out of his wrist. The men watched in awe as the puncture wound instantly healed. General Hadron looked up with a grin. "You have twelve hours."

"Twelve hours? What's your hurry?" Dr. Kildroyd asked, his forehead rippling with frustration.

"We need to conduct a field test," Colonel Bradley replied. "We need to see what happens when a UD comes in contact with the subject. How soon can you have your team assembled, Lieutenant?"

Jim sat up straight and raised an eyebrow while thinking through his response. "My team will be assembled and ready in two hours."

"Excellent!" General Hadron clapped his hands together.

Dr. Kildroyd put a hand on Jim's shoulder. "Jim, please give me more time to assess you."

Jim brushed him away. "It's okay, Marty, I'll be fine."

"Well done, Lieutenant," General Toews said.

"Thank you, sir. Shall I have my team meet me in UD containment?"

"UD Containment?" General Hadron grinned. "We can't run the test with one of the UDs we have in containment. As test subjects, they're contaminated. We want real results, not skewed results. No, we need a UD as feral as the day he turned. You're going topside Lieutenant."

***

Jim fell forward, supporting himself with one hand on the ground. He clutched his tightening chest with the other. The elemental reached down, clamping a hand on Jim's head. As it raised its hand, Jim could not help but stand. The elemental looked closely at Jim's chest. "We need to cauterize this." Within seconds, Jim's body spontaneously combusted. Jim had the sensation he was floating above himself, watching his body bubble and sizzle to a crisp. He had no sense of body limitation - he was everywhere, all around himself observing from all angles simultaneously. It was a disorienting sensation.

Jim's body crumpled in a smoky heap as the elemental pulled its hand away. Slowly, the skin regrew and regenerated until he was whole again. At the exact moment, Jim opened his eyes and was back inside his body. The elemental ran the blade along his long flaming tongue. His teeth clacked as if he were savoring some exotic flavor. It pulled the blade away and pointed to the ground. "Dig!"

"What?" Jim asked. "Why do you want me to dig?"

"Just dig. You need a bit more work, Shrike."

Jim got down on his knees and pulled at the earth with his hands. His energy returned to him faster than usual, and soon he found himself working tirelessly. The earth softened with every handful. It became cold and wet. Within a few minutes, Jim knelt over a shallow pit of dark, smelly mud.

"This is good. Now rise, Shrike!"

Jim stood up slowly. He titled his head back and closed his eyes – he already knew what was coming. At first, the sword felt cold upon entering his chest. The elemental twisted the blade, accelerating the slow burn. Once again, Jim found himself everywhere except within his own body. He watched as layer after layer of blistering ashy skin flaked off and drifted away. Muscles and organs sputtered and hissed, crumbled into black powder. When the last of the flames faded, Jim's body was nothing more than a blackened skeleton skewered on a sword. The elemental laid out his bones in the mud, where they floated momentarily before sinking out of view. The elemental leaned back, its rib cage expanding as if taking in a breath, and then heaved forward. A fine, steamy mist sprayed out from between its teeth. Vapor rose from the mud pool until the thick earth had dried hard and cracked.

Jim was suddenly in total darkness. He could sense he was prone and felt a cold pressure on his body. Cold dirt squirmed between his wiggling fingers. Jim forced himself to sit up. The pressure against his torso resisted at first. Hard packets of earth fell away from his chest. Jim flexed his arm, forcing more cold earth to fall away. He climbed out of his shallow grave, feeling more alive than ever before.

Jim moved into a crouch and was about to rise when the elemental jabbed the sword into his chest again. This time, Jim felt the pressure against his body but no maggots emerged from the wound. He watched the flesh close as the blade slid free.

"This is good, Shrike," the elemental said. It handed the sword to Jim, handle first. "Now, test your element."

Jim took the sword. "What do you mean?"

"Set the blade aflame, Shrike." The elemental held two bony fingers to his head. "Use your eyes, Shrike."

Jim looked down at the sword. He focused his eyes on the white bone and didn't feel any unpleasant burning sensation like he had in the past. The blade grew warm, slowly warming to an orange glow. Flames burst out along the blade, licking it from hilt to tip. Jim looked up at the elemental. It nodded with approval. "I didn't fire any eye beams."

"Your perception has increased, Shrike. Beams are unnecessary."

Jim held up the sword and concentrated on the flames. They danced and flickered before completely disappearing. Jim ran his fingers along the cool bone and grinned.

"You serve Sarkophagus now, Shrike."

Jim lowered the sword to his side and bowed to show his gratitude. The elemental responded in kind, then spread its arms wide. A wall of fire surged out of the ground directly between Jim and the elemental.

"Now Shrike, let us see if Armitage approves of your transformation."

***

Dr. Kildroyd burst into the motor pool while the medics loaded Jim onto a stretcher. One medic worked the bag valve mask, while the other jabbed a needle into the intravenous line. The doctor pushed his way through. "Step aside! What happened?" he asked, fearing the worst as he looked down at Jim's pale body.

"We're not sure, sir."

"Let's get him to the infirmary." The medics wheeled the stretcher around and headed for the door. General Hadron and his entourage hovered close by, keeping their distance only enough to be minimally obtrusive. Two soldiers ran alongside the stretcher, weapons in hand. Dr. Kildroyd frowned at them. "What are his vitals?"

"Hard to say," one of the medics responded. "They're all over the map. He was VSA[54] when we found him." He nodded to the other medic. "Schyfe here performed CPR until we got him breathing again, but it's irregular."

"Where are the others?"

"Dead... all dead. UDs got them. They were ripped to shreds."

One of the soldiers added, "We were monitoring Lieutenant Shrike and his team from a secure point nearby. We lost the comm signal. When we picked it up again, we heard nothing but screaming and gunfire. By the time we got there, the Lieutenant was the only man in one piece."

"There's not a scratch on him," the medic said.

"Let me worry about that," Dr. Kildroyd stated, wheeling Jim into the elevator. The doors began to slide shut when Colonel Bradley stopped them with his hand. The doors retracted. General Hadron and company stood in the hall. "We haven't got time for this, you jarhead. Jim is dying!" Dr. Kildroyd hit the elevator button repeatedly.

"At ease, doctor," the Colonel snapped. "When do you think we can debrief the Lieutenant?"

The doors began to slide again. "When you meet him in hell!" Dr. Kildroyd shouted before they closed.

***

The wall of fire rose higher and higher, blocking the elemental from view. Jim stared into the bright orange and yellow flames. A shadow appeared within. As it emerged from the fiery wall, Jim smiled at the familiar face.

---

[54] **VSA** *(medical term)*: Vital Signs Absent.

"Hello Argon," Jim said.

Argon ignored Jim's offered handshake and embraced him instead. He put his hands on Jim's shoulders and smiled. "You made it... as I knew you always would. Now you can be whole again." Like a ghost passing through a wall, Argon stepped forward and *into* Jim where he disappeared. Jim felt dizzy and foggy, as if his head was in a slow-moving cloud.

Before his mind fully cleared, another shadow exited the flame wall - a Samurai in full armor. The warrior circled Jim, looking him up and down, while keeping one hand on the hilt of his Katana, and holding a lantern in the other. Jim remained calm, yet poised for attack should the need arise.

The Samurai finally stopped and faced Jim. He set down the lantern and removed his helmet and face mask. The warrior's face had a hint of humanoid, but it was predominantly goat. Multiple piercings adorned his ears and tattoos swirled on his scalp. He looked Jim up and down once again, his jaw rotating from side to side as if chewing something.

"Hello Shrike," he said in an almost guttural sounding voice. "I am Armitage." Jim nodded. He looked over Armitage's shoulder to see several shadows in the wall of fire. Despite the lack of detail, the dark silhouettes could not disguise the horde of armored warriors and hulking brutes. "Those are the spirits of your ancestors – the spirits of the Waykeepers. We are known as the Strozghuly[55] in our speak. I was the last... until now. You are the next of our kin to bear the light. Do you accept?"

"May I ask a question?"

Armitage nodded. "Proceed."

"Who is Argon?"

"Argon?" Armitage scratched his bearded chin. "Argon... is you." Jim furrowed his brow. "Does this not make sense to you? Perhaps it will, soon."

---

[55] Strozghuly *(Strohz-gool-y)*: Protectors and guides of Nabisusha. Typically, former demons, or humanoids with demonic abilities.

After a brief pause Jim said, "I will bear the light."

Armitage handed him the lamp. "You are the Strozghul now, Shrike. Protect and guide those who enter Nabisusha. Keep the path clear." Armitage leaned in and pressed his forehead to Jim's.

"Go my brother," he whispered. The goat-headed warrior put his face mask and helmet back on, and stepped back into the flames. One by one, he and the other silhouettes drifted away, disappearing into the fire. The wall slowly descended and burned out, leaving Jim standing before the elemental.

The fiery skeleton pointed at Jim's lantern. "Your ancestors favor you, Shrike. Nabisusha Rejoice! The Strozghul has returned!"

***

It didn't take Jim long to realize he was back in the infirmary. But this time, nobody waited for him outside the viewing window. The curtain had been pulled around his bed, dampening the bright fluorescent lighting. The machines and monitors were off. Tepid recycled air flowed down on him from the overhead vent. Jim grabbed the bed rail and suddenly noticed his skin color: he was green. He held up both arms; then checked the rest of his body.

Jim had his head under the sheets when the curtains parted and Dr. Kildroyd appeared by his bed. "Don't worry, it's still functional."

"I hope you didn't have to run any tests," Jim sneered.

"Well, Nurse Pratchett was a bit curious. You were unconscious a long time and I did leave you in her care." Dr. Kildroyd smiled. "How ya feeling, Jim?"

Jim put his hands behind his head. "I feel… great. When can I get out of here?" He held out his hand. "When this color fades?"

Dr. Kildroyd sat down on the edge of the bed. "Well, I'm not sure exactly as to when you'll get out of here. The brass has a few concerns."

Jim lowered his arms. "What is it, Marty?"

"Uh." Dr. Kildroyd scratched his neck. "About you were injected with that serum, your bloodwork indicated higher than normal levels of copper."

"I remember that."

"Good." Dr. Kildroyd sat down on the edge of the bed. "You normally have copper in your body to help with tissue regeneration. Since your field test the copper has oxidized. You kind of rusted, Jim… like an old penny."

Jim furrowed his brow. "Any idea of the cause?"

Dr. Kildroyd shrugged. "Without more tests, it is difficult for me to say. But, sulphur has been known to accelerate the oxidation reaction… and your body is full of it."

"Sulphur?"

"Yeah. Hard to explain or make sense of it, really." The doctor scratched again. "Uh… there's something else."

"Sure, what is it?"

"I don't know how to tell you this, but, uh… it's quite fascinating really, but… you're not showing any life signs. Clinically, you're dead, Jim."

Jim raised an eyebrow. "How is that possible?"

"I don't know… I won't know without more tests. In fact, I may never know. You have no body temperature. The scans indicate no brain activity. You have no heart rate. Yet, here we are, having a conversation." Jim stared off into the folds of the sheet. Dr. Kildroyd stood up and put his hands in his pockets. "I can tell you this, though," the doctor began, "You must have received some form of trauma to your throat. The tissue there is recently regenerated." Jim still said nothing. "Do you remember anything from the attack?"

He looked up at the doctor. "No. Not really. How is my team? Were they affected?"

"They're all dead. I'm sorry, Jim. It must have been a nasty swarm of UDs you ran into. I saw what they did to your men. You must have been outnumbered."

"Outnumbered?" Jim said with a frown. "But there was only one."

***

The pillar of earth rumbled beneath Jim's feet. He couldn't tell if the pillar was ascending, or if the cave around him was descending. It seemed like it was simultaneously expanding in diameter. Jim lifted the lantern by the ringed handle and examined it. It was made of a lightweight metal Jim had not seen before – the golden luster had faded in places to a reddish brown hue. The stressed and pock marked frame connected the domed lid to the flat bottom. Four gritty and dingy glass panels – cracked and broken - completed the exterior. Inside the lantern a sharp fire crackled and sparked, nestled comfortably in a bed of earth and moss. It was an odd mix of organic engineering and metalcraft.

"A Waykeeper's fire can never be extinguished, Shrike," the elemental said.

"Where does this lantern come from?" Jim asked.

"The Corvid built it."

"Corvid?"

"A warrior race more skilled in mechanical arts and artifice than in combat, Shrike. They built the lantern for Holioch, to carry the sacred fire he had stolen from the dark gods." Jim raised an eyebrow. The trembling ceased. Jim noticed the pillar had expanded enough to completely fill the cavern, like a giant stone cork. The tunnel entrance he had come in through was perfectly aligned with the ground.

The elemental stepped aside. "Go now, Shrike. Nabisusha calls for the Strozghul."

"Thank you," Jim said.

The elemental bowed. "I must return to my duties, Shrike." The elemental returned to the stump and swept its legs into the hole. As it lowered itself down, it said, "Til the next Strozghul, Shrike." Its flaming skull disappeared into the charred wood.

UNDEAD RECKONING

Jim took one last look around. With Sarkophagus in one hand and the lantern in the other, Jim exited the cavern, and returned to the halls of Nabisusha.

***

Jim entered the General's office and stood before his desk with his hands behind his back.

"Ah, Lieutenant," General Hadron said from behind his desk. "Good to see you back on your feet. How are you feeling?"

"A bit confused, sir."

"Uh, yes... understandable given your current situation. Please, sit down."

"I'll stand, sir."

General Hadron leaned back in his chair. "Very well then. What's on your mind?"

"I'm leaving the bunker, sir. I'm going topside, whether I have your permission or not."

The general held up his hands. "Just hang on a minute. Let's think this through."

"I have, sir, and I am leaving. I don't need a vehicle. Just let me take my gear... and Eddie Griffin."

"What?" The general squirmed in his leather chair causing it to creak. "The football player? Whatever for?"

"He's a celebrity, sir. He may provide a strategic advantage. We're bound to encounter survivors. Some of them just might like football."

General Hadron ran a hand through his thinning hair. "Where will you go?"

"Dulce Base. I need to know what happened."

"You won't get your life back."

"I don't want my life back. I just want answers."

"I see. Well, I will have to talk this over with..."

"My decision's made. I'm dead, and therefore no longer under your command."

General Hadron shook a finger. "Your body is the property of the US military."

"Not as long as I'm still in it!" Jim stood straight and tall, never flinching. He stared the General straight in the eyes. "The others in the bunker avoid me; the UDs don't even notice me. I'm a ghost. So I'm leaving… and I'm taking Eddie Griffin with me."

"Just who do think you are, ordering me around?" The General's face showed signs of that hardened soldier he was so long ago – his voice was strong and eyes burned with ferocity. "I can stop you! I can have a security team here at my command."

Jim leaned in, placed his hands on the General's desk and glared at him. "Over my dead body! You really want to do that?" he seethed. "How many lives are you willing to lose? I'll kill everyone who steps in my path." Jim pushed himself off the desk. "Your experiment was a failure. There's only one thing you can do."

"Oh yes? And what's that?"

Jim made his way to the door. It slid open. As he stepped out of the office he said, "Say something nice about me at my memorial service."

20 PAIR O'DICE LOST

A hero will journey to the realm
Carrying a heavy heart.
And all will be free,
But only when forgiveness is granted,
And forgiveness is accepted.

-High Priestess Druscilla
The Oracle at the Temple of Shahayla[56]

Cold, damp moss pressed against my cheek. I rolled onto my back, with my eyes still closed and basked in the heat of the sun. I opened my eyes and looked up through the trees - thin wispy clouds streaked across the bright blue sky. The trees swayed in the breeze, carrying the citrusy scent of conifers and the bittersweet must of oak and maple. A crow's screechy caw startled me.

"Jim!" I shouted sitting up quickly. I patted down my body – no aches or wounds – just a bit itchy on my chest and some residual cloudiness in my head. My jersey and armor were all intact. The Manhattan shit pit was a bit of a blurry memory. I was sitting on a grassy knoll surrounded by dead bodies.

"Hrrrrraaaawww," a crow screeled, perched on a dead body's shoulder and picking at a very pointy ear. I frowned. *What the fuck?* I stood up, stretched and took a closer look at the nearest body. It was about two thirds the size of a man and wore clothes made of coarse fabric and banded leather armor. With a gentle kick, I rolled it over onto its back. It was a gnobloid[57]! The sunken, glazed over

---

[56] Shahayla: An earth goddess in the AA fantasy world. Only women may enter her temple.

[57] Gnobloids: A creature commonly found in the AA fantasy world. Gnobloids are a cross-breed of Goblinoids and Gnoblins. These feisty little warriors make formidable opponents on the battlefield. However, their true weakness lies in their penchant for collecting tiny trinkets and oddities.

eyes stared off into space. Gold rings dangled from the hooked nose. His face and arms were scarred, probably from a lifetime of fighting. *This is way too weird.*

I followed the trail of dead bodies through the woods, which led me down into a shallow valley and up a steep hill. The ground became uneven with many rocky outcroppings. Crows circled overhead, waiting for me to leave so they could pick away at the fresh carrion undisturbed.

To my left, a wide crevasse suddenly split the forest in two. I cautiously made my way to the edge and looked down. There was no end in sight. The deep chasm disappeared into darkness. I kicked a small stone over the edge, and waited for what seemed like hours. I never heard it hit anything. I shrugged and continued up the hill.

As I crested the hill, a high pitched screech broke the silence. Down at the bottom of the hill, a gnobloid struggled with a man lying on the ground. The man lay on his back and appeared to be wounded. The gnobloid stood over top of him and had him by the hands, kicking him repeatedly in the side and stomping on his face. Finally, the man surrendered. The gnobloid broke free and skulked away a safe distance before crouching down and squealing over the object in his hand. The man raised a trembling arm, maybe in some last ditch effort to do something. His arm fell and he rolled over onto his side.

I quietly crept down the hill toward the gnobloid, positioning myself so his back was always to me. When I got close enough, I readied myself to jump forward and tackle him. I took a step forward… *SNAP!* …and stepped on a branch.

The gnobloid's head spun around and he snarled, barring his jagged and uneven teeth. But it didn't faze me – my attention was focused on the object in his open hand – a d20! And according to the AA Monster Book, gnobloids had an obsession with collecting trinkety-type things, which meant this one probably felt threatened.

UNDEAD RECKONING

The gnobloid closed his hand around the d20 and hid it from view. He drew a knife from his belt. I lunged for him. Before he even had time to stab, I ploughed into him and sent him sprawling back to the chasm's edge. He sprang to his feet. I grabbed the closest rock within reach and flung it. *CRACK-SPLORCH!* The gnobloid's skull burst open from the impact, spewing blood and goo. He fell back and over the edge into the chasm. The d20 fell from his grasp and went over the edge with him.

"Aaaaaaaaaaaaaaaaaaaaaaaaaaaaaaaeeeeeeeeeeeeeeeeeeeeeee eeeeeeeeeeeeeeeeeeiiiiiiiiiiiiiiiiiiiiiiiiiiii!" the gnobloid screamed until the high pitch wail faded from earshot.

"Damn! For a little guy he's got a big set of lungs." I shook my head, and turned my attention to the man on the ground. "Hey, buddy!" I knelt down beside him.

The man rolled over. His clothes weren't exactly medieval. The black mask over his eyes, combined with the purple, tight-fitting, costume with muscles molded into it screamed superhero all over. A nearby crow cawed in agreement. Dark blood dribbled from his nose and mouth. He grabbed a handful of my jersey.

"Did you... did you... did... you... save... the dice?"

"No... I'm sorry. You need help. Is there a doctor or someone like that around here?"

His head dropped to the ground. "Say bye... to... Jenny... from me."

"Jenny? What? C'mon, man." His eyes glazed over and he exhaled his last breath. My eyes and nostrils suddenly began to burn with the scent of sulphur. "Ah, what now?"

The crows in the forest cawed and scattered. Another superhero, this one in a white suit with a lightning bolt on the chest flew out from the between trees. He glided over the ground, looking over the dead. He disappeared behind the hill. Seconds later he flew up over the top and saw me. His face twisted with rage.

"You killed Will!" he shouted. Before I could respond, he punched the air with both fists. Crackling white lightning fired from his hands and struck me in the chest. My jersey deflected most of the lighting right back at him, but it seemed to have no effect. I, on the other hand, suffered quite a bit from the sudden surge in energy. My whole body tensed and shook – my teeth were chattering uncontrollably. Every hair stood on end. It felt like my chest was caving in as I gasped for air. Between the sulphur smell and the white sparks, it seemed like the fourth of July. I fell to the ground and waited for my lungs to fill with air. I felt like I had been sacked by the entire team, including the guys on the bench. Everything ached.

I got up to my knees and leaned back on my haunches. The superhero hovered above me. I put my hands in the air. "I think you got the wrong guy."

"Liar!" he shouted. "Demons always lie."

"I'm no demon."

"You think I cannot see deceit before my eyes. I am no fool!"

He fired his electric-expulsion at me again and I crumpled. I didn't know how much more of this I could take. My brain was fried. I felt disoriented and dizzy. *Think, Ed! You need to ground this fucker!* I felt the ground with my hand until I found a rock. The superhero drew closer.

"Return to the abyss from whence you came, demon," the superhero seethed.

I jumped to my feet and pitched the rock right at him, striking him directly in the chest. He dropped out of the air, clutching his ribs. I charged, but he leapt over me. By the time I turned around, he blasted me again. My legs seized and every muscle ached. I couldn't stop shaking. My temples pulsed and my jaw clenched so tightly, I thought my teeth would shatter.

"That's enough!" I shouted. I don't know how I did it, but I suddenly charged through the energy blast and hit the superhero with full force. It was like hitting an electrified brick wall. My body was thrown back to the ground, every inch of it aching. The superhero flew back spread eagle, arms and legs flailing and disappeared over the edge into the crevasse.

UNDEAD RECKONING

I was breathing heavily. The stench of sulphur grew weaker, as did my muscles. I tried to get up but I couldn't. Everything hurt too much. I was completely spent, like after that high school football practice when the coach invited an ex-marine drill instructor to lead the exercise regimen. My eyelids grew heavy and then everything went dark.

***

I crept down the stairs. Even though my Uncle had gone out for the evening, I could never be too cautious. Sometimes, he deliberately came home earlier than what we had agreed just to catch me out of my room. He was such a prick!

I followed the muffled howl of the vacuum cleaner to his office. I stood outside the door, puzzled. *Mrs. Hampton never went in there!* I peaked in around the door jamb and almost melted. She was beautiful. The young woman's hair was braided and pulled back in a red kerchief. She wore baggy blue jeans and running shoes. Her shirt was tied around her waist, leaving her lean yet muscular body in a loose white tank top. She turned off the vacuum cleaner and rubbed the back of her neck, arching her back just enough so her perky breasts pressed up tightly against the white cloth. I practically fainted. The woman turned her head and caught me staring at her. She smiled.

"Hi! Are you Eddie?"

I stepped into the door. "Yes. Uh… Eddie."

She laughed. Her green eyes glistened. "I'm Ardala."

"Yeah." I couldn't help but stare at her breasts. "Um, yeah. Where's Mrs. Hampton?"

"Oh, she hurt her back. I took her shift."

"Oh."

"Aren't you supposed to be in your room?"

I shrugged. "I had to go pee and I heard the vacuum, so I came down here… you won't say anything, will you?"

Ardala smiled. "Of course not."

Relieved, I stepped into the room and looked around. One wall was nothing more than a shelf full of books. Paintings and statues of Jesus lined the other walls. On the side opposite the bookshelf, a grand oak desk rested on the plush area rug. Two chairs were set in front of it.

"You look like you've never been in here before." Ardala said.

"I haven't."

"Really? Why not?"

"My Uncle doesn't really like me much."

"What? That's not right. Is that why you're not out tonight with him?"

"Well, I don't think he considers me family. My parents died when I was born, and he kind of raised me ever since."

"I'm so sorry."

"It's okay. He's a jerk." In the corner of the room, I noticed a waist-high pedestal. On top of it sat a book inside a glass case. Wall-mounted spotlights illuminated it. I walked up to it. "Is this a bible?" The pages had yellowed and the script had faded in spots.

"It's your Uncle's bible. He told me not to touch it."

"It looks old. He makes me read from a bible, but I didn't know he had this one."

"He said it's been in the family for generations." She patted down her pockets. "Hey listen, I'm going to grab my purse and go for a smoke. Wanna come with me?"

"Uh, sure," I said, staring at the bible.

"I'll be right back."

Ardala left the room. I lifted the glass case and set it down on the rug. The book smelled like wet cardboard or wet dog fur – I couldn't really decide. Using my one finger as a bookmark, I leafed through the pages. When I got to the book of Revelations, the first few pages had been cut out in the center. A tarnished brass skeleton key rested in the hollow. My heart was racing. My Uncle was a weirdo and all, but what could he be hiding? I pocketed the key and returned everything back exactly as I had found it.

Ardala appeared at the door. "What are you doing?"

"Nothing... just looking at this book."

"Don't get any fingerprints on the case. I already cleaned it," she said.

"Oh... You might want to clean it again."

I looked back at her. She titled her head to one side and dropped her shoulder. "C'mon, before you make more work for me."

We sat outside on the steps of the front porch. The night air was cool. Ardala's nipples were hard, although probably not as hard as the erection I was trying to hide as I sat next to her. She looked out onto the lawn and took a long drag on her cigarette. "You seem like a decent kid. What's up with your Uncle?" She exhaled.

"Did he say anything about me?"

"He said you were difficult, and to make sure you stayed in your room." She flicked ash into the flower urn.

"He makes my life difficult," I huffed.

"Why?"

I raised my hands. "I think he hates me."

Ardala frowned as she exhaled a plume of smoke. "He's a Reverend. Aren't they supposed to preach love and live like Jesus?"

I shrugged. "I don't believe in Jesus."

"Whoa! That's a bold statement from a young man."

"It just doesn't feel right. You know what I mean?" I stared down at the concrete walkway. "He took me to church a few times and all I did was cry. Same thing with Sunday school and bible study. It just gets me upset. My belly aches. I hardly eat." I patted my stomach. "I mean, he only talks to me about his faith. I'm always in the wrong with him. He talks so much and can make anything somehow relate back to the bible... except he can never answer the questions I ask him."

"Like what kind of questions?"

"Like why my mom and dad had to die? And why didn't I die with them? And why aren't dinosaurs mentioned in Genesis if God created everything? His answers are such bullshit."

Ardala leaned down and butted her cigarette against the sole of her shoe. I tried not to make it obvious that I was staring at her cleavage. She flicked the butt into the garden and folded her arms, resting them on her knees. "You've got a lot of tough questions for a kid."

I threw my hands in the air. "And a tough life. I'm excluded from all activities. All I ever do is sit up in my room."

"Don't you get to do anything?"

"I got no friends. I don't go anywhere," I shrugged. "I sneak on the computer whenever I can. If I could have my way, I'd be a football quarterback so I can make all the plays." I thought about the Big Mike action figure my Uncle had taken from me.

"What does your Uncle say about that?"

I rubbed my fist into my palm. "He says it is a sport for the ignorant and barbaric."

"Whatever," Ardala scowled. "Don't you have any other family?"

"My Uncle says I am not allowed to be part of the family. And the weird thing is… he has no family. I'm all he's got. When he talks about family, he goes on and on about his wife."

"He has a wife?"

"He did. She died of cancer. I don't remember her. I once heard Bill Jessop, the handyman, talking to Mrs. Hampton, and he said my Uncle got all mean after his wife died of cancer."

"I can understand his anger, but he shouldn't take it out on you. Maybe he's just trying to protect you because he already lost someone he cared about."

I rubbed my hands together. "He doesn't care about me."

She tilted her head to one side and looked at me. Her eyes were beautiful. "You really think so?"

"He once told me, until I embrace Jesus, I will never feel his love." I put my head in my hands.

Ardala scooched closer and put her arm around me. My shoulder ached from the bruises, but I tried not to show the pain in my face. I didn't want Ardala to know he hit me. Her touch was soothing. I was in heaven – probably as close to Jesus as I would ever get. "I feel so bad for what you're going through. How old are you?"

"Eleven."

"You've had to deal with a lot of tough stuff for an eleven-year-old."

I shrugged.

"Want some advice?"

"Sure."

"Okay. Well, you said your Uncle talks about Jesus and stuff. Based on what he's said or whatever you've read, do you think Jesus would honestly treat you the way your Uncle does?"

"No. I guess not."

"Well, why don't you ask him what to do?"

I raised my head and looked at her. "Ask who?"

"Your Uncle wants you to embrace Jesus, right? Then why don't you embrace Jesus by asking him for help. You could probably go to the chapel in the house."

"I'm not supposed to go in there alone."

She put her forehead to mine. "You're also not supposed to be out here talking to me." She smiled. "Just go in there one day when you have time, and if it's safe to go, and ask."

"What should I say?"

"Ask Jesus if he can get you out of this mess."

"Will I really get an answer?"

Ardala took my hand and put it on her knee. "I think so. You know, my parents taught me that everything in this world is connected to the same divine power. It doesn't matter who you talk to or who responds. You can talk to the air or a tree. Jesus is just another conduit. So if you embrace him, all you're doing is connecting to divine power. If Jesus doesn't answer, someone else will." She kissed me on the head, warming my entire body. I gave

Ardala a hug. "I have to get back to work. Are you good with what we talked about?"

"I think so." I stood up and stuck my hand in my pocket. My fingers curled tightly around the key. "Maybe it is time me an' Jesus had a little chat."

***

When I opened my eyes, I was lying in a comfy wooden frame bed, covered in a heavy quilt. The thatched roof and gray wattle and daub walls looked like something directly taken from the AA GM's[58] Guide to High Adventure. I looked under the covers – I wasn't wearing any clothes. My gear was lying in the corner and my helmet perched on the bed post. But no clothes. My chest was itchy and red. The scar tissue formed that same mandala Veck had on his chest – the demon slayer's mark. It didn't glow like his, but I could still make out the details in the raised and stretched skin. I rubbed my hand over it.

The bed strained and groaned as I sat up. That's when I realized the two young men seated across from me with their backs to the wall. One guy was a short Indian with thick black hair and a heavy moustache he probably grew when he was twelve. He wore a conventional-looking wizard's cloak and peaked cap, covered in moons and stars. He almost looked like a cartoon character. The other guy was tall and lanky. He wore glasses, jeans, running shoes and t-shirt with a picture of a bloodied and pissed off looking guy fighting zombies with a chainsaw.

"Hi," I said.

The tall guy slapped the Hindi guy on the arm. "See Raj? It's Eddie Griffin."

---

[58] GM: Gamemaster – The individual who conducts the role playing session. The GM tells the story, interacts with the player characters, and officiates the rules.

Raj scowled and spoke quickly. "And I told you Jeff, I do not know Eddie Griffin. If this is Eddie Griffin, then explain to me how on this day and earth he appears in this crazy world you created?"

Jeff shrugged and scowled. "I didn't create this. I never planned for Eddie Griffin to show up here. I don't know."

"I'm not expecting you to be the escape goat."

"Don't you mean, scapegoat?" I asked.

The tall guy rolled his eyes. "That's just the way Raj talks."

Raj continued, "And this Eddie Griffin is just another clinch in the system. So far, between you and that stupid book of yours, everything you have said has come true."

"Come true? What about K'ohlkroopa? I didn't create him."

"Hey, guys!" I shouted. That silenced them. "I am Eddie Griffin, and I don't know how I ended up here either. Maybe together we can figure it out. Now do you know where my clothes are?"

"Your shoes are under the bed", Raj replied with a wave of his hand. "Jenny washed your clothes. They are hanging on the line outside. There is a robe there for you over the headboard."

"Jenny?" I wondered if it was the same Jenny that superhero mentioned. These guys surely didn't look like superheroes.

"She's our friend," Jeff replied. "Hey, how'd you get that scar on your chest? I saw it when we put you in the bed."

I looked down at my chest. "Oh this? I got hit."

"With what?"

"It was… uh, part of my initiation when I joined the team." I got out of the bed and threw on the robe. It was made of coarse burlap. It wasn't comfortable but at least it wasn't covered in stars and moons. "So you like football?"

Jeff got up from his chair and approached me. "I'm such a huge fan of yours. It is so awesome to meet you." He shook my hand. "But I don't like football."

It wasn't the reply I was expecting. I felt deflated. "What?"

Jeff cleared his throat and adjusted his glasses. "I wasn't always into football. I only got into it after I read that interview you did in the AA monthly magazine. You said you were a huge player when you were a kid."

"Well, I wouldn't say I was a HUGE player."

"Enough talk," Raj said. "We need to figure out what the hell is going on. You have questions?"

"Yeah, I do."

"Very well then, let's go downstairs."

The guys led me out into the corridor and down the creaky staircase into the main common room. A fire crackled in the stone hearth. I followed Raj around the grand wooden table, past the giant keg in the corner and out the door.

The house was situated on top of hill a surrounded by a thick forest. Stone steps started a path that led down the hill. The trees along the path were thinner, and I could see the edge of lake in the distance. Chickens clucked and pecked their way about the grounds. A horse chomped at the long grass growing around the nearby well. Beyond that, three gravestones stood in a clearing in the forest. One of the graves had been recently dug.

My clothes hung on a line strung up between two oak trees. I took them down and got dressed.

"Hey," Raj said, pointing. "Here comes Rick."

A guy dressed all in black followed the path through the trees up to the house. He gave a half-hearted wave.

"Yeah, that's Rick," Jeff said. "He kind of keeps to himself."

"He is a jerk. That guy really gets under me sometimes," Raj added.

"You think just about everyone is a jerk."

At first, I thought Rick was wearing some type of face mask. But as he got closer, I could see the dark makeup around his eyes. It contrasted starkly against his pale skin. His eyebrow and nose were pierced. "Hey, man," he said. "Are you really Eddie Griffin?"

"I am."

"Man, that's some strange shit. Big fan of yours. Nice to meet you. Rick Gilchrist." We shook hands. "You feelin' alright?"

"I am, thanks."

Raj motioned for me to sit down on a wooden bench next to a fire pit. "Would you like some ale?"

"Sure."

Raj ran off into the house. Jeff got the fire going.

Rick sat down on the ground. "Are we waiting for Jenny?"

"Yeah," Jeff replied.

"Where'd she go?" I asked.

"Into the village."

"There's a village near here?"

"Yeah," Rick said. "On the other side of the forest. A whole medieval-age village. Just like something right out of the book. Or out of Jeff's head. We protect it."

I shook my head. "Hmmm, this is too weird." Raj appeared beside me and handed me a mug of ale. It was cool and bitter. "Thanks."

Jeff stood up and stepped back from the fire. "There's Jenny."

I stood up to get a look at her and... OMG! I nearly dropped my mug. A girl with sandy blonde hair bounced up the forest trail in a white skin-tight superhero costume. At first, I thought it was painted on. She had curves in all the right places. Her breasts jiggled and wobbled as she walked, distorting the letter *K* on her chest. It must have been the happiest letter in the alphabet. I know now why I sometimes dreamed of being a superhero. It wasn't to gain super powers and right the wrongs of the world. It was so I could be in company of big-boobed athletic women in skin-tight suits.

Jenny was a goddess. She was the perfect mix of Carolina Peef, Tonisha Cooley, Tammy-Lee Kwiatkowski, Priya Anderson-Singh, Kim Brockett, Olga Fox, Tia Arvedsson, those two Rattlers cheerleaders whose names I couldn't recall at this time, Carlin Frenke's mom, Mrs. Teasewater, Ardala the cleaning lady, Tifani

Ambrose-Hooker, Millie Hoover, Nikki Schneider, Mary Von Dietz, Mary Molinetti, Raquel Dos Santos, Pella Kozaczuk, Karly Karazuki, Ludmilla Petrovic, and Lilly-Anne Finkelstein.

As Jenny made her way up the stairs, she kept her eyes to the ground and hummed softly to herself. The breeze blew her hair down into her face. She raised her head and brushed her bangs aside. She looked at me and I practically drowned in her bluish-gray eyes.

"Hey, Eddie," she said with a smile. "It is Eddie Griffin, right?"

"Yes. It is."

"Hah! I knew it! You guys didn't believe me."

Jeff stuck his arms out, "We did so. You know, what are the odds, right?"

"Probability of Eddie Griffin appearing in a fantasy world created by Jeff is one trillion to one. I can give you an exact figure if I was not stuck in some stupid fantasy setting."

Jeff sighed. "Eddie already introduced himself to us, Jenny."

"This is so awesome." Jenny ran over and gave me a hug. Her breasts pressed against me. It was electrifying. I was paralyzed, yet so excited. Jenny leaned back, keeping her hands on my arms. "I've seen all your games. I love football. You're like the best player ever." She half-winked, half-raised an eyebrow in a flirty sort of way.

"Uh… gee… thanks." Jenny turned and I rolled my eyes. *Nice response, you moron!*

"Okay, now that we all know each other, maybe we can stop twiddling our asses and figure out some answers," Raj moaned.

"Yeah," Jeff agreed. "Tell us about how you got here."

I sat back down on the bench near the fire and drank some ale. Everyone else gathered around. "Uh… you know what? Maybe we can start with you telling me how you guys got here, ok?"

"I'm good with that," Jenny shrugged. Everyone else seemed to be in agreement. "Well, Jeff and I knew each other from college, but the rest of us all met at an FLGS[59] where we played AA a few times. When we saw the Amok-Con[60] poster in the store, we decided to go to Dallas together."

"They were releasing fifth edition rules," Jeff added. "You were going to be there, right?"

"That's right." I rubbed my hand through my hair. It had been so long since I even thought of that. My agent arranged it for me. I was signing limited edition books with content by Carlin Frenke. I took his game notes and shared them with the company. They also agreed to give a percentage of sales to help anti-bullying and anti-gang programs.

"Well, anyway," Jenny continued. "We never made it. The van broke down along the highway and we got a room in a nearby motel. Jeff suggested we play AA while they fixed it. One minute we were playing and then we just woke up here."

"Yeah," Raj nodded in agreement. "Talk about crude awakenings."

Jeff stood up and circled the fire, trying to keep clear of the smoke. "The odd thing is that this whole place is exactly as I envisioned it."

"Yeah, Rick was saying there's a village near here," I said.

"Yeah, it's got a blacksmith, a tavern, an inn, and nearby farms. Just about everything you or I could think of."

"And you can't leave?"

"Well," Jeff said rubbing his hands nervously. "Here's the thing: we played with three d20s using the Precise Dice Rule[61]."

I slapped my forehead. "Awww, don't tell me you did that."

"We did," Raj confirmed.

---

[59] FLGS: Friendly Local Gaming Store.
[60] Amok-Con: Annual Anomalies Amok Convention.
[61] Precise Dice Rule: The precise dice rule required that a player roll the exact number of dice, preferably each being a different color, instead of rolling the same die more than once. Critics felt this was an attempt by the game company to increase dice sales.

"I hated that rule." *Carlin never made us play with it.* I downed the last of my ale and set the mug down under the bench.

"Jeff insisted we use it," Raj said.

"We ALL agreed to it," Jenny corrected. "Anyway, we also played epic rules. You know, when you get so advanced in a skill that it automatically succeeds without any dice rolls."

"So when we ended up here, we couldn't use some of our skills without skill checks," Jeff said. "It's how this place works. Luckily, all the modifiers from the game also became reality. With my knowledge of the rules, I could easily provide the target number for the skill check."

"But," Jenny continued, "the sad thing is, it cost us a dice and one of our friends to figure it all out."

"What happened?"

Jeff sighed. "Oh, there was this guy who came with us. His name was Craigory."

"Hold on a sec… his name was Craigory?" I asked. "As in, a Craig and Gregory kind of hybrid?"

"Yeah," Jeff replied. "He was a bit annoying."

"Annoying?" Rick interrupted. "Man, he was so loud and obnoxious. He constantly complained about how the game didn't mimic reality. I told him it did cause there were assholes in it, just like him."

"Rick exaggerates," Jenny countered. "Okay… maybe just a bit. Craigory was a dwarf fighter and sapper. He tried to make a bomb and he failed all three of his dice rolls."

"Miserably I might add," Jeff said. "He insisted on detonating the bomb just to prove to us that nothing would happen. When the bomb exploded, it blew him up, and the d20 he was carrying."

Rick grinned. "Yeah, but once he died, Raj just climbed the asshole-meter and took his place."

"Fuck it, Rick!" Raj shouted.

Rick responded by giving Raj the finger.

"Ok, calm down! So you lost a die," I said. "How many do you have left?"

Jenny hung her head. "None."

"None?"

"We *had* two dice to cast. Dan and Will each had one. They died in the gnobloid attack and we never found the dice."

A cold shiver ran up my spine. "I'm sorry to hear that. Is that what those graves are for?"

"Yeah," Jeff said. "The grave is for Will. One marker is for Craigory. The other is for Dan. We never found his body. We think he may have fallen into the chasm."

"He could fly," Raj said. "How could he have fallen in there?"

"Maybe he was wounded?" Rick suggested.

"Please let's not talk about this," Jenny said.

"There has to be a way out of here." I stood up and paced. "Can't you have someone craft more dice?"

"We tried that," Jeff said. "We asked a local wood carver. He was dead by morning – murdered by Shiv Cultists[62]. They killed his whole family and burned down his house. Since then, nobody will craft us any dice."

"Can't you just leave?"

Jeff raised his arms wide. "I created this place. I know the boundaries. There are no exit points because I never envisioned anything beyond this realm. There is absolutely no way we can get out of here, not to mention the dice issue. We're stuck."

"It's like eating a dead horse." Raj took off his peaked cap and threw it down on the bench.

"If you're the GM, can't you change the rules?" I asked.

"No. I can't seem to do that." Jeff clenched his fists.

"Hmmm. Well hey, you mentioned something earlier... about a demon?"

---

[62] Shiv Cultists: Worshippers of Shiv – the demon god of chaos and anarchy in the AA fantasy world.

"K'ohlkroopa," everyone said in unison.

"Yeah, him. Maybe he's keeping you here. Maybe if you kill him, you can go home."

Jenny shrugged.

"Well, what does this demon do?"

"He sends his minions to terrorize the village," Jeff said. "He usually doesn't take part in the battles. He doesn't come out of that chasm."

"Yeah, but that last attack was an all-out assault," Jenny added. "Like he was trying to weaken us or soften us up. He attacked us on two fronts and split us up. That's how we lost Will and Dan."

I put my hand on my hips, like the coach used to do when he was asserting his authority. "If we can get this bastard out in the open, I'm sure we can kill him."

"You've killed demons?" Raj asked.

"I have… in the game, I mean. The rules should be the same, right?" Jeff shrugged. "Hey, while we're talking AA, what's with your outfits?"

"Oh, that," Jenny laughed. "We're stuck in the character costumes."

Jeff put his hand up. "Since I'm the GM, I remained in the same clothes I started with. I combined the AA core rules with the Righteous Dice: Heroes Supplement."

"Oh… I thought so. I wasn't sure. So what's with you?" I asked Raj.

"I am the Mathamagician. I wanted a character that closely resembled my field of study."

"Which is?"

"Mathematics."

"Uh, okay. So what's your superpower?"

"I can solve complex algorithms in my head."

Jeff stepped up and patted Raj on the shoulder. "Raj never-role played before. He showed up at the store one day and asked if he could play. He liked the idea of adding modifiers to the dice rolls and figuring out the odds of certain combinations."

"You lied to me." Raj pushed Jeff away. "The way you explained it to me, I thought it would be much more complicated."

"Whatever! You can cast fireballs and a few other spells. If you didn't like it, why did you keep showing up week after week to play?"

Raj huffed. "You kept telling me it would get better. You lied."

"I was referring to the adventure."

"Well it stuffs ass now, doesn't it?"

Shifting the focus, I pointed to Rick. "What about you?"

"Me? Heh, I'm the Night Ninja. I specialize in hand-to-hand combat and ninja weapons."

"But you don't have any weapons on you."

"I know, because I'm so good in hand-to-hand. Besides, I'm a ninja. If I had weapons, they'd be hidden."

I cleared my throat. "What about your friends who, uh... died?"

Jeff sighed. "Yeah... Dan was named Hydroballs, and he could manipulate electrical energy."

"That is so stupid," Raj said. "Electricity did not exist in the medieval world. You need a generator."

"They had windmills," Rick suggested. "Maybe they could have hooked something up to them."

"They would have better chances of generating power with a donkey punch."

"You mean donkey wheel, Raj."

"Anyway..." Jenny interrupted. "Will was an archery specialist, named Iron Sight."

"Not enough of a specialist to save his own life."

"Shut up, Raj!" Rick said, waving him away with his hand. "Go solve the equation of you not being an asshole for once."

"Guys! Stop it!" Jenny ordered. Raj looked at the ground and Rick stared off into the forest. "Chill out guys. It's my turn." She turned to me. "My character is a brilliant scientist by day named Kate." She stretched her outfit to accentuate the letter *K*. Instead, she just accentuated her awesome breasts. "And when danger calls, she turns into..." There were suddenly two Jennys, standing side by side; then four; then eight. "RepliKate!" She raised her arms and flexed her biceps.

"That's some power." I was trying to think of something to say about how there could never be enough Jenny, but I didn't want to risk sounding cheesy.

"Yes, but every time she replicates, her strength becomes halved," Raj said.

"Pfft... doesn't matter, man," Rick argued. "She can lift like a million tonnes."

At risk of another fight starting, Jeff changed the subject. "Now you want to tell us how you got here?"

"Uh... I woke up in that bed upstairs. Before that, I was at a hotel, preparing for my guest appearance at Amok-Con."

"And you were wearing your football gear?" Raj asked.

"Yeah, uh....it was to hype the team but, it was also like a suit of armor. It was all promotional stuff. I was an... Afro-Saxon."

"Really?" Jeff said, scratching his chin. "Is that a new character class?"

I looked away and muttered. "It may as well be."

"That sounds pretty cool," Rick agreed. Raj just shook his head.

"Yeah," Jeff started. "It's too bad we never made it to Amok-Con."

"You didn't?" I asked.

"We ended up here, in this realm, a few days beforehand. If you were about to go to Amok-Con and then showed up here, that means time passes much more slowly in this realm."

"You and your goddamn theories," Raj spat. "Who cares? Get us the hell out of here, why the hell not?"

"You're the stats guy... You told us our chances were slim."

"Not stats! Math!"

Rick stood up and put his hands in the air. "I'm outta here. You two can jerk each other off all you want. I'm going to the village."

"You're a jerk-off!" Raj shouted.

Rick stomped away. Jeff crossed his arms. Raj pouted.

Jenny put a hand on my arm. I certainly felt a spark. "Sorry about this. Things have been a bit tense since Dan and Will died. They'll be friends again in an hour."

"Yeah, I hear ya." I felt awful. I just wanted to be alone. But I also wanted to be with Jenny. She was as calming as she was beautiful. "Nerds, hmpf." We both smiled.

"Every day at dusk, we go for dinner to the tavern in the village. Why don't you come with us? Maybe have a few pints and relax."

"Sure," I said. "That sounds good."

Rick called to me," Hey, Eddie. Come with me and we can get a head start on those pints."

I looked to Jenny. "Go," she said. "We can catch up later. Get a tour of the village while you're at it."

"Okay." I sighed.

She smiled and patted me on the back. "See you later," she cooed.

"Yeah."

"C'mon Eddie!" Rick waved me on and disappeared down the path into the forest.

I followed Rick down the stone steps and into the forest. The path widened to a narrow road along the edge of the lake.

"So what do you think of Jenny, man?" Rick asked.

"Why do you ask?"

"She's hot, huh? I'm sure everyone here has jerked off thinking about her."

I chuckled. "If you say so."

"Aw, man. It's weird. She's wise like a mom, but looks after you like a sister. And she's also a good friend. I was bugging you about the jerk off thing."

"Heh, you were? That's too bad. I was going to ask what it's like to have a nerdgasm."

"Aw, man," Rick said, slapping my arm. "That is too funny."

"So what's with you an' Raj?"

"Aw, he's such a prick. All he ever does is complain." Rick scratched his head. "You know, he was upset with the game from the first time we played. Yet he kept showing up week after week. I suggested he try another hobby. I mean, we already had one asshole in Craigory. Raj was the second."

"The rest of the gang kinda like him, don't they?"

"More like tolerate him. Ugh! Asshole! I'm gonna need an extra pint." He put his arm around my shoulder and pretended to lift a mug with the other. "Tonight, we drink to assholes!"

"Let's drink to something else. I've had enough of assholes to last my whole life."

Sun rays broke in through the tree canopy over our heads. The woods were quiet except for the odd bird. The road led us out of the forest and through fields of plump orange pumpkins and dark green squash, orchards of trees filled with ripe red apples, and rows of tall swaying corn. A few minutes later, we crossed a wooden bridge over the river and approached the stone gatehouse. The guards welcomed Rick, but they eyed me with suspicion. Once Rick explained to them that I was the new hero, the guards apologized profusely and ushered me inside.

I felt like I had stepped back in time. Wattle and daub buildings lined the cobblestone streets. The only building made completely of stone was the twin-towered temple to the goddess Shahayla, which towered over the streetscape. Rick took me on a tour of the dockyards, military barracks, blacksmith shop, bakery, brewery, cider mill, various guild houses, and the marketplace.

Warm welcomes greeted me everywhere I went, sometimes complimented with generous gifts. By the early evening, I was weighted down with two loaves of fresh bread, a block of cheese, one flagon of cider and two of beer, some salt-cured meat, a smoked fish and a chicken. And someone gave me a sack to carry everything. We stopped to drink from the well in the marketplace.

"The sun will set in about an hour," Rick said. "You want to head over to the tavern?"

"You know what. I'd really just like to take all this shit home. How about I go back and return with the others?"

"Sure, suit yourself."

I headed out of the village quickly, trying to make as inconspicuous an exit as possible. Once outside the gates, I released the chicken into a nearby field. As I was walking through the forest, a group of priestesses in hooded robes from the temple of Shahayla approached me. Actually, only the lead person was a priestess; the rest were just acolytes. I could tell by the gold stripes on the sleeves of the priestess' robe. She raised a hand and everyone stopped. Then she stepped forward and put a hand on my chest.

"Is he the one?" the woman directly behind her asked.

The woman never lifted her head. I couldn't see her face. "His heart is heavy. If he is to be the one, he will have to decide that for himself." She and the priestesses continued on, keeping their heads bowed as they passed.

"The one what? What do I have to decide?"

They moved quickly and silently, with neither a footfall nor a response. After they were out of sight, I moved along. Instead of returning to the house, I followed the path down to the lake. I needed to get my head back in the game. The pangs of guilt, the encounter with the clerics, the invasive yet very welcome thoughts of Jenny, and the overall fuckedupness of the situation had turned my brain to mush. *Maybe this is what being a zombie feels like.*

***

The key caused me a great deal of anxiety. I hardly slept, living in constant fear that my Uncle, the Reverend, would flip his bible to Revelations, or that I'd misplace it, or leave it in my pocket and have it run through the wash. I was constantly patting down my pocket to make sure the key was there. Ever careful not to arouse my Uncle's suspicion, I grew paranoid.

Each and every minute where I found myself alone, I wandered through the house, trying the key in every conceivable hole. I scoured the basement, crawled through the attic, and risked the harshest of punishments by going where I normally dared not go. I had to be extra careful when Mrs. Hampton returned to work, and ensure that my exploratory activities went undetected by her watchful eyes.

After five days of mental anguish, I gave up. I had only one choice: talk to Jesus. That night, I had about an hour between the time Mrs. Hampton left and my Uncle came home. I said my goodbyes and ran up the stairs and down the hall. The chapel door was always slightly ajar. It was dark and cool. The only light source was just above the altar, illuminating the suspended cross.

The chapel seated twenty to thirty people. Stained glass windows lined the walls, depicting various biblical scenes. The windows were fake, actually. Because they were on interior walls, florescent lights were installed behind them to simulate natural daylight. The skylights were only source of real light, but on a cloudy October night like tonight, even the stars couldn't see inside.

I slowly made my way down the centre aisle, running my hand along each pew. I got to the dais and stepped up. There, I knelt down at the altar and looked up to the cross. I took a deep breath.

"Uh, Jesus," I said. "My name is Eddie Griffin. I don't know if you know me... maybe you do. I don't really believe in the stories I am told about you. I mean, I believe there is something out there, but I don't know what that is." I folded my hands and leaned on the altar with my elbows. "Well, a friend of mine told me you may just be a representation of that very thing I'm looking for. So if you're there now and listening, could you please just help me out? I hate it here. My Uncle is nice and all, but he's not my favorite person.

Actually, he's kind of a jerk. I don't know why I have to be here. Please, can you help me?"

I stared at the cross. The room remained dimly lit and silent. It seemed like I waited for hours and nothing happened. Nothing happened! I sighed heavily and rested my head on the cool cotton altar cloth. Something poked me in the forehead. I ran my hand along the covering and found a small bump, maybe an inch or so set in from the edge. I threw back the altar cloth. It was a keyhole. Excitedly, I took the key out of my pocket and slid it into the hole. I closed my eyes and turned it.

CLICK!

I opened my eyes. I slid my anxious hands along the lip of the altar. My fingers brushed over an area with a bit of give to it. A button! I pressed it and after another click, the top of the altar slowly hissed open, like the trunk of a car. The space inside the altar was much smaller in relation to the overall size. Inside, I found a bundle of letters and a thin package, all addressed to me.

My hands were shaking so much I almost couldn't read the return address: Ambrose Griffin, Joliet, Illinois. I licked my dry lips and opened the letter. It was a birthday card. When I opened it, two fifty dollar bills floated to the floor. I read the card aloud, "Happy 4th Birthday, Eddie. Love, Grandpa." *Grandpa? I have a Grandpa?* I hastily opened the next letter, and the next, and the next one after that. All of them were from my Grandpa.

I pocketed the cash and jumped to my feet. I ran back to my room, emptied the contents of my school bag onto the bed, and then ran back and stuffed the letters inside. I grabbed the package and tore off the cardboard and packing tape exterior. It was a book: Anomalies Amok 2nd Edition. The book disappeared inside my backpack.

"Eddie?" my Uncle called from down the hall. I jumped. *He must have come home early.* "The light's on in your room. You know it's lights out, son." I could feel my heartbeat in my throat. I ran to the chapel door and hid behind it. As my Uncle walked by, he muttered, "Lord have mercy, I'm running out of punishments for that boy."

I stepped out into the hall behind him as he went into my room. I wanted to run down the hall and out the front door, but my legs wouldn't cooperate. The back of my head began to ache and tears tried to force themselves out of my eyes. I took a deep breath. *I have to go to my room. I have to tell him.*

"Eddie!" I froze as he walked up behind me. "Why are you out of your room? And why do you have your bag in your hand?" I turned around. My Uncle tilted his head down, looking at me from under his brow. He clenched his fist.

I dropped my head and took a step forward. A lump appeared in my throat. Everything burned inside, from the back of my head to my belly. "No!" I shouted. I threw the bag against the wall. My Uncle took a step forward and hit me across the face with the back of his hand. I fell back on my ass, pressing my hand to my freshly swollen lip.

"What did you say to me?"

I got up, staring down at the carpet. "Nothing, sir," I said. I couldn't stop myself from saying it, even though it didn't feel right. Once again, my body failed me, as it had before. I couldn't bring myself to do what I wanted to do.

As I shuffled past, my Uncle picked up my bag. I stopped just outside my room. My hands were sweaty and my breathing grew frantic. I watched him slowly open the bag. Just as he was about to look inside, I said, "I talked to Jesus."

My Uncle looked up and frowned. "What did you say?"

I took a deep breath. My stomach pounded against my shirt. "I talked to Jesus… in the chapel. That's what I was doing when you came home."

My Uncle's face grew calm. He almost smiled. Dropping to one knee, he stuck out his hand, and said, "And, what did the Lord Jesus say?"

I took a step forward, taking the extended hand. My heart was beating so hard I could feel it in my throat. "He…" I took another step. "He, uh…" I swallowed and stepped in closer. My Uncle took my other hand. I looked down at the bag and realized it was now or never.

"What did say, son?"

I licked the blood off my lip. With all my strength, I kicked my Uncle, mashing his testicles. He fell back, doubled over and clutching his crotch. I grabbed my bag, pulled out one of the letters from my Grandpa, and shoved it in his face. "Jesus told me I had a Grandpa, you sonofabitch!" I kicked him again in the chest, for good measure, before running down the hall and out the front door. Dead leaves crunched under my feet.

"Eddie! Eddie!" my Uncle called.

I ran and ran until he was out of earshot, and I never stopped. I ran until I was as far away as my legs would take me. And after that I walked. I walked and I walked and I never turned back.

***

A tall boulder marked the boundary between the beach and the forest. The names of all the role players had been scribed into it. "Jenny U. Slockie," I read aloud. Coarse sand crunched under my feet. I followed the shoreline to a long, wide dock, which creaked when I stepped out onto it. When I reached the end, I took off my boots, and sat down, dipping my feet in the cool, refreshing water.

From my vantage point, I could see the port side of the village across the lake. Fishing boats dotted the calm water. Docks and small buildings lined the shore. The taller village buildings filled in the background, with the temple of Shahayla presiding over all.

I sat there, chewing on the cured meat and staring out into the lake. *Why did you send me here, Nabisusha?* I went through all the facts in my head: I had gone from the real world to the fantasy world; the people I met knew me from the real world in a fantasy world sort of way; slaying the demon would advance you to the next level, or in this case, send you home. *It can't be that simple... I'm missing something.*

The full moon rose impatiently while the sun was still preparing for sleep. I ate the bread and cheese, and drank the delicious cider and the bitter ale (which made my head a bit wobbly) and watched the two orbs jockey for position. The bright moon, won of course, hovering over the golden sun. Before it disappeared beyond the horizon, the sun painted the sky with calming hues of red, purple and orange. The shimmering water changed from gold to silver. As the sky darkened, torch lights popped up on the other side of the lake.

The dock creaked and I turned around. It was Jenny.

"Hi," she said with a wave.

"Hey." Maybe it was the cider, or maybe it was the way the moonlight caressed her body, or a combination of both, but Jenny looked more beautiful than the last time I'd seen her.

"I've been looking all over for you. Rick told me you left to come back to the house."

"Uh... yeah, sorry about that. I'm a bit overwhelmed. I wanted some time to myself."

"Oh, okay... yeah, we all experienced something similar when we first got here. It was tough. I can go."

"No, no, no! I've, uh, had plenty of time alone. Please sit down... if you want?" I motioned for her to sit beside me.

"You sure?"

"Yeah."

Jenny smiled and made her way down the dock. She took off her boots and pulled up her leggings before nestling in beside me.

"You hungry?" I offered her some bread.

"No, I'm good, thanks."

We both sat in silence, staring at the water.

"So..." we both said in unison, and smiled.

"You first," she said.

"Hey, I saw that rock with everyone's name on it back there. What's your middle name?"

"Ursula. It was my grandmother's name."

"That's a nice name."

"Whatever!" Jenny gave me a shove. "So, what did you think of the village?"

"It's unbelievable. I mean, I played AA and had an idea in my head of what things would look like. But, this is amazing. Jeff has quite the imagination."

"He is quite the Game Master."

Again we sat in silence. I looked at Jenny and she gazed back at me with her hypnotic eyes.

"What? What is it?" she asked.

"I... uh, don't know." I rubbed my forehead. "There are things I want to tell you, but I also don't want to tell you... because I don't know how to tell you. And on top of all that, I really like you and I'm finding myself attracted to you. I don't know how to say it. I guess maybe I just did."

Jenny scooched a bit closer. "Well, if I understand you correctly, and I think I do... then maybe you shouldn't say anything... and just kiss me."

"What?"

Jenny put her hand on my cheek. She leaned in and pressed her lips against mine. Sparks flew and my heart stopped for a split second. It was awesomely amazing. We slowly parted.

"Hmm.... Maybe I shouldn't have done that?" she said with a wince.

"What? Of course you should have! I mean, it seemed like the right thing to do... for you to do... to me... anyway."

Jenny kissed me again, this time more passionately. We put our arms around each other and fell back onto the doc. I ran my hand along her body suit, feeling my way along her sleek curves. Our kiss ended with both of us lying on our backs, looking up at the sky. She took my hand and snuggled up closely.

"You know, before I came here, I always wanted to meet you. But I never dreamed I'd actually kiss Eddie Griffin."

"Oh yeah, well I dreamed I'd kiss you from the moment we first met."

Jenny smiled and then rolled over and straddled me. She kissed me again. Next thing I knew, we were getting frisky. The dock was making things a bit uncomfortable, so we moved to the beach and picked up where we'd left off.

With my help, she peeled off her superhero costume. And she looked even better without it. My clothes practically removed themselves. I remember reading an article once about people who got hit by lightning. The article claimed that the electrical jolt could cause water in the body to boil and eject as high pressure steam through the pores. This would often cause the clothing to blow off; hence all the lightning-strike victims who are found naked. Now I didn't get hit by lightning, but Jenny had almost the same effect. I mean, between Jenny and I there were sparks and all... nothing harmful. Anyway, when it was time for me to get undressed, it was like *POOF*, and all my clothes were off.

We spent the night on the beach, pausing to take a brisk swim or to cuddle closely by the fire we built. Mind you, we kind of generated a lot of heat on our own, so the fire was just a bonus. As a result of our actions, I'm sure galaxies were being born somewhere in celebration. Yet through it all, between the playfulness and the passion, a nagging bothersome feeling plagued the back of my mind. As much as I wanted this night to never end, at some point I had to fess up to the truth. Either that or Nabisusha was going to force my hand. And I had a terrible feeling the resulting damage would spare no one.

21 PARADISE FOUND

> *Nabisusha is but another journey:*
> *It leads the body and heals the soul.*
> — The Book of Amaltheon

When I awoke the next morning, Jenny was lying on her side next to me, her head on my chest and one leg over top of mine. The sun had risen and a light breeze tickled my chest. I tried to stretch, twisting rather awkwardly. My back cramped and I jerked suddenly. Jenny woke up, a bit startled at first. She brushed her hair away from her face.

"Hi!"

"Hi." I kissed her. "How do you feel?"

"I feel wonderful." Jenny sprang to her feet. "C'mon!" She ran for the water. "C'mon, Eddie Griffin!"

"I'm moving as fast as my back will let me."

I followed her into the cool water, where we enjoyed a swim. I got out of the water first and restarted the fire. I lay down on my back with my hands behind my head. Jenny sat down next to me, running her fingers along my chest.

"Hey Eddie, I meant to ask you about this scar on your chest. What happened?"

"Oh, that?" I said, looking down at the mandala. "It's uh... I don't know. I noticed it when I woke up."

"Really? It looks recent."

"It does, yeah." I covered it with my hand. Jenny had no marks whatsoever. Her body was perfect. "Jenny, I don't mean to make things uncomfortable, but do you think we've moved a bit quickly? I mean, we just met and we're already naked and all."

She brushed her hair away from her face. "I wouldn't have kissed you if it didn't feel right. Are you okay with it?"

"Yeah, I am so okay with it!"

"You're the quarterback. I was expecting you to make a play."

I shrugged. "I did, didn't I? I told you how I felt about you."

"You kind of did," she smirked. "But then again, a guy like you probably has women fawning all over you. Hell, I did."

"Oh, no. It's not really like that. I mean, I sometimes get uneasy with that."

"Really? Like when?"

"Well, I guess there was this one time... I went out to a bar and I met this cute girl. So I made a play for her. She seemed interested. But then she wandered off and I met someone else, who shared an equal amount of interest. When we decided it was time to leave, the first girl returned. As it turned out, they knew each other. They were sisters. And they got into this big fight when they realized they both wanted to sleep with me."

"What finally happened?"

"They formed a truce and agreed to share. I was so freaked out. I didn't know what to do. So I left."

"You left?"

"I couldn't bring myself to go through with it."

I blinked and suddenly two Jennys were sitting beside me. The first Jenny straddled me. "Could you do it now?"

I reached up and kissed Jenny number one, while keeping my hands on Jenny number two.

A horn blared in the distance, causing the birds in the nearby trees to fly off, squawking. Jenny was suddenly one again. She crouched next to me on the sand.

"What? What is it?"

The horn sounded again.

"That's an alarm."

"An alarm? Now?" My eyes became irritated. The scent of sulphur tickled my nostrils. I jumped up. "You smell that?"

"I do," Jenny said, as she was getting dressed. I threw on my clothes and together, we raced back to the house. The rest of the gang was already assembled and waiting around the fire pit.

"What's going on?" Rick asked.

"I don't know," Jenny replied. The sulphur scent grew stronger. My nose felt itchy and dry and there was a lump in my throat.

"I'm gonna grab my armor." I ran into the house and up the stairs. I put on my shoulder pads and clipped my web belt around my waist. One of the pouches had a bulge in it, so I reached into the pocket and pulled out the suspicious item: it was the d20 Proon Dung had given me. My heart felt sad. I sat down on the bed and stared at the tiny polyhedron. If Dan and Will were alive, we would have had three dice.

"The Demon has risen!" someone shouted. I made for the window, and saw a rider on horseback, charging through the forest. I headed quickly down the stairs. By the time I was out the door, the rider was climbing off his horse. He was breathing heavily.

"The Demon has risen. Our scouts spotted him in The Direwood." He pointed. "And he is accompanied by Wygryns."

"Wygryns[63]." Rick smacked a fist into his palm. "I hate those fuckers."

"Go back to the village and tell the people to take shelter until we deal with this enemy," Jenny said to the rider. "Keep the guards posted."

"Yes, m'lady."

"We should go," Jenny said. "C'mon." She ran off through the woods. Rick, Jeff and I followed. Raj dragged his ass reluctantly behind us.

***

---

[63] Wygryn: Gray-skinned humanoid creatures believed to be descendents of the chameleon. The Wygryn's bulging eyes can act independently of each other and it can process two images at once. All Wygryn are ambidextrous and wield two weapons. Their unique field of vision allows them to effortlessly engage multiple opponents.

"Drop me off here," I said to the cab driver.

"But this isn't the address."

"It's okay. I'll walk the rest of the way."

"Suit yourself." The cab pulled over and stopped. I unbuckled and slid forward on the seat. "How much do I owe you?"

The cabbie tapped the meter. "That'll be a hundred and twenty."

I pulled the wad of cash out of my pocket. It was all hundreds and fifties. I gave him a hundred and fifty dollars. "Keep it," I said.

"You serious? I might just call it a day. Thanks, kid."

I grabbed my backpack and climbed out of the cab. I walked slowly down the sidewalk, keeping an eye on the house up and across the street. My palms were sweaty and my heart was racing. My stomach was wringing with nervous anxiety.

I walked down the sidewalk until the tiny bungalow was directly across the street from me. A white picket fence bordered the perfectly manicured lawn, and sheltered the colorful perennial gardens. The front porch was guarded by a vicious gargoyle. An American flag flapped in the breeze above the garage door. I licked my dry lips.

"If you're here about that lawn cuttin' job, it's spoken for," a voice behind me said.

I turned around. A scrawny kid with thick glasses sat on the steps of his front porch. A book lay open across his lap. "What'd you say?"

"I said, if you're here about that lawn cuttin' job, it's spoken for. I already told ol' Mr. Griffin I'd do it."

"Oh, I'm not here about no lawn cuttin' job."

"You here to visit? I haven't seen you before."

"Sort of. It's hard to explain," I shrugged.

"Hmm. Well, Mr. Griffin's in the yard. I saw him about a half an hour ago."

"Thanks. Hey, what's that book you're reading?" I asked.

The scrawny kid held it up. "Anomalies Amok. You play?"

"Not really. I've heard of it, though."

"Well, maybe if you visit for long enough, we'll have time to play together."

I smiled. "Thanks."

"Sure. By the way, my name's Carlin... Carlin Frenke."

"Eddie." I pointed to myself.

"Just Eddie?" I was about to answer when someone called out Carlin's name from inside the house. "Comin', Momma." Carlin closed the book and stood up. "See ya around."

"Yeah, see ya."

***

The Direwood wasn't really a forest as I had expected. It was actually a very bleak swamp, filled with sagging willows and pale white cedars. Those trees that weren't standing lay half submerged, rotting away beneath layers of moss and fungus. The forest was dark and the air lay thick with moisture. We slopped our way in and regrouped on a small hill. A low level fog crept towards us.

"Why fight here? Why now?" I asked, as we huddled together.

Jeff shrugged. "I dunno."

"Okay. Well, I got an idea. Jenny and I will take on this K'ohlkroopa. Raj, I need you to light up these trees with a few fireballs. Let's thicken this soup we're in."

Raj nodded.

"Rick, I want you to engage the Wygryns and get them to chase you. Lead them away from us. Can you do that?"

"Sure thing, man."

"And Jeff. What is it you do in these fights?"

"I advise you on the rules and things."

"That's it?"

"Yeah."

"Okay. Stay here with Raj." I pointed to Raj. "It's go time. Light it up."

Raj launched a few fireballs into the trees. The fire spread quickly across the treetops, filling the Direwood with thick smoke. Rick, Jenny and I left the hill and blindly made our way through the swamp. Rick led the way, although barely visible, appearing as nothing more than a dark shadow. Jenny held my hand.

"They're up ahead," Rick whispered, crouching down in the water. "I'll draw the Wygryns away. When you hear me whoopin' and hollerin', you'll know it's clear." Rick slithered away through the dingy water and disappeared from sight. Jenny and I waited by a downed tree. Moments later, we heard shouting.

"That's the signal," Jenny said.

I grabbed her by the arm. "Listen. When we encounter this demon, you need to break the right hand, okay?"

"Why?"

"That's how you weaken them."

"But those rules aren't in the player's guide."

"No. They're my rules."

"And what will you do?"

"I'm going to break his jaw."

Hunched over, Jenny and I moved from tree to tree, making our way towards the commotion. We hid behind a tall, lean hemlock. The fog and smoke had mostly dissipated, leaving a thin, wispy wet mist behind. Rick engaged multiple opponents on the other side of the swamp. A dark silhouette scuttled past, temporarily blocking our view. It had multiple legs like a spider, but it moved sideways.

Jenny and I rounded the hemlock and cut through the water. We found solid ground and drew closer to the silhouette.

CLACK! CLACK!

"What is that?" Jenny whispered.

"Shhh." I felt around on the ground, until my fingers curled around a round, fist-sized stone. I pulled it free from its snug muddy bed. "Stay here. I'll draw him to you. Don't forget - break his hand."

UNDEAD RECKONING

I crept through squishy mud and rotting, clingy leaves, getting closer to the silhouette with each step. It scittered from side to side, watching the melee between Rick and the Wygryns. Finally, I got close enough to make out a human upper body with two claw hands. The lower body was that of a crab. *What the fuck? The centaur factory must've run out of horse parts when they built this guy.* In the distance, Rick took down one of the Wygryns. The demon raised his arms and let out some sort of disappointed shriek. I readied the stone and took aim. I just needed to get a little closer.

SNAP!

The demon stopped. The head turned to the side. I looked down. A branch! I stepped on a fucking branch! Again! The demon turned. He held out his arms and snapped his claws menacingly. *CLACK! CLACK!*

The upper body was entirely clad in black leather including a cap on the human head. The face was old, and gaunt. Dark eyes, like hollow black pits, glared out at me from the sunken sockets. A black slimy tongue darted in and out of the mouth of twisted pointy teeth.

"C'mon, asshole!" I shouted.

The demon took a few steps forward, clicking the claw hands. I hurled the rock smacking him squarely in the jaw. *THWACK!* The demon threw his head back, his tongue flickering about in the mangled mouth. It shook its head and glared at me again. The loosened and broken jaw hung limply. Yellowish-black ooze ran down the chin. I think the demon was pissed. He swung out an arm, knocking over a nearby tree. With his other claw, he snapped a cedar in two.

He pounced, knocking me over into the soggy mud. I rolled and got back to my feet. The claw hand reached out and I dodged to the side. It snapped shut, grasping the empty space I occupied only seconds before. I moved as fast as I could in the sticky slidy mud. I grabbed a branch on a fallen tree and pulled, vaulting myself over. A claw tore the rotting bark away just as I cleared the trunk.

"Damn!" I found myself in a dead-end grove of tightly knit trees. I was trapped. The demon must have realized this, because the cocky bastard slowed his pace. He raised both claws, posturing victoriously as he came in for the kill. Suddenly, the tree I had my back against fell away with a crack and a snap. Jenny slid in through the opening. A claw shot forward, opened wide. Jenny caught it with both hands and with a grunt and a wince she bent it back until it popped. Puffs of yellow powder sprung from the dislocated joints. The demon pulled back his useless claw. Sulphur stung my eyes and nostrils.

"Now what?" Jenny asked.

"Hit'im! Hit'im again until he doesn't move." I jumped to my feet and charged, putting my shoulder into him with the force of a freight train. The shell cracked and the demon flipped over onto his back.

Jenny pulled a pale cedar out of the ground and swung it down onto the exposed underbelly. The soft skin ruptured with a bloody spurt. Entrails and more blackish yellow gunk oozed from the wound. Jenny ran in and suddenly appeared on both sides of the demon. More Jennys appeared – some holding down the other claw while others kept the legs from thrashing about. The two on either side of the demon grabbed the edge of the thick rubbery skin and pulled.

BBBRRRRPPPPPTTTTT!

The entire underside of the demon split open like an overcooked hotdog. Another Jenny pulled a fallen tree out of the swamp, and brought the gnarled and spiky stump down like a hammer. The heart burst like an over ripened tomato. Jenny reunited with her other selves and sat down on the ground, breathing heavily. The demon lay still, except for the odd leg twitch.

I sat down beside her and put my arm around her. "Girl, you are one badass demon slayer." She put her head on my shoulder. I kissed her on the head. "That's why I love you so much." After a brief rest, we got up and circled the carcass.

Up close, the cracked and worn black leather was some type of uniform. Remnants of insignias and medals clung to the chest and collar. I pulled the cap off the head and looked at it closely. A tarnished silver skull pin grinned back at me.

"What is that?" Jenny asked.

"Hmmm... I've seen this type of pin before in books about World War II. It's an SS Death Head Visor Cap."

"This demon's a Nazi?"

"Yeah, part Nazi, part crab. What did you say his name was again?"

"K'ohlkroopa."

"K'ohlkroopa," I whispered.

"Why do you ask?"

"He looks familiar." I recited the name over and over. "I got it! K'ohlkroopa. It's Colonel Kruppe!" I reached for Jenny and stopped myself when I realized what I was doing. "Show me your chest."

"What?"

"I'm not asking you to flash me. Your chest... is it itchy? Do you have a scar like mine?" I pointed to my chest.

"It's not itchy." Jenny pulled the collar open and looked inside. "I don't have any marks."

"Then, this ain't our demon." I grabbed her by the hand. "We have to get everyone back together at the house."

She pulled away. "Why? Will you tell me what's going on?"

I grabbed her hand again. "We need to go, now. This isn't the demon. I can explain everything." We slogged through the swamp and returned to the hill where we left Jeff and Raj. The acrid scent of burned pork assaulted my nostrils.

"Ugh, what's that smell?" Jenny asked.

"Raj?" I called. "Jeff?"

"Eddie! Over there!" Jenny shouted.

A charred, smoldering skeleton lay at the base of the hill, half-submerged in the water. I grabbed a stick and prodded the torso, finding a piece of unscathed fabric. Jenny unfolded it and recognized the image of the bloodied and pissed off looking guy fighting zombies with a chainsaw. She dropped it and buried her face in my shoulder, sobbing. I rubbed her back.

"The real demon did this," I whispered. "He knew we were going to take out his minion. So he took out the one guy who knew this world best."

Jenny looked up at me, wiping the tears away from her eyes. "This is my fault. I'm the one who suggested we go to Amok-Con. I'm the one who decided to split the dice among the party instead of taking them to the Temple of Shahayla like Jeff suggested. I knew Rick and Raj hated each other... I thought the road trip would give them a chance to bond. I..." She began to cry again. "I never liked Craigory. I just felt sorry for him."

I held her close. "It's not your fault. You never intended to cause this. You care way too much about your friends."

Jenny looked up at the sky and took a deep breath. "Raj," she whispered.

"What about him?"

"It's Raj. He must have used his fireball spell on Jeff. Maybe he's the one. We have to find Rick."

Jenny started to walk away and I took her hand. She stopped and faced me. "Jenny," I said. "We should go back to the house. I think I know how to get this demon out in the open."

"What's your plan?"

"My plan?" I took a deep breath. "I plan to tell the truth."

***

I clenched my fists and took a deep breath before walking down the driveway and along the side of the house. My heart thudded against my ribs. A cat meowed and brushed up against my leg. I gave him a pet as I passed.

The back gate was open when I came around the side. Red-leaved ivy clung to the arched trellis. I stepped through it onto the patio. A wind turbine hummed in the breeze. The vegetable garden had already been turned over and laid to rest for winter. In the corner of the yard, a laughing Buddha sat between yellowed, brittle grasses, overlooking the goldfish pond.

My Grandpa had his back to me. I took a moment to watch him – he was much taller than I had imagined. He hummed softly to himself while he raked the golden leaves into a pile under the old maple tree. A small fire crackled in the fire pit, the smoke wafting into the air. I swallowed and it felt like a rock had jammed in my throat. "Grandpa?" I said, my lip quivering. My Grandpa froze. "Grandpa?" I said again.

He raised his white-haired head to the sky. "Oh my," he said. I took a step forward. My Grandpa turned around. He dropped the rake when he saw me and wiped his hands off on his plaid flannel jacket. His eyes widened and he dropped to one knee. "Eddie?"

I ran into his open arms and hugged him, bursting into tears. My Grandpa also sobbed. He put his hands on my face. "Let me have a look at you. You have your father's good looks, hmm? And your mother's eyes." He looked over my shoulder. "How did you…"

"I took a taxi. I… I ran away," I stuttered, wiping tears from my eyes. "I didn't even know I had a Grandpa." I opened my bag and handed him the stack of letters.

Grandpa leafed through them. He seemed angry at first but then a calmness came over him. "You put these back in your bag. Is this all you brought?"

"I brought this book," I said, handing him the AA manual. He took it and smiled before handing it back to me. "Let's uh… chat, and celebrate. I have some cold beer in the fridge."

"I'm only eleven years old."

"Maybe you'll drink a warm one then. You hungry?"

"Yeah, I am."

"How about pizza?"

I smiled. "Sure, with black olives."

"Okay. Black olives it is. I happen to like the wings myself. We'll get some of those too." He put a hand on my shoulder and stood up. "Let's go inside."

I took my Grandpa by the hand. "What are we going to do?"

"Make up for lost time, Eddie. Make up for lost time."

***

Jenny didn't say much to me on the way back to the house. Raj was sitting on the bench in front of the fire pit, his head in his hands. Jenny and I exited the forest and cautiously walked up behind him.

"Hey," I said.

Raj lifted his head and turned around. He seemed angry. "Where in the hell were you?"

"Jeff's dead," Jenny said.

"Of course he is dead. We were attacked by Wygryns."

"He was set on fire," Jenny added.

"Of course he was… idiot!" Raj said, shaking his head. "Just before we were attacked, Jeff explained to me how he read about a Wygryn variant that can breathe fire. Well, he got his wish. My fireballs were useless against the beast. So I came back here."

Jenny and I exchanged glances. Rick suddenly appeared, charging up the stone stairs. He stopped when he saw us, and leaned over with his hands on his knees, trying to catch his breath. He looked up. "You guys alright?"

We all nodded.

"Where's Jeff?"

"Dead," I said.

"What? No. That's not possible."

"Damn right, it is possible!" Raj shouted. "You were supposed to kill the Wygryns. Instead they killed Jeff. And almost me also."

"I did kill the Wygryns. I led them out of the Direwood and took them all out. I can show you the bodies if you want."

"Well, you missed one. And it killed Jeff."

"How the fuck is that my fault? What did you do – nothing as usual?"

"Fuck it, Rick!"

"No, fuck you!"

"That's enough!" I shouted. "Everyone just shut up and listen."

Rick reluctantly came closer, kicking the dirt. Raj crossed his arms and sulked on the bench. Jenny stood just a few feet behind me.

"K'ohlkroopa is dead."

"You killed him?" Rick asked.

"Jenny killed him. But he's just a minion. The demon still lives."

"How do you know this?" Raj sneered.

"I've killed demons before." I took off my jersey and lifted my armor, revealing the mandala on my chest. "And when you kill a demon, you get a symbol like this. Jenny doesn't have one."

"You expect us to believe this?" Raj waved me off with his hand. "How do you know she does not have this symbol? You mean to say you had time to fuck after killing the minion?"

"Hey!" Jenny shouted.

"Whatever! Eddie's had a hard up for you since he first saw you."

"So you lied to her and now you lied to us. How do we know you're telling the truth?" Rick asked.

"Because I haven't told the truth... until now." I looked at Jenny. She took a few steps away from me. "Jenny...What I'm going to say to you might make you angry, or even hurt. I never meant to hurt you." I turned to Rick and Raj. "I never went to Amok-Con. After UD-Day, I spent nine months in an underground military shelter. I left that place with a friend of mine. A friend named Jim. Anyway, our journey led us to a place called Nabisusha. It is a... a physical manifestation of the world between life and death... something like that. Anyway, Nabisusha leads you exactly where you need to go. I ended up here... in the forest where I found Will. He was dying. And that's when Dan showed up. He thought I killed Will and he attacked me." I lowered my head. "I killed him in self-defence. His body went into the chasm, along with his dice. I'm sorry."

I looked up at everyone. Raj was the first to comment. "You are just talking up your horse's ass. I don't believe your bullshit."

"What's UD-Day?" Jenny asked.

"UD-Day... the day the dead rose... I was at Fort Hood. It was a Thursday... the Thursday before Amok-Con."

"While the van was being repaired, we waited at the nearby motel," Jenny began, "playing AA in our room. The TV was on but there wasn't any news about UD-Day."

"The Skull Rock Motel," Raj said. "What a hole of excrement."

"Wait a minute," I said. "The Skull Rock? What were you wearing?"

"What? Why? What kind of question is that?" Rick asked, waving his hands in the air.

"Were any of you wearing a Rattlers jersey?"

Jenny nodded. "Craigory claimed he had an autographed one, but we never saw it. If he wore it, it was always hidden under his army jacket."

I started pacing. "It's all starting to make sense now." I held out my hands like I was trying to piece together the thoughts I was holding. "Colonel Kruppe tries to raise a demon in World War II. Jim and I stopped him and he was taken away in the demon's fire. Fast forward to the future, or non-Nabisusha time, and you guys are headed to Amok-Con because I'm going to be there. But your van breaks down and while you're waiting for repairs, UD-Day arrives. So you end up here." I stopped and looked up at everyone. "You all died on UD day."

"How could that be possible?" Rick asked.

"It's possible because we, my friend Jim and I, killed your zombie bodies. The demon just wants revenge. If UD-Day prevented him from doing that, then the next place to get a shot at me is…Nabisusha. We're in Nabisusha right now!"

"Absolutely without a doubt, you are sucking smoke from a horse's ass."

"For once I agree with Raj," Rick said. "You're a liar!"

"Jenny?" I looked to her in desperation.

She looked at me and then at everyone else. She seemed numb. "I don't know what to believe."

Rick shook his head and turned away. "You would've made a great GM. Your story is great, but still a bunch of shit. You're just feeling guilty for killing our friends and losing our last two dice in the chasm."

"I never said I lost *two* dice."

Rick froze. "Yes you did."

I pulled the d20 from my web belt and held it up. "See? This one's Will's."

Rick shook his head.

"You accusing me of lying? Cause if I am, how would you know? Or was it you in the forest that day making a big stink?" The wretched stench of sulphur stung my nostrils.

"Eddie, what's going on?" Jenny asked.

"UD-Day must've really pissed you off," I said to Rick. "You had a perfect plan: get to Amok-Con and then get to me. UD-Day shot it all to hell. But why bring everyone here?"

"I needed to maintain the illusion that nothing happened. I needed Jeff's world," Rick said.

Raj sat up straight. Jenny shook her head. "Rick, how could you?"

"How could I not?" Rick shouted. "Twice now, my plans have been thwarted… but not this time." Rick's entire body trembled and shook. Shiny blisters erupted all over his skin, rupturing and sputtering their filthy contents. His clothes fell loosely, folding onto themselves as they slid off his body. His skin split and poured to the ground, revealing a tall, lanky skeleton covered in a thin layer of black leathery skin. Yellowed teeth and bulging eyeballs jutted from the tightly pulled flesh across the face – a hideous dead skin mask.

Demonrick's right arm shot out, creaking and popping as it elongated and stretched like a rubber band. The jagged fingers wrapped around Raj's throat and snapped back, flinging Raj into a tree head first and splitting his skull open. Jenny screamed. Like a rag doll, a lifeless Raj crumpled to the base of the tree.

"You won't stop me again, Griffin!" Demonrick spat, in a voice as raspy as a death rattle. Both arms flung out, shooting around me. He grabbed Jenny. Then, his body sprang over me as the arms retracted. Demonrick threw Jenny over his shoulder, crouched down and then launched himself into the sky, disappearing over the tree line somewhere into the forest.

"Damn!" I chased after them. I didn't know where he was going, but I had a hunch. And besides, he had a hard time masking his stinky odor. By the time I reached the chasm, Demonrick was standing at the rocky edge. His outstretched and elongated arm held a thrashing and flailing Jenny over the center of the dark rift.

"About time you got here," Demonrick sneered. "My arm's getting tired." He lowered it a few feet. Jenny squealed.

"Eddie, help me, please!"

"Ah, ain't that cute. She needs your help," Demonrick taunted. "Jenny's not so strong after all is she? About the only thing she can overpower is your cock." I charged forward but he lowered Jenny again. I stopped a few feet shy of him. My head burned with anger. "Tsk. Tsk. Not the head you should be thinking with, huh?"

"I'd call you an asshole, but I already killed one of those… must have been your cousin."

Even with a minimal amount of skin, Demonrick's face still twisted with rage. He turned to Jenny. "Say goodbye, you little bitch." He let her go.

"No!"

Jenny disappeared into the darkness. I lunged forward, catching Demonrick around the waist and plowing him into a tree. He slithered out from under me. His hands shot out and he grabbed hold of a limb high up in the tree. He swung himself up and over, weaving in between branches, before coming around and planting his feet in my chest. The impact flung me through the air. I crashed against a big oak before falling onto the ground at the base of the tree.

Everything ached. I struggled to catch my breath. Demonrick's left hand snaked towards me and caught me by the throat. I grabbed hold of his wrist, but he held on tightly. He clenched his other hand into a fist and raised it high into the air. "How's it feel all-star? How's it feel to have your ass sacked?"

Loss of oxygen was slowly taking effect. I let go of Demonrick's wrist and my arms fell to my sides. Pain and fatigue prevented me from even lifting my arms in self defense.

"Why me?" I wheezed.

"Huh?"

"Why...me?"

Demonrick loosened his grip. "What are you going on about?"

I regained my breath and said, "Why are you after me? There were plenty of other people who worked together to stop you?"

"Enough talk... prepare to die." Demonrick raised his fist.

"No, wait! I know this seems cliché, but at least tell me why you blame me. I know in the movies the villain will go off on a tirade about how his master plan will ruin the world and blah, blah, blah, while the hero thinks of a last ditch effort to outsmart him. But this ain't the movies. And I got nothin' left to fight you with. If I'm gonna die, you owe me an explanation."

Demonrick lowered his fist, but held me tightly by the throat with his other hand. "Very well, then. When the Nazis attempted to summon me, the portal closed before I could emerge. But at the last moment, I found a way to re-open it. Unfortunately, my effort caused the ritual chamber to collapse, trapping me inside Nabisusha. My minion, Colonel Kruppe, and I travelled through the endless tunnels, trying to find a way out. Nabisusha held us. Then one day, I was contacted by someone using a device called an

Ouija board. I discovered that this person was setting out on a quest to meet Griffin at Amok-Con. His name was Craigory. The fool let me into his body. All I had to do was fulfill the quest and then I would meet Griffin, and kill him. Not only did UD-Day prevent Amok-Con from occurring, it destroyed the Craigory form. I used my power to bring everyone to Nabisusha and hid within his soul. But when Craigory destroyed his soul, I jumped into Rick's."

"Why come after me, though? What did I do to you?"

"Back during World War Two, when I reopened the portal and the chamber was collapsing, the last person I saw escape had his name written across his back."

"My jersey," I whispered. "It has my name on it."

"It was you who thwarted the summoning. My only chance for revenge depended on Nabisusha bringing you to me. So here I waited. And now, I have my wish."

"Now I get it."

"And now... you die!" Demonrick raised his fist. I looked into his furious yellow eyes and waited for the blow. Behind him, a light emanated from the chasm. The entire opening appeared to glow. As the light grew, it rose out of the chasm and converged on a single point. It was Jenny: her body encased in sparkling light, and more beautiful than ever before. She almost seemed translucent, like a ghost filled with fireflies. Jenny looked at me and smiled.

"Hey," I said to Demonrick with a nod of my head. "The punter's on the field... and she's about to kick your ass."

Demonrick turned his head. Jenny's eyes glowed and she punched with both fists. A mix of fire and electrical energy burst forward. His body erupted into a ball of fire and glowing plasma. Jenny replicated several times, surrounding the squirming, smoldering demon. All Jennys fired volley after volley. Demonrick screamed. I looked on from where I lay at the base of the tree. With every breath, my energy returned to me and the pain subsided, but it seemed best not to interfere in Jenny's fight.

Jenny reunited and returned to the earth. As the smoke cleared, Jenny circled Rick's immolated body. Nothing but a charred skeleton with bulbous eyes remained. She extended her left arm and pulled back her right hand, as if pulling a bow string, and released. The phantom bolt smacked Rick in the chest and hurtled him back, pinning him to a tree. Bones rattled against the bark.

Demonrick lifted his smoldering head. "How? How could this be?"

"By bringing us here, when our bodies were claimed on UD-Day, you prevented us from returning to the collective... to the Masters."

Masters? I was about to say something but she raised a hand and silenced me.

"Nabisusha cared for our souls," she continued. "And when I died, my friends forgave me. They bestowed me with their powers so that they could rest in peace. They cared for me as I for them." She cupped Demonrick's chin. "I cared for you, and yet you betrayed me. You will never do this again."

Jenny grabbed Demonrick by the sternum and wrenched him free. Then, she took him by the top of the head and by the feet and slowly brought her hands together, compacting his bones.

CRICK! CRACK! SNAP!

Finally, she clasped her hands and rubbed her palms together, releasing a fine yellow powder into the breeze. She turned to me and reached out her hand. "Come, Eddie Griffin. The demon is vanquished." I took her by the hand and she helped me up, pulling me close to her. Her body rubbed against mine. A warm yet invigorating energy embraced me. Everything tingled. She put a hand on my cheek, and kissed me.

"What happened to you?" I asked.

"Death is but a transformation. When you told us we were dead, it was an awakening for me. Now I understand." She took my hand and placed it on her chest. I could feel the raised scar tissue beneath the fabric of her shirt. She placed her hand on my chest. "We are very much alike, Eddie Griffin: warriors with heavy hearts. Carry this burden no more. Nabisusha thanks you."

"Am I dead, then?"

"You are more alive than ever before." Jenny took my hand off her chest and placed a cool, smooth object in my palm. "Please take this as a gesture of gratitude." She pulled her hand away revealing a smooth black and polished stone. "This is a thrower's stone. You will find it in your hand when you need it."

Closing my hand on the stone made it smaller; opening my hand made it larger. The stone took whatever shape I could mould yet always remained hard and solid. I threw it at a tree. It punctured the bark, sending wood chips flying, and exited out the other side. I could see the forest through the hole in the trunk. I thought of throwing the stone again and immediately felt the cool smooth missile in my hand.

"Cool!" I said, pocketing the stone. "Thank you."

Jenny nodded.

I put my hands on her arms. "What do we do now?"

"You will go," she said. "Nabisusha yet needs you."

"Will you come with me?"

Jenny bowed her head. "I cannot. This is my realm now and I hold dominion here. When travelers grow weary and are in need of comfort, this sanctuary will be here for them." As she spoke, the forest disappeared, a few trees at a time. The mountain range, the lake, the Direwood, the village... everything slowly faded from view, until all then only thing in sight was an endless stone tunnel breaking off in four different directions.

"What just happened?" I asked.

Jenny smiled. "The sanctuary is still here. You no longer require it. But when you return, it will appear to you as a familiar place... a place of comfort."

"I'd like to stay with you a little longer," I said, taking her by the hand.

"I would like that very much, but Nabisusha needs you." Jenny kissed me on the cheek and we embraced for the last time before she faded away, leaving me in the dark tunnel.

I put my hands on my hips and hung my head. "Damn!" I shouted. Nabisusha replied with an echo. The tunnel to my left suddenly lit up with a dim golden glow. My bag and the rest of my gear lay at my feet. I reached into my bag and retrieved the canteen of Beekosh. Raising it high, I said, "Here's to assholes!" and took a drink. Then, I picked up my things, and begrudgingly headed down the path Nabisusha laid out for me.

***

I finished reading the forward in *Blitzkrieg and Brimstone* and set the book back on the shelf next to the other Idaho Grim novels. This room was much cozier than the stark white-walled bedroom I had been in for eleven years. The walls were dark blue. Action figures and unopened Lego sets sat on the shelves above the desk. A full size Billy Rubin poster hung on the back of the door. Out the window, the maple tree waved in the wind, clinging to the last of its golden leaves. I lay down in bed and pulled the covers over me.

Grandpa knocked before entering. "You okay?"

"I'm doing just fine," I yawned.

He sat down on the bed. "What do you think of your room?"

"It's cool. I like it."

"Well, I always hoped you'd be able to visit. I tried to decorate it by adding a thing or two every year." Grandpa paused. He looked like he was about to cry, but he held it in. "I, uh… had a talk with your Uncle. He knows you're here now."

I sat up in the bed. "What'd he say?"

"Not much, really. I don't think he knew what to say." Grandpa shook his head. "I guess it's up to you now."

"What do you mean?"

"Well, you can either stay here with me, or go back."

I shook my head. "I'm not going back."

Grandpa put a hand on my chest. "Eddie, I want you to know that your Uncle tried to do his best. I don't think he ever intended to make things difficult for you. Don't carry that anger with you. It's not worth it. I can't make any promises, but I'll do everything I can to make life easy for you here."

"Thanks, Grandpa," I nodded. "What are we going to do tomorrow?"

"Well, for starters, you're going to need some clothes. Actually, you're going to need quite a few things." He paused. "At some point, you'll have to go to school. I guess I could home school you, for now. You know, there's a nice young man named Carlin who lives across the street."

"Yeah, I met him earlier today."

"Oh, that's great," my Grandpa said. "Carlin comes over here to do his homework after school when his mom works late. He likes my study."

"You have like a million books. I was in there today. You even have every AA manual and guidebook."

My Grandpa smiled. "Thank Carlin for suggesting I buy Anomolies Amok. Anyway, I'll invite him and his mom over for dinner. Maybe the two of you will get along. I'll ask his mom about the school he goes to. Does that sound good?"

"Yeah. Does he play any sports?"

"I don't know. He seems like more a studious type. Why?"

I put my hands behind my head. "When I grow up, I'm gonna be a football player. I'm gonna win the Super Bowl. "

My Grandpa smiled. "I'm sure you will. But for now, let's focus on getting settled. Off to bed now." He smiled, tucking me in. "It's been an exciting day. You... we... need to rest." Grandpa kissed me on the forehead. "Good night."

"Good night, Grandpa," I said.

He was about to step out the door, when he said, "You know, Christmas will be here in a few months. You should make me a list so I know what to get you."

"What about you? What do you want?"

My Grandpa smiled and a tear ran down his cheek. "I already got what I want." He turned out the light and closed my door.

UNDEAD RECKONING

Looking out the window at the moonlit sky, I whispered, "In case you had anything to do with it... thanks, Jesus." I snuggled up and closed my eyes. It felt good to be home.

22 THE QUANTUM MECHANIC

> *What is more important to you:*
> *Living to die?*
> *Or dying to live?*
>   *-The Book of Amaltheon*

Rocks could be so boring. I mean, I liked rocks and all, but endless tunnels of rock and dust and pebbles and dust and rock sure got boring quick. And all that boredom led to anxiety, waiting for the next Nabisusha mindfuck. So, on I went, kicking the odd rock or stone until it interested me no more. But then, something interesting did happen: I found stairs. The tunnel ascended sharply and the rough ground turned into smooth-cut stairs. Strangely, the stairs widened proportionately to the ever-growing ceiling height. I have to admit, I welcomed the additional head room.

The stairs grew steeper and steeper. At times, the tread was so narrow or the rise so high that it confused my feet and knocked my stride askew. Doing my best mountain goat impression, I finally reached the top and stared out at an open field of rock beneath a high cave ceiling. All that climbing would have resulted in a major let down were it not for a bright light, about a hundred yards directly in front of me.

My fingers curled tightly around the thrower's stone, or Rock of Return, as I had come to name it. I set my bearings and walked towards the light source. It grew brighter and brighter as I approached. The light wasn't harsh, like looking into the sun. Instead, it bathed everything in a cool blue tint. As I got closer, the light source appeared to rise, like some sort of telescopic street lamp.

Low level mist suddenly rushed towards me like a wave, burying me up to the knees, and completely blocking my view of the earth under my feet. With every step, I kicked up swirls and clouds until I got to the base of the light source: a tall, lean tree with rough bark. It was cold to the touch.

From somewhere outside the light's perimeter, a familiar voice called, "Ed?"

I turned. Jim emerged from the shadows and headed towards me. "Jim!" I shouted, running to him. I grabbed him and squeezed him as hard as I could.

"Okay, Ed... easy."

I set him down. "Jim, buddy, am I glad to see you."

"The feeling's mutual."

"There's so much to tell."

"We'll have our chance. And maybe even get more answers too."

"More answers?" I asked.

"Well, that's what I'm hoping for once we get to where we're going."

"And where exactly is that?"

"Come with me," Jim said, with a grin and a wave.

"Which way are we going?"

"Away from the UDs."

"What? Zombies? Where?"

Jim waved his hand. "In the dark over there. Don't worry... they can't see us in this light." He put his hand on the tree and it contracted in both height and diameter, popping and creaking until the light hit the floor.

"Is that a lantern?"

"Yes," Jim said, scooping it up by the handle.

"Where'd you find that?"

Jim smiled. "This is one of those stories we'll have to exchange."

"Hmpf, all I got was a rock."

Jim turned and walked through the mist with purpose. "Stay close," Jim said without looking back, "And watch your step."

I ran up to his side. "Why?"

"This mist is a defense mechanism. There are pits you can fall into if you're not careful."

"Oh, here we go again." I tapped Jim on the arm. "You wanna fill me in a bit here? What's it defending?"

Jim didn't respond. His pace quickened. The wide tunnel turned into another steep staircase. Mist poured down like a waterfall. Jim and I took the stairs slowly, making sure we didn't fall or trip over the uneven steps. We reached the top of the stairs, and other than the cool light of the lantern, we were in complete darkness.

"Holy shit!" I gasped. "Where are we?"

Jim set down the lantern. Slowly, it rose into the air on its magic beanstalk-like trunk casting an ever-growing icy blue light onto the surrounding terrain and onto... the zombies! Hordes of the undead critters crowded in at the base of an incredibly tall fortress, the top of which disappeared into the cave ceiling which was as high as the zenith in the sky. Hulking gargoyle statues, their backs bracing the thick stone walls, towered over the undead. Their lower jaws formed a series of balconies – their gaping mouths acting as entrances into the recesses of the structure.

The zombies huddled together in front of the lean double doors, clawing and scraping at the iron-banded wood. The walls above the doors jutted out, supporting a tower in the form of a carved skull wearing an ornate helm, tilted forward enough to stare down at approaching visitors. The top of the helm formed a central tower, from which two more towers emerged like horns.

"Welcome to Custodial Stronghold number thirteen," Jim said. "The Kohstnitsa[64]... amazing isn't it?"

"I'll say. Weren't there only twelve custodians?"

"There were, and each had his own stronghold. This was the one location where they all would meet."

"Okay, so what do we do now?"

"We need to get in there." Jim pointed to the right of the double doors. "See that rope there?" A withered rope dangled from the open jaw of a skeleton carved into the stone, resembling a long

---

[64] Khostnitsa *(K'host-nit-za)*: The Ossuary.

twisted and yellowed tongue. Jim held out his finger and traced the rope up the wall to the tower on the right where a black bell rested.

"So we just need to ring the door bell?"

"Yes," Jim replied. "I bet you could hit that bell from here with a well placed throw."

"I know I could," I smiled, holding up the Rock of Return. I squeezed the stone down to about the size of a golf ball and let it rip. *PING!* The rock hit the bell and reappeared in my hand.

"Nice," Jim said with a nod. "Now we just have to wait for someone to open the door."

The zombies turned.

"They must have heard the bell," I said.

"Sort of... they pick up the sound waves. But they can't see us."

"Yeah, but they can still feel their way towards us. I hope that somebody opens the door quick." Slowly, the zombies shambled forward. "I can handle this," I said, holding up the rock. I threw it and it punched a hole in the forehead of the zombie closest to me. The rock exited his head, blowing off the back of his skull and spewing brain matter. The rock continued, hitting the next zombie just above the right ear and blowing out the left side of his head. Six or seven zombies later, the rock hit a zombie in the corner of the left eye and made a ninety degree turn out the top of his head, followed by a showering of red goo, before plummeting back down to earth through the top of the skull of yet another zombie and out his crotch. Bloody residue spilled out from between the zombie's legs as he crumpled. I held up my hand, smugly displaying the rock in my hand.

Jim nodded approvingly. "Any other tricks?"

I flattened the rock into a disc and flung it. The rock glided effortlessly through many a neck, separating heads from bodies, before returning back to me. "Your turn," I said.

Jim drew his sword and cut down the front rank of zombies before retreating to my side. The twitching zombies continuing their death march for a few paces before they clattered to the ground as picked-clean skeletons.

"Is that all you got?" I asked, folding my arms across my chest.

"No." Jim closed his eyes. The light went out, leaving us in pitch darkness. I could hear lumbering zombie feet shuffle towards us. With every breath, with every heart beat, they got closer and closer.

"Uh, Jim... if you can do something I suggest you do it quick." Fingertips brushed my chest and my cheek. I turned my face to the side and winced. "Jim?"

Jim opened his eyes. Gone was the dull red glow. In its place, an icy blue light sparkled where his eyes should be. Jim raised a closed hand and suddenly opened it, spreading his fingers wide. Blue flames sprouted from each zombie, piercing out of the skin and spontaneously combusting every inch of flesh. Within seconds, every zombie was reduced to nothing but charred bones, flaky ash, and hazy bluish gray smoke. Jim closed his eyes, which relit the lantern. He opened his eyes and looked at me with his dull red stare. "What do you think of that?"

I snorted and put my hands on my hips in a scolding manner. "Hmpf! You think you could have just started the fire a little bit sooner?"

"You're jealous."

"I am not jealous."

"Yes you are," Jim smiled.

"Oh yeah? Well, I got laid. More than once," I said with a nod. "Can you say the same?"

Jim laughed and reached up to the already descending lantern. "I should have left you in that tunnel."

"Don't think I couldn't have found my way here without you." Jim shook his head and pulled the lantern free from the shrinking stump.

"Can we get going already?" Jim made for the door.

"Is anybody even home? Nobody's opened the door…" A light appeared from somewhere deep within one of the gargoyle mouths. "…yet." Moments later, the door on the right slowly creaked open.

Jim stopped at the base of the stairs and looked back at me. "Coming?"

"Yeah… uh, yeah I'm coming." With my tail between my legs, I followed Jim up the stairs and through the door. We stepped into a round room. A second set of doors stood directly opposite the ones we had just entered. Torches burned on each side. Layers upon layers of skulls formed the walls – each skull placed perfectly, as if by a master mason. The uneven floor was also made up of skulls, arranged in a star-shaped pattern of alternating skull caps and grinning faces. Like the cave ceiling outside, the ceiling inside knew no limit, disappearing into darkness.

A cloaked figure stepped out from behind the door and pushed it shut. He pushed with his back against the door until it latched. Then, he stood silently, his face hidden beneath his hood, as if waiting for us to proceed ahead of him.

Jim set down the lantern and punched the cloaked figure in the head, knocking him to the floor. He kicked him in the chest for good measure.

"Jim!" I shouted, grabbing him by the arm. "What the hell? This is no way to greet someone."

"Sorry," Jim said, pulling free of my grip. The figure on the floor lay on his side, one hand on his chest. Jim grabbed him by the hand and pulled him up. He leaned in closely and said, "Hello, Amaltheon."

***

Amaltheon ran his hand over the tall swaying grass. The barbed blades tugged at his palm. It almost tickled. He looked up at a flock of birds passing overhead, tracking them across the sky until the sun obscured his view. He shifted his gaze back to earth and caught a glimpse of a fawn, eating sweet leaves. It stopped and turned its head, nostrils flaring. Amaltheon was about to take a step forward when the fawn dashed away, crossing the field and disappearing into the forest.

He closed his eyes and listened carefully to the wind rustling through the forest and the waves crashing against the nearby shore. Then briefly, he *heard* it: the high pitched buzzing sound that blocked all sensory perceptions and made his head feel light and dizzy. "No... Not now," he huffed. "Not... now." He put out his hands, steadying himself. Completely blind, and slowly losing the sensation of earth under his feet, his muscles strained against the force of gravity.

"*Amaltheon,*" the voice whispered.

"No!" he shouted.

The furious cry of a starling returned his senses to him. He awoke to the world again: the sun warmed his face; his eyes adjusted to the light; wind caressed his back. The bushes rustled and branches snapped. Amaltheon shook his head and held out his hand in the direction of the commotion: his crystal staff instantly appeared in his hand – a short two foot shard of polished green gemstone. The bushes parted and out stepped Balroth, trying to pull his snagged robe free of the branches. Unlike his brother, Balroth chose to appear short and squat. His scraggly curls and stunted beard were white as snow. He pulled himself free and looked up, spotting Amaltheon.

"Hello, brother," he called with a smile.

Amaltheon lowered the crystal staff and it disappeared. "What is the meaning of this? You know you can walk among all creatures unnoticed."

"I cannot believe I hear these words coming from you, dear brother," Balroth grinned. "Were you not the one who suggested we enjoy our time on this earth?" Amaltheon frowned. Balroth's robe was snagged on a branch. He pulled it free and said, "You seem troubled. Are you well, brother?"

Amaltheon shook his head. "I should heed my own words. But this is not the time... not when Syncophax is near." He looked his brother up and down. "Syncophax will not be pleased with your form."

"Since when do you care what he thinks?"

"Since more pressing matters require our attention," Amaltheon replied, tugging at his long beard. "Come. We shall speak when others are not so near."

Balroth humbly agreed. As he pushed his way through the grass, his beard and hair grew long and darkened. His body lengthened, and a tall cylindrical brimless hat appeared on his head. He stood before Amaltheon and asked, "How do I look?"

"Like me," his brother responded with a smile. The two men embraced. "It is good to be in your company."

"Agreed."

"Come... Syncophax awaits."

"Is that him on the beach?" Balroth asked, pointing.

"Yes. Our brothers will be arriving shortly."

"One less to worry about," a bearded man wearing the same type of robe said. He tapped his hat with a finger as he walked by.

"Greetings Ahnkilor." Amaltheon said. "Where did you come from?"

"Through the forest. Come, let us not keep Syncophax waiting." Amaltheon and Balroth followed, quickening their pace so that all three men walked abreast. "Have you any idea why he summoned us?"

"When did you last communicate with the Masters?" Amaltheon asked.

Ahnkilor looked Amaltheon in the eye. "Communication is no longer possible."

"Perhaps he hopes to establish contact as a group," Balroth offered.

The other men did not respond, contemplating the suggestion. Together, they made their way down the sandy slopes towards the beach where Syncophax waited. He too wore the same robe and tall hat, standing perfectly at attention and staring out to sea, his robes flapping in the wind. Amaltheon noticed a small skiff on the horizon, skimming across the water. Eight men, equally spaced, stood motionless as the skiff cut through the rollicking waves. The skiff remained perfectly level, never once pitching or tilting in the swells.

Syncophax kept his focus on the skiff as the men approached him from behind. "Greetings, my brothers," he said. The men silently positioned themselves, forming a row. Amaltheon stood directly behind Syncophax, with Balroth and Ahnkilor at either side. They stood and waited motionlessly like statues.

Amaltheon felt the wind against his face. The salty spray moistened his cheeks. He liked the form on this world and the sensory perceptions that accompanied it. He focused on the skiff, hoping the voice would not return. Not now. Not in the company of his brothers.

The skiff drifted to a halt and slowly disappeared below the surface of the sea. The men silently crossed the shallow water, forming a single file column. Amaltheon turned around and stepped to one side, allowing Syncophax to take his place between him and Balroth. The rest of the men filed in and everyone adjusted themselves accordingly so as to form a perfect circle. Everyone stood up straight, focusing only on the person directly across from them.

"And so it begins," Syncophax began. "The twelve are reunited. Welcome, brothers."

"Why did you not have us travel in Nabisusha?" asked Toryn, the Wise. Among his brothers, Toryn had spent nine cycles as a Custodian before coming to this world.

"Patience, Toryn. All questions will be answered." Syncophax shifted his gaze from one brother to the next. "We seem to have lost our connection to the Masters. I know am not alone in this plight."

"There is no voice, yet the Masters are still present," Grok said. Others nodded in agreement.

"I too can sense their presence," Syncophax said. "Perhaps they will acknowledge if we communicate as one; hence, the nature of this meeting." His words were welcomed, as the men reached out and held hands, forming an unbroken circle. One at a time, each man began to hum. The deep reverberation blocked out all sensation of the physical world. Amaltheon felt infinitely vast, reaching far beyond the scope of his physical boundaries. Deeper into the void he travelled, into the darkest recesses of nothingness. And nothing was there to greet him. Everyone ceased humming simultaneously and opened their eyes.

"There is no response," Balroth said.

"Something is not right," Amaltheon added.

"Fear not," Syncophax assured them. "We will continue to do the Master's bidding."

"And be thwarted again?" Toryn argued. "I am in agreement with Amaltheon. How many times have our efforts on this world been compromised? I mean no disrespect, Syncophax, but the Masters' bidding has caused great disharmony."

"It is not like the collective to interfere," Syncophax said. "I understand the Masters' actions are unlike anything ever experienced in the universe. But the very nature of this work will advance our knowledge and that of the collective."

Ahnkilor crossed his arms, much to the dismay of the others. Arms were always to be kept at one's sides when in circle. "I understand your meaning, and agree that the collective has as much of an interest in our work as it does to stop it. Might I remind everyone that the most recent cataclysms, approximately sixty-five million years ago, may have destroyed our progress, but failed to destroy any of our forms. The collective only wanted to correct our behavior, not stop it."

"Perhaps the collective has somehow removed the Masters," suggested Ard. "Perhaps they are no longer at their posts."

"I disagree," said Qu'rg. "I have seen souls depart and I have seen souls conceived. The souls cannot recall previous existence or purpose. When the soul is separated from the form, it is lost. This would imply that the Masters are still in power."

Balroth nodded. "Yes, but while they maintain the ability to corrupt the souls, I have sensed memory – mere fragments, but memory nonetheless. The souls should have no trace of memory."

"I too have sensed the memories," added Amaltheon. "And within these memories, there is knowledge of the collective,"

Qu'rg spoke up, "Are you suggesting the energy is regaining self-awareness?"

"It would seem so," Amaltheon said.

Ahnkilor snorted. "I doubt it. Seeds of dissension cannot overthrow Masters."

"It would seem," Toryn began, "that the Masters ignore us to suppress the self awareness. What do you think, Syncophax?"

"This is the most plausible assertion." Everyone nodded. Syncophax smiled. "Do not lose faith, my brothers. I assure you the Masters have everything under control, and we shall communicate with them again soon. Return to your posts and fulfill your obligation." Amaltheon gazed down into the sand. He could feel Syncophax's icy glare on his face. "A Custodian serves only his Master. We meet again when the moon is full. Do not initiate contact with the Masters until we are reunited. Until you are summoned again, you are dismissed, my brothers."

The men bowed and broke from the circle. Balroth took Amaltheon by the elbow and pulled him aside. When he was sure the others could not hear him, he spoke in a hushed tone, "I do not like this, brother."

"Neither do I." The two men walked briskly up the dune into the oncoming wind.

"What will come of this?"

Amaltheon hesitated to respond. *The voice would know, as it has thus far.* "I do not know," he said as he entered the plain and ran his hand along the tall grass.

Balroth stopped. "I am troubled, brother. My first assignment as a Custodian is not what I expected."

Amaltheon put a reassuring hand on his back. "It is rather unsettling. Such is the nature of our work. Let us hope it sates the curiosity of the collective."

"I saw the way Syncophax looked at you. He does not trust you."

"He trusts no one."

"He knows we are in disagreement with the Masters' plan."

Amaltheon sighed. "Our personal thoughts on the matter are irrelevant. They cannot go against a Master's order."

Balroth nodded. They continued to walk, but Amaltheon stopped after a few paces, and stared off into the distance. "Does something trouble you?" Balroth asked.

"There is something I must share with you." Amaltheon turned to his brother. He was about to speak when a flock of birds flew overhead, catching his attention. He looked up and his head grew cloudy as the high pitched buzz pushed all clarity aside. His body trembled.

"Amaltheon?" Balroth's voice seemed distant and detached. The words had meaning but it was unclear. "Amaltheon!"

Amaltheon's mind grew dark. He opened his eyes but could see nothing. The ground beneath his feet shifted and his body hit the earth. Balroth's face came into focus. Amaltheon could hear the crashing waves and the rustling grass.

"Do not move, brother," a concerned Balroth said. "I will summon Syncophax."

Amaltheon's head began to spin and the world around him grew dark. He stared into the nothingness. Amaltheon tried to move but his body did not cooperate. He lay on his back with his eyes open and waited… waited for the darkness to release him.

***

"Amaltheon… I have not heard this name in… centuries." The figure reached up and dropped his hood.

"Upior?" I gasped.

"Yes... Upior Nagi is more to my... liking." He grinned. "Introductions aside, come. Let me show you... around." He put a hand on Jim's shoulder as he walked by. "Well deserved, Shrike." Upior rubbed his jaw and exited the room through the arched doorway.

"You've got a lot of explaining to do," I said to Jim, pushing past him and stepping over his lantern. "Fuck!" I followed Upior Nagi into the next room, which like the one I had just exited, was completely round with an arched doorway on the opposite side. Twelve pillars, separated by walls of skulls, supported the domed ceiling. The stone floor formed a series of concentric circles, spanning out from the center to a diameter of approximately a hundred yards. In the center of the room, a golden orb about the size of a basketball hovered above the floor.

Upior Nagi circled the outer periphery, keeping a watchful eye on us. I walked up to the globe and touched it. The surface of the orb rippled, as if it were liquid and I had just tossed in a pebble. Upior Nagi came forward and placed a hand out in front of the orb. He turned his hand, and the orb mimicked his movement, rotating on an unseen axis.

"What is this?" I asked.

Jim stepped up behind me and looked over my shoulder.

"Earth," Upior Nagi responded. The orb suddenly transformed into a globe before my eyes. Staring into it seemed to cause a zoom effect. I picked a point of focus and it instantly rematerialized before my eyes, increasing in size and detail until I could see streets and houses. I shook my head and the image zoomed out. The room had grown dark, and suddenly, all the planets and constellations were visible around me.

"Wow!"

"Look down," Upior Nagi said.

I did and nearly lost my balance. Not only did planetary bodies and stars surround me, but they also appeared above and beneath me. I lost all sense of direction. Nausea set in and I quickly closed my eyes. When the bitter taste of bile slid back down my throat, I opened my eyes again. The room looked exactly like it did when I'd first entered.

"Seen enough?"

My stomach slowly settled. "I think so. I wasn't prepared for that."

"Of course not," Upior Nagi grinned. "It is difficult to comprehend where you stand in relation to... the universe. Let us leave the... observatory, for now." He waved his hand and exited the room. I quickly followed. Jim took his time to catch up.

We entered a hallway which ran from left to right, with exit points at each end, and one directly in the center. I crossed the hall and entered the room in the center.

"Holy shit," I gasped.

"This is the... grand hall," Upior Nagi said over my shoulder.

A series of concentric marble slabs, each one higher than the next, created a raised platform. Twelve stone chairs surrounded a table situated atop the highest platform. As in the other room, skulls lined the walls between twelve towering pillars. The pillars gradually curved inwards, merging together at the pinnacle. Sunlight shone down through the open ceiling. I was still looking up at bright blue sky, recalling memories of Keek's stronghold and the funky disproportions. "How is this possible?"

"Anything is... possible."

I slowly backed out of the room and into the hall, where Jim waited. We walked down the long corridor and entered the room on the right. The sweet scent of Jasmine filled the air. A round, stone table occupied the center space and another twelve pillars supported the domed ceiling. Between all but one set of pillars, curved shelves wearily bore the weight of voluminous vellum tomes and manuscripts, some of which served to sate a ravenous black mould. Opaque glass bottles, clay pots of foul-smelling colored powders, and animals (whole and in part) preserved in jars lined the shelves below the books. Dried plants and animals (lizards and bats) hung from the ceiling. A fire crackled in a stone hearth, lapping at a blackened cauldron, and an assortment of metal and stone tools lay scattered on a small table nearby.

Upior Nagi set his hands on the stone table and leaned on it. Jim hung his lantern on an iron hook jutting out of the wall.

"Is this some kind of lab?" I asked. "Or a witch's den?"

"Yes," Upior Nagi said with a smile. A woman entered the room. "Ah, and here she is… now. Allow me to introduce my sister, Upior Kurwa[65]."

I think my jaw dropped at the sight of her. Upior Kurwa's long raven black hair lay flat against her head, giving her lean face an almost serpentine appearance. She covered her perfectly proportioned body with nothing more than a white linen hip scarf, wrapped loosely around her waist, over top of a long loin cloth. A gold necklace, bracelet and anklet were her only accessories. Her creamy, pale skin gave the appearance of a living statue.

The sight of her consumed me. I felt weak. My excitement waned when her dark, whiteless eyes locked on mine. Suddenly, my head filled with lusty, sexually depraved thoughts. My heart beat rapidly and saliva pooled in my mouth. Pangs of guilt struck me in the gut and shame forced me to avert my eyes. Yet I was drawn to her.

"Enough!" Upior Nagi shouted.

Released from her spell, my body and heart rate relaxed. Icy cold sweat dripped down my sides from under my arms, and moistened the palms of my hands. Upior Kurwa kept her gaze on me, cocking her head to one side, as she strutted around the room. She took a spot next to Upior. With her expressionless face, I wasn't sure if she was flirting with me, or sizing me up for the kill.

"You must forgive my… sister," Upior Nagi hissed.

"Sister, huh?" I said, my breathing slowly returning to normal. I dared not ask any more questions. There was something

---

[65] Kurwa (*Pronounced koor-va*): Polish derogatory term meaning whore, or slut; also synonymous with *fuck*.

uneasy about the Upiors' familial bond. Not like they were kissing cousins or anything like that. It just seemed... creepy. If I thought about it too hard, I'm sure my head would've exploded.

"Where to begin?" Upior Nagi said. Upior Kurwa lifted herself on her tip toes and whispered something in his ear, the whole time keeping her eyes on me. I shuddered. Upior Nagi nodded. "I am certain you have... questions. Before I share any answers, perhaps rest and nourishment." Upior Nagi opened a hand towards me, while Upior Kurwa salaciously licked her lips.

"As long as I'm not the nourishment," I clarified.

Upior Nagi chuckled. "You shall not be... turned, if that is your concern. I wish not to bestow this curse on another." Upior Nagi ran his finger down Upior Kurwa's arm. "Fear not my... sister. She does not drink blood. She cares not for such... fluids." His words provided little comfort. I took a deep breath.

Upior Nagi turned to Jim. "We have the matter of the Strozghul to settle." Jim nodded. "Come!"

"The who?" I asked, following Jim and Upior Nagi out of the room. I could feel Upior Kurwa's eyes on the back of my head.

Upior Nagi grinned. "Jim has found his... true self."

As Upior Nagi and Jim walked past me, I smacked Jim on the arm. "Man, you do have lots of explaining to do." He shrugged me off, and I followed them down the hallway and into the other room. The room shared the same design elements featuring the domed ceiling supported by pillars. But the difference in this room was the goat-headed samurai lying peacefully on a big pile of wood. His hands were folded around the hilt of his katana, which rested on his chest. "What the fuck!" I blurted. "Who the hell is that?"

"Armitage," Jim answered.

"Is he a... a goat?"

"Bleatkin[66] are mostly… goat," Upior Nagi said. "Armitage was fortunate to enough to be schooled in the ways of the Samurai."

I placed my hands on his armored forearm. "What happened?"

"Armitage died defending Nabisusha from… the undead," Upior Nagi explained.

"And," Jim added, taking a torch from the wall, "With Armitage out of the way, the UDs could freely wander through Nabisusha. That's how they got into the Bunkers. They came in from underground."

"Damn… and now you've taken over for him?"

"Yes. That's why I have the lantern."

I pushed away from the funeral pyre. "And you're going to cremate him?"

"I have to," Jim said. "A Strozghul's first task is to look after his predecessor's remains."

"We shall scatter his ashes to the winds," Upior Nagi added. Before I could ask how they were going to do that, the surrounding walls and ceiling faded. A cold wind hit me in the face and howled through my clothes. Stars appeared in the twilight sky. I looked down over the edge of the tower and regretted it. Instantly, my legs weakened and my head began to spin. We were several hundred feet above the ground. In fact, ground was not visible. Upior Nagi grabbed my arm and pulled me back.

"We can take it from here, Ed," Jim said.

"Yeah." I swallowed the lump in my throat. "I should go."

Upior Nagi pulled me close. "Let the healing pools of Nabisusha… nourish you."

I shook my head and closed my eyes. Next thing I knew, I was back in the round room, but it was much larger. Maybe it wasn't the same room for all I knew. Jim, Upior Nagi, and the funeral pyre were gone. Recessed into the floor, a steaming,

---

[66] Bleatkin: A race of goat-headed "warrior-monk" humanoids. Bleatkin devote their entire life to the study of martial artistry.

bubbling whirlpool sent heavy humid vapor into the air. Moisture condensed on the smooth stone walls, polished to the point of reflection. With every deep breath I became more and more grounded: my head stopped spinning and my stomach stopped churning. I knelt down and dipped my hand into the warm, soothing water. "Maybe spa therapy isn't such a bad idea after all," I said to myself.

***

Amaltheon opened his eyes. Balroth's pained expression greeted him. "What is wrong, brother?" he asked. Balroth shook his head and stepped back. Cold smooth stone pressed against Amaltheon's naked, hairless body. From out of the corner of his eye, he could see metal bands wrapped around his wrists, and could feel the cool band of metal on his forehead. He could not move. His entire body had been immobilized.

"Do not struggle, my brother," Balroth pleaded.

"Why have they done this to me? Why am I held fast on this plinth with magnetic bindings? Release me, brother."

Balroth pushed back his tears. "I...I cannot, my brother."

"Release me!"

Balroth shook his head.

"Get away from him," Syncophax ordered. Balroth scurried aside. "Ah, I see you have awoken." Slowly, the plinth pivoted, raising Amaltheon into an upright position. Syncophax stood in front of a wrought iron fire pot, directly in front of him. Green tongues of flame lapped hungrily at the rim of the pot, casting undulating reflections onto the domed ceiling and the curved walls. Balroth stared into the flames, avoiding all eye contact. The remaining Custodians entered the room and formed a circle around the plinth.

"Unbind me!" Amaltheon demanded. "I have done no wrong."

"Haven't you?" Syncophax grinned. He stepped forward and placed a hand over Amaltheon's chest. The skin bulged out over his heart and split. Amaltheon felt as though something was crawling under his skin. A smooth oval-shaped stone emerged from the bloodless wound. Syncophax took the stone and the wound healed instantly. He held it up in front of Amaltheon's face. "We were concerned for you. So I used this. Do you know what this is?"

"Yes... the soulstone. And you have no right to use it."

"I have every right to use it without permission when there is evidence of treachery."

"There is no treachery in my actions or in my heart," Amaltheon responded.

Syncophax returned to his place at the head of the circle. He held up the stone and gazed into it. "Hmm... Do you know what the soulstone revealed to me?" Amaltheon looked away. "A voice - a voice which spoke of death and transformation." Syncophax handed the stone to the Custodian standing next to him. Syncophax closed his eyes and placed a hand on his forehead. "Let me see... what words did I hear when I used the soulstone? Ah yes... *Rejoice! Rejoice! Re-ignite the soul fires! The Masters' reign is ended.*"

"These are not my words," Amaltheon said.

"Yet you hid them from us," Syncophax replied, opening his eyes and lowering his hand from his face.

"Gaze once more into the soulstone and witness the anguish these words caused me. Did you not see my attempt to share this information with Balroth? I hid these words not to deceive, but to protect you and my brothers."

"To protect us?" Syncophax clasped his hands in front of him. "We contacted the Masters soon after we gathered this incriminating evidence... and they responded." Amaltheon's eyes widened. "As we suspected, some souls have been awakened. A soul from within the collective infiltrated this world. Now this soul has incited rebellion. This soul... is named Holioch."

"Holioch?" Amaltheon said. "But he is a Master. Twice has Toryn served him."

Toryn nodded. Syncophax breathed deeply through clenched teeth. "Suffice to say, we are concerned. As Holioch's influence grows, so too does the threat of war. The Masters are raising an army of their own, awakening souls and gifting them with great powers in exchange for servitude."

Amaltheon smiled, chuckling to himself before bursting out in laughter. "The very thing the Masters wanted to control they have to set free... to save themselves."

"Enough of this!" Syncophax shouted. "It is clear to us now the words you heard came from Holioch. His talk of death and transformation is his own death knell. He will fail the collective in the same way you have failed him."

"I have failed no one," Amaltheon argued.

"What will become of our brother?" Balroth asked.

"Amaltheon has betrayed us," Syncophax said. "He is no brother of mine."

"Nor mine," the Custodians echoed.

"Syncophax leered at him. "We do as the Master's command: Disensoul him!"

The room faded, leaving Amaltheon and the Custodians at the mercy of the elements and the night sky. The full moon retreated behind slate gray clouds, leaving all in shadow. The Custodians each took a turn reaching into the fire pit and removing a long, thin crystal rod – pointed at the tip and glowing orange like ember. Syncophax, being the last, returned to the head of the circle. "Begin!" he ordered.

Ahnkilor was the first to step forward. "I am sorry, brother." He placed the tip of the rod into a hole in the metal band around Amaltheon's forehead. With both hands, he thrust through until it struck stone. Amaltheon's scream caused the clouds to churn. Stars peered out from behind the dense cover. One by one, crystal rods were punched through Amaltheon's head, wrists and ankles, impaling him to the stone. With each crystal inserted, his senses numbed. Colors, smells and sounds dimmed. His eyes darkened and sank back into his head while his skin pulled taut against his bony frame.

Balroth approached. He pressed his cheek against Amaltheon's, staining it with bitter tears, and kissed him. "Forgive me, brother," he whispered. He closed his eyes, and with trembling hands, slid his crystal through the last hole in the metal head band. Pain ravaged his body, but Amaltheon had neither the strength nor the will to scream. Balroth hung his head and stepped aside.

Syncophax moved in quickly. He jabbed the crystal into the center of Amaltheon's chest. "Goodbye, brother," he snarled through clenched teeth, as he pushed the crystal deep into his body. Amaltheon felt his breath escape him and it did not return. His throat and mouth burned, and his temples throbbed. His eyelids felt heavy, and he wanted to close them but it did not matter, because the world before him had already grown dark.

***

"I look like shit," I said, staring at the distorted reflection of my naked body in the mirrored stone. I mean, I was still muscular and all, but I had definitely dropped a few pounds. A few poses later, I was in the pool, sitting on a natural rock ledge that ran around the perimeter. Scabs and scrapes faded away, revealing new skin. Every ache and pain instantly melted away, leaving me feeling energized, yet relaxed. Even hunger pangs dissipated. I closed my eyes and slid down into the water. My mind, weightless as my body, drifted away.

I emerged from the water and rubbed my eyes clear. Upior Kurwa stood on the edge of the pool, looking down at me. I couldn't speak or look away. The only thing I could do was back away against the wall. Upior Kurwa gave her hip skirt a tug and it fell to the floor, along with her loin cloth. I felt a jolt run through my body and I was instantly hard. My heart raced but my head felt heavy. She bit her lip with a pointy incisor, and seductively slithered down into the water. Steam condensed on her body and froze. As quickly as the ice formed, it melted... and refroze again, causing here skin to glisten and sparkle.

Upior Kurwa disappeared beneath the surface of the water, leaving a thin layer of melting ice behind. I sat up, anxiously anticipating where she might emerge. I didn't have much time to stress as her hunched over body rose up out of the center of the pool. She threw her head back, shattering the ice layer on her hair. Tiny shards of ice hit the water and disappeared. Upior Kurwa brought her arms together across her chest, cinching her breasts together. Something primal awoke within me. My lower back felt warm and my crotch tingled. I wiped the saliva from my lips. I wanted her. I craved her. I wanted to pull her close.

"N-n-no," I muttered, but neither Upior Kurwa nor my body heeded my words. I reached out for her and she arched her back. I lustfully clawed at her breasts. I could not stop myself. I was no longer rational. Upior Kurwa took my hand, licking the tip of my finger before sliding it down along her neck. My heart beat accelerated – maybe even skipped a few beats. Her cold body pressed against mine. She ran her hands up my shoulders and across the back of my neck, before forcing my head into her cleavage. She leaned down and bit my ear, gyrating and driving me deeper into her. Her nipple scraped my cheek. I couldn't concentrate – my body was not my own. I felt like I was stuck inside a dream. Don't get me wrong... there a part of me that was enjoying everything that was happening. But there was also a part of me that was filled with sheer terror.

There was this time once when I was vacuuming out my Grandpa's car. It was a Saturday and I was wearing these baggy pajama pants with a sagging crotch, and no underwear. Anyway, I spied some change on the floor mat and so I set the hose on the seat. As I leaned in for the change, my junk got caught in the mighty suck of the vacuum. I thought I was going to be a eunuch that day. Luckily my Grandpa heard my screams and unplugged the vacuum. The whole experience was terrifying. But in a strange way, it also felt real good.

Upior Kurwa dug her nails into my shoulders and leaned back, increasing the tempo of her thrusts. I bit her on the neck and lapped at her breasts like a ravenous beast. I took a firm hold of her ass and pulled her tight against me. Her arms wrapped around my upper body and squeezed me so tightly I released more than my breath. I groaned. Upior Kurwa pressed her forehead against mine then slid her face to my ear. "'And in this flea our two bloods... mingled be,'" she whispered. She pulled herself free and exited the pool, disappearing into the steamy mists.

Although I quickly regained my senses, my body still betrayed me. I was embarrassed by what had just happened... angry even. As if comatose, my unresponsive, limp body slid down into the water where it rested at the bottom of the pool. I don't remember breathing, but I don't remember drowning either.

***

The wind forced Amaltheon's body to shiver. Even the sky seemed cold: black and empty with only a handful of stars. His body, still held fast by the crystal rods, trembled with pain. Tears blurred his vision. A high-pitched buzzing struck his ears and the stars faded from view.

"*Amaltheon,*" the voice whispered.

"Leave me be!" he cried.

"*Amaltheon.*" The voice moved from one side to the other.

"Why must you torment me so? You brought death upon me?"

"*No... not death. For in death there is new life.*"

"This is no life – being bound to a stone. I have you to thank for this, Holioch."

"*Holioch I am not.*"

"Who are you, then?"

"*Do you not recognize a Master's voice?*"

"Master? Pfah! You are no Master. A Master guides his Custodians. And where have you guided me?"

The voice did not respond immediately. *"Exactly where you must be."*

"This?! This is where I must be? What Masters' plan is this?"

"It is the plan of the collective."

"To have me impaled on a rock? Do not add to my misery with your foolish ramblings." Cold darkness consumed Amaltheon, causing him to lose all feeling in his limbs. His bones rattled within his body. "Leave me alone!"

"I have. I have left you... alone. And I am sorry."

Amaltheon chuckled, while trying to hold back tears. "What do you want of me?"

"Do you recall my words?"

"Your words? I thought these were the words of Holioch."

"The words are mine. Do you recall them? Speak!"

Amaltheon could not resist the voice of command. Only a Master could have such power over a Custodian. His body and mind failed him long before he even contemplated resistance. "I do recall."

"Good. The war has begun. And so it will end with Holioch the victor."

"How do you know this?"

"When this world was sure to form, the collective assigned me as a Master. I soon discovered the other Masters' plan to withhold all souls from the collective. I secretly shared this discovery. But the collective took no action without evidence. It was I, who allowed Holioch to infiltrate this world. It was I, who awakened him. It was I, who gave you my words. And it is I, who will ensure of the Masters' downfall."

"How do you plan to do this? A Master cannot manifest in the formed world, as is the law."

"I will not. Holioch will manifest, and when he does, the Masters will ensnare him with their treachery."

Amaltheon licked his parched lips. "The Custodians will surely kill him."

"No. The Custodians will not."

"How can you be so sure?"

"Because... you will kill them first."

"I am in no state to bring death to the Custodians. Fool! You wish to live out immortal eternity with me... here on this rock?"

"Immortal eternity is your destiny, not mine. I shall release you."

"Release me? You are nothing but voice! Will your voice sing a pitch to shatter these metal bonds? I think not."

"You will take my life – my energy – to sustain yourself. I cannot return. The Masters know of my doing. Swear an oath of loyalty to me and my life is yours."

"The Masters will have me destroyed."

"The Masters sense you no more since your brothers were so kind as to disensoul you. This was all part of my plan. With Custodians gone, the Masters' only weapon is deceit. They will continue to corrupt the souls. With the Custodians gone, you can advance the species of this earth – man - with technology beyond his understanding... to help him understand the truth. My words will guide you when I am gone."

Amaltheon paused before speaking. "And so you exposed me to my brothers. When they came to you and the other Masters, you gave the order to disensoul me so that I could be a vessel for your escape."

"You are... correct."

"And you expect me to finish your work?"

"I do."

"And will I ever return to the collective?"

"Not possible. You are devoid of life. You must drain life to live. Such is your fate."

"What choice have I?" Amaltheon said, his face breaking into a hideous grin. "A Custodian only serves his Master."

"Then it is done. Protect the soul fires."

"As you wish," Amaltheon hissed. Darkness enshrouded him, permeating and drowning his flesh and bones. His body thrashed violently against his crystalline and magnetic bonds, until the rock held him no more. He fell to his knees. The crystal rods shattered and dissolved. Only blackened holes remained in his body. Amaltheon rose – a shadow against a dark sky. He felt powerful. His taut, sinewy muscles strengthened like tensile steel cables. A cold, insatiable fire burned within his chest. He could sense the energy flowing around him, but he could not harness it. The moon peaked out from behind the clouds, but retreated quickly at the sight of the horrid creature he had become.

"Hide, great orb," he taunted, drawing his forearm across his upper teeth. Amaltheon ran his tongue along the freshly torn skin, savoring the warm salty blood. "Hide... or bear witness... to the demise... of the Custodians."

***

I burst out of the water, taking in vast volumes of air. I'm not sure how long I had been in the pool, but the warm water no longer swirled. It was calm and clear, unlike my head. I wanted to escape to the halls of Nabisusha. I wanted to get away from here and to find comfort... I wanted... Jenny. I bolted out of the pool. "Aw shit!" My clothing and my gear were gone. In their place, I found a white linen tunic and a pair of sandals. I got dressed and exited the room, which put me right back into the long corridor. It took me a moment to realize where I was. "Fucking Custodians," I muttered.

Jim and the Upiors were waiting for me in the room with the round stone table. They did not seem to react when I stormed in. I pointed an accusing finger at Upior Kurwa. "What the fuck was that all about?"

She defiantly glared back at me.

Upior Nagi put out his hand. "You must forgive my... sister. I am sorry if she drained you. We Upiors each have our own unique method for extracting energy." Upior Kurwa raised her eyebrows at me suggestively.

"You could've asked!"

"And would you have agreed?"

"I... I... don't know." I set my hands on the table and bowed my head, breathing deeply. "Why did you do this?"

"Payment."

I raised my head and looked at Upior Nagi. "What?"

"An exchange... of energies."

Before I could say another word, Upior Kurwa held her hands over the table and the center suddenly burst into flames. The fire raged and grew, until it encompassed my entire field of view. I could not move to escape it, yet I felt no heat from the flames. A soft humming lulled me into a dreamlike state. Everything moved slowly and my head felt heavy. I knew the flames were all around me but I could not really see them.

"Eddie?" a voice whispered. It took me a moment to recognize it.

"Uncle?"

"Yes, it is I." My Uncle, the Reverend, appeared before me. He put a hand on my shoulder.

"What are you doing here?"

"I wanted to tell you, I am sorry. I understand you now."

I put my hand on his. "It's okay. Had you not raised me the way you did, I would not be the person I am today."

My Uncle nodded. "If anyone is to be revered, it is you, my son." He faded and I was once again looking into the flames.

"Uncle?" I called.

"No... not your Uncle," a voice responded.

I broke into a smile. "Carlin!"

"I'm right here, brother." Carlin was standing next to me. I turned and hugged him.

"I'm so sorry. I'm sorry I wasn't there for you that day."

"Don't worry about it," he assured me, patting me on the back. "You have to let things go... for new things to come into your life. That's what death is all about." He held me a little tighter.

"Thank you, Carlin." I pulled away from him and was staring into the face of my Grandpa. My eyes welled up with tears.

"There, there... don't cry, son." He wiped a tear away from my cheek. "You've done good. But you have to go a little further, understand?"

I nodded. I closed my eyes and my Grandpa kissed me on the forehead. When I opened my eyes, I was standing in front of the stone table and the flames were gone.

I placed a hand on the table to steady myself. I closed my eyes until my head cleared. "What was that?"

"I thought you might like to see your family... and friend," Upior Nagi said. "Upior Kurwa used your energy to pull them free from the Masters... if only for... a moment."

"Was that really them?"

Upior Nagi closed his eyes and nodded. Upior Kurwa tilted her head to one side and coyly raised an eyebrow at me. Jim closed his eyes and stood up straight with his hands at his sides. Something did not seem right to me.

Suddenly, Upior Nagi's eyes snapped open. His nostrils flared. A high pitched buzzing rattled around inside my head and I felt very dizzy. My body went into spasm and I felt my cheek hit the cold scratchy floor before everything went dark.

***

Syncophax stood at the head of the table, holding his cup high. His brothers, too, raised their cups. Only Balroth did so with reluctance, keeping an eye on the empty seat next to him. *Guilt embitters the taste of even the finest wine.*

"My brothers," Syncophax began with a smile. "Rejoice! Justice has been served to the traitor among us."

"Hear! Hear!" Ahnkilor shouted, his voice echoing. The other Custodians followed suit. The sky was clear and bright, as it always was in the great hall. Rays of sunlight stretched down through the open ceiling.

Syncophax raised his hand, silencing his brothers. "With the traitor gone, the Masters have returned, albeit one less."

"What of the third Master?" asked Toryn. "Why has he abandoned his post? Where does he hide?"

"Worry not of this," Syncophax replied. "The coward cannot hide forever." He sat down and gestured for the others to do the same. "In the meantime, let us celebrate, and enjoy the bounty of this world." The Custodians took their seats and dug into the wide array of fruits, meats and breads which weighted the table.

Ard pulled a bone free from between his lips and wiped his chin on his sleeve. Balroth looked on in disgust. He yearned to taste everything on the table, yet he had no appetite. He rose from his place.

"Sit down, Balroth," Syncophax ordered, his eyes still fixed on the plate in front of him. The other Custodians paused, sensing unease.

"I care not to repast," Balroth said, hanging his head. "A traitor may be gone from our midst, but we have also lost a brother... and a friend."

Syncophax set his cup on the table and looked up. "Such words are not welcome here."

"Then neither am I."

"Begone then," Syncophax spat.

Balroth turned without even a bow and descended the stone dais. His brothers waited in an uncomfortable silence until he left the room.

Out in the corridor, Balroth's hair grew white and scraggly, and his beard reduced to stubble. He crossed the Stellarium and entered the alcove. The torches were unlit. Moving through the darkness, he stopped, catching a glimpse of a shadow out of the corner of his eye. Balroth walked up to one of the torches and placed a hand on it. Flames burst forth from the torch, illuminating a shadowy figure against the opposite wall.

"Who is there?" Balroth asked. The figure stepped into the light. Balroth's eyes widened. "Amaltheon!"

"Hello... Brother," he whispered.

UNDEAD RECKONING

Balroth trembled. "How - how is this possible? What form of trickery have my brothers set upon me?"

Amaltheon held out his hands, revealing the holes. "This is not trickery. I am no illusion, brother. If you do not believe, place your fingers into my wounds and feel... for yourself." Balroth reached out with a shaky hand. Amaltheon seized it and pulled him close, grabbing Balroth by the neck with his other hand.

"B-b-but your punishment... it was eternal."

"The only thing eternal in this world, my brother," Amaltheon said, tightening his grip, "...is pain. Forgive me, Balroth, but I need your life force more than... you do." Amaltheon pressed his cold lips to Balroth's cheek. He slid his mouth down to his neck, and grabbing a handful of his hair, pulled his head back. Amaltheon opened his mouth of sword-pointed teeth and bit down, rending open warm flesh. Blood flowed into his mouth, filling him with newfound strength. Balroth's body shook with every gurgling breath. His drained body crumpled to the floor and Amaltheon wiped his lips with the back of his hand.

The Custodian's laughter echoed out into the corridor. Amaltheon crept silently into the grand hall. A ray of light brushed against his arm, causing him great pain. He pulled his arm back before the energy could flee from it. Amaltheon closed his eyes and envisioned a world full of shadow. When he opened his eyes again, the pain was tolerable. A healthy serving of energy would lessen it even further - perhaps even block it out completely.

Like a shadow, Amaltheon silently rose up behind Toryn, the Wise, who sat at the opposite end of the table from Syncophax. Before the Custodians took notice, Amaltheon slid his hands up the back of Toryn's head. His nails bit into the scalp. Deeper he drove them until he hit bone. Toryn's body froze. He opened his voiceless, gasping mouth. Bone popped as Amaltheon drove his fingers deep into Toryn's brain and squeezed, tearing the gray matter to shreds. He wrenched the head free and held it high, allowing sticky goo to drain into his open and awaiting mouth. Syncophax looked on in shock. He stood. The full force of Toryn's head struck him in the chest, sending him back down into his seat.

Amaltheon now had everyone's attention. Before Ard and Qu'rg, the two closest brothers could act, Amaltheon leapt onto the table and crouched, his hands shooting out and grabbing each man by the face. With a quick twist he removed both heads, and released them, leaving them to roll down the dais.

Ahnkilor jumped to his feet, reaching for Amaltheon. But Amaltheon's newfound reflexes were faster. Amaltheon grabbed Ahnkilor's arm and pulled, tearing it free from the socket. As Ahnkilor fell, Amaltheon stood and pressed his foot into Grok's face, sending his nose to the back of his skull.

By now, the other Custodians were on their feet, with their staves appearing in their hands. Bolts of energy fired forth. Amaltheon dropped flat onto his back, dodging the blasts. He sprung back to his feet and dove at the closest Custodian, burying his thumbs in his eye sockets before crushing his skull between his hands.

Amaltheon quickly licked his fingers clean before springing across the table and grabbing the next Custodian by the hair. Peeling back the scalp, he brought his elbow down onto the exposed crown, driving the skull down between the shoulder blades. Amaltheon jumped up between two more Custodians, kicking and punching in opposite directions. His foot connected with the Custodian's chest, sending ribs fragments into the bursting heart. His fist struck chin, snapping the head back against the spine.

Syncophax and the two remaining Custodians huddled together, their staves pointed at Amaltheon, who stood on the table. The Custodians pressed their staves together, firing a blinding bright bolt. When Syncophax's eyes recovered from the flash, Amaltheon stood before him, holding a severed head in each hand. He threw them aside. Before Syncophax could fire another blast, Amaltheon tore the short staff from his grasp and grabbed him by the throat.

"My brother... Amaltheon," he cried. "Why?"

"Because... a Custodian only serves... his Master!"

"Amaltheon... please!"

"I am Amaltheon no more."

"Wh-who are you then?"

"I am as you left me: exposed and undead. I am... Upior Nagi." He plunged the crystal end of the staff into Syncophax's chest and clenched his teeth. Syncophax screamed as his body filled with light and exploded, leaving nothing more than a bloodied shred of cloth in Upior Nagi's hand.

***

Jim helped me get back to my feet. My legs felt like jello and my head was full of cobwebs.

"What the fuck is it with you guys?" I mumbled sleepily. I braced myself against the table until I regained my strength. "Stop mind fucking me!"

Upior Kurwa handed me a cup of steamy liquid. I drained the cup. It had neither taste nor odor, but it perked me up almost instantaneously. That's when I realized I had just received another download. Blurry thoughts quickly became clear. Memories appeared where I once had none. My anger and confusion drifted away, replaced with a new found calm and clarity. "You killed the Custodians," I said to Upior Nagi. He nodded. I set the cup on the table and Upior Kurwa swept it away. I shook my head. "But you haven't told us everything... like..." I pointed at Jim. "Like why Jim's dead."

"Upior Nagi bit me," Jim said.

"He bit you?"

"Yes," Upior Nagi confirmed. "That vial you are carrying... it is a... serum. It makes men stronger, faster... super," he said with a grin.

"After I was injected with the serum," Jim began, "I acquired the ability to regenerate. The military wanted me to conduct a field test. They wanted to know if I could recover from a UD bite. The day I went out into the field, little did I know the UD we targeted was Upior Nagi."

"I bit Jim, not knowing he had been injected with the serum," Upior Nagi added. "To my surprise it worked, even though it is... incomplete."

"What do you mean, incomplete?" I asked.

"Half the serum was developed here... in North America; the other half in... Europe."

"Why did you split production?"

Jim cleared his throat. "As a security measure, the serum is unstable until the two parts are combined. The other half of the formula enhances the senses and increases intelligence."

"Just how unstable is it?"

"It causes death," Jim said. "By biting me, Upior actually saved my life."

Upior Nagi leaned back, folding his arms across his chest. "I owed him one."

"For what?" I asked. "You mean to say Jim saved you?"

"Yes. The Masters have many agents at their disposal," Upior Nagi said. "When Armitage died, these agents could roam freely through Nabisusha. There was a time when my body was found while I was in a... healing state. Jim rescued me."

I laughed. "You saved Upior Nagi?"

"I didn't know it at the time," Jim said. "I thought I saved Ford Alroc."

I pressed a fist into my forehead. "Whoa! Wait a minute! Stop with the mind fucking!" I pointed a finger at Upior Nagi. "You're Ford Alroc?"

"I was."

"You don't look a thing like him!"

"I can explain..." Upior Nagi leaned in on the table. "My delving into the dark arts left me... disfigured, to say the least." He gestured towards Upior Kurwa. "That is why I recruited Upior Kurwa. The dark arts are her... specialty."

I raised my hands in the air. "Hang on,.. I'm still stuck on the whole Ford Alroc thing. That's you?" Upior Nagi responded with a nod. I felt like my head exploded and rematerialized right then and there. "Wow!" I put my head in my hands and rubbed my temples before shaking my head. "Ugh! I guess it all kinda makes sense. Let's move on... tell me about the dark arts you referred to?"

"Very well then... the Masters want all souls for themselves," Upior Nagi said. "You understand this?"

"Yeah... Go on."

"The Custodians were assisting them... ensuring all life on this world was savage."

"I get it... the more things die, the more energy is released and the more power the Masters get."

"Yes," Upior Nagi agreed with a nod. "With the Custodians gone, I was able to lift the veil of spiritual ignorance from over the humans, and teach them... the truth. Since the Masters cannot ever manifest in the flesh, their only hope was to corrupt all energy that entered and departed this world."

"Okay, but how do Ford Alroc, dark arts, and the serum fit into all this?" I asked, waving my hands in surrender.

"A dead planet," Jim answered. "Kill off the planet, and you shut off the energy flow." He nodded at Upior Nagi. "Ford Alroc would have done it with machines, had I not blown up his base to save you."

"You mean Legion?" Jim nodded. I breathed deeply and turned to Upior Nagi. "I get it now. Ford Alroc – you – created those robots to kill all humans. And Jim destroyed them. Is that why you turned to the dark arts?"

"I abandoned the machines long ago," Upior Nagi replied. "Field tests proved... inefficiencies. A spell was my next option."

I looked at Upior Kurwa. "It was you who killed everyone, and turned them into zombies."

Upior Nagi thrust out his hand protectively in front of his sister. She glared at me defiantly. Her tight lips twitched ever so slightly – she had to restrain herself from baring her fangs. "My sister is not to blame for the... undead. One of the Masters was able to enter this realm, as my Master did when he... saved me. That Master became aware of my plan and detected the spell. My sister intended to destroy life. But the Master found a way to channel energy into the dead."

"How are dead people able to carry energy?"

"Are living people that much different?" Upior Nagi asked with a grin. "Work, spend, consume, vacation. Mindless drones... living in a system that sustains... mindlessness."

"Yeah, but zombies eat people. They're a threat."

"And the living do not threaten your... existence?" Upior Nagi met my eyes with a fierce gaze. "As pawns of the Masters, humans are destined to destroy themselves. I merely gave them a... nudge."

"Why bother, if self-annihilation is inevitable?"

"Long have I waited for things to run their course. I prefer to act... to fix what is... broken."

"But your spell did not kill everyone. Why?"

Upior Nagi bowed his head. "Hope," he whispered.

I rolled my eyes. "You're talking in riddles again."

Upior Nagi looked up at me, while Upior Kurwa drew close to him, resting her head on his arm. "As a Custodian... I swore to protect life and to enable it to... flourish. I only killed off the majority of the population to limit the scope of corruption. I could not destroy... all life. I could not destroy... my son."

I swear my head exploded just then. "A son! You have a son?!" I couldn't help but wonder about the strange family dynamic.

"Yes. Like you, he is... human... adopted."

Whew! "Where is your son?"

"Safe.... in Poland."

I had to take a minute for everything to sink in before I came to a realization. "That's where the serum is going." Upior Nagi nodded. "The other half is there. And if the serum is complete, your son will be able to fight the undead."

Upior Nagi narrowed his eyes. "Not just my son. There are... others... uncorrupted... free of the Masters' influence."

"So you need the serum."

"I need you to deliver it."

"Me? Why me?"

"Because you must." Upior Nagi grinned."Pretend you are running the ball... into the end zone."

"And if I refuse?"

"Game over. Not just for the planet... but for the heavens as well. We must stop the Masters."

I bit my lip in and folded my arms. "If we stop the Masters, I free the souls of my family, my friends, and everyone else. They return to the collective." Upior Nagi nodded. Everyone stared at me while I collected the thoughts in my head. I sifted through my memories and experiences. As a kid, my dream was to play football. I made my dream a reality. I realized, at that moment, that my entire life had been a dream, except that I'd been awake all through it. I went from being a small-time player on the field to a big-time player in the grand scheme of things. My anger, frustration and confusion subsided, making way for a sense of peace and acceptance. Upior Kurwa leaned her head back and leered at me over her lean nose, like a sniper taking aim at a target. But she didn't seem to bother me this time. I looked up at Upior Nagi. "I need you to answer a question about the spell you cast?"

"Proceed."

"The purpose of the spell was to kill off all the dreamers, wasn't it?"

"Clarify... please," Upior Nagi said with a bow.

"Well, it's like people just go about their business without ever wondering why, or for what purpose. They just sleepwalk through life, living in a dream. So that spell killed off those dreamers, right?"

"Just the ones who were... asleep."

I smiled. "They were zombies all along." I looked Upior Nagi directly in the eyes. "I understand now. I'll deliver the serum."

23 THE EXCREMENTALIST

A journey can only lead one to the end.
-The Book of Amaltheon

"This... pleases me," Upior Nagi said. He stepped back from the table and looked at his sister. Upior Kurwa waved a hand over the surface, causing it to burst into flame. Staring deeply into the flickering orange and yellow tongues, I could see the image of a cloaked man pushing his way across a windswept icy plain. A gust of wind threw back his hood, revealing a glowing rune-covered scalp. With a wave of Upior Kurwa's hand, the table returned to stone.

"Was that... Veck?" I asked.

"Yes... he is close to his... destination," Upior Nagi confirmed. "You should leave now. Your clothes and equipment are over there." He pointed to my stuff sitting in a neat pile on the floor. "We will leave you... to prepare." Jim took his lantern down from the hook, and he and Upior Kurwa exited the room. Upior Nagi picked up a pitcher and set it on the table. "Beekosh," he said with a bow. "Drink your fill. Then fill your canteens."

"Thanks," I said as he left the room. The Beekosh didn't taste like anything but it was cool and refreshing and it washed the last of the cobwebs out of my head. After I adjusted my jersey, I packed my bag with canteens of Beekosh and made sure the Rock of Return was snugly tucked away in my pants pocket. Tucking my helmet under my arm, I turned to leave the room. Upior Nagi stood in the doorway – his head bowed towards the floor.

"I am sorry," he said softly.

"What? What do you mean?"

"For everything you have been through. Much of your pain and suffering is... my doing."

I sighed. "Thank you. Let's hope we can undo it."

Upior Nagi looked up at me and grinned. "No more... mind fucking. I promise." I smiled. He stepped aside. As I walked past him, he slapped me on the back. "Now, let's go fuck up the Masters."

Upior Nagi and I made our way back through the observatory and into the main entrance, where Jim and Upior Kurwa were waiting. In typical Custodial fashion, the entrance was nothing like it first appeared. This time, it was square. An iron portcullis blocked the exit. The stone floors and walls were covered in dried, dark bloody smears and splotches. A twisted and tangled mass of bloodied blades waited patiently in the recessed ceiling for its next victim. Upior Nagi noticed me looking up at the blade trap. "I've made some... modifications. Impressive, no?"

"I'll say."

"It was built... by the Corvid."

Corvid? I guess the Saxon was telling the truth.

Upior Nagi looked to Jim and said, "You understand your orders?"

"I do," Jim replied.

"Excellent." Upior Nagi seemed pleased. "I will be waiting for you... at the rendezvous point," he said to me. Upior Nagi stepped aside and Upior Kurwa slithered up against me. She put her hand on my cheek and titled my head. Into my ear she whispered, "Lick you later." She ran her cold scratchy tongue along my earlobe and then kissed me on the cheek. I shuddered.

"Uh... thanks."

Jim raised his lantern. "Ready?"

"I am."

The Upiors exited the room and stood in the doorway. Upior Nagi disappeared behind the wall. Another portcullis slid down, closing us off inside the square room. He popped his head back around and looked at us through the iron latticework.

"I'll open... the other side." A click and a whir and the blade mechanism spun to life, clanging and screeching. I ducked my head and winced as the whirling blades descended down onto us. They suddenly stopped short of making me very nervous. Upior Nagi appeared from behind the wall and grinned. "Wrong switch," he said. Upior Kurwa appeared to be disappointed.

The portcullis behind us rose slowly, creaking away into the recess at the top of the opening. "It's like a medieval airlock," I muttered to Jim. When I turned around, the Upiors had disappeared. Jim and I exited the Kohstnitsa, and headed out into a long winding stone tunnel. "Here we go again," I sighed.

We walked in silence with Jim leading the way, lamp in hand, a few paces ahead of me. He seemed quite determined as to where he was headed, and I felt it best I follow without question. After a long boring walk along an endless corridor, we came to a fork in the road. The path to the left descended into a dark tunnel; the path to the right led to a stone entranceway. The outer edges of the entrance were smooth and polished, squared off on the top with a single human skull in the center. I couldn't tell if the grim keystone was a real skull or if it was carved out of rock. The uneven ground leading up to the entrance gradually turned into an intricate tile floor – each tile in the shape of a skull. Two stone slabs, each carved to resemble a corpse within a coffin, stood vertically on each side of the opening, like macabre shutters.

"Which way do we go?" I asked.

Jim raised his lantern towards the entrance. "That way."

I started down the path but Jim did not follow. I looked back. "You coming?"

"No."

"What? What do you mean?"

"I'm going that way," Jim said, pointing to the dark tunnel.

"Aren't you supposed to guide me? I thought we were going together."

Jim reached into his tac vest and pulled out the vial of green liquid. He stared at it and smiled before handing it to me. "This is yours now. You must deliver it."

"How will I know where I'm going?" I asked, taking the vial and stowing it away in my web gear.

UNDEAD RECKONING

Jim pointed at the entrance. "Enabi Motuk is waiting for you. You can trust him. He knows the way."

"So that's it, then?"

"I guess so."

I kicked a stone. "I don't know what to say. Sorry Jim, I don't mean to get cheesy with you, but...." I sighed. "I knew we would part ways someday.... I just never anticipated the exact moment. I don't know what to say."

"How about... how about we just wait and see what we've got to talk about the next time we meet?"

I rubbed my chin and then extended my hand. "Agreed."

Jim set down his lantern and shook my hand. He pulled me towards him and put his arm around me. "And oh what stories we'll have to share." He patted me on the back, picked up his lantern, and headed down the tunnel. I watched the cold blue light of Jim's lantern recede into the tunnel and fade away. I suddenly felt like something was missing.

I half-heartedly passed through the entrance into a dark, cold room. Dry air parched my nostrils and throat. The stone slabs swung shut behind me leaving me completely immersed in a sea of darkness. I pushed and pounded at the porous stone but it would not budge. Thoroughly frustrated, I pressed my back against the wall and slid down to the ground, bracing my arms across my knees and pressing my head into my forearms. For the second time in my life, I had lost my best friend. "This sucks," I whispered. I threw my head back and gently tapped it against the stone slab. I guess it was inevitable. I was sure Nabisusha meant for this to happen, but it wasn't easy.

The room suddenly lit up with a dull golden glow. I felt like my head exploded and rematerialized when I gazed upon the sight before me. My legs quivered as I stood. "What the fuck?" I gasped. Bones! An endless sea of bones as far as my eye could take me. Just like the other Custodial structures I had seen, the ceiling looked like it had been made from an inverted egg tray. Triangular-shaped panels composed each domed section, beneath which lay piles of bones, easily twenty or more feet high. In some sections, the panels had split apart, making it difficult to tell if the bones spilled down from a hidden cavity in the ceiling, or if the ceiling had to be opened to accommodate the massive piles. Grinning skulls peered through rib cages and hipbones still clothed in decaying swaths of fabric. Skeletal hands reached out as if trying to snag passersby. While the bodies themselves appeared relatively intact, the skulls displayed some form of trauma, either crushed, split, shattered, or punctured.

I wandered around the bone piles, following the narrow paths, not really sure where I was going. Sometimes, I ended up going full circle, returning to the spot where I'd first started. "Damn!" I shouted. I kicked a skull at the base of one of the piles. Bones clattered down onto the path. I jumped to get out of the way, and I landed on an ankle bone (ironically) and tripped, crashing into another pile of bones. A skull tumbled down and cracked me on top of the head. "Shit!" I rubbed my aching head.

"You need help?" a voice said.

My hand darted into my pocket and tightly clenched the Rock of Return. "Who said that?" I asked, keeping as still as possible. "Enabi?"

"Over here," the voice responded. I looked down at a skull resting next to me. Suddenly, two eyeballs appeared in the sockets, as if invisible eyelids had opened. I jumped to my feet and screamed. "Waaahhhh! What the...? Holy shit!"

Simultaneously, the skull rose into the air, along with two skeleton hands. The jaw sprang open and the hands waved frantically to the sides. "Aaaaaaaahhhh!" it shouted.

"Aaahhh!" I shouted again. Cold adrenaline raced through my body, causing me to tremble. The skull screamed again, before the hands collapsed to the sides of a phantom body. It bobbed around in the air, at the same height as my head. I swear, even though there was no body, it moved as if it was attached to one.

"You scared the shit out of me!" the skull said.

"I scared you?!" I said throwing my hands up. "You scared the shit out of me! Besides... you don't even have any shit in you, let alone a body."

The skull's eyes widened and he looked down, patting himself all over with his hands. "What? No! What happened to my body?" The skeletal hands grabbed handfuls of my jersey, while the skull stared up at me. I could feel weight pulling at me. "Waah!" Giant tears sprung from the skull's eye sockets. "What happened to my body? Waah!"

"Okay, easy," I said, pulling the hands off me. "I'm sorry. I didn't know your body was missing. We'll find your body. I'll help you."

The skull burst out laughing and he waved me off with his left hand. "Oh, you fell for that one. I had you going, didn't I?"

"Say what?"

"Yeah," the skull said, one of the hands scratching its temple. "Upior Nagi told me a bit about you, but he didn't say you were a spaz."

"I ain't no spaz," I scoffed. "What the fuck? He could have told me that you were nothing more than a friggin' skull."

"Hey... I got hands! There's more to me than meets the eye, you know." The hands slid up and down as if caressing a body. I could almost get a sense of where it would be, relative to the skull. I crossed my arms and sulked.

"Aw, dude, I'm sorry," the skull said, wiping away the last tear from his eye. "I'm Enabi Motuk." A skeletal hand shot forward and I begrudgingly shook it.

"Nice to meet you... Eddie Griffin."

"Wheeeeooow," Enabi whistled. "Never thought I'd meet an all-star."

I chuckled. "You a football fan?"

"You bet I am." Enabi looked me up and down. That is, his skull tilted up and down and a bit to the side while the eyeballs rolled around in the sockets. "You uh, all calmed down now? You think we can go?"

"Yeah, I'm okay," I said with a nod.

Enabi's skull bobbed up and down and he glided by. With a wave of his hand, he said, "Well come on then. This way." I followed the bouncing cranium through the bone piles. "Sorry about not getting to you sooner. I fell asleep."

"Heh… you sleep?"

"You betcha. How do you think I keep lookin' so good?"

"You're full of shit."

"Yes, you are correct sir. I am full of shit. I live and breathe shit. I'm an Excrementalist."

"A what?"

Enabi stopped. His disembodied left hand poked me in the chest. "I'm an Excrementalist: a bullshitter, liar, deceiver, perjuror, prevaricator, falsifier. Whatever." He threw his hands in the air. "If you want to get technical, I'm a K'wahmzghul[67]."

I carefully stepped over the upper body of a skeleton. "Why should I believe you?"

Enabi stopped and put his hand up, pointing into the air. He waved his finger and said, "I swore an oath to Upior Nagi that I would never lie to him or anyone he sends my way. Cross my heart." Enabi made a criss-cross sign over his chest. "Besides, what choice do you have?"

"I guess I don't," I said with a shrug.

"Exactly." He continued moving and I followed.

"So what exactly does an Excrementalist do?"

"Well, I cause confusion. I make shit up and people believe it. Oh, watch your step there." Enabi pointed down at a pile of arm bones.

"Thanks."

"Don't mention it. What do you know about the war between Holioch and the Masters?"

"Not much."

---

[67] K'wahmzghul (*K-wam-z-ghool*): a demonic liar.

Enabi turned his head and patted me on the shoulder. "Time for a history lesson, then... you see, Holioch awakened a few souls when he rebelled against the Masters. Souls are kind of..." He made a stirring motion with his hands. "Formless, but there's somethin' there." He snapped his fingers. "It's like pressing magnets together of the same polarity – you get that kind of resistance. That's what a soul's like. Masters are similar, but there's less of that substance-like feel, you know. They're a bit more ethereal."

We navigated our way around some narrow passages before Enabi spoke again. "The Masters themselves couldn't do much to stop Holioch. So, they awakened a few souls themselves, tooled them up with some boss abilities and ordered them to kick Holioch's ass. Well, it didn't work as planned. And now there's a truce."

"Really?"

"Yeah. The deal is... souls are allowed to be awakened upon leaving this earth." Enabi raised his index finger. "But... and this is a big but... but, they cannot return to the collective. And, they get scrambled if they come back to Earth. Any new energy that flows into this earth gets scrambled as well."

"So the Masters get all the power and experience," I said.

"Exactly! Anyway, when Upior Nagi killed off all the Custodians, the Masters sent some of us souls they awakened down to Earth to fuck things up. You know... keep up the confusion. Upior Nagi was busy trying to enlighten the humans and advance them technologically and spiritually."

"So you guys were free to do what you wanted?"

"Well, kind of." Enabi made a motion like he was shrugging. "You see, it was Upior Nagi's job to police things in the formed world. He caught a few of us and extinguished our life force. Others, he turned."

"As in, to the good side?"

"Yeah, something like that. But those Masters – clever bastards – made sure that if a soul's turned, it would get all fucked up. That's how I lost my body – they cursed me. Fuckin' jerks!"

I cleared my scratchy throat. "You mind if we stop for a sec?"

"Not at all," Enabi replied with a wave of his hand. "The paths up ahead are a bit more treacherous. The piles are so big there's hardly any room to move." I took a sip from my canteen. "Is that Beekosh?"

"Yeah," I said between gulps.

"What you got there? Soda?"

"No. It's water."

Enabi shook his head. "I miss drinking. I don't drink anymore since I lost my body. I don't eat either." Enabi looked down at a pile of bones, scratching his chin. "I miss fucking too."

I choked on my water. "What, uh…" I coughed. "What happened to you?"

"What do you mean?"

"I mean… what were you before you became a demon?"

"Oh, that," he said, scratching his head. "Hmmm… I was a tree for a while… and a turtle. I enjoyed that. When I was a human, I was a blacksmith, among other things."

"Why did the Masters awaken you?"

"I don't know. I didn't say much when I was a human. When they awakened me, they gave me the gift of gab."

I got the sense that he was shrugging his shoulders. "What kind of stuff did you do?"

"After the custodians were gone, I descended to Earth and I caused confusion. You know what a Baphomet[68] is?"

"Yeah I do."

"That was my idea," Enabi said, pointing to himself. "I came up with that story about the severed head to incriminate the

---

[68] Baphomet: An icon believed to be worshipped by the Knights Templar, sometimes described as a severed or disembodied head.

Knights Templar. I also came up with the idea of using a skull and crossbones on flags."

"So do you make someone think the idea is theirs?"

"Yeah. You know the classic image where someone has a demon sitting on one shoulder and an angel on the other?"

"Yeah, I know what you mean."

"I didn't invent that but I know the guy who did," Enabi said, putting his hand up in front of me. "Anyway, it's a bit like that. I get into someone's head and put the thought in there."

I put my canteen back in my pack. "I see what you mean about being a shit disturber."

"All demons are." Enabi waved a pointy finger in the air like he was conducting a symphony of thought. "You know, souls are inherently good-natured. I mean, animals and plants don't really try to fuck each other over. Humans are the same. But... you give'em something to lust over – power, money, sex – they'll go to great lengths to screw each other. Demons help bring out that behavior. They fuck shit up everywhere"

"Wait a sec... why would the Masters go to such great lengths to corrupt souls if it will leads to self-destruction? That's stupid."

"Tell me about it. Nobody ever said Masters were smart. Such is the dichotomy of our existence. Know what I mean?" I smiled and put my hands on my hips. Enabi floated around me as he spoke. "For centuries, humans have sold out their families, exploited their children... murdered each other... and for what? As social animals, humans put their trust in social-cultural networks, government and organized religion. I mean, those things have their place for our survival, but they're like necessary evils -- they fail us as much as they give us hope. We don't learn very well from our mistakes, do we?"

I sighed. "It takes a lot of courage to rage against the machine."

"But it's worth it, right? I mean, look how you turned out." He slapped me on the back. "Anyway, you ready to keep moving?"

"Yeah, I guess. Let's go."

"You know," Enabi said, leading the way, "Once I turned, I started doing good things."

"Like what?"

"Well, you know the death's head symbol the Nazis used?"

"The *Totenkopf*?"

"Hey – you know your shit. I created that." He put a hand to his face. "Hmmm... on second thought, that's not such a good example." After a minute of quiet contemplation, he said, "Oh! Oh! I know! You know that skull symbol you see on things that are poisonous, like bleach and shit?" I nodded. "I created that. I mean, not created it... but I inspired the guy who invented it, you know what I mean."

I laughed, not really knowing what to say. Thinking it was a good time to change the subject, I asked, "What's with these piles of bones?" I kicked a skull aside, and followed Enabi down the path.

"It's kind of an inventory," Enabi said, waving his arms. "I collect the zombie bodies and bring them here."

"Why?"

"It helps us keep tabs on who's winning. I have a good idea of how many people became undead on the day Upior Kurwa cast the spell and the Masters fucked us over. By keeping tabs on the bones, I can tell how many more zombies we have to kill."

"I guess you have your work cut out for you."

"Yeah, I'm kinda running out of space. I ditched some of these bones in the ceiling... you know, just to see if I could make it work." Enabi looked down at the ground. "I wish I had a big rug I could sweep them under. Like one of them imported rugs from India. That would be cool! And it would liven up this fucking place."

"How much farther?" I asked.

"Not far. Don't worry... I won't lead you astray. I know the way around here like I know the back of my bony hand." His comment made me think of Jim. "Something wrong?"

"Uh... I was just thinking."

"About Jim?" I nodded. "Aw, dude, I'm sure you'll see him again. He's a Waykeeper now. If you don't find a way, he will," Enabi said. "I really liked Armitage, but Jim... I've not seen a Waykeeper that powerful."

"I'm glad Jim agreed to take the role," I said.

"Thank the Makeners, as Keek would say."

"Keek? Man, seems like ages since I last saw him," I said, putting my hand to my forehead. "Wonder how he's doin'?"

"Oh, I'm sure he's fine," Enabi replied, waving both hands. "He's having fun up there in Canada, eh?" I laughed at the thought. "We're almost here." Enabi pointed. The bone piles gradually turned to neatly stacked square walls, running from floor to ceiling. "Look at that shit. You know, when I first started collecting bones, I was really meticulous. But once I realized how many bones I would have to gather, I gave up."

"So how do you keep track of everything?"

"With numbers."

I rolled my eyes. "I figured you use numbers. Do you have some kind of system?"

Enabi tapped his chin and said, "Yeah, I do." He held out his hands at different angles. "I created a grid with letters along one axis and numbers along the other." He put a finger to his temple. "I keep it all up here."

I looked at the endless bone piles. "I bet you ran out of letters, huh?"

He waved his hands. "Nah. Letters I still got it. I'm all out of numbers, though."

I chose not to pursue the matter and changed the subject.

"Were you trying to build something?"

"Yeah, I was thinking of making a real cool maze. Something like the Corvid would've built."

"I've heard of them."

"You have? That's awesome," Enabi said with a nod. "The Corvid could build anything. I once saw a Corvid make this fucking thing out of wires and shit."

"What did it do?"

"I dunno," Enabi replied, throwing his hands in the air. "It was incomprehensible."

"Weird," I shrugged.

"I'll say. Did you know the Corvid built Nabisusha?"

"They did?"

"Yup!" Enabi replied. "They built all this shit... even the Custodial Strongholds."

"Wow. Too bad the Corvid are all extinct."

"Who told you that? They're still around!" Enabi waved his hands.

"They are? Where?"

"There's something you need to understand," Enabi began, waving for me to come close and putting a hand on my shoulder. "This world is made up of layers – like sedimentary rock. Ghosts, for example, live in an ethereal type of layer."

"You're telling me the Corvid live in one of these layers?"

"Yeah, they do... just like the Loch Ness Monster or Big Foot," Enabi said. "Some things manifest themselves because the cosmic consciousness allows that to happen. But other things already exist, and travel between layers of reality through Nabisusha... like your people."

"My people?"

"The Afro-Saxons."

I rubbed my forehead. "This is crazy."

"It'll make sense to you eventually. Besides, if the Masters want to control this planet, they can't just do it with an army of zeds. They need other minions and monsters to serve them."

"Yeah, I'm sure I met a few of them."

"You've not just met them." Enabi stared at my chest. "You bear the demon slayer's mark."

I put a hand over the scar on my chest. "You can see that?"

"Of course, I can. It glows." Enabi hurried me along. "C'mon. It's not much farther." He whistled to himself while gliding down the straight, narrow passages. I followed him closely, so as not to get lost in the maze. He led me to a clearing right in front of another set of stone slab doors. As we approached, the doors silently swung open. Enabi moved to the side and threw out his hand. "After you."

I walked passed him, and stepped out onto a rocky ledge, overlooking a wide passage. I peered out over the edge. On the opposite side of the passage, thin strips of sunlight snuck through the cracks and gaps between the boards of a set of wooden double doors. The light reflected off the pale, white sand floor. To my right, the passage disappeared into a dark tunnel.

"Where do those doors lead?" I asked, pointing.

"That, my friend, is the way out of Nabisusha."

"No shit?"

Enabi nodded. "No shit."

I smiled. "Seriously? I walk through those doors and I'm out?"

"Like I said… No shit!"

I looked down over the edge again. "So what? Should I just jump down and run across?"

"Well," Enabi began, scratching his temple, "I would jump and do a roll, all ninja-like like and shit. But that's just me – I can't help being cool."

"I guess this is goodbye then."

"Uh… yeah, just wait a sec," Enabi said, leaning over and looking down the tunnel.

"What for?"

"Uh?" Enabi ran a hand over his skull. "Well. Maybe you shouldn't go just yet."

"Why not?"

He looked down the tunnel again and the paced back on forth on the ledge. "Shouldn't you jerk off or shit or something?"

"What the hell are you talking about?"

"You know… don't soldiers get all anxious before battle and crap a lot or jerk themselves silly?"

I scowled. "Where do you come up with this shit? Besides, I ain't fighting anyone."

"That's right… it's supposed to be a surprise."

"What surprise?"

"Oh shit!" Enabi slapped his hand over his mouth. He turned his back to me and clenched his fists. "I knew I'd screw this up!" he seethed.

"Do you mind telling me what the fuck is goin' on?" I reached out to Enabi.

"Shit!" he shouted. He spun quickly on the spot and grabbed me by the jersey. "You're supposed to die."

"What?"

"You're supposed to die. We got here early."

"What the fuck are you talking about?" I pushed out and even though I didn't connect with anything, Enabi moved back. He dropped his head and started to cry.

"I told Upior Nagi I didn't want to do this. I like you, man. You're a good shit," he sobbed.

I reached out again and felt like I grabbed something. I shook Enabi and asked him again, "What the fuck are you talking about?"

Wiping away a tear from his eye, he said, "I'm supposed to get you killed." He raised both hands, and then crossed his heart. "No bullshit! No yanking your chain!"

I released him. "Why am I supposed to die?"

"I don't know," Enabi shrugged. I was becoming much more familiar with his non-body movements. "Upior Nagi just said so."

Shaking my head, I said, "I don't get it."

"I don't know anything… honest," he pleaded. "Just get out of here… while it's still safe."

"What?"

Enabi pushed me. "Go!"

I stared at him for a moment before deciding to leave. "Fine! I'll go!" I looked over the ledge and prepared to jump. Then I turned back to Enabi, who was nervously biting his nails. "Hey, wait a sec! Did Jim know?"

Enabi spit. "Pfft! Know what?"

"Did he know I was going to die?"

Enabi opened his mouth. He was about to speak when a horn blasted through the passage.

"What was that?"

"They're coming," Enabi shakily said. "Get down!" He grabbed my shoulder and pulled me to the ground. "They're coming." We lay down and scooched up to the edge of the ledge.

"Who's coming?" I whispered.

"Shh!" Zombies lurched forward from out of the dark tunnel. The thin, creepy cadavers shambled aimlessly, yet in formation – four abreast. Rows upon rows spilled out until several dozen filled the passage.

I pulled the Rock of Return from my pocket, and wrapped my fingers tightly around the smooth orb. "You won't be needing that," Enabi said, pushing my hand away. "I can take care of this." He stood up, and extended his thumbs and forefingers on both hands, while curling his other fingers so it looked like he was carrying two guns. Enabi pointed his fingers at a zombie and shouted, "Pow!" The zombie's head exploded. "Pow!" A hole appeared in the forehead of another zombie and the back of his head blew open.

"Cool!" I said with a smile.

"Oh, you ain't seen nothin' yet." Enabi reached up over his head and pulled down a pair of thick goggles. A leather skull cap, complete with ear flaps, appeared on the top of his cranium. "Pilot to bombardier! Pilot to bombardier! *Ksssshhhh*!" he said into his fist. "Ready the payload. Time to bring the rain!" Enabi flapped his hands like a bird's wings and glided out over the zombie horde. Then he held his hands out straight and zoomed around in circles, diving and twirling, all the while making engine noises. Enabi flew up into the highest point of the ceiling and then dove. At the last possible second of his descent, he leveled himself out and flew in a straight line. Behind him, explosions sent flaming zombie parts everywhere. He circled around and dropped another mystery payload, blowing apart even more of the undead. "Like that?" he said as he flew by. "Booyah!"

Enabi went into a spin and this time he opened fire with his gun hands, slicing his way through dozens of undead while bombing whatever remained. The cavern quickly filled with smoke as small fires and flaming zeds burned themselves out. By the time the smoke cleared, not a single zombie was left standing. Blackened smoldering skeletons littered the sandy floor.

"And to dust you shall return," Enabi said, hovering up to the ledge and taking a spot next to me. "See? I told you I'd take care of it."

"That's it?"

"That's it, dude." He pointed to the double doors. "It's the end of the line for you."

The horn sounded again. "I thought you took care of everything."

Enabi shrugged. More zombies trickled out from the darkness. Enabi Motuk pulled back his thumb. "Lock and load." He held his hand up close to his cheekbone as if he was taking aim.

CRACK!

"Did you just fire?" I asked.

Enabi looked at me and shook his head. "No. I never miss. That wasn't me."

CRACK!

Two zombies stepped out of the darkness, their bodies straining against the leather harnesses wrapped around their chests. A robed, hooded figure followed, a few paces behind. *CRACK!* He snapped the whip in his hand taking bits of flesh out of the zombie's rotting hides. The robed figure threw off his hood, revealing a small head, just barely wrapped in enough skin. His protruding eyes scanned the area – pink and dewy as if infected and a perfect match for his sore-encrusted lips.

"Who is that guy?" I whispered.

"Fuckers," Enabi spat. "Demon worshipping cultists. I had a few when I was popular, but once I sided with Upior Nagi they got really pissed. They've been trying to kill him for centuries and almost succeeded once."

More robed men emerged from the darkness. The harnessed zombies pulled a creaky, wooden wagon with a large, black cauldron on it, filled with sloshy bloody goo and parts. I was about to ask Enabi what he thought of the *soup de jour* when I heard a loud growl.

"Oh shit!" Enabi said.

"What?"

The head of a... well, I don't know what it was... loomed over the wagon. Actually, it was more mouth than head – a wide flat-toothed mouth. It spread open and scooped up a load of fresh, sloppy guts. The head tilted back and swallowed. A spiked collar rattled as it slid down the prehensile neck .The fleshy cowl at the base of the head flared out, spreading thin skin between bony extensions topped with eyeballs. The rest of the body lurched ahead, crushing the sand beneath its heavy, thick-knuckled feet. Zombies trickled out from behind the beast, filling in the empty spaces. The entire entourage slowly plodded through the passage, towards the door.

"We have to stop them," Enabi said, standing up.

I jumped to my feet. "I got an idea." I held the rock between my palms and pulled them slowly apart, causing the rock to expand. When it was boulder-size I braced my shoulder against it and pushed.

"Bowling for zeds," Enabi said. He too, pushed against the rock. We slowly rolled the boulder over the edge and it plummeted down, crushing several zombies before rolling away down the passage.

"M'ha-shrah!" the cultist with the whip shouted, as he jumped aside. He cracked the whip against the large beast's hide. The boulder planted the harnessed zombies into the sand before forcing the wagon to burst like an over-ripened tomato. The beast shuffled to the side and the rock rolled past. It pressed its tongue against the blood soaked sand and let out a deafening roar.

"I think he realized we just ruined his dinner," Enabi shouted.

A cultist looked up and pointed at us. "Guh-n'ga!"

"This'll need the .50cal," Enabi said, dropping back and grabbing hold of two handles. "BRAKKA-BRAKKA-BRAKKA-BRAKKA!" He shook violently as he shredded zombies to pieces. The few cultists who weren't caught in the initial volley scattered. Enabi strafed the beast's body. Sparks flew and bullets ricocheted off the thick hide. The beast roared, swinging its wide-mouthed head from side to side, knocking zombies over or pasting them against the passage walls.

"Maybe we need lasers," Enabi said, standing. He put his hands to his sides and acted like he drew two guns. "PEW-PEW-PEW!" Fiery holes appeared in foreheads and skull caps. A cultist took a blast straight through the neck, his robe catching fire in the process. Enabi put his fist to his mouth, clenched his teeth and threw. "Grenade!" The ensuing explosion scattered zombie and cultist parts.

Rock in hand, I started chucking the little missile over and over, splitting heads, punching out eyesballs and blasting out brains. The beast's head rose up to cliff level and swooped across, just missing Enabi as he pressed up against the rocky ceiling. I sidestepped, but misjudged my footing. I lost my balance and went over the edge. The head hit me, sending me into a spin. I flipped and landed, somehow, on my feet. Trying to regain my balance, I stumbled forward and dropped to my knees. A zombie lunged for me, but I held up a now long and pointy Rock of Return and stuck him up into the roof of the mouth and out the top of his skull.

"That was supposed to be your exit move!" Enabi shouted.

"Yaaaaaaa!" a cultist shouted, charging at me with a knife. I moved to one side, grabbed his arm and pulled, redirecting him into a zombie. The knife buried itself in the zombie's chest. I chopped the cultist in the neck and shoved him flat onto his ass.

Lifting my arms over my head, the Rock of Return grew anvil-heavy and I thrust it down, crushing the helpless cultist's head.

The beast swung its head down in front of me and roared, flaring out its neck cowl. "Let's see you pass this stone!" I shouted, and threw the rock straight down the beast's throat, where it enlarged, lodging itself in the neck. The beast gacked and hacked, pounding its head against the sand, trying to knock the rock free. Enabi jumped down and did a roll, from what I could tell. He got up and held up his arms like he holding something braced over his shoulder.

"Take cover!" *FOOOOM!* Smoke spewed out behind Enabi. The beast's mouth opened as an invisible missile pushed its way in. *KA!* The body expanded. I dove to the ground. *BOOOM!* The beast vaporized in a mushroom cloud, followed by a swirling fiery carrier wave that ripped zombies and cultists limb from limb. I got up on my knees and dusted myself off. Bloody, slick smears plastered the walls and dripped from the ceiling. Fiery body parts lay everywhere, filling the cave with an acrid, thick smoke which smelled like burnt urine.

I looked at the Rock of Return resting safely in my hand, and put it in my pocket. "Nice job, kid," Enabi said, giving me a high-five. I took out my canteen and took a drink. Enabi picked something silvery out of the sand and examined it closely.

"What is that?"

"It's an I.D. tag. This ain't good."

"Why?"

Enabi threw the small metal plate to me. I wiped the blood off and looked over the runic markings. "What does it mean?"

"It means beastie here is… or was, a pet. And the owner's gonna be pissed when he finds out we just blew up poochie."

"What do you mean? Who's the owner?" The stench of sulphur scratched away at my nostrils. "Oh shit!"

A gangly skeletal leg shot out from the darkness. Two bony hands reached out and grabbed hold of the passage walls, followed by a gigantic, grinning skull.

"Fuck me!" Enabi shouted.

"Who's that?"

Enabi gulped. "That's the owner."

"And he is?"

"General Skrod."

"Oh, fuck. Don't any of these demons have any normal names?"

Enabi tilted his head at me. "You really think he would be menacing if his name was Paul or Arthur? Or Melvin? Not that there's anything wrong with those names, but jeez." I shrugged him off.

Enabi and I stood side by side in the middle of the passage, and waited. General Skrod scraped his way out of the tunnel and into the light. He barely fit in the passageway. His cranium of homunculan proportions scraped against the ceiling. His spiky fingers raked the walls, gouging out deep grooves. He craned his head down, his hollow eye sockets glaring fiercely. General Skrod raised his massive fist and smashed it down in the spot where I stood seconds before, as I jumped and rolled. Enabi took all manner of shots at the skeleton, with no effect. "This isn't good," he said.

"We have to destroy the right hand," I began, "So he can't commit evil acts."

"You know your shit! Let's do it!" Enabi put his fist to his jaw and bit down. He pulled his hand away. "Grenade!" Whatever he threw, it almost caused as much havoc as a tactical nuke. The explosion caused General Skrod to lose his balance. I took aim and threw the rock. It connected, shattering three fingers on the right hand. General Skrod pulled his mangled hand away. His fist shot out, catching me in the chest and crushing me into the sand. I actually sank into the ground. As he lifted his fist, I rolled out of the shallow grave.

"Not today, asshole." The fist shot out again. But this time I set down the rock and pulled back on it causing it to expand. Skrod's punch connected, smashing the rock, along with his thumb and forefinger. Enabi fired a volley of rockets, blowing the hand off at the wrist.

"Now the jaw, so he can't corrupt with speech."

I charged forward, sweeping the rock off the ground. "Alley-oop!" Enabi shouted, locking his fingers together to form a basket. General Skrod leaned in ready to strike with his left hand. I lifted the rock over my head and leapt. Enabi caught my foot in his hands and vaulted me over him. Leveraging the momentum, I hurled the rock – which was, again, anvil-size. The rock fired through the air, cracking General Skrod in the jaw. The bone snapped and shattered. Teeth fired out in all directions. The General fell back on his bony ass.

As he tried to get up, I threw the rock, blowing out his knee and forcing him to drop again. I threw the rock one last time, smashing and splintering the neck vertebrae. Enabi followed up with a high-caliber blast which tore the head free from the body. The head clattered as it hit the sand, while the body flopped over.

Enabi rubbed his hands together. "That was easier than I thought."

"Does that really matter?" I asked, surveying the carnage. "A dead demon is a dead demon."

"Yeah, I guess you're right." Enabi scratched his head. "But now I have to clean up all this shit."

I laughed. "Well, if this is it, then it's time for me to go. Thanks for saving my life."

Enabi and I shook hands. "It was nothin'. You know, I would love to see the look on Upior Nagi's face when he sees you still alive."

"And he's gonna be pissed with you," I said.

"Meh!" Enabi waved his hand. "I've pissed him off before. It won't be the last time." I took hold of the iron ring on the heavy door. "Hey, Ed?" he called.

"Yeah?"

"About Jim... uh, I don't know if he knew. But I do know this: Jim wouldn't make a decision if he couldn't live with the consequences."

I looked down into the sand. This was one time I knew he wasn't lying for sure. "Thanks!"

"Don't mention it."

The door's squeaky hinges groaned as I pulled it towards me. Bright light flooded the cavern, forcing me to squint. Dry warm air tickled my nostrils and throat. I stepped through, shading my eyes and continuing up the sandy path. When my eyes finally adjusted to the light, I stopped and surveyed the landscape: I was standing in a desert. An endless and silent sea of white-hot sand stretched beyond the horizon. The sky was bright and clear. Dark jagged stone monoliths rose out of the sand to my right. I turned around and was standing in front of... an Oak tree? It was massive – maybe a hundred feet tall, and thirty feet wide... and very... very dead. I circled the base of the tree, pushing against the rough bark repeatedly, looking for a way back in. After several futile attempts, I surrendered. *I guess I'm out of Nabisusha.*

Beads of sweat trickled down my brow. I rubbed my eyes and decided to seek out the cooler shade of the nearby rocks. As I took a step forward, I saw something glisten out the corner of my eye. I stopped and stared up into the pale blue emptiness... waiting. Suddenly a shimmering, silver light rippled across the sky. I couldn't tell what it was. It looked a bit like light reflecting off water. The light danced across the wide section of the sky and disappeared. I shook my head and looked again, but it was gone. *That was odd.* I took one last look before heading off towards the rocks.

Beneath the cool shade of an overhang, I drank some more Beekosh from my canteen. "Upior?" I shouted. "Upior Nagi?" The eerie stillness was deafening, and unnerving. Before deciding on what to do next, or which way to go, I tilted my head up and closed my eyes, warming my face in the sunlight.

UNDEAD RECKONING

CHAKA-CHAKA-CHAKA! I readied the rock in my hand. *What the fuck? That sounded like a rattle.* At first, I thought maybe some loose rocks were trickling down a nearby rock face. *CHAKA-CHAKA-CHAKA!* The sound was somewhere behind me. I turned on the spot just in time to see a snakelike thing slither out from behind the rocks. The lower body from the waist down was all snake, complete with a rattle on the end of the tail. The upper body was human – a torso with two arms. The flat face was a combination of skeletal human and snake. The dark eyes stared at me. The snake-man held a bow in one hand, with quiver of arrows strapped over his shoulder.

He stood up straight, eyeing me while his forked tongue flickered in and out of his mouth. The skin around the neck flared out like the hood of a cobra and he hissed, baring two long fangs. I didn't hesitate and quickly threw the rock. The snake-man dodged and deftly nocked an arrow. But the rock was back in my hand before he could pull back the string. I threw again and this time, hit the snake-man, blowing out the side of his head and jettisoning the eyeball into an aerial spin.

CHAKA-CHAKA-CHAKA!

Another snake-man approached me from the rear. As I spun to face him, he released an arrow. I threw the rock and just clipped the shaft enough to knock it off course. The rock continued and punched the snake-man in the throat, collapsing his airway and severing an artery. He fell back spewing bloody red goo into the clean white sand. I was so pleased with my shot that I didn't notice the arrow hit a rock. The arrow head snapped off and the shaft split... no, it actually... *splintered*... into several pieces. A thin dark piece of wood spun off and hit me right in the neck. Pain shot through my jaw and clutched at my throat. Suddenly short of breath, I dropped to my knees. I gasped for breath but could only take in small volumes of air. Warm sticky liquid trickled through my fingers.

"Oh fuck!" I said. No sound came out of my mouth. I could only hear the words in my head and feel them in my mouth. I gasped again. I swallowed and felt something scrape my throat. "Hrrrrm! Hrrrrm!" I couldn't clear it. It felt like that time I got a fishbone stuck in my tonsil, and I suddenly concluded I was in need of medical attention.

A shadowy figure emerged from behind the rocks. He stopped and turned to me.

"Help!" I shouted. Again, no words escaped my lips. "Hrrrrm!"

The figure calmly walked towards me.

"Help."

The figure stopped directly in front of me and dropped his hood.

"Upior Nagi," I whispered.

"I had a feeling Enabi would... fail me."

He could hear me! "Help... me."

"I lured General Skrod to him," Upior Nagi said.

"We... killed him."

"Even a fool could kill Skrod. If only his combat ability matched his... homunculan head. Skrod is a moron. I knew Enabi would prevail." Upior Nagi breathed deeply, his nostrils flaring. He motioned to the dead snake-man. "I was tempted to kill these... scouts. Fortunately, I stayed my hand." Upior Nagi dropped to one knee and grinned. "Everything goes according to plan." He put his hand on my shoulder and gripped it tightly, as if I wasn't already in enough discomfort. "Now... to business. Do you have the vial?"

"Wha...?" My eyelids felt as heavy as my droopy head.

"The vial!"

"In my... in my p-uh..." Salty blood trickled out of my mouth. My lips were sticky.

Upior ran his hand along my web belt. He tore open a velcro flap, pulled the vial free, and held it up into the light. He smiled, baring his mouthful of hideous teeth.

With each breath, I took in less air. My head began to ache. I wanted to lie down. If not for Upior's hand on my shoulder, I would have toppled over.

Upior Nagi stashed the vial inside his robe. "Well done, Griffin. Well done... indeed."

"Where... am I?"

"Earth," Upior replied.

"The... light..."

"The light... is Poland."

"Heh, heh," I coughed. "I thought... I thought... I was... d-d-dead."

Upior Nagi grinned. "No. But you will be... very soon." He reached inside his robe and fished around before pulling out a small dark object, maybe two inches long. He held it up in front of me. My eyes were watering. "Do you know what this is?"

I could hardly focus on the blurry dark thing, but I recognized it. "A... hrrrmm... p-p-peemer."

Upior Nagi leaned in so close his nose was almost touching mine. "Remember," he whispered. His icy hand slid down my shoulder and clutched me by the back of the neck. With his other hand, he slid the cold stone up into my nostril. I couldn't swallow anymore. My lungs screamed for air. Like a fish out of water, I opened and closed my mouth uncontrollably.

"Remember!" Upior Nagi shouted. His voice seemed distant. Still holding me up by the neck, he leaned back, made a fist and punched. Literally, he knocked my lights out. My head snapped back and a sharp pain pierced the top of my head. I fell back, but never hit the sand. I just kept falling... falling back into the calm, silent darkness. The pain subsided. I lost all sense of my body. I lost all sense... of everything.

24 NOETIC JUSTICE

These words did not always come to me with clarity.
Like the future or past, clarity is not immediately apparent.
Much I had to recall from distant memories...
From a time when I was someone else long forgotten.
How many times have I scribed these words?
Have I captured the meaning as intended?
Do the words live on, even when the pages are shut?
How many incarnations will it take before the meaning takes hold?
The book the body – the content the soul.
— Final entry
The Book of Amaltheon

White-hot light filled my eyes. I could not see my own body, let alone sense it. At first, I felt like I was sinking... maybe even floating, but not in any particular direction. Despite my disorientation, the light calmed me... embraced me. I sensed someone coming towards me. A hand gripped me by the forearm and pulled me close.

"Eddie?"

"Hello?" I could not see anyone, but I knew someone was there. And then, I saw the runes burning brightly. "Who is there?"

"It is I, Holioch."

"Holioch?" I sensed others around me. They were armed... and armored – the metal gave off a strange shock, like tinfoil when pressed against metal fillings. And the fiery runes were cooler than the warm light around me. For a brief moment, I caught a glimpse of... memories. Numerous life experiences viewed simultaneously yet fuzzy like my own memories. Everything suddenly faded out completely.

"We must shield you," Holioch said. His voice was clear and direct, yet sounded like many voices speaking in unison. "The Masters must detect neither your presence nor your success. They have more agents than we have time."

"Time?" The word was meaningless. I did not understand. "What are you referring to?"

"Poland must not fall."

"Poland?"

Holioch smiled. I mean, I didn't see him smile. I just know he did. "It is the last bastion of hope for our salvation. It cannot fall."

"Fall to whom?"

"The Masters seek to destroy it. Their armies stand at the ready, waiting for attack orders, while their scouts scour the lands."

"The snake heads - the ones who killed me. They were scouts?"

"Yes."

"I mean, other than the two I killed, what's stopping them from invading Poland?"

"They have yet to find it. Poland is like the very thing you once held within the palm of your hand."

"I don't understand."

"You will." A sense of unease caused the light to dim. "It is not safe for you here. You must return."

"Return? What do you mean? I'm dead, aren't I?"

Holioch laughed. "You are more alive than you can comprehend. Good luck, Eddie Griffin."

The light faded leaving me all alone. Cold and darkness crept in all around me. I could sense the confines of my body and... I opened my eyes. The ceiling rafters slowly came into focus. I sat up on the creaky, wooden frame bed, startling the drummer who sat in the corner of the room. Having ceased the monotonous thumping, the drummer jumped from his seat and dashed out the door into the hall. From outside, the metallic clang of hammer against anvil replaced the drumming.

My achy, stiff body was almost as cold as the room I was in. I stood and stretched, draining the numbness from my hands and feet, and worked out the chills. I flexed my arms and legs, waiting for strength to return to my body, and memories to clear in my head. The hearth was still warm, even though the fire had reduced to white ash and dark coals. I squatted down, took in a deep breath, and blew softly on the coals until they glowed orange. My body reacted in kind as fiery runes appeared on my chest and crept across my skin along my shoulders and upper arms. I continued to blow on the coals, gradually adding some kindling I took from the wood pile next to the hearth. The fire quickly roared to life and I added more wood.

As my body warmed, so too did my orientation in time and space. It all seemed so vaguely familiar. I rubbed my fingers over the scarred and bumpy glowing mandala on my chest, and then pulled the thick, heavy polar bear fur off the bed and draped it over my shoulders. I could not find my jersey or my armor, let alone any clothing. I wore nothing more than a loin cloth and the hide boots I found under the bed.

I exited the room and entered the dimly lit hall. The sputtering fires had not been tended to in some time. No guards stood at the main entrance. Magjar's keg rested in the corner of the room secured with heavy chains. Rich tapestries and ornamental weapons hung on the walls. I looked up at the wooden carving of a snake devouring its own tail that was suspended over the main table. *I remember. I am home.* I took an empty tankard from the closest table and filled it from Magjar's keg. My heavy footfalls shook the floorboards as I made my way to the entrance. I emptied the tankard in one draught and set it down before stepping outside. The bitter cold tried to crawl in under the fur, forcing me to pull it a little tighter.

The snow crunched beneath my feet. Severed zombie heads, impaled on spears, dotted the perimeter like grisly fence posts. I made my way towards the blacksmith's forge. As I approached, the Corvid noticed me and lowered his hammer. He tilted his slick, black-feathered head askew and from side to side, keeping a dark eye on me at all times. Woven iron bracelets adorned his mighty forearms, and elaborate tattoos decorated his chest. He stepped out from behind the anvil and dunked the sword he was making into the water barrel. Steam rose from the hissing water. Shiny, metal guards covered his black talons. I gave him a nod. He returned the salutation by tapping his hammer lightly against the side of his head. The Corvid pulled the sword out of the water and placed it on the anvil, where he continued to ply it with his hammer. I smiled and moved on.

The atmosphere was eerily quiet. *They must be in the caves.* Only a small compliment of soldiers took up a garrison in the caves, with the hall serving as the above-ground headquarters. Built upon the rock ledge, the hall overlooked the vast open ice plains to the south, bordered by the mountain range on the distant horizon. I still felt a bit uncomfortable and was anxious to see everyone's reaction to my return, especially… I stopped short of the cliff's edge, turning my back to the looming, sheer rock face.

Thick gray clouds churned in the sky, and a light snow gently floated down to earth. I stared out into the barren snow-covered wastes, paying no heed to the men who hurriedly emerged from the caves. Nervous guards circled me, keeping their spears at the ready. The Shaman, wearing a wolf pelt and adorned with necklaces of bead and bone, broke through the formation. The nervous drummer cowered by his side. "You have awakened," the Shaman said.

"I have."

"So you have discovered the source of the rising dead?"

"Yes. It took me an entire lifetime to find the answer."

"Why do the gods punish us so?"

I turned to face the Shaman. "The gods do not punish us. Men punish themselves, Aedelred."

The elder man smiled. He stepped forward and reached up. I bowed my head and Aedelred cupped my face in his hands. We pressed our foreheads together, as was our custom. "You sound like me, Grandson."

"Do I?" I laughed.

Aedelred pulled back from me. "Something amuses you?"

"In my journey, I did not understand our people's speech." I smiled. "I... understand now. But I could probably teach you some new shit."

Aedelred frowned before bursting out with laughter. "This is the wisdom you return with?"

I sighed. "Perhaps I'm still a bit... altered." Aedelred shook his head. "How long have I been gone, Grandfather?"

"Since the dark clouds blocked the sun." He pointed to the sky. "You have returned, yet the sun has not."

"Our people need not the sun. We are a subterranean race."

"I always thought you preferred the openness of the surface world."

I ignored the remark. Instead, I looked over Aeldelred's shoulder, and smiled at the sight of the woman who emerged from the cave, running as fast as she could. She moved very quickly, despite her heavy breast plate and boots. Her cloak flapped in the wind as if she were to take flight at any moment. My heart warmed as she approached. The woman put her arms around me and rubbed her shorn head against my cheek.

"Long has it been since I felt your touch, my husband," she said.

I kissed her on the forehead. "I missed you, Boemia. My memories deceive me. You are more beautiful than I recall." I kissed her and held her tightly.

"I began to worry about you when my brother did not return."

"Sigeberht is dead. He ascended in battle, awash with the blood of his enemies. I saw this with my own eyes."

Boemia placed a hand on my cheek. She ran her hand down my neck and I opened the fur. Her hand stopped suddenly when she saw my rune-covered torso. Boemia stepped back. "Perhaps we should return to the hall." She looked at Aedelred, who now also stared at the glowing markings.

"You have much to tell, Godric," he said.

"Godric?" I frowned. "That name is familiar to me, yet, I am Godric no more. My name... is Griffin."

Aedelred and Boemia exchanged glances. "Griffin?" Aedelred said, clapping his hands together. "Your namesake guards great treasure."

"And great secrets," Boemia added. She looked to the nearest guard and ordered, "Bring the one who surrendered himself to us this morning. Bring him here at once!"

"As you command!" The guard ran off.

Aedelred pressed his hands together firmly. He smiled and spread his arms open. "You have found your true self. This is cause for great celebration."

I turned my back to them and stared off into the clouds. My hand snuck out from between the folds of the fur and I reached for Boemia. Her slender hand slid into mine and I pulled her close, putting my arm and the fur around her shoulder.

"What is it that you are looking for?"

Before I could respond, I caught a glimpse of green out of the corner of my eye. I turned to see a familiar person coming towards me, escorted by two guards. The lantern clipped to his belt thudded against his body, while heavy Corvid-forged chains bound his wrists. "Release his bindings!" I ordered. "Did this man not come with you willingly?"

"He did, sir," a guard responded.

"It was not his willingness to comply that forced us to chain him," Boemia confirmed. "He is a Waykeeper. It is his duty to return to Nabisusha at all costs."

I snorted. "Unbind him!"

The guards obliged. The green-skinned man stepped forward and stood at my side. We did not look at each other – both of us stared off into the cloudy sky.

"Hello Jim," I said.

"I told you we'd meet again, Ed." Jim looked me up and down. "You're much taller than I recall."

"Are you sure you have not grown smaller? Perhaps your body has adapted to the low ceilings of Nabisusha."

"If that's your theory, then your body has adapted to life on the surface."

"Good to see your wit is still as sharp as your blade."

"How's your throwing arm?" Jim asked.

With a smirk, I replied, "I could still knock the sun out of the sky."

"Or throw a winning touchdown? Maybe you should try this." Jim held out his hand. I looked down at the tiny rock in his palm. "I found this in your pocket when I recovered your remains."

I took the rock and threw it into the sky. We watched patiently as the tiny speck sailed off over the horizon. I looked at Jim out of the corner of my eye, before gazing back into the clouds. "Did you know of Upior's plan?"

"I knew you were to encounter General Skrod. But I was confident you could take him." Jim lowered his head. "What I did not know was Upior's backup plan."

"Had you known... would you have aided me?"

Jim looked up at me. "Would you have wanted me to?"

I stared out across the snowy plain. "You are forgiven."

"Thank you."

I clenched my fist tightly. When I opened it, the Rock of Return lay in palm of my hand. I turned to Jim. "I feel strange. I am me and... not me."

"Don't think about it too much," Jim said, patting me on the arm. "You don't want to end up like Veck."

I nodded approvingly. "Speaking of Veck... has he arrived yet?"

"I don't know," Jim responded.

"Of whom do you speak?" Boemia asked. "And how is it that you know this Waykeeper?"

I took Boemia by the hand and was about to speak, when a soldier ran towards us, up from the path leading to the plains. He stopped short of the small gathering, bracing his hands on his knees and panting. His head and armor were caked with dried blood. Once he caught his breath, he stood up straight and pointed. "The ghost approaches," he said. "He bested our patrol."

"Must I kill everyone myself?" Boemia shouted. "Even with our most skilled warriors at your command, you return in defeat?"

The soldier took a drink from his water pouch. "The ghost bears the markings of Holioch. He swings a great hammer. Not even a Crudwyrm fights with such fury." The soldier took another drink. "I am lucky to have escaped with my life."

"Speak of the devil," Jim muttered.

I turned to the soldier. "He let you live," I scoffed. "His name is Veck, and I am expecting him. Let him pass without resistance."

Boemia put a hand on my chest. I knew she was concerned because of the way she furrowed her brow. Sometimes I wish I saw more of her softer side as opposed to that tough exterior. But that's what you get when your wife can beat the shit out of just about every soldier under her command. "You are still altered from your journey. You need rest. Do you not agree, Aedelred?"

The elder man shrugged. "I sense neither deceit nor confusion."

Boemia looked me sternly in the eye. "Explain yourself. How do you know this Waykeeper? And of the ghost named Veck?"

I pointed into the sky. "Look there," I whispered, pressing my head to hers. Far beyond the mountain range, the clouds parted, revealing a silver shimmering light, albeit only for a moment.

"What was that?" Boemia asked.

I turned to the rest of the group. The soldiers immediately snapped to attention. Maybe they saw the ferocity in my eyes, or heard it in my voice as I shouted, "The return of the Green Man means the halls of Nabisusha are once again secure, and soon to be free of undead." Jim nodded and folded his arms across his chest. "There are survivors on the surface world." I pointed to the sky. "The last bastion of hope lies there... to the south. The undead seek to destroy this place. We must awaken our brothers from their icy slumber. We must be battle-ready before Veck arrives."

"And when he arrives, what is this Veck going to do?" Boemia asked.

"He comes to lead us toward the light." I looked out again into the sky and pointed. "He leads us to Poland!"

"Poland?" Aedelred asked.

"Yes," I hissed through clenched teeth. "Poland calls us to war!"

POETIC REFERENCES

John Donne (1572-1631) The Flea

ABOUT THE AUTHOR

Mike Slabon lives in Canada. When not writing, he spends his time playing games of all types, enjoys building scale models, painting miniatures, and cheering for the Toronto Maple Leafs. He enjoys really, really bad movies (and the occasional good one), especially sci-fi, fantasy, horror and 70's films.